The SPY'S REWARD

NITA ABRAMS

ZEBRA BOOKS

Kensington Publishing Corp.

www.kensingtonbooks.com

ZEBRA BOOKS are published by

Kensington Publishing Corp.
850 Third Avenue
New York, NY 10022

All Kensington titles, imprints, and distributed lines are available at special quantity discounts for bulk purchases for sales promotion, premiums, fund-raising, educational, or institutional use.

Special book excerpts or customized printings can also be created to fit specific needs. For details, write or phone the office of the Kensington Special Sales Manager: Attn. Special Sales Department Kensington Publishing Corp., 850 Third Avenue, New York, NY 10022. Phone: 1-800-221-2647.

Zebra and the Z logo Reg. U.S. Pat. & TM Off.

ISBN 0-8217-7854-4

First Printing: February 2006
10 9 8 7 6 5 4 3 2 1

Printed in the United States of America

To JR, Mary, Rachel, Sarah, Will, and Nora:
Poor Abigail—she has Leah, while I have you

PROLOGUE

London, December 1813

Everyone was wearing black except Abigail. All the Harts, of course: Aaron's widow, Belinda. His brother, Stephen. Stephen's wife, Danielle. Stephen's cousin and business partner, Joshua, who, as the wealthiest of the Harts, was the unofficial head of the family. Even Abigail's own sister was wearing black gloves. Leah was sitting next to Danielle, forming a solid female block of disapproval, and the two of them were explaining the new rules.

"Now that my brother-in-law is dead," Danielle told her, "things will be considerably less awkward. We believe"—four severe faces nodded in agreement—"that it will be acceptable for you to refer to yourself as a widow. Belinda intends to return to her family in Hamburg, and those who knew Aaron well will understand the situation. It is for Diana's sake."

Diana was wearing black as well, but she was upstairs with Fanny, Abigail's companion. Danielle and Leah did not believe seventeen-year-old females should be present at serious family conferences. Diana had changed dramatically in the nine months since Abigail had last seen her: her daughter had grown up; she was a young lady now instead of a girl pretending to be a young lady. Abigail thought of the havoc that would ensue if Diana's stepmother had charge of her and shuddered. Belinda was a timid, unworldly woman who had barely been able to discipline Diana when Aaron was there to reinforce her. It was obvious the Harts had no confidence in her: Why else was she being sent back to Hamburg when by rights she should be raising her own young son, Diana's half brother? Instead Robert was going to live with Joshua, and the Harts were giving Abigail back her daughter. With certain conditions attached.

"You will go into mourning for at least six months," Danielle continued. Again there were four nods of agreement. "You will live quietly." She looked around her, taking in the simple furniture and spare decoration in Abigail's drawing room. "This is not what Diana has been accustomed to, but it is pleasant enough."

"Would you prefer me to take Diana out of London?" Abigail tried not to sound too eager.

Joshua cleared his throat. "We thought to keep her here where she could see her father's family regularly, at least at first. But perhaps this summer you might visit one of the watering places. Tunbridge Wells. Or Ramsgate, if you prefer the sea."

Abigail turned to her sister. "And may she continue to see her grandmother?"

"This has also been discussed." Leah paused for

the inevitable nods. "Mother has agreed to allow Diana to visit, accompanied by me or by Danielle."

Everyone shifted uncomfortably in their seats. Abigail's mother had not spoken to her since the divorce.

"Now," said Danielle. "The question of Diana's marriage." Everyone sat up straight. "Joshua has kindly agreed to take charge of this matter. There is no hurry, of course, but we will all keep our eyes open for suitable prospects. As she will be residing here with you, Abigail, it may happen that you yourself will observe that Diana has a partiality for one or another of the candidates we present to her. Leah and I have persuaded your mother that an arranged marriage of the old-fashioned sort is not appropriate for Diana."

Abigail suppressed a snort. What they meant was that Diana had been having her own way for years and would likely prove very uncooperative if they attempted anything like the formal, negotiated marriages of Abigail's own generation. Danielle had always been a realist.

"We believe we can trust you to prevent any unacceptable attachments," Danielle said.

This time there were no nods. Abigail guessed that "we" was Joshua and Danielle. Leah pursed her lips, Stephen frowned, and Belinda looked terrified. There had probably been a ferocious argument on this question. Most members of the Hart family regarded Abigail as the very last person they would choose to advise a young woman on female virtue. She had failed not one but two of the Hart brothers: her first husband, Paul, by letting him die of a mere cold in the chest; her second, Paul's brother Aaron, by insisting on the divorce.

"Naturally, you will tell Joshua immediately of any suitors, welcome or unwelcome, and he will take whatever steps are necessary. After six months, you and Diana may entertain quietly here." Danielle surveyed the room again. "You may wish to purchase some new furniture; Joshua will reimburse you for any expense."

"Thank you, but there is no need for him to do so," Abigail said stiffly.

That was part of the problem, of course. The Harts could have forgiven her for forcing Aaron to divorce her if she had been left poor and helpless. But Abigail Hart was a very wealthy woman. She could refurnish this drawing room twelve times over, and they knew it. When she left Aaron she could have purchased an enormous, elegant home in a fashionable neighborhood. She had chosen instead to buy a small house in Goodman's Fields, which she had furnished to her taste rather than to her pocketbook. Still, she knew that to Diana her home would seem shabby, and she wanted Diana to be comfortable inviting friends here. "I will be glad to assume the expense of redecorating. Perhaps Diana will help me select new things."

Belinda spoke for the first time. "Diana would like that very much." Her watery blue eyes met Abigail's and for a moment there was something like friendship between them. Belinda, Abigail was certain, was glad to be a widow.

"Well." Danielle rose. "It is all settled, then. Belinda, you may fetch Diana down to us."

There was an awkward silence while Belinda was

gone. Then she reappeared, followed by Diana and Fanny.

Danielle beckoned Diana over. "Child, we are leaving. Make your curtsey to Mrs. Asher and to your mother."

Stiffly, Diana nodded at Fanny. Then, to Abigail's surprise, Diana came over and kissed her quickly on the cheek, darting a quick glance at her two aunts.

"Until Thursday, then." Danielle herded Diana out the door, and the rest of the party took their leave as quickly as possible. Only Joshua lingered behind. He had always had a certain sympathy for Abigail.

"I hope you are pleased," he said.

"I am," she assured him.

"There will be a certain awkwardness at first, but Diana is a lovely girl."

Fanny said quickly, "Oh, indeed she is!"

Abigail sighed. "Joshua, you can speak plainly with me. She has been indulged and flattered by everyone in that household so outrageously that it is a wonder she behaves as well as she does. She is far too pretty for her own good, and an heiress besides. You may be sure I will keep a close eye on her. I advise you, however, to send Belinda to Germany as quickly as may be, because I predict that Diana will be pleading to return to her care within a week."

"But Diana was delighted when we proposed this!" He looked around the room, just as Danielle had. "You must think her spoiled indeed if you believe she will care about how big your drawing room is, or how many footmen you have."

"I certainly hope she is not so petty! No, what she will care about is that I am far stricter than Belinda. Naturally she is eager to come and live with me. She has not been allowed to see me for more than a few hours at a time since she was a little girl. I am forbidden fruit, and you know Diana has always chafed at restrictions of any sort. Right now I represent freedom. After three days here, she will realize that rules in my household do not have exceptions for her."

"We have every confidence in you." He bowed to Fanny. "And in Mrs. Asher."

"Well?" said Fanny eagerly, after the door had closed behind him. "Is it settled?"

"Oh yes. It is all arranged. There are now two widows in this house. I am to wear black, and live quietly, and prevent Diana from forming unsuitable attachments. If I am very, very good, I may be permitted to take Diana to Tunbridge Wells this summer." She began to laugh, but there was an edge to the laughter, and Fanny's eyes filled with tears.

"But you must be happy? Surely you are happy? I know I am!"

Abigail thought that Fanny's gentle patience would be sorely tried in the months ahead. "Yes," she said. "I am happy. I would have agreed to almost anything to have her back."

1

London, February 1815

Eli Roth stopped dead in the doorway of the breakfast room at the sight of the elegant form of his
brother-in-law sipping coffee in a chair facing the
window. It was half-past seven, and the waxing daylight revealed that Meyer was not only up but dressed
for a formal morning call—his jacket pressed, his
neckcloth carefully folded, and a heavy gold ring (a
gift from the Duke of York, which he rarely wore)
gleaming on his left hand.

"Nathan!" said Roth, startled. Meyer rarely breakfasted before nine these days. "This is certainly an
unexpected pleasure. I had not thought to see you until
this evening."

"I have an appointment." The dark head was
bent over the coffee cup, eyes half-closed.

Roth wasn't deceived. His brother-in-law was at his
most dangerous when he looked sleepy. "Whitehall?" he queried, hoping the government was not
going to frustrate his plans at the last minute. "More

trouble in Austria?" In theory Nathan's service as an unofficial intelligence courier for Wellington was over. But as Roth himself had pointed out to his fellow bankers only a few days earlier, peace was sometimes as dangerous and unpredictable as war, and Meyer had already been to Vienna twice to "assist" the British delegation at the Congress.

"No, nothing of any importance," said Meyer, still gazing into the unfathomable surface of his coffee. "A courtesy call." His tone was pleasant, but discouraged further prying.

Roth narrowed his eyes and considered this response for a moment. Then, apparently changing the subject, he said, "Did you by any chance have time to consider the matter we discussed last night?"

"Good morning, Louisa," said his brother-in-law courteously, rising and turning as Roth's wife entered behind him.

"How do you *do* that?" Louisa Roth waved him back to his chair with an irritated gesture. "I could have sworn I made no noise at all, and you were talking to Eli with your back to this door!"

"Your elegant perfume," suggested Meyer, beginning to smile. "It preceded you into the room."

"I do not wear perfume during the day, as you know very well."

"The whisper of your silk skirts."

"Wool," she pointed out, spreading the soft maroon fabric out for inspection.

Still standing, he bowed. "On you, my dearest Louisa, it glows like the finest satin. Hence my misapprehension."

"Your misapprehension," she said tartly, "consists of the belief that you must be on the alert twenty-four hours a day, lest some French villain attack us here in the heart of London nearly a year after Napoleon abdicated." Without pausing to acknowledge Meyer's wry grimace, she turned to her husband. "And what, pray, were the two of you discussing last night?"

"I beg your pardon?" hedged Roth.

"I saw you giving Nathan those little glances after dinner," she said, folding her arms. "The I-must-speak-with-you-alone glances. I therefore obligingly retired early. But now I see Rodrigo is upstairs counting Nathan's clean shirts, a postboy has just left a message in the kitchen about a vehicle for Wednesday morning, Nathan is at breakfast two hours earlier than usual, and you are interrogating him about some mysterious proposal. I assume all these events are connected."

Roth brightened at the mention of the postboy. "You'll do it, then?" he asked, turning to Meyer.

"I don't see why not." Meyer picked up his cup and drained it. "It will be a bit dull, I expect, but traveling in France under my own name still has the charm of novelty. I'll come round to the bank this afternoon and you can give me the particulars. For now though, I must beg both of you to excuse me. My appointment is in less than an hour, and the gentleman who awaits me is greatly enamored of the virtue of punctuality." He bowed slightly and vanished.

Louisa Roth stared at the now-empty doorway. "Where is he going?"

"Whitehall, I would guess," said Roth slowly, putting all the pieces together. That was not what she had meant, of course.

His answer did serve to distract her for a moment. "He denied it—I heard you ask him."

"He was lying." Recollecting his brother-in-law's precise words, he amended this statement. "Or rather, speaking disingenuously. I suspect the courtesy call is on Colonel Tredwell at the Horse Guards." He stepped over to the table and pulled out a chair. "Some coffee, my dear?"

"No, thank you." Distractions rarely worked on Louisa Roth for more than a minute. She moved to face him, and since he was rather short, her piercing blue eyes looked straight into his. "When I asked that question, I meant where was he going on Wednesday. France, it seems."

"A quick trip. Nothing dangerous, no intrigues or burglaries, I promise you. I got word from a friend that a kinswoman of his was stranded south of Grenoble without a suitable escort. I thought Nathan could use a bit of mountain air, a change of scene."

He could see from her expression that she no more believed his story than Nathan had last night.

"Eli, you are matchmaking again," she said flatly.

"Nonsense."

She sighed. "Nathan can fool me when he lies. You, however, cannot."

"Well, what if I am matchmaking, as you call it?" he asked, exasperated. "You are just as eager as I am to see him remarry."

"No, I am not. Eli, I believe this has become something of an obsession with you. I know that having Nathan in residence here, still unmarried after so long, is a daily reminder of his loss—and yours. But he has proposed moving out several times since the war ended, and perhaps you should agree the next time he does so. It might help you to remember that he is a grown man, that you are not responsible for his happiness."

"I do not believe I am responsible for Nathan." He scowled at his wife. "And I thought you enjoyed having him lodge here with us."

"I do," said Louisa, unruffled. "What female would not?"

It said a good deal for his relationship with his wife that he had never had a single qualm about housing his brother-in-law, even after Nathan's children had left the house. Eli was short, round, balding, and nearsighted. Nathan was tall, slim, dark-haired, and possessed of a commanding pair of nearly black eyes.

"*But,*" she continued, "pleasant as I find Nathan's company, I will have to dispense with it if every time you see him you feel an overwhelming urge to drag him under a wedding canopy."

"Louisa, my sister died more than fourteen years ago. It was understandable that he should grieve for a bit, but his refusal to consider taking another wife after so long is absurd, especially since he and Miriam were wed so young that he is still at an age when some men are marrying for the first time. I admit that our attempts to find him a bride have miscarried a few times—"

"More than a few," muttered his wife.

"The situation is different now." Roth gestured at the newspaper lying neatly folded and unread by Meyer's abandoned cup. "While the war was on, he distracted himself with his work for the army, with disguises and ciphers and forgeries and midnight landings on hidden beaches. But now the war is over. He no longer even has a father's responsibilities to occupy him; Rachel and James are settled in households of their own. He is bored and restless, ready for a change. I could see it in his eyes last night when I proposed this little jaunt to him. And observe: he has already agreed to go. He did not even take a day to think it over."

She still looked skeptical. "Who is this friend of the family he is supposedly rescuing in the mountains of France?"

"A very suitable prospect," he assured her. "A cousin of Joshua Hart, well educated, eager to travel, said to resemble her mother, who was a great beauty. Of course, I did not tell him that Miss Hart was an eligible young woman. I believe I gave him the impression that she was a bit of an invalid, taking the waters at Digne-les-Bains for her health."

"He'll see right through your little plot the moment he meets her."

"I think not." Roth gave a satisfied smile. "This is one of my better schemes. After all, even Nathan is not omniscient."

"Oh?" said his wife. "Then how is it that between ten last night and seven this morning he has recalled his most trusted servant from Kent, arranged for a post chaise, and scheduled an appointment at Whitehall, where he will no doubt offer to carry confidential messages to France? Or are you going to pretend that he knew nothing of this request of yours until nine hours ago? That Rodrigo's return and Nathan's meeting with the colonel are happy coincidences?"

Roth drew himself up magisterially. "I will not deny that Nathan is uncannily observant. Clearly he got wind of this somehow last week, when I first received Hart's letter. But anticipating a voyage to France on the strength of gossip at our bank is not the same as anticipating what will happen when he gets there."

"I know what will happen," she retorted. "He will be his usual courteous, impenetrable self, he will escort Miss Hart back to England as quickly as possible, and then he will stalk in here and raise his eyebrows at you just as he did after your other attempts. If I am lucky, the disappointed bride-to-be will not fall desperately in love with him, as two of the others did, and I will not have to spend months avoiding her and all her relatives."

"We shall see," said Roth, turning back to the sideboard. "I am two moves ahead of him this time, my dear. And matchmaking is not a game familiar to Nathan."

She frowned at him. "You are keeping something from me."

He did not respond, but picked up the coffee pot.

"Are you afraid I will tell Nathan?"

"No," he said, pouring her a cup and setting it at her place. "I am afraid you will say 'I told you so' if it doesn't work."

Not for nothing was Louisa Roth the wife of a financier. "What are the chances of success, in your estimation?"

"Something like one in ten."

"Well," she said, settling into her chair, "for an affair involving Nathan and a marriageable female, those are quite respectable odds."

2

Digne-les-Bains was larger than Meyer had remembered. His previous visit, if one could call it that, had involved skirting the town by night with a terrified royalist partisan as his guide. He had slept in a hollow beneath a large rock and had dined on water and two-day-old bread. He was therefore unacquainted with the town's inns and dismayed to find there were over two dozen such establishments. His informant, a stout porter at the main post house, told him proudly that several new hostelries had opened recently.

"All very superior, monsieur, and patronized by foreign gentlewomen such as the one you seek. Times are good here now, by the grace of God."

"Digne did not prosper, then, under Bonaparte?"

"Bonaparte!" The man spat reflexively. "He nearly ruined us. Who comes to take the waters when all of Europe is under siege? But since the tyrant's abdication, it is a different story. Every room at every inn is taken, even now, in winter. I have made more money in pourboires in six months than in the past three years. This means, of course, that I carry dozens of portmanteaux every day, and as I also direct most of the visitors who arrive on the diligence to their lodgings, I have too many clients to remember one English lady. The town is full of English ladies." The mention of pourboires suggested to Meyer that the porter's memory might be assisted by a small coin. The man pocketed it with effusive thanks—but still could not recall an ailing Englishwoman who had arrived three weeks ago with a companion and a servant. "Well," said Meyer, producing another coin, "where would a wealthy invalid from London be likely to stay? She is taking a treatment at the baths, of course."

The porter thought for a moment. "Hôtel du Petit Paris, by the cathedral. Or perhaps . . ." He paused, clearly hoping for another coin, but something he saw in Meyer's face made him resume hastily. "Hôtel d'Angleterre, just inside the Porte des Bains. If she is very wealthy, the Auberge des Cygnes."

"And what is the attraction at the Auberge des Cygnes?" asked Meyer, finally producing the long-awaited third coin.

"It is very well appointed, monsieur. The emperor's own sister stayed there several years ago." The porter seemed to have temporarily forgotten that Napoleon was a villain and a tyrant. "And it is the only inn near the baths, which are a league east of town. I can guide monsieur, or I can procure a gig and driver, or perhaps monsieur would like me to call the ostler back before he stables monsieur's horse."

"Thank you, no." Meyer was already scanning the rooftops of the town, looking for the cathedral. If only Rodrigo were here. Somehow his manservant always knew just which inn to try first. But Rodrigo was many hours behind him, bringing up the carriage he had hired in Barrême. Meyer might not have remembered how big Digne was, but he had certainly remembered the appalling state of the roads, and had concluded that it would be prudent to hire the first vehicle he saw which seemed sturdy enough to have a chance of reaching the coast with all four wheels intact. For a moment he toyed with the idea of sitting down to a long, leisurely meal at the post house. Let Rodrigo canvas twenty inns for news of the woman. But after hours in the saddle, he needed a walk in any case. He gestured towards an elaborate ironwork bell tower some distance away. "Is that the cathedral?"

"Indeed, monsieur. Take the first turning to your right and continue up the hill and you cannot miss it." Meyer reflexively spun him a fourth coin and set out for the center of the little town.

Naturally, there was no Miss Hart at the Hôtel du Petit Paris. Nor was she nearby at the Angleterre, in spite of its name. They did have a room available, however, and he booked it as a precaution. With a weary sigh, he retrieved his horse from the post house, dispensing yet another coin to the porter, who evidently acted as an intermediary between the inn's grooms and their customers. At this rate he would dower the porter's daughter before he found Eli's damsel in distress.

He could, of course, have tried the other hotels in town first, but something about the description of the Auberge des Cygnes made him think it very probable that Miss Hart would be there. He pictured her, from Eli's vague description, as one of those perpetually ailing maiden ladies who drift from spa to spa, always certain the cure for their infirmities is just ahead in some yet-untried hot spring or some newly compounded tonic—the more expensive and fashionable, the better. She was probably around thirty; Eli had mentioned an older woman, a companion, and if Miss Hart were herself elderly she would likely have someone younger, to run errands and fetch shawls. She would wear a cap, he thought, and look a bit faded and pinched. To him she would be civil, and speak in a low, fluttering voice, but in private, with her companion, she would be shrewish and demanding.

He had no illusions about Eli's purpose in sending him here. His brother-in-law was once again attempting to find him a wife. He was not sure who was more embarrassed by these futile episodes—Eli, Louisa, the potential brides, or himself. Luckily the attempts were relatively infrequent. Eli put forward only candidates who met his own demanding requirements as a replacement for his late sister: cultured, well dowered, reasonably attractive women of his own faith. Meyer was not in danger of falling for someone who enjoyed languishing at spas, however, even if she was an heiress. No matter how wealthy she was, he was wealthier. And the more Eli had emphasized Miss Hart's money, the more he had insisted that she was not really ill, the more certain Nathan had become that Eli must be losing his touch. It was in part, then, out of amused pity for his brother-in-law that he had agreed to go—pity, and, he admitted to himself, curiosity. Why not return to France?—the country he had, in some small way, helped in its battle to expel the usurper. Admittedly, wearing his own clothing and traveling under his own name made him feel exposed and vulnerable, but even that anxiety had its own charm. It was pleasant to feel reckless, after years of caution and secrecy.

His reflections were interrupted by a sudden jolt. His horse had stopped. They had been ambling up a wide thoroughfare along the river valley, and now the road suddenly forked. To the left was a long building tucked underneath the low cliffs that rose behind the river. The domed roof and classical porticoes proclaimed its therapeutic function. He saw an old man in an invalid chair being wheeled along the colonnade by two uniformed attendants, and a matron shepherding her children into the central hall under the dome. The right-hand fork led to a handsome stone inn. The wrought iron gates into the yard were decorated with swan medallions, and the drive swept up to a porch flanked by two statues of swans.

"Auberge des Cygnes," Meyer told the horse, giving it a nudge. He had hired it in Barrême, but it was either very knowledgeable about the inns of Haute-Provence or it preferred the smell of hay and oats to the smell of mineral-laced steam. It turned right obediently and trotted up to the gates. A very supercilious ostler raised his eyebrows at the sight of the shaggy animal. "Hold him," said Meyer curtly. "I may only be here a moment." He swung off the horse and strode into the building, ignoring the boy's stammering protests.

The interior of the building was even more richly appointed than the exterior. The floors were black-and-white marble, and a massive staircase led up to a gallery beneath a central skylight. To the left was a dining room. Liveried servants were laying the tables for dinner with silver and crystal. To the right was a glassed-in terrace overlooking the river. Elegantly clad guests were sitting at small tables or strolling by the windows. Meyer scanned them idly, wondering if his quarry was there. He saw a number of ladies in bath chairs, most of whom were dozing. They were quite elderly, and their attendants seemed to be younger. There were two women of the right age talking at a table near the entry, but they were speaking Italian. At the far end, closest to the river, were several older couples and a large family. In the center of the room, surprisingly, was a group of lively young people—or rather, a group of six young men, surrounding a petite, fair-haired, young woman who was startlingly pretty, and clearly well aware of that fact. She was flirting with all six admirers simultaneously, her posture and expression so blatantly inviting that for one moment Meyer wondered if she might be a courtesan. No, he decided, she was too tastefully dressed. And she had a chaperon, of sorts: an older woman, some sort of superior servant, sitting stiffly in the corner with her eyes fixed on the coquette in fascinated disapproval.

A cough at his elbow announced the innkeeper. He was even more supercilious than the ostler, and his profound regrets that all of his rooms were spoken for were offered in a very perfunctory manner. His eyes lingered expressively on Meyer's riding clothes. Clearly the guests of the Auberge des Cygnes were expected to arrive in carriages.

"I am not seeking accommodation," said Meyer. "Not yet, at any rate." His tone was perfectly pleasant, but the innkeeper shifted nervously under his stare. "I am seeking a countrywoman, a Miss Hart, who is having a treatment at the baths."

"Ah—Mademoiselle Hart." The innkeeper coughed and looked even more nervous.

Good. He would not have to canvas twenty-one more inns. "So she is staying here?"

"Yes, indeed, monsieur."

"I am expected, I believe." He handed the innkeeper his card.

"Of course, of course." The man was steering Meyer back to the central entryway, peering quickly over his shoulder as he did so. "I will send your card up at once, monsieur. If you would care to wait in one of the salons? A room has been reserved for you, near the suite occupied by the ladies, but it is not yet made up." He beckoned urgently to a servant and sent him running off with the calling card while herding Meyer toward the staircase. "And I wish to assure you that mademoiselle has been attended at all times—at all times, monsieur. You need have no concern. Many English believe that we here in France have no care for the proprieties, but I can promise you that is not so, especially here at the Auberge des Cygnes. This is a place where any young lady may confidently make herself at home, may even—dare I say it?—indulge in some youthful high spirits, secure in the knowledge that her elders are watching over her to check any rash impulse that might be misunderstood." He gave another anxious glance back at the terrace.

Meyer added two and two without much difficulty. He stopped, shook off the innkeeper's tug on his sleeve, and turned back to the terrace. "That, I take it, is Miss Hart?" he asked, gesturing towards the blonde Jezebel holding court in the center of the crowd. She was not wearing a cap, and she was most definitely not an invalid. In fact, she looked to be bursting with health. Eli must have thought it a great joke to send him here expecting a sickly spinster.

The innkeeper's mouth made a little *O* of surprise. "But—monsieur is not the cousin of the young lady? You are not acquainted?"

"I have never met her, no. I am a family friend. I had business in Nice, and her kinsman asked me to escort her home when she became stranded here with her companion."

"Stranded?" repeated the innkeeper, bemused. "Companion?"

"I am afraid there has been a misunderstanding," said a woman's voice in English behind him.

"Ah, madame," said the Frenchman with obvious relief. "Here is Monsieur Meyer, who says he is expected."

Meyer turned, startled, to find a slender, green-eyed woman gazing at him warily and holding his calling card at the end of her fingers as though it might burn her. This woman was, in fact, wearing a cap—a very expensive one, edged with Brussels lace. But judging by the thick, light brown hair under the cap and the color in her cheeks, she was not an invalid either. She took in his windblown hair and riding boots and the slight frown on his face.

The red in her cheeks deepened, but she did not lower her eyes.

"I must apologize, Mr. Meyer," she said. Her tone was not apologetic. It was embarrassed and not a little annoyed. "You have traveled all this way, evidently in some haste, for nothing. My cousin can sometimes . . ." She paused, and began again, more courteously. "I do not know how you came to be so misled. Far from being 'stranded,' as you put it, we have been ready to set out for England for over a week. Joshua wrote me that he would be in Grenoble and would like to travel back with us. We have been waiting here for him to join us. Only this morning did I learn that you—a complete stranger—were coming instead."

He looked over at the laughing group in the terrace room. The girl was reading aloud from a piece of paper—a love letter, perhaps, or a poem. Then she rolled it up and tapped one of her admirers on the cheek in mock reproof.

"You are saying that Miss Hart does not require an escort." A brigade of duennas, perhaps, but not an escort.

Her eyebrows went up. "She is with me."

Eli had not mentioned the companion's name. "Ah. Yes. Mrs. . . ."

"Hart," she said impatiently. "Abigail Hart, Diana's mother. And if you think her own mother insufficient protection, perhaps it will ease your mind to learn that we are traveling with two maids, a footman, a coachman, and a courier."

Meyer shot another glance at the girl, then back at the woman. Her mother. The same fine features, yes, the same smooth forehead and level brows. There was a glint of gold in the light brown hair under the cap. Not as pretty as the daughter; her face was sterner, quieter. The eyes were compelling, though: green edged with black, very clear. At the moment they were also very cold. He was beginning to be annoyed and embarrassed on his own account. What could Eli have been thinking? It was not like him to be so careless, sending his victim off to play Sir Lancelot to a maiden who was traveling with her mother, a staff of four, and a professional guide.

"A very reputable gentleman, madame's courier," the innkeeper whispered to Meyer. "A former military man, from a good local family." Evidently the news that Meyer was no relation to Miss Hart had not blunted the innkeeper's impulse to reassure him about her safety.

Abigail Hart held out the calling card. "We are very grateful for your consideration on our behalf, and I deeply regret this inconvenience." She paused, and then added stiffly, "We would invite you to dine with us, but we will be busy preparing to leave early tomorrow."

"Naturally." Meyer gave a slight bow. "I will be staying at the Angleterre, should you require any assistance getting under way in the morning." He ignored the card. If she wanted to insult him by returning it, she would have to put it in his pocket herself. After a moment her hand dropped.

"Good-bye, Mr. Meyer."

"Madam, your most obedient servant." He did not bow this time.

Diana waited until late in the evening, when Abigail was tired and cross. "That will be all, Lisette," her daughter said to the maid, holding out her hand for the hairbrush. Abigail's shoulders, unconsciously braced against the maid's inexpert tugs, sagged in relief as the girl bobbed her head and withdrew. "We should have brought your maid," Diana said, lifting her mother's heavy hair and gently untangling the ends with little swipes of the brush.

Abigail sighed. "Fanny needed Rosie in London. And I thought it would be simpler to hire servants here, people who speak the language and know how to go on."

"Our coachman has become lost several times," Diana observed, moving around behind her mother. "Lisette cannot dress hair to save her life. Mademoiselle Esmond looks more like a vulture than a chaperon. And Captain Hervé is very gallant, but a bit impractical."

"He seems to think I am paying him to kiss my hand and protest his eternal devotion. Rather than to organize our route and book rooms and make sure we have decent horses. You should have seen his dismay when I told him I wanted to leave at nine tomorrow morning."

"He is always shocked when either one of us appears before noon," Diana said. "Poor man, I feel sorry for him. What is a cavalry officer to do when the war is over and his side has lost and he has no pension? He can hardly take up ditch digging."

Abigail tilted her head back, letting Diana run the brush all the way through from the top of her head. "You could be a ladies' maid if we lost our fortune," she said. "You are almost as good as Rosie."

"Mmm hmmm," said Diana, still brushing. Abigail

could see her face in the mirror. Her eyes were lowered, and she looked very demure.

"Well then." Abigail sat up suddenly, putting an end to the performance. "This is all very nice, but what do you want?"

"Am I so transparent?" Diana tried a rueful smile, a mixture of charm and repentance.

That smile had worked quite well on Diana's father. It did not usually work on Abigail. "Yes," she said tartly. She pulled her hair forward and began to braid it in quick, expert movements. "I cannot in all honesty say that I prefer Lisette's attacks on my scalp, but it has not escaped my notice that every time you offer to brush my hair on this trip you lull me into a trance and then make some outrageous demand. So, what is it this time? Could we possibly put off our departure tomorrow, because another young man has invited you on an outing to another ruined castle, and you will never have such a chance again, and it would be so very lowering to have Mademoiselle Esmond or even worse, your mother, along, so just this once would I be willing to let the young man's sister or aunt or ex-mistress be the chaperon—"

"Mama!" Diana flushed in annoyance; she hated it when Abigail was sarcastic. "She was *not* his ex-mistress."

"She was not a respectable woman."

"Well, neither are *you*," snapped her daughter, before she could stop herself. Then she turned bright red. In the mirror Abigail could see the panic in her eyes, quickly replaced by mortification. "Oh!" She threw down the hairbrush. "It is *your* fault I am so horrid! I was never like this with

Papa!" Turning, she ran out of the room, leaving the door open behind her.

Apparently she had forgotten that in order to accommodate the anticipated arrival of Cousin Joshua she had given up her own bedchamber and was now sharing with Abigail. Abigail counted to sixty: ten for Diana to reach the door of her former room, ten for her to remember that it was no longer hers, ten to try to open the locked door anyway, and thirty to concoct some new scheme to placate her disobliging mother. At the end of sixty Abigail still heard no footsteps outside. She shrugged, closed the door, wrapped herself in a shawl, and sat down by the lamp with her book. In the fifteen months since she had become reacquainted with her daughter there had been many similar scenes.

Five minutes later there was a tap on the door, and the handle turned gently. Diana peered around the edge of the door, looking, for once, rather unsure of herself. She stepped in and took a small, nervous breath. "I am very sorry, Mama." Her face, without its usual practiced repertoire of expressions, was the face of an eighteen-year-old girl rather than that of a sophisticated young lady.

Abigail moved over and made room on the settee. After a few minutes of silence—not an uncomfortable silence—Abigail asked gently, "Should I ring for a tisane?"

Diana shook her head.

"What did you want to ask me?"

The blond curls hid her daughter's face. "Nothing."

"I might say yes." Abigail paused. "Unlikely, of course. When you were little you once asked me if I ever said yes. And when I answered 'yes' you stamped your foot and told me that that particular yes did not count." That elicited a choked-off laugh. "Is it something about our journey tomorrow? Did one of your admirers ask to come with us? Or do you want me to protect you from Captain Hervé's attentions?"

"I do not find the captain difficult to manage." Diana sounded more like herself now; there was an amused arrogance in her tone. So far as Abigail could see, Diana did not find any male difficult to manage. Years of manipulating her father and half brother had honed her skills to a terrifying edge. It was her mother—her long-estranged, cautious, unsociable mother—whom Diana could not manage. And vice versa.

"If you must know . . ." A small, slippered foot scuffed carefully in a rectangle over the carpet. "I wondered if you might change your mind and ask Mr. Meyer to travel with us."

Abigail blinked. Diana had not been introduced to the unwelcome Mr. Meyer this afternoon. She had not even seen him—had she? Abigail had not shown her Joshua's letter; had only said, this morning, that there had been a mix-up and their cousin would not be joining them after all.

"I saw you speaking with him." More scuffing. "And I asked Monsieur Jusserand who he was."

The innkeeper was, of course, putty in Diana's delicate little hands.

"It was all a misunderstanding," Abigail said. She knew her voice sounded stiff; she knew Diana could sense her uneasiness. She tried to sound unconcerned. "Why would you want to change our arrangements, in any case? You just told me that you have no objection to Captain Hervé."

"I have no *objection*, no. But Mr. Meyer is far more . . . presentable, do you not think?" She shot her mother a look under her lashes. The minx look, Abigail had dubbed it.

"I did not notice." Abigail used her most repressive, motherly tone.

"Mother! He is *very* distinguished-looking. Everyone on the terrace said so."

It was no surprise that Diana would want to trade in the portly Hervé for the tall, keen-eyed man who had bowed over Abigail's hand this afternoon. Her daughter collected attractive males like ornaments. And Hervé was already her slave. She wanted a new challenge.

"It would not be right to impose on Mr. Meyer. We will do very well as we are."

"Why? He rode all the way here from Nice! It is rude of us to send him away like a piece of unwanted baggage!"

Abigail sighed. "Please trust my judgment on this, Diana. It would make me very uncomfortable to accept his offer, although it was well meant. If you are pining for another glimpse of Mr. Meyer, I suspect we will see him once or twice en route. There are not that many inns between here and Grasse."

There was another little silence. "Are you glad to be going home?" Diana asked hesitantly.

Abigail kept her tone neutral. "I suppose so. Are you?"

"I shall certainly be delighted to see the last of Digne-les-Bains."

"Well, we never intended to stay here quite so

long." Abigail rose and took off her shawl. She risked a teasing smile. "Were you very bored, dear?"

Diana made a face. "It is so *respectable*! We might as well have been in Bath or Tunbridge Wells."

"Had we been staying in Bath," Abigail pointed out, "those charming young English officers you tormented yesterday on the terrace would likely not have spoken to you. In France you are a countrywoman; at home you are Hebrew."

Her daughter flushed. "Even so, I am very glad to think I will never see Digne again after tomorrow morning."

3

Grasse, March 1

At the age of twenty-five, Anthony Roth reflected bitterly, he was already a laughingstock in four countries. Oh, not to the man on the street, of course. Merely to his very extensive family and their even more extensive network of friends and business associates. Like this man, a perfume broker, an important client of his late father, who was staring at him seemingly in horror, clearly looking for something in his appearance or manner to explain the stories.

"Is monsieur *the* Anthony Roth?" the Frenchman had asked just now. *The* Anthony Roth. The one who had been jilted by two fiancées within the space of six months, fiancées who had known him since childhood. Cousins, in fact. Anthony had the distinction of being both the first *and* the second Roth ever tossed into the dustbin by his betrothed. No wonder the man was staring. Surely there had to be some hidden defect when a wealthy young man with no obvious bodily affliction could not even manage to wed one of his own cousins in an arranged marriage. Or perhaps he did have a bodily affliction. He was not tall or muscular. He was not graceful or musical. He was a pale, short, nearsighted young man with a very good head for numbers and a reputation for skill and diplomacy in the international financial markets. The latter reputation, however, was fast disappearing this past year, since Anthony had become somewhat thin-skinned after the second broken engagement.

"What do you mean, *the* Anthony Roth?" he snapped, abandoning diplomacy once again.

"The author, of course."

Taken aback, Anthony blinked. "Author?"

"Of this treatise." The perfumer pulled down a document box from the shelves behind his desk, untied the ribbons, and extracted a pamphlet with a long title in Latin advertising it as the work of one A. Roth. He held it reverently, smoothing out the corners. "This has increased my clients' yield of tincture of lavender twofold."

"Oh." So the man had not been staring in horror. He had been staring in awe. At the wrong cousin. Anthony sighed. "No, that is my cousin Anselm. He is a chemist."

"A brilliant man." The perfumer carefully replaced the pamphlet, closed the cover, tied the ribbons in perfect, symmetrical bows, and set the box in exactly the same space on the shelf. "A brilliant, brilliant man."

Anselm was indeed brilliant. He was also married to one of Anthony's former fiancées, Elena Mendez. Elena had not intended to jilt Anthony. She had been on her way across Europe to the wedding, in

fact, when she had fallen in love with Anselm. As she
had explained in her very long and very apologetic
letter, it was impossible for a young lady of sensibil-
ity to remain indifferent to someone when she had
seen him wounded during a duel in defense of her
honor. Anthony had spent weeks after the receipt of
that letter imagining himself as a famous swords-
man and deadly shot. He had even gone to a shop
in Naples and looked at a few pistols, and a friend
had given him the name of a fencing master. But he
had been very busy at the bank—especially this last
year, when the end of the war threw all the financial
markets of Europe into chaos—and nothing had
come of his sanguinary ambitions.

"Still," said the perfumer, with a last, reluctant
glance at the box, "it is, of course, an honor to have
you here, Monsieur Roth. Normally it is Monsieur
Gibel who comes to meet with us."

Every year at this time, the perfumers of Grasse
estimated the spring lavender crop and negotiated
loans with the Roth-Meyer Bank for the expensive
process of production. Winter still lingered at the
higher elevations, but here in the coastal hills of
southern France the spiky purple plants were already poking out of the soil. Apparently this would
be an exceptional harvest—and, with peace in
Europe for the first time in over ten years, the perfumers were confident that they would sell every
drop they produced. Since the loan amount was so
large, and since Anthony was en route to London
in any case, he and his mother had agreed that it
would be appropriate for a Roth family member to
go in person to this year's meeting. His mother had
also hinted delicately and then much less delicately

and then almost belligerently that he might wish to travel on from Grasse with his uncle. As everyone in the family knew, Nathan Meyer had been lured to France in the hopes that he might wed Joshua Hart's beautiful young cousin.

"I think it might be a bit awkward," Anthony had said to his mother, after the first delicate hint.

"No," he had said, after the second, less delicate hint.

"Absolutely not!" he had shouted, after she had come out and told him that Nathan was impossible with females and would probably welcome his nephew's company and if by some chance Miss Hart did not suit Nathan, perhaps Anthony himself might offer the young lady an alternate choice within the family.

And that was the point, of course. Keep those large, lovely Roth-Meyer bank accounts from being frittered away in dowries and marriage settlements. The best solution was to marry a kinswoman, but since Anthony had clearly bungled his chances for a cousin, his mother was willing to settle for second best: an heiress like Diana Hart.

"I am *never* coming within fifty miles of any courtships, engagements, or weddings involving any member of the Roth or Meyer families ever again," Anthony had said in a tone of voice he did not even know he possessed. "Do I make myself clear?"

The subject had not been mentioned again. Nathan Meyer was the father of Anthony's other ex-fiancée; and although he did feel just a bit guilty about avoiding his uncle, Anthony preferred to meet him in company in London rather than travel in close quarters with him for ten days. The Meyers terrified him, frankly. It had been almost a relief when Rachel broke their engagement. She was taller than he was, she was more athletic than he was, and she was depressingly full of energy. Her younger brother was even worse: James had taken a false identity as a Christian in order to hold a commission under Wellington, and the exploits of Captain James Nathanson were famous all over Europe. Duels, secret missions, three daring escapes after falling into French hands, women swooning at his feet, etcetera, etcetera. In the company of his Meyer cousins, Anthony had always felt as though they were painted in color and he was a faded gray. As for his uncle—he was the most terrifying of all. He was not lively and charming, like Rachel, or notorious, like James. He was a quiet man, unobtrusive without being timid or humble. His work in the family bank had been competent, no more, and he had spent very little time there since the death of his wife. No one who met him would suspect that he spoke six languages fluently or that he was deadly with a knife or that he could memorize the contents of a desk drawer in a few seconds, down to the last crumb of dried snuff. He had, in fact, been Wellington's principal intelligence agent in Spain and France, and was the most dangerous man Anthony had ever met. No, Anthony would attend tonight's dinner with the perfumers, sign the papers for the loan tomorrow morning, and head back to the coast as fast as he could go. The bank's very efficient courier system would keep him informed of his uncle's movements, and he would take care not to get on the same boat from Antibes, or even to stay in the same town as Nathan Meyer.

The perfumer was asking him something—had he had a chance to rest, to change his clothing? With an effort, Anthony returned his attention to the business at hand. It was nearly time for the dinner, which was at the hotel where Anthony had taken rooms. He let the broker lead the way down the steep hillside and managed to pay attention as the man pointed out shops and factories belonging to his clients. They were deep in a discussion of the new French tariffs when Anthony became aware of an odd, insistent noise. It sounded like shouting. It was coming from the foot of the hill, and now he could see bobbing lights gathering below and hear individual voices.

"*Nom de Dieu*," said the Frenchman, shocked. "A brawl, so early in the evening?"

There was a sudden pounding of hooves, and Anthony jerked his companion back just in time to avoid being run down in the narrow street. Two riders thundered by, and from the sound of it, more were on their way up the hill. He hauled the perfumer into the nearest alleyway and watched, stupefied, as shouting men ran up the street alongside the next wave of horsemen, waving their arms and slapping the horses' flanks to make them go faster.

"What is happening?" he asked, stunned. "This is no brawl."

The broker shook his head. "I do not know. Something terrible. The English have invaded, perhaps."

"Nonsense." Anthony was quite sure the English had not invaded. Why bother? The newly restored Bourbon king was in London's pocket.

"Austria, then."

A woman ran by, sobbing, her feet slipping on the muddy cobblestones. Anthony caught her arm. "What is it, madame? What has caused all this commotion?"

She wrenched her arm away and stumbled on up the street, but he had seen her face in the light from the lantern above the door. Those were tears of joy.

It was only six leagues from Digne to Barrême, but they were six nearly vertical leagues, ascending several thousand feet to cross the Col de Chaudon, and then dropping down sharply to the hill that cradled the smaller town. The road as it approached the pass was in fact little more than a cart track, and Meyer abandoned the jouncing carriage at the first halt, explaining to the coachman that the horses would find the vehicle easier to pull empty.

"Suit yourself," growled the man.

Meyer's servant, Rodrigo, said nothing, but handed him the bridle of the familiar shaggy horse with something like a smile.

"Did *you* ride in the cursed thing on the way to Digne?" Meyer demanded.

"Certainly not, señor." Rodrigo glanced back at the steep descent into Digne. "I, ah, felt it was my duty to observe the road carefully. So as to be prepared for any difficulties when we returned with the young lady."

"The young lady and her mother and two maids and a footman," Meyer reminded him. "Imagine trying to bring that lot across the pass."

Rodrigo looked over at the horses, straining a bit

on the steep slope even with no passengers in the carriage. At the summit, half a league ahead, there was still snow. "We would have needed a second carriage, of course."

"Yes, double the chances of a broken axle." Meyer paused to adjust one stirrup. "I'm well out of it. Let Mrs. Hart's French captain hire drivers and horses and inspect harness and retie bandboxes onto the roof. We shall proceed at our leisure into Barrême and have supper at that excellent hostelry you discovered."

"The Cheval Blanc."

"That's it, yes. By tomorrow night we should reach the coast." He glanced down at his mount. "On a more prepossessing animal, I trust."

"And will you send a message to Mr. Roth about Miss Hart?"

The Roth-Meyer banks maintained an extensive and remarkably fast courier system all over Europe. Meyer had made good use of it during his work for the British army.

He thought for a moment. "It would be prudent, although I am tempted to let him stew as the rumors begin trickling back to London."

"You agreed to come over here and escort her," Rodrigo reminded him.

"So I did. And look to have escaped undamaged, for once."

"I did not meet the young lady. What is she like?"

"Fair hair, just out of the schoolroom, and the most accomplished flirt I have seen since Elena Mendez." He added, after a short pause, "One wonders what my brother-in-law Roth was thinking. She is certainly very pretty, but unless I miss my guess she is a five-foot-tall bundle of willful mischief. I do not envy her future husband. Or, for that matter, her mother, who has charge of her at the moment."

The track now became very steep, and for several minutes the two men rode on in silence, shifting their weight carefully in the saddle as the road angled up to the summit. Meyer was looking back, checking on the progress of the empty carriage behind them, when Rodrigo reined in beside him with an exclamation. He pointed up the hill to a level stretch just below the pass. "Would that, by any chance, be Miss Hart's party?"

Two carriages were drawn up across the road. At the side of the leading vehicle, whose horses had been unhitched, a stout man in a tricorn was leaning over, talking to another man who was halfway under the body of the carriage. A third man was attempting to hold both the unyoked animals and the pair still poled to the second carriage. Four women stood huddled together a short distance away in one of the few spots not dusted with snow. One, the smallest, had spotted the approaching horsemen. She took two steps towards them, stretched out a tiny, gloved hand in mute appeal, and then crumpled to the ground.

"That is Miss Hart." Meyer's voice was dry. "The one who just fainted."

"Is she an invalid, señor?"

"No. A comedienne." He spurred his horse forward, but the girl was being helped to her feet already, and by the time he arrived she was being settled in the rear carriage with some rugs.

He turned to the mother, who was looking more

exasperated than concerned. "May I be of some assistance, Mrs. Hart?"

"Thank you, no. My daughter tripped on a rock." Out of the corner of his eye, Meyer saw Diana Hart's eyes flash as her elegant swoon was converted into a stumble. "She is already recovered, as you can see."

Miss Hart was duly introduced, and assured her would-be rescuer that she was only a bit shaken.

"And the carriage?" he asked, looking again to Abigail Hart.

"A broken strap." She gestured towards her coachman, who had emerged from underneath the lead vehicle. "Jacques tells me the wheel is sound. We should be under way within half an hour. Excuse me one moment." She went over to the stout man and said something. He removed his hat with a flourish, bowed, and made a long reply, accompanied by more flourishes, which she eventually cut off with a curt gesture. "We will move our second coach to the side," she said, returning. "I do apologize for blocking the road."

By this time Meyer's own carriage had come up. "My vehicle is at your disposal," he said, indicating the shabby barouche drawn up behind him. "It would easily hold you, your daughter, and your maids; there is no reason for you to wait in the snow while repairs are made. They may take longer than your coachman supposes, and this spot is rather exposed."

It was a raw day, and the wind was cold. He could see her hesitate, but then she shook her head. "I would not wish to inconvenience you."

"Hardly an inconvenience. I am not using it at the moment."

He saw her flush in embarrassment as she realized

that the carriage had in fact been hired for herself and her daughter. "Some fresh air will do us all good. Please do not let me keep you, Mr. Meyer."

That was a dismissal if he had ever heard one. He touched his hat and rode on.

Rodrigo, who had remained behind to help move the second carriage out of the road, caught up to Meyer about ten minutes later. They were just beyond the summit, and both men reined in for a moment, looking down the steep, winding road that led into the cloud-covered valley.

"I checked the brakes, señor."

"On our carriage?" asked Meyer, surprised. "I thought you did that this morning."

"On the ladies' carriage."

"No business of ours."

Rodrigo opened his mouth to object and then wisely shut it again.

"I don't suppose you also made sure that they had a proper strap to use as a replacement," Meyer said after a moment.

"They do. And tools. And even a spare wheel rim."

Meyer grunted. "So that French lieutenant, or captain, or whatever he is, is less of a fool than he looks."

"Oh no, señor. Your impression was quite accurate. He is a fool. The coachman told me that Mrs. Hart arranges everything."

"I see." He nudged his horse back into motion. "Well, they certainly have no need of us."

"As you say, señor."

"Mrs. Hart has made that abundantly clear."

Rodrigo coughed. "The señora did tell me to thank you again."

They rode on in silence for another five minutes. "How many rooms are there at the Cheval Blanc?" Meyer asked finally.

"Five, sir. A parlor and four bedchambers."

"Go on ahead. Book those rooms for Miss Hart and her party, and then find us somewhere else to stay."

There was only one other decent hostelry in Barrême, a tiny posting station right on the main road. It had mediocre food, no private parlor, and only one bedroom. The wine was good, but Meyer did not get to enjoy much of it, because the host announced at ten o'clock that he was closing up for the night. When Meyer asked for a bottle to take up to his bedchamber the man looked at him as though he had proposed to host an orgy. Barrême, it was clear, was not a place for those who kept late hours. Meyer, a light sleeper, was therefore somewhat surprised to be awakened in the middle of the night by the unmistakable sound of hoofbeats cantering up to the inn. He wrenched open the casement and looked out onto the road. It was still well before dawn, perhaps an hour or more. There was very little light, certainly not enough for ordinary travelers to feel comfortable riding these mountain roads. And yet here were five riders, approaching the inn at a dangerously fast pace. In the next minute three of the riders had flashed by, still heading north on the road, although their horses were laboring. The other two were beneath his own window, pounding on the door and calling the tavern keeper by name. They sounded drunk. They must be drunk. Surely what they were saying was a jest, a prank. Meyer pulled on his breeches and boots and ran down the stairs, just in time to see the half-dressed innkeeper snatch up a lantern and run headlong out the door, leaving it wide open.

Meyer stood in the doorway for twenty minutes, watching lights gradually go on all over the village, listening to the shouts and catcalls, the anxious female voices, the sound of wagons rumbling onto the street. More riders went by, and one group of men on foot, arguing ferociously with each other as they walked. Rodrigo had come down some time ago with two loaded pistols and was standing next to him. The sky grew lighter and lighter, and still Meyer leaned against the door frame, stunned and horrified. There was another emotion buried beneath the disbelief and the revulsion, but he refused to acknowledge it right then.

The passing groups became less frequent, and the sun was nearly up. Meyer was hazily thinking that he should move, go inside, finish getting dressed, when a lone rider pulled up his horse suddenly and jumped off nearly on top of him. Even half-frozen with shock Meyer had his pistol up instantly, but in the next moment he saw who it was: a short young man with strands of sweat-soaked hair plastered to his forehead and the marks of a pince-nez on each side of his nose. He was breathing hard, and he staggered slightly as he stepped away from the horse.

"Uncle Nathan," he croaked. "Thank God I spotted you. I've been riding all night, hoping to find you. You've heard the news?"

Meyer nodded. He was so numb that he didn't

even think to ask how his nephew Anthony had come to be in France.

"Is there no ostler?" the younger man asked, looking around impatiently.

"He ran off." Meyer gestured to Rodrigo, who took the horse and led it away.

Anthony limped inside and collapsed into the first chair.

"Something to drink?"

His nephew nodded. "No innkeeper either, I take it?"

Meyer strode over to the low door that led down to the cellar. "He ran off before the ostler did. I'm afraid we'll have to serve ourselves. Just a moment." He cocked his pistol and blew the lock off the door.

Anthony flinched at the noise. "I thought you could pick locks."

"I felt like shooting something." An understatement. He grabbed a lantern and returned a minute later, slightly dusty but triumphant.

"That's not wine," said his nephew, peering at the bottle. "That's brandy."

"Not just any brandy, my boy." He went behind the bar and found two glasses. "A 1785 Armagnac. It isn't every day Napoleon escapes from Elba."

Anthony took a healthy swig out of the glass Meyer handed him. "What have you heard?"

"Not much. Most people have been running by shouting, *'Vive l'Empereur!'* He landed yesterday evening?"

"Yes. About an hour before sunset. Landed on the beach, not at Antibes."

"There's a royal garrison at Antibes, of course he

didn't land there. Go on. How many men did he have with him?"

Anthony shook his head. "I've heard every number from fifty to five thousand. More every minute, that's clear enough. That fat Bourbon fool we put on the throne last year is not very popular with his subjects."

"Rabble joining up will only slow Napoleon down," muttered Meyer. "He had his personal troops on Elba, over a thousand men, many of them from the Old Guard—they will be with him." He paced up and down, unable to stand still. Now that the shock and anger were wearing off he felt almost elated. Some part of him had been asleep since Bonaparte's abdication last April. It was coming back to life, and it was starved for action. There was an enemy again; there would be troop movements and supply trains and weapons distributions—numbers, names, places. He itched to collect them and pass them on. Supposing, just supposing, Bonaparte chose to come into the mountains? To come this way? It was not impossible. In fact, it was very likely. "Has he sent out any advance parties? Given any indication of where he is headed?"

Anthony drained his glass and set it carefully on the table. "If he has, they're still well behind me. Never ridden so fast in my life." He was looking even paler than usual and Meyer suddenly recalled that Anthony was not one of Wellington's young intelligence officers, but the pampered, sedentary heir to a banking fortune.

"When did you last eat?" he demanded.

His nephew's smile had an odd sideways tilt. "Yesterday morning."

"Go on upstairs and try to get some sleep. I'll see what I can find in the way of food."

Anthony nodded and limped towards the stairs. "Which room upstairs?"

"There's only one," Meyer told him. "Not up to the bank's usual standards of accommodation, I apologize."

"Well, if I owned a cellar full of that brandy, I wouldn't bother about bedchambers either," Anthony said sleepily. "That stuff is, what, ten guineas a bottle in London? Perhaps we should buy some to take with us."

He frowned as his nephew disappeared. Eli had mentioned something about Anthony coming to England, and that final comment seemed to confirm it. The last thing Meyer wanted at the moment was a traveling companion, but he might have no choice. At least he was not saddled with Miss Hart and her mother.

4

The first council of war, as Anthony would later call it, was convened at half-past seven on the second of March 1815, in the best (and only) bedchamber of the Auberge de Barrême. It consisted of Anthony Roth, banker, reclining; Rodrigo Santos, manservant, seated; and Nathan Meyer, retired spy, standing. Or rather, not standing. He was pacing back and forth so quickly the floor vibrated beneath his feet.

"Would you mind sitting down?" Anthony was propped up in bed, somewhat cleaner than he had been two hours earlier, eating a poached egg that his uncle had managed to produce in the inn's kitchen. "You're making me dizzy."

"That's the brandy," said Meyer callously. "And there is only one chair. Which I have given to Rodrigo, since he has already ridden out twice this morning to see what he could discover."

"Is there any more news?" Anthony had been asleep during both of Rodrigo's expeditions.

"Yes. No." His uncle waved towards a piece of paper on the table, which called on all brave Frenchmen to rise against the puppet king installed by the tyrannical British. "A handwritten copy of the proclamation issued last night after Napoleon's landing. They had it at the bakery. What they did not have was bread, and that is a very bad sign. When the bakers of France are not baking, the entire fabric of the nation has collapsed." He stalked over to the window again. "Obviously, I should do *something*. But what? Wellington is in Vienna, should I head east? Or west, to the royalist troops stationed near Avignon? Perhaps I should get down to the coast and sail back to England. I need more information, and all I have is this damned proclamation."

"Nearest bank courier is in Nice," muttered Anthony. "A day's ride there, and a day's ride back. What about the French military semaphore stations? Isn't there one at Toulon?"

"They cannot use the semaphores at night," Meyer reminded him. "Or when there is fog." He nodded towards the gray mizzle outside the window.

Rodrigo pushed himself up out of the chair. "I will ride south, señor, at least as far as Senez. The news is all coming from the south; the closer we are to events the more likely we are to have an accurate report."

"No, I'll go." Meyer was shrugging on his coat. "You've been out enough. Get yourself something to eat, lie down."

"It is much safer for a Spanish servant to make enquiries right now than for an English master," Rodrigo objected. "The royalists and the Bonapartists are agreed on only one thing: if something bad is happening, it is England's fault."

"Good point." He took off his coat again, but when

Rodrigo started for the door he stopped him. "Sit back down. I don't need you, I need your clothing."

Anthony watched, fascinated, as his uncle exchanged boots, shirts, and jackets with his servant. Meyer was whistling as he left.

"I've known you for years and never noticed: you're nearly the same height and build as my uncle," Anthony said, staring at the olive-skinned servant. "Is that why he won't go anywhere without you?"

"He just did go somewhere without me," the Spaniard pointed out. He grimaced. "Did you hear him? Happy as a lark, as you say in English. When he first heard that Napoleon had landed, he was shocked, angry. But now he has a chance to pretend to be a Spanish servant, and he is like a child with a new toy. He will speak French with a Spanish accent, he will use Spanish gestures—even that song he was whistling is an old folk song from Andalusia. And the possibility that some mob of drunken Provençal villagers may beat him to death for asking the wrong question makes him enjoy it all the more." He stomped over to the door. "What is more, I must now go out in *his* clothing, and I look perfectly ridiculous."

Anthony did not think Rodrigo looked ridiculous, but Rodrigo did not seem to have his master's knack of taking on the personality along with the costume. He looked like a Spaniard who had switched jackets with an Englishman. "Why must you go out?"

"We need to buy food. Barrême is on the verge of full-scale panic, and the first thing a fearful populace hoards is food. Also, there is one little matter I forgot to take care of when I went out earlier."

"Can it not wait?" Anthony was (not unreasonably, in his opinion) a trifle uneasy at the thought of remaining alone in a deserted inn while the south of France erupted outside the unlocked door.

"Perhaps," was the enigmatic reply. "Perhaps not, however." Confirming Anthony's fears, he tossed him a pistol as he left.

"Do you know how to use it?" he asked, seeing Anthony's horrified expression.

"No."

"Point it and look grim, then," Rodrigo advised. "And don't speak French if you can help it. You have a pronounced English accent."

Anthony spent five minutes pointing the pistol, very carefully, and practicing a grim stare. Then he gave up and went back to sleep.

He woke up to the sound of feet pounding up the stairs and voices in the room below. Sitting up with a jerk, he flailed around under the bedclothes looking in vain for the pistol. Luckily, the feet belonged to Rodrigo.

"What is it?" Anthony asked, alarmed at the servant's tense expression.

"Complications. I've told them you will be down immediately. Shall I help you get dressed?"

"Told whom?" He swung his legs down to the floor and nearly screamed at the pain in his thighs.

"Two Englishwomen, who were abandoned this morning by their French servants. The maid at least had the courtesy to tell them she was leaving. The others just vanished. Their courier, a retired army captain, had most of their money in his possession."

"Captain in which army?"

"Napoleon's, of course."

"Then he is no longer retired, is he?" Wincing, Anthony staggered across the floor to the basin and rinsed his face and teeth. "Is one of these abandoned ladies by any chance Miss Hart?"

Rodrigo looked surprised. "You know about Miss Hart?"

"My mother," explained Anthony apologetically. "She is, um, very devoted to the family interests." He grabbed a hairbrush, presumably his uncle's, and swiped it over the top of his head. Then he attempted his stockings and boots. "Perhaps it would be best to bring the ladies up here," he said when he was finally dressed. "More privacy." And he was honestly not sure if his aching muscles would make it down the narrow stairs.

"I suppose you are right," said Rodrigo. He straightened the bedclothes, threw the wash water out the window, and disappeared. A moment later he was back, holding the door open. "Mrs. Hart and Miss Hart, sir."

Luckily, Anthony was standing with his hand on the back of the chair. Otherwise, when Diana Hart walked into the room, his already strained legs would have given way. She was the most beautiful girl he had ever seen.

Abigail was normally a light sleeper, but she was very tired, and the Cheval Blanc was quieter and more secluded than the Auberge de Barrême. Consequently, she did not realize there was anything wrong until she woke up and discovered that it was eight o'clock. Lisette had been instructed to wake her at six. Not only that, but no one had been in to make up the fire, and there was no water in her washbasin.

Frowning, she rang the bell and waited. Two min-

utes passed, then three, then five. Nothing happened.
She opened her door and peered out into the hall. Agitated voices could be heard arguing down in the
public rooms below. With her shawl thrown over her
nightgown, she darted out and tapped softly at the
door of Diana's room. There was no response, but her
daughter was often difficult to wake in the morning.
By now Abigail was beginning to be puzzled. Whatever
her other faults, Lisette had always been cheerful and
reliable in the mornings. Glancing quickly around to
make sure no else was upstairs, she marched down to
the other end of the small corridor and banged on the
door of the room Mlle. Esmond and Lisette were sharing. It swung open, with a sad creaking noise.

The room was empty. Crumpled bedclothes, open
drawers, and a still-burning lamp bore mute witness
to an early, hurried departure. Propped on the night
table was a folded piece of paper. More and more bewildered, she took it up. It had no superscription,
but there was no doubt it was meant for her. Printed
in smudged pencil, it read:

Most esteemed madame,

> *It is with desolation that I must leave your very
> gracious employment in some haste and without
> taking leave of you and Mlle. Hart. In this emergency I must, however, rejoin my family in Nice
> immediately.*

> *Please be assured, madame, of my most respectful
> devotion.*

Juliette Esmond

Her first thought was *Good riddance,* and she immediately felt guilty. She knew all too well how difficult the life of an unmarried, middle-class female could be. And Miss Esmond, unlike Abigail, did not have a substantial personal fortune to ease those difficulties. Her only saleable assets were her rigid aura of propriety and a talent for intimidating servants at the various superior inns the Harts had patronized during their stay in France. Abigail had been very thankful, at least at first, to have an ally in the battle to keep her daughter's wilder impulses in check. She sighed and refolded the note. Only then did she notice the scrawled postscript, on the outside: *Lisette will accompany me to Castellane, where her brother resides.* Abigail raised her eyebrows. She had not thought there was any love lost between Lisette and the prim older woman, but obviously somehow Mlle. Esmond had persuaded Lisette that her own need of a companion outweighed Lisette's obligation to her employers.

Thinking dark thoughts about unreliable foreign servants, she headed back to her daughter's bedchamber. A second tap on the door produced the same response as her first attempt. Waking Diana sometimes required prolonged, loud knocking, as she knew from experience, and she was not prepared to stand here in her nightgown. She retreated to her own room and got dressed as best she could with no wash water and no one to help put up her hair. She was very annoyed. Even if Mlle. Esmond and Lisette had, for some unaccountable reason, suddenly gone off early this morning, surely the inn had its own serving girls? She marched downstairs determined to give the innkeeper a piece of her mind.

The agitated voices were louder now, coming from the front room of the inn. She opened the door and stepped in. Six people were clustered by the window that overlooked the street. She recognized Munot—the innkeeper—and two of the maidservants; the others, all male, looked to be townsmen. One of them was wearing stockings of two different colors and had what looked very much like a nightshirt stuffed into his breeches. They fell silent as she entered—a cold, wary silence. Munot would not meet her eyes. Last night he had hovered over their table at supper, pressing his best wines on them and joking with Captain Hervé about his good fortune in obtaining such lovely clients.

"I rang several times," she announced. "My own maid has been called away by a family emergency."

At this two of the men coughed.

Ignoring them, she turned to the nearer of the two maidservants, trying to sound firm and composed. "I require hot water and fresh towels, at once. Also, the fires in our rooms are out. Is Captain Hervé still abed?"

The maid glanced nervously at the door leading to the back rooms: the parlor and downstairs bedchamber.

Abigail did not wait for a reply. "Please ask him to wait on me at his earliest convenience."

She turned and left the room, but not without hearing the innkeeper say in a low voice, "That is her—the Englishwoman."

Five minutes later, the maidservant appeared. She had no hot water and no towels, and she was clearly very frightened. "My regrets, madame, but Monsieur Munot says that you must leave at once.

It is not safe for you here; there is strong feeling against the English now."

"But we have Captain Hervé, and our coachman. Surely there is no real cause for alarm?"

"Both men are gone, madame. Very early this morning." Bobbing a curtsey, the woman scuttled away.

"What is it, Mama?" Diana, in a lace-edged wrapper, had emerged into the hall.

"I don't know," Abigail said, worried. "Our servants have all vanished, and the innkeeper seems to have taken us in aversion." She was trying to remember how much money she had given Hervé last night. Quite a bit—there were the charges here at the inn, and two sets of horses, and the new, larger carriage she had bespoken for this morning. Perhaps he had left the purse with Munot.

The maidservant reappeared. "A gentleman to see you, madame." Booted feet were coming up the stairs, and Diana fled with a small shriek into her chamber.

It was Meyer's manservant. She recognized him at once, although he was dressed rather oddly, in an elegant shirt and jacket quite unlike the usual garb of a valet.

"I beg your pardon, Mrs. Hart, for venturing to come up uninvited, but I—" He cleared his throat. "Perhaps you recall me from yesterday. I am Rodrigo, Mr. Meyer's man. He is extremely concerned for your safety. He proposes that you and Miss Hart and your maids join him at the post house immediately."

"My maids have left," said Abigail in a voice that did not sound like her own. "Everyone has left." She took in a shaky breath. "Something has happened, but no one will tell me what it is." Diana had opened her door again, just a little.

He was taken aback. "You have not heard the news?"

"*What* news?"

"Napoleon landed near Antibes last night with a force of unknown size. He has pledged to reclaim France from its enemies. The first reports arrived here some hours ago, and the entire region is in chaos."

God help us. She leaned against the wall. Decades of conflict in Europe had finally ended last year— the same year that her nine-year exile from her daughter had been revoked. Two long-held, long-cherished fantasies, combined in one: to travel to the great cities of the continent with Diana. It had been her idea, her plan. She had made all the arrangements, hired Hervé, read dozens of now-outdated guidebooks and memoirs, pored over maps. And now her daughter—her sheltered, spoiled, impulsive, beautiful daughter—was trapped in a town full of Bonapartists in the middle of what had just become a war zone.

Abigail would, under ordinary circumstances, have kept Diana as far away from Nathan Meyer as possible. Her daughter was too young to be married; Abigail would not let Diana duplicate her own error if she could prevent it. And even if the notion of Diana's marriage had been more acceptable in the abstract, she would have been opposed to this particular match. Joshua Hart's clumsy maneuvering had made her furious. Luring them to Digne—*not* a town on her carefully compiled list of worthy sights for their tour—and then foisting Meyer on them at the last minute was, in her opinion, despicable. The letter extolling Meyer's qualifications as a bridegroom had enraged her even further. A gentleman of leisure! Received by such notables as Sir Charles

Barrett! What was admirable about leisure? What Jew was a gentleman? As she saw the women she had grown up with presiding over country homes and riding in carriages on the Sabbath and appearing in public with their arms bare, she despised them for aping the manners of a society that would never accept them. Meyer's own daughter, in fact, had recently married a Christian. The man was a profligate, an apostate, a disgrace. Had Abigail been on her own, she would have hesitated a long, long time before approaching Nathan Meyer for help. But she was not on her own, and so she did not hesitate at all.

"We can be ready in five minutes," she told the servant.

He nodded. "I will remain here, in the hall. Call if you need assistance. Bring only what you can carry yourselves, and dress warmly."

Twenty minutes later, she and Diana were ensconced in the bedchamber of the little post house, hastily cleared for their use by Meyer's nephew. Rodrigo had found them hot water and towels and even some breakfast. The street was quiet at the moment; the only sound was Diana's soft humming as she pinned up her hair. Abigail wanted to grab her, to shake her, to scream that the world could not be pieced back together by means of a washcloth and a cup of chocolate. But she said nothing, and when Diana asked her to help with the pins, Abigail stepped over and held them in hands that did not tremble.

The second council of war was convened in the public room of the Auberge de Barrême at a little past ten in the morning. It consisted of Diana Hart, seated; Abigail Hart, seated; Anthony Roth, seated; Rodrigo Santos, standing; and Nathan Meyer, standing. For this meeting, Meyer had decided to play the role of obliging family friend. He drew up chairs for the Harts at a table by the window and, after a moment, another one for Anthony.

"I assume that you wish to return to London," he said, addressing Abigail Hart. "As quickly and safely as possible."

She nodded.

"It is unfortunately not easy to determine the best means of achieving that object."

She stared up at him. "What do you mean? I thought you said a few minutes ago upstairs that you now knew where the invasion force was."

"Yes. I know where it is, and how large it is, and I was even able to obtain some information about their projected route." He flipped open a book lying on the table—he had borrowed it from her— and unfolded the map bound into the front cover. "We are here." His finger stabbed down just north of the town of Castellane. "Napoleon, with some fifteen hundred troops, is here." The finger moved south of Castellane to Grasse. "A small advance unit, under General Cambronne, is here." He pointed to Seranon, halfway in between. "Cambronne has sent a request to Castellane for provisions. Provisions for five thousand."

He saw both women swallow nervously as they looked at the map. Castellane was less than five leagues from Barrême.

"They are obviously headed to Castellane," said Meyer. "What I do not know is what they will do when they get there. They may turn west. There is a narrow pass from Castellane through the hills; in two days they could reach the Rhône, and have an easy route to Paris. They could also continue north, pass through Digne, and go up into the mountains."

"That was not a mountain?" Diana asked in a small voice. "The pass yesterday?"

"The range between Digne and Grenoble is, er, a bit higher," Anthony offered.

Nearly ten thousand feet higher, as Meyer calculated it, but the girl would likely be discovering that for herself very soon.

He captured Abigail Hart's gaze with his own. "We—you—have several choices. First, you can simply remain here. The army may well come through, but they are unlikely to molest a small party of visitors. After they pass, it might be easier to travel."

She shook her head. "I—I must confess that it was rather frightening to see the change in Monsieur Munot at the inn this morning. And I am anxious to leave before more recruits join the invaders."

"I take it, then, that for the same reason you would not wish to go south and attempt to reach the coast? That would be the second option."

She blinked. "Would that even be possible?"

"Possible, yes. But the roads to the south are jammed at the moment with panic-stricken farmers running away from trouble and bored young men running towards it. I would not care to travel in that direction escorting two women." He leaned over the table. "To my mind, the practical choice is between north and west. And that choice depends, of course, on where Bonaparte is planning to go."

"Where do *you* believe he will go?"

Meyer studied her, calculating his strategy. Her

green eyes narrowed. She was studying him in return. He could feel her suspicion, her hostility. Good.

"I believe he will go north." His voice was soft. "There are too many loyal garrisons in the Rhône Valley, and the people of that region have always supported the Bourbons."

"And we, therefore, should turn west."

"It is what I would advise."

"But"—her hand shot out and came down across the line representing the Rhône River—"if there are so many royalist troops here, do we not risk trapping ourselves between two opposing armies?"

He looked down, shrugged. "I cannot make this decision, Mrs. Hart. You are responsible for your daughter's safety; it must be your choice. Both routes have their dangers." He added after a moment, "You may also wish to consider that the northern route is extremely difficult. Yesterday's road is as nothing compared to some of the passes closer to Grenoble."

Abigail Hart was not a stupid woman, he decided. She did not like him, but she did not underestimate him either. He could understand her dilemma: was he urging her to go west in the hope that she would agree—or in the hope that she would rebel? The thread running between the two of them was stretched taut. Would she tug back? Or let go, and watch him stumble?

She bowed her head. All he could see of her now were her cap and the edge of her smooth, golden-brown hair. "Is your preference for the western route an overwhelming one?" she asked, very low. "Do you believe the choice is clear?"

He held very, very still. "It is not clear at all. That

is why I am so reluctant to endanger you without giving you a say."

"I would prefer to go north, then." She looked up at him. "I cannot like the notion of heading directly into a valley full of newly mobilized soldiers."

"I could, of course, ride west today. I would rejoin you in Digne two days from now with more information about the state of things near the Rhône. You could travel with my nephew in the meantime."

"No!" cried Diana immediately.

Anthony flushed and bit his lip.

"It might be best to stay together," Abigail said. Her face was tinged with red, although it was not as red as his nephew's.

"Very well." Meyer turned to Rodrigo. "Can you have the horses harnessed in half an hour?"

"Yes, señor." His expression was very cold. So Rodrigo, at least, had understood what was happening.

"And you, Mrs. Hart? Will that be enough time for you and your daughter? Are your bags packed?"

Her expression was just as cold as Rodrigo's. "We have one bandbox apiece, Mr. Meyer, and a small valise. I daresay we can manage to put on our bonnets and close up three bags in thirty minutes. If you will excuse us?" Without acknowledging his bow, she led her daughter off towards the bedchamber.

Rodrigo did not move.

"The horses?" Meyer prompted.

The servant gave him a fierce look. "What would you have done if I had told her the truth?"

He sighed. "What truth?"

"That you know France like the back of your hand. That entire divisions of the British army followed your recommendations for their line of march. That it is absurd for anyone else in this party to have any say in this decision whatsoever. Now you have reeled in that poor woman like a fish on the line, so that you can absolve yourself of blame later. You know Napoleon will head for the mountains, and you goaded her into proposing that route for us."

"I am not omniscient," said Meyer wearily. "I believe he will go north, yes, but it is not certain."

"I pray that he does go north," Rodrigo said, still glaring. "Because if he goes west, you will abandon the ladies and go after him, and I will be ashamed that I ever served you."

"*Do* you serve me, Rodrigo Santos?" His voice was low and hard. "Or do you serve some dream of Iberian chivalry? I did not ask you to go to the Cheval Blanc this morning. I did not authorize you to bring those women here and offer my services as escort."

"Would you have left them here unprotected?" Rodrigo asked, shocked.

"Perhaps." He stared out the window for a moment. "But it is too late now. You offered them my help, and they accepted. I will keep them safe, if I can."

5

"We have been traveling for two days and we are back where we began," Diana said, tossing her bonnet onto the bed. "In tedious, tedious Digne-les-Bains. Only *now* we have a horrid little room in a horrid little inn instead of our lovely rooms at the Auberge des Cygnes."

The Auberge had been full—or rather, Abigail suspected, reluctant to house English guests. It had taken Rodrigo several hours to find them accommodation for the night, and she shuddered to think what they were probably paying for the two grudgingly conceded bedchambers at Le Mercure. She did not know precisely what the charges were, because Meyer had refused to let her pay them. Or to pay for the horses, or the carriage, or the hamper of food Rodrigo had somehow procured before they left Barrême, or even for her lodging at the Cheval Blanc. He had pointed out this morning that thanks to Hervé's treachery she had very little ready coin and her letter of credit was unlikely to be honored in the small mountain towns on their route. She had conceded this and had proposed—quite reasonably, she thought—to keep an account and repay him when they reached London. But in a typical display of high-handed male arrogance, he had informed her that he had better things to do with his time than collect receipts for every coin they spent. Then he had stalked off before she could reply.

That was the first argument. The second argument was about their papers. Meyer had asked for them before setting off from Barrême and had then, without so much as a by-your-leave, taken them away.

"What have you done with our papers?" Abigail had asked when he had returned empty-handed.

"Put them somewhere safe." He was tightening the girth on his horse, not looking at her.

"Where? What if I need them?"

"I will fetch them out."

"Mr. Meyer." She spoke softly, slowly. Now he did look up. For some reason he seemed almost amused, and that enraged her further. "Those are my papers, mine and my daughter's."

"I do not dispute that."

"Then why have you stolen them?"

"I have not 'stolen' them. But I do not wish you to show those papers to any Frenchman with a sash on his coat who asks to see them. I am charged with your safety; in the interests of that safety I must reserve the right to decide when to show our papers and to whom."

She forgot to be angry for a moment; she was too shocked. "But—we cannot refuse to show our papers!"

"There will be many travelers without papers on the roads of France this week, I assure you. A few coins will be just as welcome in most cases, and far safer." He gave one last, savage jerk on the strap and walked away, adding, over his shoulder, "And unfortunately for your accounts, I am afraid that it is not customary to give receipts for bribes."

She was not going to let him march off like that twice in a row. Abandoning dignity, she ran after him.

"Mr. Meyer!"

He turned.

"You do understand that without those papers Diana and I cannot go anywhere on our own? That we are virtually your prisoners?"

"It is at the very least a mutual bondage, madam." His mouth was set in a grim line. "I cannot leave you; I have pledged my word to protect you. We travel at your pace, along a route you have chosen, to your destination. You will forgive me if I attempt to ensure that we reach that destination without attracting the attention of Bonapartist mobs."

That time she had been the one to walk away, resolving not to speak to the insufferable Mr. Meyer for the rest of the day. Perhaps he had read her mind; perhaps he had made a similar resolve. It was now nearly ten hours later, and she had caught no more than a glimpse of him in that entire time. He had ridden outside the carriage throughout the journey back to Digne, even though it was a cold, dreary day. At every halt he had vanished, reappearing only as they were about to get under way again. When they reached the little spa town he had vanished again. He was making it quite clear that he wanted nothing to do with the Harts.

Unfortunately, one of the Harts was behaving equally badly. While the uncle had been pointedly

absent, the nephew had been gracious and attentive. It was young Roth who had chatted with
determined cheerfulness in the carriage, Roth who
had handed them in and out of the vehicle, Roth
who had procured hot drinks, Roth who had remained with them at Digne's posting station while
the servant hunted for lodging, Roth who had escorted them, a few minutes ago, to this room and
tipped the servant who carried their meager luggage. And every overture by Anthony Roth had
been met with the coldest, most contemptuous response imaginable on Diana's part.

"Have you visited this part of France before, Miss
Hart?" Roth would ask.

"No, I have not." In a tone that might have been
acceptable if Diana were traveling on a stage coach
and some stranger had leered at her. Or perhaps
not even then.

At this point Abigail would hastily break in. "It
has been so difficult to travel, of course, while the
war was on. Although I understand that you have
been doing business in Italy for some time now. In
Naples? We very much enjoyed our brief stay in
Italy. Diana, did you not say only the other day how
charming you found Florence?" And so on. Abigail
did not have a talent for babbling; her efforts had
likely only rubbed salt in Roth's wounds.

Abigail took off her bonnet and put it down next
to Diana's. Part of her knew that ten hours of rough
roads, combined with her irritation at Meyer, might
make this a poor moment to speak calmly and
firmly to her daughter about her rude behavior.
But she felt obliged to make the attempt.

"Diana, if today was a sample of how you mean to

treat Mr. Roth I warn you right now that I will not tolerate it," she said. "How could you be so uncivil?"

At Abigail's indignant question, Diana lifted her chin. "I did not wish to encourage his attentions."

"You cannot tell me that you do not know how to discourage a young man's attentions in a less brutal manner. I have been watching you encourage and discourage would-be gallants all over France for many weeks now."

"Do you think me a flirt, Mama?" She lifted one eyebrow in a manner calculated to remind her mother of just how flirtatious she could be.

They had had this conversation before, including the eyebrow. With an effort, Abigail repressed an impulse to stalk across the room and shake her daughter until her teeth rattled. For someone who had seen her mother only twice a year from the age of eight to the age of seventeen, Diana had an uncanny instinct for the precise phrase and gesture that would irritate Abigail the most.

"We are not discussing flirtation. We are discussing common courtesy."

Diana raised both eyebrows this time. "Oh? It seemed to me that you were not very courteous to Mr. Meyer earlier today."

Abigail thought of several responses: "Two wrongs do not make a right." Or, more to the point, "Mr. Meyer is the most provoking man I have ever met." Instead, she took a deep breath and said quietly, "I did not behave well, I admit it. But I was hoping that you would make up for my lapse. Instead you outdid me."

That spiked Diana's guns; she had expected Abigail to defend herself. She looked down, uncertain how to respond, then capitulated—not without a small grimace of distaste. "I will try to be more polite, Mama, but he is very tedious."

Everything was tedious today, according to Diana. The carriage, the weather, the meager luncheon at the mountain tavern, the book Abigail had offered to lend her.

"I found him a very pleasant and well-informed young man."

"That is not what I meant, Mama. It is his *manner.* You know what I am talking about: the way he turns red when I look at him, and stumbles when he helps me out of the carriage, and stares at me when I pretend to be asleep so as to escape his attention."

Abigail did indeed know what Diana was talking about. Roth was clearly smitten, and he was not the type to interest Diana. He was short, with a pale complexion and fair hair. He had nice eyes—at least Abigail thought them attractive—but they were blue. And at the moment, he could barely walk properly; evidently he had ridden hard the day before and was still recovering. Diana preferred tall, dark, athletic men. Like Nathan Meyer.

On cue, her daughter strolled over to the window and said pensively, "Mr. Roth does not look much like his uncle, does he?" A pause. "By the way, will Mr. Meyer be joining us for supper?"

"We will be eating in our room."

"What?" Diana spun around.

Abigail held up the note the inn's servant had brought up with their bags. "Mr. Meyer sends his compliments, but there are no private parlors available. He will arrange for a meal to be brought up to the room, since we are fatigued and will wish to retire early." She did not bother to conceal the irritation in her voice.

"Well!"

And before Abigail could stop her, Diana had marched to the door and was headed downstairs, with Abigail hurrying after her. She could not prevent Diana from making a scene—she had tried twice before on this trip, and failed both times—but she might be able to contain the damage. Although if Diana was planning to light into Nathan Meyer, Abigail was not sure she wanted to stop her.

There was no scene. Diana, and Abigail behind her, took one look at the boisterous crowd in the public room of the Mercure and retreated precipitately back upstairs. Diana even locked the door. They looked at each other sheepishly.

"Our room seems very clean for—for this sort of place," Diana said tentatively. Then she started to giggle. "Mother, did you *see* what the fat woman in pink was wearing on her head? It looked like a dead rabbit!"

Meyer was getting ready to leave again. He opened the shutters and peered out at the sky. "Still cloudy. I hope the moon comes out; that road will be nearly impassible in the dark." It would not be an easy trip even if the moon did appear. He had been on horseback all day, and now he was facing an additional forty-mile roundtrip over two passes.

"You should know that road quite well by now," Rodrigo said dryly. "I believe this will be your fourth encounter with the Col de Chaudon in two days."

Nathan slung a battered dispatch case over his

shoulder. "Get some sleep. If they do not turn west at Castellane, it will be your turn tomorrow night."

"They will not turn west," the servant said gloomily. "You are never wrong about this sort of thing."

No, they would come north. Nathan was sure of it.

Rodrigo handed him two pistols. "What shall I say if you are not back by the time Mrs. Hart is dressed tomorrow morning?"

"Tell her I have ridden out to get more news of the invasion. It is the truth, after all."

"And Master Anthony?"

Meyer looked nervously at the bed. "For God's sake, don't call him that when he is awake. He already thinks we are patronizing him." His nephew had fallen asleep the minute he had pulled off his boots and lain down. "Best to tell him as little as possible. He might conceive that I was endangering Miss Hart with my plan."

"You are," Rodrigo said. "As you are well aware."

"It is a very small risk. As *you* are well aware. Anthony, on the other hand, may prove more of a challenge as far as safety is concerned."

"I was surprised when he continued on with us today," Rodrigo said. "I had thought he would be returning to Italy."

Meyer shook his head. "He was on his way to London. But in any case he would have followed Miss Hart."

"Ah, yes. That."

"That, indeed. Precisely what I meant when I said that his safety will be more difficult to guarantee." Meyer sighed. "Five francs says that he is injured 'protecting' Miss Hart within three days."

"Too easy. Make it one day."

"Done."

They clasped hands.

"I have won the last three," Meyer reminded his valet.

Rodrigo shrugged. "I am due for some luck."

"Do you suppose there are other men who make wagers with their servants?" Meyer asked as he wrapped a muffler around his neck.

"Most men stay in one place long enough to make some friends."

"You would be utterly wretched if I were to marry again and settle down," Meyer informed him. "You know that perfectly well." He picked up his hat and headed for the door. Then he turned. "Oh—and make sure the women don't go downstairs. It's a bit rough down there."

It was nearly dawn by the time Meyer rode into the yard behind the Mercure, so tired that it took him several tries to open the stable door. Rodrigo must have been listening for him, though, because he had not even finished unsaddling his horse when the Spaniard materialized at his elbow.

"Buckle is stiff," Meyer muttered, fumbling at the bridle.

Rodrigo pushed him aside. "Go on in, there's coffee."

"Anyone else awake?"

"Two servants in the kitchen."

The haze of fatigue turned black for a moment, and he leaned against the stall door, blinking to clear his vision. He cursed under his breath.

"Don't look to me for sympathy." Rodrigo threw

a blanket over the horse. "You know my opinion of this scheme. Riding that road, in the dark, in your condition, is madness—and the roads will only get worse as we proceed."

"I'm out of practice," he admitted. "It used to require several days of this sort of thing before I wilted." He looked at his servant. "You will go tonight?"

"So, they are coming north."

"Yes."

Rodrigo looked as though he was not sure whether to be grateful or dismayed at this news. "I will go. But if we continue at this pace, we will soon be too far ahead of them to double back at night. Have you thought of that?"

Meyer shrugged. "We can always contrive something. A broken wheel, a lame horse. But we do not need to manufacture any delays right away; we will not be traveling at all tomorrow."

Rodrigo frowned. "Why not?"

"The Sabbath," Meyer reminded him. "At sundown tonight."

His servant shot him an incredulous look. "You—worrying about the Sabbath? While Napoleon is forty miles away? Master Anthony—" He hastily corrected himself. "Señor Roth, I mean, will call your bluff if you attempt to use that as an excuse to delay us. He knows quite well that you travel on the Sabbath."

"I will not be the one making the request. Have you noticed how careful Mrs. Hart has been about what she eats? She is far more observant than I am. She will not wish to ride on a Saturday, and I will, of course, respect her wishes."

"I see." Rodrigo opened the stall door, then paused. "Someday," he predicted, "someday very soon, I think, you will regret making Señora Hart one of your pawns." He stomped out of the stall and scooped up an armful of hay from the nearby bin, radiating righteous disapproval.

Meyer followed him out and nearly tripped over the baskets. He had forgotten all about them. A startled flapping and cooing erupted.

"Madre de Dios," said Rodrigo, turning and dropping the hay. "Is that what I think it is?"

"Yes, I've brought us a little present. I sent down to Grasse for them yesterday and prayed they would be delivered in time. Amazingly, they survived the trip." He hastily picked up a small metal tin from behind the baskets and stashed it away before Rodrigo could ask him about it. Sending messages was one thing. It was a bit dangerous, and scouting every other night would tax both of them severely, but Rodrigo would go along with it—after a certain amount of grumbling. If he found the jar of sulphur inside that tin, however, there would be open rebellion. And if he found the map and the notes tucked into the lid of the tin, he would probably turn Meyer over to the nearest insane asylum.

Rodrigo lifted the baskets and peered inside at the disgruntled birds. "How are you going to explain the sudden presence of two sets of carrier pigeons to Mrs. Hart?"

A very good question. Abigail Hart was an intelligent woman, that was already clear. And she didn't trust him at all. He wished he could have seen the letter she had received from Joshua Hart. He barely knew the man, but his impression was that Hart was a pompous boor. A recommendation from Hart would probably incline the widow to despise Meyer before she had even met him. He remembered her narrow, assessing stare during the delicate negotiations this morning—no, yesterday morning. If she suspected what those pigeons meant, his careful balancing act would come crashing down. He would have to think of some plausible tale to account for the birds—once his brain was working again.

"I'm going to get a few hours' sleep," he said. "If the others wake early, tell them I have been taken ill."

"You *have* been taken ill," muttered the servant. "Napoleon fever. Incurable disease. Likely fatal."

Meyer pretended not to hear that remark.

6

Three hours' sleep proved insufficient to inspire an explanation for the pigeons. They could not possibly be concealed, however; the throaty cooing was far too distinctive. He concluded that the best approach was to act as though there was nothing at all odd about them. Perhaps his talent for prevarication would miraculously return before someone thought to question their presence.

When the women emerged from breakfast, therefore, Rodrigo was in the process of strapping the cages beneath the coachman's bench of today's carriage. Considerably smaller than yesterday's barouche, this small, two-wheeled vehicle might well have been described as a farmer's gig had it not possessed a stained canvas cover and a small perch for a driver. Meyer saw Diana pause, shocked, her brows drawing down as she took in the open sides and the single horse standing in the traces.

"What is that?" she hissed to her mother, pointing at the carriage.

Abigail Hart, more tactful, greeted Meyer with a wary, "Good morning."

He raised his hat. "Good morning, Mrs. Hart. Miss Hart." He was glad to see that both of them were warmly dressed. "I trust you slept well?"

"Quite well, thank you." Only now did Abigail permit her gaze to settle on the carriage. "Is this ours?"

"I am afraid it is. The road is too narrow for a larger vehicle."

"Any vehicle would be a larger vehicle," he heard the girl mutter under her breath.

"We are taking a spare horse"—he indicated a sturdy chestnut, already fitted with packsaddles—"and will hope for the best."

"You meant it when you said this route was more difficult, I see." The widow's voice was dry.

He saw a challenge in her clear eyes and could not resist testing her again. "It is not too late to change your mind, Mrs. Hart. I will speak plainly: depending on the weather, two days from now we may be riding mules." Napoleon, he had discovered last night, had abandoned his heavy gun carriages and had transferred all his baggage to mules: an unmistakable declaration that his goal was now the mountains.

"I have traveled on mules."

Not at this time of year, he thought. Not at four thousand feet, with snow underfoot and the wind howling and particles of ice stinging the side of your face so that you could see out of only one eye. Even for the pleasure of shaking Abigail Hart out of her eternally calm, self-possessed shell, he could not wish for a reprise of his last trip over the Col

Bayard. "And you, Miss Hart? Have you some experience with mules as well?"

She swallowed, but nodded.

Anthony came hurrying up with several large carriage rugs. His eye fell on the cages, and he looked startled. "Pigeons!" He swung around and looked at Meyer, who was hastily searching through his extensive mental file of plausible lies hoping to find one labeled "carrier pigeons." "You had them sent up from Grasse, didn't you?"

Had his nephew been eavesdropping in the stable at dawn? No, Anthony had still been fast asleep when Meyer had stumbled into the room just before six. He shot a quick glance at Abigail Hart and saw that she was looking puzzled and suspicious.

"Well—" he started to say, then stopped, not sure what was coming next. He really was out of practice.

But Anthony, full of energy after twelve hours of sleep, did not wait for him to continue. "You know, my father always used to say that you were the most farsighted man he knew, and this proves it." He grinned. "Sending for our pigeons! That's famous!" He turned to the Harts and explained. "The bank has a courier system, you know, and for emergencies we use these birds. We can get a message from Italy to Paris in a day, and from Paris to London in another day. When the news about Bonaparte came into Grasse—the perfume town, south of here—I rode off to find my uncle at once, abandoning one of our biggest clients. I've been fretting about it since I woke up this morning. But now, of course, I can send word to them." He seized his uncle's hand and shook it. "Thank you, sir. You just saved my neck."

"Not at all," said Meyer politely.

Rodrigo, completely expressionless, finished stowing the rest of the luggage and climbed into the driver's seat.

"Oh," said Anthony, disappointed. "Er, I had thought I might drive the ladies."

Meyer was so grateful to his nephew that he almost agreed. Then he thought of the likely condition of the road north of Digne-les-Bains. It ran along the Bléone River, which was currently swollen by snowmelt into an unnavigable torrent. He led Anthony out of earshot of the Harts. "May I offer you some advice?"

"Certainly."

"It is only natural that you should find Miss Hart's company preferable to mine."

Anthony looked uncomfortable, and started to stammer some polite disclaimer.

Meyer waved it off. "Take a good look at the driver's seat on that gig. It is set well forward of the passenger seat, and is higher up, to boot. How easy do you think it would be to hold a conversation with someone sitting both behind you and below you? You will do far better riding alongside, where the road permits."

His nephew eyed the vehicle thoughtfully.

"Furthermore, my experience traveling with your cousin Elena two years ago suggests to me that young ladies are inclined to take attentive suitors for granted, and to take more interest in those whose companionship is less frequently offered."

"I am not a suitor," Anthony protested, looking even more uncomfortable.

Too late Meyer recalled that he, in theory, was the suitor. "I was, er, speaking metaphorically," he said.

But as he mounted up and turned into position in front of the gig, he resolved to make himself scarce at the midday halt. When he wasn't mooning over Diana Hart, Anthony's intelligent expression and well-cut features made him reasonably pleasant to look at. If his nephew could somehow engage the girl's affections, it would solve two problems. First, it would free Meyer from his brother-in-law's clumsy matchmaking. And second, he would be able to stop feeling guilty every time he saw Anthony. It was not his fault that his daughter had jilted her cousin, but guilt was not always a rational emotion.

Shortly before noon the party reached the town of Malijai, where they stopped for lunch. Meyer promptly put his campaign to promote Anthony's welfare into action. Pleading concern about one of the horses, he disappeared into the stable with Rodrigo. There were no other animals there at the moment, and he gratefully made himself a bed out of horse blankets in the tack room and fell asleep.

He was already up, brushing bits of hay from his jacket, when Rodrigo came to wake him an hour later. At least, he thought, he had not yet lost the knack of waking himself at set intervals, a skill he had perfected over many years of irregularly snatched naps in dangerous locations.

"Am I presentable?" He turned his back, and the servant quickly dusted off his shoulders.

Rodrigo shook his head as he surveyed him. "As your valet, I should resign from your service immediately. Or perhaps shoot myself."

Meyer ran his hands hastily through his hair and straightened his neckcloth. "Luckily, you are not merely my valet. You are also my coachman and my bodyguard." He opened the stable door and peered out. Anthony was just emerging from the inn. He was scowling ferociously. Obviously the opening round of the campaign had not been a success.

Meyer waited an hour before bringing his horse alongside Anthony's. The scowl had faded; Anthony merely looked tired and uncomfortable. He nodded morosely to Meyer but said nothing.

"I am sorry I was unable to join you for lunch," Meyer said, testing the waters.

The scowl immediately returned. "Not as sorry as Miss Hart. Do you remember your theory that young women prefer the absent suitor to the present one? It has been fully confirmed."

Meyer grimaced. "An unintentional effect, I assure you. I had forgotten all about that hypothesis."

"Well, Miss Hart compared you to Byron. She said you were"—he gritted his teeth—"romantic and inscrutable."

"Are those compliments?"

"Apparently. She also asked me whether you had ever killed anyone."

"What!" He reined his horse in. "What made her ask such a question? You young fool, you didn't tell her about my work for the army, did you?"

"Of course not! What do you take me for? She saw the pistol in your saddle holster."

He raised his eyebrows. "Miss Hart seems to have a vivid imagination. I trust you assured her that I am in fact rather dull and not at all bloodthirsty?"

Anthony twisted in the saddle slightly so that he could look Meyer full in the face. "Sir, *are* you courting

Miss Hart? My mother seems to believe that it is all arranged."

Meyer coughed. "Yes. So does your uncle Eli. And it is all arranged." Anthony took a deep, painful breath.

"Save for the little matter of consulting the two interested parties."

"Oh." His nephew digested this in silence for a moment. "You . . . are not partial to Miss Hart?"

"I believe the correct expression is 'We would not suit.'"

Anthony looked torn between relief at this news and outrage that any man could be insensible to the attractions of a girl like Diana Hart.

They rode on for a few minutes without speaking. It was raining lightly, but a breeze was sweeping the clouds away ahead of them, and they could see the town of Sisteron rising on its rocky plateau some miles ahead.

"Uncle Nathan?" Anthony's voice was so low it could barely be heard over the noise of the river below them.

Meyer turned his head.

"*Have* you ever killed anyone?"

His jaw tightened. "Yes."

Fascinated and horrified, Anthony stammered, "With—with a knife? Right there, touching them? Or only with a gun?"

"Both." And before his nephew could ask any more questions, he spurred his horse forward and reclaimed his position in front of the carriage.

7

Abigail was pleasantly surprised when they reached Sisteron before sunset. She had vowed that she would not say anything if Meyer wanted to continue after dark. She would not even request a halt for tomorrow. Yesterday's argument about the papers had left her shaken. She still believed that she was perfectly capable of taking charge of the documents. But the expression on his face when he had informed her that he was responsible for her safety had told her that the situation was far more serious than young Roth was letting on. Meyer's nephew treated the invasion as a temporary inconvenience. He cheerfully assured Abigail and Diana that it would be suppressed within a week or two, that the French government troops were well prepared for such an attempt.

When Roth informed her that the party would remain in Sisteron for two nights, therefore, her immediate reaction was not gratitude but anxiety. She had come down to the small parlor adjoining the rooms booked for the male travelers—her own

88 *Nita Abrams*

room was up on the top floor—and she could not help glancing at the door of Meyer's room.

"Is your uncle anywhere about? Might I speak with him? I would not like him to think that I have insisted on our remaining here tomorrow."

"He is leaving, or has just left."

She had barely seen Meyer the entire day; he had ridden either ahead of or behind the carriage and had disappeared at lunch. "Where is he going?" she asked, before she could stop herself.

"As I recall, up to the Hôtel de Ville, to see what he can learn. But he told me earlier today that he believes we are comfortably distant from Napoleon's forces."

"If he is still here, I would like to ask him a few questions."

Diana appeared, freshly washed and combed, and Roth's face immediately went carefully blank.

"I will be back in a moment," she told her daughter, taking up her shawl. "I am going to see if I can find Mr. Meyer before he leaves."

"Oh, is he gone again?" Diana looked a bit disappointed. "He seems vastly busy, always off on some mysterious errand, even at mealtimes."

Abigail saw Roth frown at this observation, and attributed his unease to jealousy of his uncle. She felt very sorry for the younger man. In Diana's absence he was perfectly presentable; in her presence, he became a wooden lump. At least Diana was now being civil to him, in a distant and very patronizing fashion.

Roth escorted Abigail out to the inn yard. It took some time to determine that Meyer had indeed left; the ostler had a very thick accent. By the end

of the interrogation they had several curious on-
lookers. Very thankful that Diana had not come out
with her—several of the bystanders had been just
the sort of bashful young rural giants she enjoyed
reducing to stammering idiocy—Abigail returned,
escorted by Roth, to their parlor.

It looked very welcoming after the long and uncomfortable day in the poorly sprung gig. There
were two chintz-covered armchairs by the fire,
which had now been lit. Opposite the chairs was a
long sofa, with a footstool at one end. A maidservant had brought in a pot of tea, and on the tray
were little pastries with fruit centers. Diana was at
one end of the sofa, putting sugar in her tea.

She looked up as her mother came in. "Should I
have waited? I am sorry. I did not know how long
you would be gone."

"Three lumps is too many, dear," Abigail said automatically.

Diana made a face and put the last one back into
the bowl.

"Would you like some tea, Mr. Roth?" Abigail
asked.

He turned red and stammered that he would be
much obliged.

It was an extremely uncomfortable half hour.
Roth sipped his tea and tried to make polite conversation. Diana studied her saucer, apparently
absorbed in the slight chip on one side. Abigail
thought longingly of her book, sitting on the table
by the tea tray. Finally Roth made some excuse and
retreated to his room. It really was too bad, Abigail
decided, that the parlor adjoined the two lower
bedchambers. Poor Roth must be acutely aware

that Diana could hear every move he made. Sure enough, a minute after he had closed the door, they heard a small crash and a stifled oath.

Diana clapped her hand over her mouth to keep from laughing.

"Perhaps we should also go upstairs and change," Abigail said, rising.

That was when the outer door opened.

Two square, red faces, belonging to a pair of rustic youths who had witnessed Abigail's encounter with the ostler, peered around the edge of the door.

"I am afraid this is a private parlor," she said politely.

One of them grinned, a loose, too-wide grin that was very familiar to Abigail. They were drunk.

Diana had also risen. "Didn't you hear my mother?" she asked sharply.

Abigail wanted to tell Diana that the last thing an attractive young woman should do when two inebriated louts arrive is to call attention to herself. And the second-to-last thing she should do is to speak in an angry tone. But Diana, of course, did not have Abigail's extensive experience with inebriated louts.

The shorter of the two intruders reached up for a hat that wasn't there, frowned in puzzlement, and settled for a crooked bow. The taller one pushed the door all the way open and stepped in.

"I must ask you to leave," Abigail said. She moved towards the bell, but the shorter youth blocked her way.

"Get out. At once." It was Roth. He was standing in the door of his room. He must have been changing clothes: he was coatless and in his stocking feet. He no longer looked blank or awkward, Abigail noticed. Unfortunately, he had not grown any taller, and the nearest lout had a good four inches on him.

The presence of a hostile male clarified things nicely for the intruders. "Damn English," the tall one said, scowling. "*You* should get out. We don't want your damn interference here."

"Damn Protestant heretic," the other one added, moving up next to his companion. This left Abigail's access to the bell unimpeded, but she hesitated, wondering whether Roth would be humiliated if she rang for help.

Unfortunately, before she could make up her mind, Diana intervened. "We are *not* Protestant," she said, nearly stamping her foot in anger. "We are Jews. This man's bank"—she pointed to Anthony— "loaned money to help your country. I think you are very ignorant and ungrateful."

Diana's French was not always grammatical, but it was disastrously clear.

The taller lout grabbed Roth and slammed him against the wall. "Is that so?"

Roth said nothing, but gave the man a look of contempt that somehow reminded Abigail of Meyer. Her hand, reaching for the bell, was frozen. Then the second man started punching, and Abigail came back to life, pulling on the bell rope for all she was worth, screaming at the men to stop. They ignored her. She turned around and screamed at Diana instead, telling her to go, to run and get help, to find someone, anyone. Diana's face was completely white. She didn't seem to understand what Abigail was saying. She kept looking over at the two thugs, who were systematically hitting Roth and swearing in rhythmical, panting bursts as they did so. Finally, as the boy sagged to his knees, she gave a small cry and darted out the door.

It did not even occur to Abigail to follow her. She could not leave; she felt, somehow, that her presence shielded Roth from something even worse than a beating. It was probably no more than a minute that she stood there, helpless, watching Roth flinch silently in time to the curses and blows. Then the door slammed open behind her; Rodrigo burst into the room. He tackled the tall Frenchman in a flying leap, and brought him down to the floor with a crash that knocked over the fire screen. Two quick blows to the side of the neck, and his opponent gurgled and went limp. The shorter man had dropped Roth and now attempted to kick Rodrigo from the side; the Spaniard rolled away, came up facing his attacker, and let fly one backhanded blow. Abigail heard a sickening crack as the second Frenchman, too, crumpled.

Diana had reappeared in the doorway, surrounded by terrified-looking servants from the dining room. She was clenching and unclenching her hands and looked as though she might faint any minute.

Rodrigo had dropped to the floor beside Roth. The younger man's eyes were closed, and he was breathing in little gasps. "Are you all right, Señor Roth?"

Roth nodded. Then he opened his eyes and saw Diana. He shot a mute look of appeal to Abigail, and said, so faintly that she understood him only by reading his lips, "Going to be sick."

Abigail whirled around. "Go, quickly!" she said to Diana. "Fetch brandy, and hot water! Send someone for a gendarme at once!"

Three of the inn's servants came in and hauled away the drunkards. One was able to stumble out on his own; the other had to be carried. Rodrigo got up hastily and went after them, clutching his right hand.

Abigail, shocked that he would leave Roth, hurried over to kneel beside him. She put her arm under his shoulder and helped him to sit up. This was a mistake; he promptly turned yellow and she barely had time to grab the slop bowl from the tea tray before he doubled over, retching.

"Thank you," he whispered after a minute.

"Is it very painful? Can you get up?"

With some assistance, he managed to struggle over to the sofa, where he sat, silent and stone-faced while Abigail dampened her handkerchief and tried to clean him up. His nose was bleeding, as was his lower lip, but he did not seem too badly damaged otherwise—or so she thought until she began brushing off his shirt. He bit his lip to keep from crying out the minute she touched his left side.

She sucked in her breath. "Where does it hurt?"

He moved his hand very carefully to the spot.

"Does it hurt to breathe? To breathe deeply, that is?"

He nodded.

"You may have a broken rib." A servant arrived with brandy, followed by a nearly hysterical innkeeper. She dismissed both of them. "Drink some of this." She held the brandy to his mouth.

He drank, coughed slightly, and winced. He kept looking over at the door, and she knew what he was thinking. At any moment Diana might return, and he did not want her to see him like this.

"Would you like me to help you to your room?" she asked.

"I am fine." He took a cautious, shallow breath, and stood up—very shakily. "Thank you. Thank you very much, Mrs. Hart. I am most sincerely sorry that you were—"

She cut him off, horrified. "Don't be absurd! I should be apologizing to you! If Diana had behaved more prudently, this would never have happened! They were disgustingly drunk, but I believe they would have left if she had not provoked them so."

"I don't know." He sighed, and then winced again. "It is my fault as well. My uncle warned me not to advertise our nationality. My poor French betrayed us. I should have sent one of the chambermaids out to question the ostler." He hobbled over to his room, and Abigail, watching him teeter slightly, hurried to help him into bed.

"I'll have them send a servant to you right away to help you undress," she promised. "And the doctor, to see to your ribs."

He shook his head. "No. My uncle can do it."

She did not contradict him, but the minute she left, she rang and dispatched one of the inn's grooms to fetch a doctor, or at least an apothecary. Roth probably didn't like being bled; most young men didn't. But she could not imagine that Nathan Meyer, a banker, had much in the way of medical skills.

Diana was hovering outside the door of the parlor when Abigail finally emerged. "Is he badly hurt?" she asked anxiously. "His face was all over blood. Is his nose broken?" She had been crying, Abigail saw. "It was all my fault, I know it was. Does he hate me? May I go in and see him?"

"Later," said Abigail. "And no, he doesn't hate you. He blames himself."

Her daughter gaped. "He does? But why?"

"Why? Because he is an idiotic young fool, just like you," she snapped, goaded beyond endurance. "You can think of nothing but yourself and your admirers; Mr. Roth, I have no doubt, is angrier at the servant who rescued him than he is at the brutes who hit him. Neither one of you understands that the incident just now was nothing, less than nothing, compared to what could happen if we are caught between Napoleon and the French army!"

Diana's eyes filled with tears again.

Abigail's voice softened. "If you would like to be of some help, go to our room and bring me down my small case; it has some medicines in it."

Her daughter gave a small, chastened nod and started up the stairs.

Abigail stood for a moment, shaken by her own loss of control. She had not wanted to frighten Diana or make her blame herself for what had happened, and now she had just done both. With a sigh, she went back into the parlor and sat down to wait for Diana to reappear with the little stock of medicines. She wondered who felt worse: the wounded knight, who had failed to save the princess from the dragon, or the princess's mother, who knew that there were hundreds more dragons out there, carrying rifles and bayonets.

Meyer knew something was wrong the moment he returned. Every single servant stopped dead the moment they saw him, then hastily resumed whatever they had been doing, making sure it took them in the opposite direction. He looked around for the innkeeper. Monsieur Busac, less cowardly than his employees, was hurrying out to meet him, gasping out half-finished sentences which veered wildly between apologies, reassurances, and excuses. All Meyer could make out was that the apothecary had been sent for, and the ladies were in the private parlor monsieur had reserved.

His first thought was that Abigail Hart had been taken ill. She was calm and cheerful with her daughter, but he had seen the strain in her face when she had thought herself unobserved. They had been traveling at a brutal pace, over very rough roads, and the gig had offered little protection from the cold. He shook off the incoherent Busac and strode up the stairs. Perhaps a slight ailment would be to his advantage—nothing serious, something he could use as an additional excuse for delay, if need be. He knew he was being callous, but it had not been his choice to travel with the Harts.

When he opened the parlor door and saw Abigail slumped in a chair, pale and distraught, with what could only be a bloodstain across the shoulder of her dress, he realized that he was perhaps not as callous as he had supposed. His initial panic subsided, however, as she rose to greet him. The blood was not hers, he saw, and she was steady on her feet. Something had obviously shaken her very badly, however, because she actually gave him a small, tremulous smile.

"I am very glad to see you. We have been wondering whether you had also come to grief."

"What happened?" He looked around the room

and saw the telltale signs of a brawl: crooked furniture, a rip in the fire screen, the print of a dirty boot on the side of the baseboard.

"Some drunken Frenchmen forced their way in here and Mr. Roth was injured when they refused to leave. He is not badly hurt," she added hastily, seeing the look on Meyer's face. "And Mr. Santos was able to evict the men."

"What of you? And Miss Hart?"

She assured him that they were unharmed.

There was a perfunctory tap at the door, and Rodrigo came in. He, too, looked relieved to see his master.

"I believe Mr. Roth could use your assistance," Abigail said to the valet. Her cool tone implied that Anthony had been waiting for that assistance for quite some time. "He would not let me help him undress, and I thought it best not to send for any of the inn's servants."

"I am very sorry, señora. I was dealing with the town officials."

She nodded grudgingly. "Now that you are here, I will go and change. Please send for me if I am needed."

Meyer followed Rodrigo into the bedchamber. He still was not sure exactly what had happened, but he could make a fair guess, and that guess was confirmed the minute he saw his nephew. Anthony was lying on his back, carefully breathing in an odd rhythm. His eyes were open, fixed bleakly on a spot just below the ceiling. There was some sort of poultice lying discarded in a damp lump on the pillow. He did not move or look around when the door opened.

Meyer tried to think of something heartening to

say, and failed. Sighing, he pulled a chair over to the side of the bed and sat down. Anthony didn't look at him.

"I didn't even get one blow in," his nephew said finally. "Not one. They held me up against the wall like a side of beef on a hook and battered me until I fell over. With—with the ladies watching." He smiled bitterly. "And then Rodrigo came tearing in and knocked both of them down. Oh, and then I threw up."

A fairly comprehensive catalog of humiliations, Meyer thought. So much for his hopes of Anthony's courtship. "How did it happen?" He kept his voice neutral.

Anthony gave a disgusted snort. "My fault. Mrs. Hart was looking for you, and we ended up interrogating an ostler out by the stables with five or six yokels as audience. Two of them deduced we were English and after a few glasses in the public room came to tell us we were not welcome."

"And Miss Hart threw oil on the fire," Meyer guessed.

Anthony sat halfway up. "She is not to blame! They were drunk, spoiling for a fight!"

Rodrigo seized this opportunity to start undressing Roth, moving very carefully. Meyer looked at the bruises across his shoulders and torso. One enormous spot on the side of his chest had already turned nearly black. "That looks bad."

"Mrs. Hart sent for the apothecary. She thinks a rib may be broken."

Meyer shot a quick look at Rodrigo.

"I intercepted the man and sent him away, señor. And I dissuaded the town guard from detaining the two drunks. I did not think you would wish any more attention called to our party than necessary."

"Good," said Meyer, abstracted. He was pressing gently on Anthony's side, behind the bruise. A gasp told him that Abigail had been correct in her diagnosis. "Get something to use for a binding," he said over his shoulder.

Rodrigo disappeared, and returned a moment later with a long strip of frayed cloth. Meyer wound it around tightly, watching Anthony's face as he did so. "Breathe," he ordered.

Anthony took a shallow breath.

"Deeper."

He grimaced, then obeyed.

Meyer tightened the bandage a bit more. "Try again."

"Better," Anthony admitted grudgingly. He allowed Rodrigo to finish undressing him in silence, but when Meyer turned to go, he said sharply, "Sir, wait!"

"What is it?"

"I—I want you to teach me to fight. To box, and shoot a pistol, and use a knife." He saw Meyer's hesitation and read it as contempt. "I know I can never be very good at it—I know James started boxing lessons at twelve—I know I'm clumsy, and small, and even riding a horse for eight hours makes my knees shake. But surely I can learn enough so that I can hit them next time. Just once or twice. Or fire a gun, if need be."

"You are in no condition right now—"

Anthony cut him off. "Will the next time wait until I am healed?"

He had a point. Meyer surrendered. "Sunday. If you still wish it." Sunday night would be Rodrigo's

turn to ride back towards the advancing troops—or
so he thought until he got up to leave. It turned out
that Anthony was not the only one who had been injured. As Rodrigo held the door open for him, Meyer
saw that the servant's right thumb was swollen to
twice its normal size. He raised his eyebrows inquiringly at the Spaniard.

"Dislocated," Rodrigo said with a sour smile. "I've
popped it back in, but it may be a day or so before
I can use it properly."

"Well." He recalled Rodrigo's careful movements
when undressing Anthony and swore under his
breath. "It seems I am to enjoy another moonlight
ride tonight."

"Señor, I can ride!"

"Don't be absurd. I won't go very far; I know my
limits."

"You can go tomorrow, during the day, while the
ladies are resting."

"Now that would be inconspicuous," Meyer said
dryly. "An eight-hour absence." He looked around
the empty parlor, frowning. "Do you think perhaps
I should exchange rooms with Mrs. Hart and her
daughter? We could have a bed made up for you out
here. I would be a bit easier in my mind if they were
not sleeping in a room which opened directly onto
the hallway."

"An excellent notion, señor." Rodrigo looked
considerably more cheerful.

"Oh," said Meyer, "I almost forgot. You owe me
five francs."

8

Meyer climbed slowly up the stairs of the inn, hoping there was coffee. He had been so exhausted when Rodrigo came out to the stable to help him unsaddle his horse he had not been able to absorb half of what he had been told. As he unlocked the door to the parlor, his nose answered the question: yes. There was a pot, still warm, waiting on the table. He silently blessed his longtime servant and swallowed a cup in three gulps, still standing; he was afraid that if he sat down he would have considerable difficulty in getting up.

He had found the journey back towards Digne exhausting and uncomfortable, but not otherwise difficult. He was not the only one on the road, however. Riders were still galloping north, some singly, some in groups. Where possible Meyer had withdrawn into the woods at the first sound of another horse. He had regretted that choice when he reached Malijai. There he had learned that one of the men he had avoided was none other than Embry, Napoleon's physician. Digne's royalist militia had stopped and searched Embry earlier in the day, and had thrown him into prison when he proved to be carrying messages to Napoleon's supporters in Grenoble. Unfortunately, Digne's municipal jailer was not as vigilant as the militia. Embry had escaped, and was now once again on his way north to prepare the way for his master. This was indisputable proof Napoleon had chosen the mountain route; Meyer had judged such a choice piece of news worth a pigeon from his precious little flock and had ridden back to Sisteron without bothering to cast any farther south for more information.

What time was it? He pulled out his watch. Nearly six. He could manage four or even five hours' sleep, since they were not traveling today. Perhaps he should plead some slight indisposition, spend the whole day in bed. It was very likely Rodrigo would not be fit to ride tonight either. He rubbed his unshaven jaw, yawned, and opened the door to his room.

It was not his room. Too late he recalled that he himself had proposed the switch. And although he had been very quiet, he could not simply close the door and leave, because Abigail Hart was sitting by a low fire, very wide awake, looking straight at him. She was wearing a dressing gown over her night-gown, and a shawl over that, and was in every way save one far more modestly covered than she had been yesterday evening in the parlor. The exception was her hair. It fell over her shoulders in a thick braid, glinting here and there as flickers of light from the fireplace ran across it.

She always wore caps, of course—and they were not token wisps of lace. He had never seen anything more of her hair than a scant half inch at the edge of her temples. Now he stood staring, in a kind of daze, noting that it was in fact many different colors: brown and light brown and dark gold and pale blond, each strand different, like the variegated wood of some exotic tree. It was long—nearly to her waist. She had not even made the token concession to fashion of cutting a few locks short in the front to curl around her face. Instead the brown-gold bands framed her wide forehead, flowing back and down into the braid at the nape of her neck. He knew he was staring but could not look away; she was staring back, puzzled and alarmed.

God, he thought, *please let me move. Let me think of something to say.*

She stood up. That broke the spell, although it also filled him with a vague sense of danger.

"I beg your pardon," he said, his voice hoarse with fatigue. "I had forgotten that this was no longer my chamber." He started to back out and close the door.

"No, wait," she said, glancing quickly over at the bed. The huddled form under the covers was presumably Diana. Abigail hesitated, then seemed to make up her mind. "Let us go out into the other room. I must speak with you."

He held the door open and followed her back into the parlor.

It was cold in there; the fire had nearly gone out. He busied himself bringing it back to life, giving himself time to prepare some story to explain his stained, day-old clothing, and, more damningly, the unmistakable smell of horse.

"I could not sleep," she said finally.

Still crouched by the hearth, he looked over. "Nor could I."

"I at least went to my room and undressed. You did not."

"No." He rose stiffly, dusting off the knees of his buckskins.

Her expression was guarded, watchful. She sat down tentatively on the edge of one of the chairs and studied him, frowning.

He braced himself for the inevitable question: *Where have you been?* He could concoct something, he supposed. Even half-asleep, he was an excellent liar. He enjoyed lying, in fact, practiced it the way singers practice their scales, telling small but unnecessary falsehoods to everyone he knew, even to his own family, as a way of keeping himself ready for future performances. But for some reason he did not want to lie to Abigail Hart. Since it would be both dangerous and unpleasant to tell her the truth, however, he was at point-non-plus.

She cleared her throat.

Here it comes, he thought. But he was wrong.

"I would like to show you something." Her expression was an odd mixture of embarrassment and determination.

He blinked, surprised.

She got up and went over to a small case full of bottles which lay open on the sofa, returning with a folded sheet of paper. "This reached me just before you arrived in Digne. It is from my late husband's cousin."

It was still too dark to read with the shutters closed; he went over and opened them. The sun was nearly up. As he read, curiosity quickly gave way

to disgust. Joshua Hart made Meyer's brother-in-law
look like a master of tact and diplomacy.

My dear Abigail,

*It is with great regret that I inform you I shall not
be coming to meet you in Digne-les-Bains after all.
Urgent business affairs have compelled me to return
to London at once. I send you in my stead, however,
a friend of the family, one who, I trust, will be very
acceptable to you, Mr. Nathan Meyer. He is widely
traveled and speaks fluent French; indeed, he will
likely prove a far more valuable escort than my
humble self. When I tell you that he is a widower in
the prime of life, a gentleman of means and leisure,
received by many notables such as Lord Wellington
and Sir Charles Barrett, you will understand that
any interest he may display in Diana should be very
welcome not only to you but also to*

Your affectionate cousin,

Joshua Hart

"A glowing recommendation," he commented
dryly, handing it back to her. "I am amazed you did
not flee Digne the moment you received it, so as
to put as much distance as possible between yourself and the paragon Mr. Hart describes."

She colored slightly. "Joshua can be rather over-
bearing, and I will confess that my reaction to his
letter was very much as you suspect. Circumstances,
however, intervened."

"I was happy to be of service," he said, still uneasy.

This conversation was safer than the "Where were you?" conversation, but not by much.

Her eyes narrowed. He had come to know that particular expression of hers quite well in the past few days.

"Were you?"

For a moment he thought, with a hollow feeling in his stomach, that she had somehow learned the truth.

But her next question proved that her fears were of a different nature. She held up the letter and asked bluntly, "Did you know of this? Was this your idea?"

"No to both questions, although I suspected something when my brother-in-law proposed that I meet your party and escort you back to England. My friends and family have been attempting to find me a new wife for many years." He added, with a dry smile, "I was led to believe that Miss Hart was an invalid, traveling with a paid companion."

A small, matching smile appeared. "You must have been rather surprised."

He bowed. "Let us say that both the invalid and her companion proved far more agreeable than I had expected."

Flattery did not sit well with Abigail Hart, that was clear. Her smile vanished. "And are you, in fact, intending to pay court to her?" she asked, raising her chin belligerently.

"Am I intending to pursue Miss Hart?" His voice grew very cold. "To take advantage of a terrified young woman who has been thrown into my company because civil war has broken out in France? I see that your opinion of me is very low, madam."

"I would not say that." She looked uncomfortable. After a moment, she added, "I apologize if my concern for Diana led me to imply that you have been guilty of an attempt to turn our situation to your own profit."

The hollow feeling in his stomach became a gaping pit. If she asked him now where he had been all night, he knew he would lie, and hate himself for lying.

She went over to the fireplace and threw the letter into the blaze. It sat for a moment atop a log, still folded, and then caught fire and uncurled. She watched the paper burn, and said, without turning around, "If, after we have returned to London, and a suitable interval has elapsed, you should wish to address my daughter, I would not object."

Wonderful. He pictured her and Eli and Joshua Hart herding him like a reluctant sheep into a sitting room where Diana Hart sat demurely waiting, while Anthony glowered on the sidelines. Perhaps he should take back his offer to teach Anthony to handle a pistol.

With a sigh, she stood up. "We should both try to get some sleep. Good night, Mr. Meyer."

"Good night." He made the phrase less absurd by closing the shutters to block out the brightening sky. In the newly darkened room, Abigail was only a shadow, moving slowly away and then vanishing into the even-darker bedchamber. He stood staring at the closed door for a long moment before going off, equally slowly, to find his own bed.

It was almost noon when Abigail finally managed to get out of bed. She had come half-awake several times since her awkward conversation with Meyer, but had dropped back off again before she could force herself to get up. When she saw the time on her silver traveling clock, she gave a gasp of dismay before remembering that today was Saturday. A day of rest.

Diana was nowhere to be seen. Presumably she was out in the parlor, or perhaps downstairs in the coffee room. Abigail hoped that she was tending poor Anthony Roth, but she rather doubted that Diana would offer; and even if she did, Roth would probably jump out the window the moment she came into his room.

When she rang, a maidservant appeared so promptly that Abigail was startled. The girl's nervous curtseys and stammered apologies made it clear that the innkeeper was trying to make amends for yesterday's incident. Abigail allowed herself to be mollified, especially when two large cans of hot water and a pot of chocolate appeared. As the maid helped her to dress and put up her hair, she found herself relaxing, savoring the thought that today there would be no freezing, bone-jolting carriage ride. She gave the girl a very large tip and sallied forth, feeling remarkably well for someone who had spent all night fretting first about her daughter and then about Napoleon. Her conversation with Meyer had reassured her somewhat about the former. The latter problem was less personal but more intractable. At least now, in the daylight, she was able to tell herself firmly that from all accounts there had been remarkably little violence so far.

Her cautious optimism lasted only as long as it took her to step out into the parlor. In the other bedchamber, whose door was open, Meyer and his servant were having a low-voiced but furious argument in Spanish. She did not speak the language, but when she heard words like *catástrofe* and *imperdonable* and *desastroso* it was not difficult for a woman who knew French and Italian to understand that something was wrong. Then the servant saw her, and made an urgent gesture to Meyer, who immediately fell silent. That, too, was frightening.

"What is it?" she asked nervously, going over to the doorway of Roth's room. The bed, she saw, was empty.

Meyer ran his hand through his hair. He was shaved and dressed, but he looked haggard. "My nephew decided that his injuries required him to travel more slowly than the rest of the party, so he left early. I would have told him he was not fit to ride unaccompanied, but I was unfortunately asleep upstairs, and Rodrigo was up at the city hall hoping for fresh news from the south."

"But we are not traveling today," she said. There was a quick exchange of glances between the two men. "Are we?"

"Anthony did not suppose we were, at the time that he left. In his note he wavered between portraying himself as an invalid who would hamper our progress and as our advance party in Gap. It is all an excuse, of course. He blames himself for what happened yesterday."

She could well imagine Roth deciding to flee from the witnesses to yesterday's affair. "Someone must go after him," she said, worried. "It will be very painful, riding with his broken rib."

"We will all go. I regret the necessity of traveling today, but Anthony is not the only advance party who has proceeded farther north than I anticipated. Rodrigo tells me that General Cambronne is already here in Sisteron, and Napoleon will be here late tonight or tomorrow morning. He must be marching his men on three hours' sleep; it is madness."

"You are a fine one to talk," the Spaniard muttered.

Ignoring this comment, Meyer asked her, "Have you breakfasted?"

The news that Bonaparte and his troops would be here, in this very town, perhaps in this very hostelry, before twenty-four hours had passed, made her dizzy. "It is no matter. I would prefer to leave as soon as possible." She looked around the parlor. "Where is Diana? Is she already outside? Have you told her our plans have changed?"

Meyer frowned. "She is not still asleep?"

"No, of course not. You have not seen her?" She turned to Rodrigo, feeling the first tendrils of panic. "You?"

Their appalled faces provided the answer.

She whirled and ran back to the bedchamber. Her daughter's side of the bed was an untidy mound of covers; there was clothing scattered on the floor and draped over one of the chairs. Her hairbrush and rouge pot were still on the dressing table. But her half boots were missing, and her warm bonnet, and her velvet reticule. Could Diana have gone off, leaving her things all over the room? The answer was, unfortunately, yes. In Diana's world someone else always picked up the stockings and screwed the cover on the rouge pot and packed the cloak bag.

As Abigail ran down the stairs she told herself that Diana had not been abducted by angry peasants. She was in the coffee room, she had gone out to the stable, she had taken a walk. Meyer, moving almost as quickly as Abigail, was giving orders in Spanish over his shoulder to Rodrigo as he clattered down behind her.

The coffee room held four parties eating an early dinner, who looked up, astounded, as Abigail burst into the room. The innkeeper's wife hurried over, all solicitude.

"Have you seen my daughter?" Abigail asked, cutting off the woman's flowery greeting. "Or has anyone else seen her? Has she come down this morning?"

"But yes, madame." The woman beamed. "Just one moment." She hurried away.

Abigail would have collapsed in grateful relief if Meyer had not steadied her.

"Voilà," said the woman, returning triumphantly. "My husband is very distracted by the news of the army, madame, so I made sure to put this in a safe place when mademoiselle gave it to him. And he wished me to tell you that it is our most reliable groom, Jean-Pierre, who has accompanied her."

The note was unsigned, but Diana's rounded handwriting was unmistakable. Abigail read it, sighed, and handed it to Meyer.

Dearest Mama,

I know it was very wrong of me, but as Mr. Roth's note had no superscription I opened it to see what it was and then I could not help but read it. I have gone to persuade him to return, as I am sure he should not ride yet. I am wearing the wool cape and

*my gloves with the fur edges and have a groom with
me, so you are not to worry.*

His mouth twisted. "It seems to be our morning
for notes from runaway children," he observed.
"Do you ride horses as well as mules?"

She nodded.

"Rodrigo can pack our bags and follow in the gig.
How soon can you be ready?"

"If you would wait here a moment?"

She ran upstairs, snatched up her bonnet and
shawl and gloves, and ran back down. He was still
standing at the foot of the staircase. "I am ready now."

He raised his eyebrows. "Without a coat?"

"Diana took it," she informed him. "Her pelisse
is too tight for riding. And no, her pelisse will not
fit me; I am too tall. My righteous anger will keep
me warm."

That provoked a wry, elusive smile. "Anger can
cool quickly, especially on a blustery day in March.
Rodrigo will find you something while the groom
saddles the horses."

9

Anthony was plodding toward Gap. It was a fairly level road, which was a blessing, since any slope—up or down—strained his taped ribs uncomfortably. He had asked for the laziest, most placid beast in the stables, and was going so slowly that even farmers' carts were passing him. Since the pass beyond Gap was one of the few permitting travelers to reach Grenoble from this region, the road was busy, and he was passed rather frequently. At least half of his fellow travelers turned around in their vehicles or saddles to stare at him, obviously puzzled that a lone rider with very little baggage should be keeping his saddle horse to a pace more natural to an ox. He distracted himself from his misery by guessing at their identities and errands as they went by. Some were obvious: the anxious priest, the peasant family with baskets of root vegetables. Some were intriguing, like the man wearing a military helmet but civilian dress who tore by at a gallop and then tore by again in the opposite direction a few minutes later.

When there was no one else in sight, however, he

invariably ended up reliving yesterday's fight in his head. No matter how many times he tried to make it come out differently, it always ended the same way, with the two Frenchmen pummeling him to his knees in front of Diana Hart. His only, tiny victory was that he had managed not to groan out loud. That was one good thing about traveling by himself: he could groan as much as he liked. The way he reckoned it, in fact, he was owed at least twenty-two groans for the twenty-two punches he had taken in silence yesterday, and he sometimes allowed himself an extra one when he was jolted painfully enough to produce an involuntary grunt.

There were also, of course, disadvantages to setting off alone. He had to be very careful where he stopped, because getting on and off the horse was a tricky proposition. Consequently, when he saw an old couple selling candles next to a roadside shrine he drew rein. There was a handy chunk of half-quarried stone to use as a mounting block, and if that was not sufficient, he could ask the man to help him. He was sidling his horse up to the piece of stone when he heard riders come up behind him and stop.

"There he is," said a female voice in French. The hoofbeats started up again, trotting towards him.

He couldn't turn around—he had already discovered that any twisting movements were agonizingly painful. So he levered his right leg over the cantle and slid awkwardly off the horse, turning his head back towards the new arrivals.

It was Diana, of course. She was wearing a thick cloak, but her cheeks were pink with cold, and little wisps of blond hair were blowing around the brim of her bonnet. She gave him a too-cheerful smile, as though there was nothing at all odd about a sheltered, eighteen-year-old heiress riding out alone to rescue an adult male. Well, not alone. There was someone with her: a groom, probably from the inn. But she clearly believed Anthony was in need of rescuing. Unsurprising, after yesterday.

"Tell my mother I have come up with Monsieur Roth," she said to the groom, handing him a few coins.

The servant nodded and wheeled smartly back towards Sisteron.

"Well," said Diana, looking down at Anthony. "You certainly did not get very far. Jean-Pierre told me that you had taken the slowest nag in Sisteron, and it seems he was not exaggerating."

"Miss Hart." He touched the brim of his hat. Bowing was not a good option at the moment.

"You are very foolish to attempt to sit a horse today, you know." She nudged her horse alongside him. "Can you help me down? Oh no, perhaps you should not." With a quick twist of the reins she brought her horse around the other side of the block and hopped off right next to him.

The old woman, seeing a potential customer, hurried over with an apronful of candles. Diana smiled prettily, and, encouraged, the woman launched into her sales pitch. This was a very ancient shrine, very famous. Many miracles had been reported here. If mademoiselle would light a taper to the blessed virgin of Le Poêt, her prayer would not go unfulfilled.

Diana bought two, handed Anthony her reins, and went over to the miniature building which housed the statue. Incredulous, he realized that she was actually lighting the candles. He had taken a savage beating yesterday after she had boasted of being Jewish, and today she was praying to the Madonna of some decrepit little village in the middle of nowhere.

"Now we can go back," she announced as she returned.

The thought of retracing his slow, aching steps back to Sisteron was unbearable, but of course he could not leave her here by herself. He groaned. Aloud.

She looked alarmed, but for the first time since he had met her, Anthony did not care what Diana Hart thought.

He beckoned the old man over. "If you could help me?" Between the stone and a few shoves from below he managed to mount again. "And mademoiselle." He indicated Diana with a jerk of his head. Once she was up, he turned his horse and without a word headed back south.

She pulled up alongside him, holding back her fresher and faster horse with a visible effort. "You are vexed with me." She sounded surprised.

"Yes, I am vexed. It was a perfectly reasonable decision on my part to leave early, so that I could travel more slowly. Now, because you sent your groom away, I must escort you back to Sisteron. I will now ride double the distance, and will be compelled to keep pace with everyone else tomorrow instead of resting." He was growing angrier by the minute. "I fail to see why you chose to meddle in my affairs. I do not need assistance from a schoolgirl. I am a grown man. I have traveled all over Europe without any assistance for five years now."

This was not quite true. Anthony usually traveled with a trusted family servant whose role sometimes was more similar to that of a nursemaid than that of a valet. When the news of Napoleon's escape had reached him in Grasse, however, Anthony had sent Battista galloping back to Naples, with instructions to stop at all the bank's courier stations en route and get the news out as fast as possible.

"But you are injured," she pointed out. Her chin had a stubborn little jut which was, he had to admit, very attractive.

Why was he arguing with a spoiled flirt? He gave an exasperated sigh and kicked his horse into a trot. His ribs gave an agonized protest. Perhaps a canter would be easier. Without looking to see if Diana was keeping pace, he kicked again.

She pulled in front of him, forcing him to a stop. Her face was white with anger, and her horse, sensing her agitation, danced uneasily beneath her. "You," she informed him, breathing hard, "are *not* a gentleman. I beg your pardon for feeling some concern for your welfare. How dared I presume to know better than you, with your *vast* experience of the world. Well, I may be a schoolgirl, but after watching you on the journey from Barrême I will tell you this: I can outride you any day of the week, even before you broke your rib. I do not need your escort. It is only twenty minutes back to the inn, and the road is well frequented. Go on, go off by yourself! And I hope your slug of a horse deposits you in the next available ditch!" With that she turned her horse, brought the animal rearing up in an impressive display of equestrian temper, and dug in her heels.

Swearing, Anthony followed as best he could. His horse did not seem to have a gallop; it subsided into a canter and then a trot after a few paces, and neither kicks nor the crop had any lasting effect. But then Anthony heard the scream. There was absolutely no doubt about whose voice that was. He leaned over the neck of the horse and brought his crop down savagely on the animal's flank. He forgot about his ribs, his still-swollen mouth, his aching shoulder. Shouting, plying the crop, he tore down the road and around the corner.

At a crossroads just ahead, Diana was sitting frozen on her horse. Three men surrounded her. One had a rifle cradled in his hand; the other two had pikes. Over to the side two more men were setting up a tent. They were all wearing bits and pieces of old uniforms; the man with the rifle was in fact the helmeted galloper he had noticed earlier. The uniforms looked depressingly familiar, at least to someone who had lived in Italy while Napoleon's troops had occupied it.

At Anthony's approach the helmet-wearer swung the gun up and cocked it. "Halt!" he called. "In the name of the emperor!"

Anthony halted, and one of the tent-peggers, at a gesture from the leader, came up and took the bridle of his horse.

"Your papers," demanded the leader.

Anthony handed them over.

"You are English," the man said coldly, scanning the folded sheets. "As is mademoiselle. Are you together?"

"Yes," he said, just as Diana said scornfully, "No!"

The man looked up at Anthony. "Mademoiselle has no papers. This is a very serious matter. And your papers are not in order. They are signed by an official of the false Bourbon usurpers."

The leader must have been some sort of regional

guardsman under Napoleon, Anthony thought. And now that Napoleon was on the march, the man had reassembled the fragments of his little patrol and was back in business, as officious as ever. More officious: in the old days, he might have taken a bribe. Not today, not from an Englishman.

"I noticed you earlier," the Frenchman said. "You were heading north, now you are going south." He sounded very suspicious. "And now mademoiselle, too, goes first one way and then the other. You are messengers, perhaps? Spies?"

"We are not!" said Diana indignantly.

Anthony gave her a glare which promised that if she said one more word he would personally gag her.

"Then perhaps monsieur can explain these odd wanderings to and fro on a road of great strategic importance?"

Inspiration came to him. Inspiration and revenge. "Mademoiselle is my fiancée," he explained.

Diana swallowed, but said nothing.

He gave the guardsman a wry smile. "We had—a quarrel. I, er, chose to travel on ahead of the rest of our party. She followed." He shrugged as if to say, *What can a man do?*

"And where are these others?" The man was still suspicious.

Diana pointed. Her voice was shaking slightly. "There."

"I hope you are not very angry with your nephew," said Abigail. They were walking their horses up a gentle hill along the right bank of the river, giving them a rest after a long, fast canter. "It was not so very unreasonable for him to go on ahead; he is right that it will be better for him to travel slowly."

"It would have been even better for him to rest," said Meyer curtly. "And to go off without any attendant! Without consulting me first! Without even telling Rodrigo, who would certainly have gone with him if he could not persuade him to stay! No, it was pure melodrama. I have always thought him very level-headed, but he has been behaving like a halfwit since—" He stopped.

"Ever since he met Diana?"

He grimaced. "Yes. Well."

She pushed back the rolled-up sleeves of the man's coat she had borrowed. "I am sorry to say that the phenomenon is now very familiar to me. In Italy, a young man threw himself into the Arno after she sent back a necklace he gave her. There was an aborted duel in Nice. And last week, in Digne-les-Bains, two elderly gentlemen came to blows over who would pull her chair out at one of the tables on the terrace."

"Did the young man drown?"

"Oh no," she said. "He was fished out quite promptly. And it had just the effect he desired; Diana loves to nurse hurt creatures. She flew to his bedside and cried over him. I had to make an excuse to leave Florence early."

"Forgive me if I offend you," he said after a minute, "but I find it difficult to believe that someone as calm and sensible as you could have raised a daughter like Diana."

"I did not raise her."

He looked at her, astonished.

"Diana lived with her father from the age of eight

until his death fifteen months ago. While he was alive, I saw her only twice a year." She paused, then said, "I do not wish you to think I am excusing myself, or apologizing for Diana. I am well aware of her faults, but she has many excellent qualities as well. She is intelligent and well educated. She is loyal to those she loves, and she can be very gentle and affectionate."

"Not to my nephew," he muttered.

"Ah, but he is injured now," she pointed out.

"He will not take kindly to being nursed, Mrs. Hart. Not even by your daughter. Nothing, in fact, could be more likely to dampen his ardor."

"Well, that is all to the good then, is it not? It would be awkward to cut out your own nephew."

"Very awkward," he said grimly. Then, in a different voice, "What the devil!"

Abigail drew herself up stiffly. "Mr. Meyer, I cannot permit you to use those—those heathen oaths in my presence."

He paid no attention to her whatsoever. He was staring at something farther down the road. After another moment, she had come far enough over the crest of the small rise to see what he was looking at. Her heart leaped. There was Diana. And young Roth. Then she realized that the men around them were not other travelers. They were wearing uniforms, of sorts. One of them had a sinister-looking helmet with a spike; he carried a rifle. Two others held the bridle of Roth and Diana's horses.

"Who are those men?" she asked, alarmed. She pulled up her gelding, but Meyer flicked its rump with his own crop.

"Keep moving," he said in a low voice. "Not too

fast, not too slow. And do not contradict anything I say. I believe you to be quite intelligent, Mrs. Hart. We will see if I am right."

"Who are they?" she repeated breathlessly as her horse broke into a jolting trot.

"My guess, from the bits of clothing, is that they are an old guard unit attached to the *Sûreté*, Napoleon's Secret Police. They have set up some sort of blockade here."

"But—under whose authority?"

"Their own, which makes this a very dangerous situation. Watch what you say; some of the *Sûreté* officers speak English."

They approached the improvised checkpoint side by side, slowing again to a walk. Now she could see Diana's face, pale and strained. Roth, oddly enough, looked slightly bored. He was talking to the man holding his bridle, and suddenly the Frenchman gave a huge guffaw and slapped Roth's leg so hard his horse shied backwards. Diana shot Roth an absolutely poisonous glare.

"Good boy," breathed Meyer. His own expression shifted somehow; it slid from fierce concentration into a combination of annoyance and anxiety. He looked coarser, less intelligent. She would hardly have recognized him.

"Mama!" called Diana, waving anxiously. Then she saw Abigail's oversized coat and her eyes widened. She had the grace to look a bit guilty.

Abigail and Meyer drew up a few yards from the runaways.

"What seems to be the problem, monsieur?" Meyer inquired courteously of the man holding the gun. His French sounded very odd, as though he was hissing slightly.

"Are these two in your party?" The guard gestured with the stock of the rifle towards Roth and Diana.

"Yes, monsieur."

"The young lady has no papers."

Abigail gave Meyer a quick glare.

"Mademoiselle left in some haste," Meyer explained. "She intended to return to Sisteron." He pulled a packet from an inner pocket and handed it to the Frenchman. "Here are the passes for mademoiselle and for madame, her mother." He indicated Abigail, who gave a stiff nod.

The man perused them in silence. "English," he said in disgust. "Pah!" He looked hard at Meyer. "And you? You are Spanish?"

Bowing, Meyer handed him yet another packet. "These are my documents, and also those of a servant, who follows with the luggage."

Suspicious again, the man looked at Diana and Anthony, and then back at Meyer. "I thought you said mademoiselle planned to return to Sisteron? Why are you now here? Why does the servant come with the bags?"

Meyer dismounted and drew the man aside slightly, lowering his voice as though shielding Abigail. "After mademoiselle left, I heard that the emperor's troop was advancing north very quickly. It is my job to keep the ladies safe. Since they are English, I thought it prudent to change our plans."

This made sense to the Frenchman; he nodded.

"Joseph!" It was one of the other guards. He was holding up a pistol, which he had taken from its saddle holster on Meyer's horse. "Look at this!"

The first man frowned. "Search him," he ordered.

Meyer made no protest as two of the other guards took off his greatcoat and quickly ran expert hands over his arms, his torso, and his legs. Abigail had assumed they would find nothing; to her astonishment and horror, he was carrying another small pistol and two knives, one of which had been concealed in the cuff of his boot. Diana's eyes went wide. Roth, she saw, was unsurprised, although he was beginning to look worried.

"You know," said the man with the helmet to one of the searchers, "I thought he had a military look. Let's have his jacket off." The man yanked it off. "And his shirt." Meyer gave a small sigh, untucked the shirt, and pulled it off over his head.

There were scars everywhere. A small, dimpled one on one shoulder. An ugly gash across his chest. Gouges on both arms. The Frenchman walked around Meyer, studying his prisoner, who stood impassively, shivering very slightly in the cold wind. "Bayonet," commented the guard, pointing to something Abigail could not see, on Meyer's back. "Gunshot. Knife, knife. This one, a saber, I think." He looked at Meyer, who nodded.

Abigail closed her eyes. She felt slightly dizzy. That lean, muscled body, inscribed with the signatures of a dozen weapons, could not be the body of a banker. Could it? She knew what a banker's body should look like. Both her husbands had been cargo brokers. They were not unattractive men, the Harts, but their chests had been paler, softer; their arms more rounded. And how did Meyer come to have papers describing him as Spanish? How, for that matter, had he learned to speak Spanish?

Where had he acquired Rodrigo, who treated him not as a valet treated a master but as a bodyguard treated a commanding officer?

"May I put my shirt back on, monsieur?" Meyer asked.

The guard tossed it to him, and the scars disappeared. Neckcloth, jacket. Now he was once more Nathan Meyer, would-be suitor, the same man who had bowed over her hand that first afternoon in Digne-les-Bains.

No, she thought. Not the same. This was no gentleman of leisure. That man had never existed. Leisure did not involve close encounters with bayonets and bullets and sabers.

The man in the helmet was frowning, studying Meyer's papers again. He pointed to the little pile of weapons at Meyer's feet. "Are these the weapons of an innocent traveler? And your scars, how do you explain those?"

Meyer shrugged and looked embarrassed. "Monsieur, I was a partisan in Spain. I will confess it to you, a fellow soldier. I came to know some English officers, and after the war ended they recommended me to their acquaintances who wished to tour Europe. Many regions are still very unsettled. The English travelers hire me to escort them. I speak French, and some English, and even a little German now. I know how to watch for bandits, for pickpockets, for ostlers who mix straw in with the oats for the horses." He indicated the silver buttons on his jacket. "I have done very well for myself. These ladies"—he gestured towards Abigail and Diana—"have asked me to guide them safely out of France, and I am endeavoring to make sure they come to no harm. Naturally I carry weapons. What fool would not, with such a charge?" He glanced pointedly at Diana. He lowered his voice. "Only yesterday monsieur Roth here was injured defending her from two drunks. And now, this morning, you see the result."

As the guard hesitated, still suspicious, Abigail saw Diana's eyes narrow. She knew that expression, it was one of Diana's few traits inherited from Abigail herself. And with Diana, it usually meant trouble. *No*, she thought, panicking. *Don't do it, whatever it is.*

But Diana, for once, did something right. She didn't say anything. She merely looked at the guard, her huge blue eyes filling with tears.

The Frenchman surrendered. "Pah," he grunted. "I will let you go. You cannot be planning mischief against the emperor traveling with two women. But your passes are not valid any longer, do you understand? You must stop in Gap and have them reissued by the municipal guard."

"Thank you, monsieur, thank you very much." Meyer took back the pile of papers. He cleared his throat. "And my weapons?"

With a jerk of his helmeted head the guard signaled one of his henchman to restore everything except the smallest dagger. "Trust a Spaniard to have a knife in his boot," he muttered. "I will keep this one."

He stepped back, motioning his men to release the bridles. "Move on. I will pass your servant through when he arrives here."

The reunited party rode off northwards at a slow trot, with Meyer a bit ahead of the two women and Roth behind them, like miniature advance and rear guards. Abigail glanced over at Diana. She was sitting very straight in the saddle, but tears were pouring down her face. "We will stop as soon as we can," Abigail said quietly.

"Oh Mother, I am so sorry!" Diana said, half-whispering, half-sobbing. "I am so very, very sorry!"

"It was not your fault," Abigail told her. Her own voice was shaking; she steadied it as best she could and said, "I was very angry when I got your note, but there is nothing like having a rifle pointed at one to restore a bit of perspective."

"I will make it up to you," Diana promised. "I will brush your hair every night. I will be polite to—to everyone. I will be more tidy." She looked at the bunched-up sleeves of Abigail's borrowed coat and winced. "And I will give you back your cloak, as soon as we stop."

They now were riding past the little roadside shrine, and the old woman there curtseyed as they passed by. Diana nodded back, looking very uncomfortable. After a minute, she said hesitantly, "Mama, I did something else I should not have."

Puzzled, Abigail turned to face her.

Diana would not meet her eyes. She took a deep breath and blurted out in a rush, "I made an offering at that shrine. That was where I found Mr. Roth, and I got off my horse, and the woman came over with the candles, and I bought two, and I lit them." She added, almost defiantly, "I made a prayer."

Abigail stiffened; her hands clenched the reins so hard that her horse almost reared.

"Mama?" Diana looked alarmed.

"My horse stumbled," Abigail lied. She forced

herself to relax, to ask casually, "So, you bought the poor woman's candles?"

Diana smiled, relieved. "You do not mind?"

"A little . . . not very much." She would have to speak with Diana later. But not now. No scolding now, no lectures. "What did you pray for?"

Hanging her head, Diana confessed, "For something exciting to happen."

Abigail looked back at the statue of Mary, who was smiling serenely at the baby in her arms as the candles sputtered by her feet. Abigail wondered, not for the first time, if God had a sense of humor.

10

"That was dangerous back there," Meyer told his nephew. "And you did very well." The party had stopped to rest at a village inn, and when Rodrigo had arrived a few minutes ago Meyer and Anthony had decided that he needed help rearranging the hastily loaded baggage. In reality, for different reasons, each man was avoiding the female members of the party, who were inside finishing a cold lunch. "You kept your head admirably. I saw you joking with the man holding your horse; that was a clever touch. What did you tell him?"

"That I was no longer so certain I still wished to marry Miss Hart." He colored. "I had told them she was my fiancée. It seemed the best thing, under the circumstances, especially as I was the only one with papers."

"She did not take it well?"

"Take what well?"

"The announcement that she was your fiancée."

"Oh." Anthony coughed. "No, she did not. But by then she had sense enough not to contradict me."

He shook his head. "I will never understand women. When I jested that I no longer wanted to marry her, she didn't like that either, and she must have known it was all an act."

Meyer remembered the furious expression on Diana's face after the Frenchman had slapped Anthony's leg. She had not been entirely playing a part at that moment, he suspected. Nor had Anthony when he announced his reluctance to marry her. His nephew was behaving like someone who had been rudely awakened from a very pleasant dream. He had tried to avoid Diana when they had stopped here to eat and rest. But the hunter had become the hunted: the girl had pursued him, puzzled and hurt when he made excuses to move away from her. Even Diana's mother could not repress a flicker of amusement by the fourth iteration of the little comedy.

Anthony was looking rather drawn, even paler than usual. There were little lines around his mouth. Meyer suspected that his broken rib was aching fiercely. "I think you should ride in the gig this afternoon," Meyer said abruptly. "It will be no more uncomfortable than trotting. And Miss Hart will be on horseback, if that is your concern."

His nephew sighed. "Was I that obvious?" He looked down at a chicken pecking at some gravel in the small stable yard. "You must think I am very fickle. A short time ago I regarded a chance to be alone with her in a carriage as a great prize."

"I think you had a very unpleasant experience yesterday, and the bruises were the least of it," Meyer said quietly. "And then you had another unpleasant experience two hours ago. You cannot tell me that you were not frightened when you found yourself alone with Miss Hart confronting five armed, self-appointed imperial police."

"I was frightened," Anthony admitted. "I was more than frightened; I was terrified. I will say for Miss Hart that she seemed remarkably unafraid, at least while it was all happening."

"Discretion is the better part of valor," Meyer observed. "The former quality being somewhat lacking in Miss Hart."

"You should have seen her yesterday, when those oafs barged into our parlor." Anthony gave a short laugh. "It was a crack-brained thing to do, to scold them like that, but she certainly had courage. I, on the other hand, did not show to advantage in that encounter."

"Did you not? Well, then, what of me, today?" Meyer's voice was harsh. "Do you think I fancied standing in front of all of you half-naked while that greasy vigilante paced around cataloguing my wounds? Do you think I did not choke, inside, while I was thanking him effusively for letting us go? In that encounter did I show to advantage, as you put it?"

"But—but," Anthony stammered. "It was an act. Of course you thanked him, of course you let him search you. There were five of them, and they were armed, and the women were there."

"And yesterday?" Meyer was angry now. "When you were outnumbered two to one, taken by surprise? Yes, Rodrigo appeared and disabled your attackers. You compare yourself to him and feel inadequate. His opponents were facing the other way, you young idiot, focused on you! The women were there with you as well. How much difference would it have made if you had known some sparring techniques? Is it not possible that resistance would have angered them even further? Or that in a three-way fight in a small room one of the women could have been hurt? I accepted my humiliation to prevent something worse from happening. Is your dignity so much more precious than mine?"

Anthony was looking a bit stunned. Meyer realized that he had been nearly shouting. It was unlike him. He was always quiet, cool, collected. For years he had worked doggedly to become imperturbable, a man ruled by logic, a man who calculated costs and benefits even when the costs were lives. Logic had told him that he should placate the man with the rifle, should allow himself to be searched and even to be stripped. But logic was no consolation afterwards. The memory of their safe escape was an abstraction—a negative, a sorrow avoided rather than experienced. The memory of standing in the wind while eight people eyed his battered torso was all too concrete.

"I am sorry," Meyer said, drawing in his breath. "I am overwrought. But think about what I said. You give yourself, and perhaps Miss Hart as well, too little credit. Our situation is difficult. We should not reproach ourselves if we sometimes make poor choices in the heat of the moment. Or even good choices with unpleasant consequences, as in your case." And in his own case as well. The unpleasant consequences had not yet arrived. But they were coming.

Anthony nodded, a little shamefaced, and started to walk away. But then he paused. "Sir," he said, turning back, "will Mrs. Hart be riding in the gig with me?"

"Very likely. Why?"

His nephew looked uncomfortable. "What shall I say? That is, if she asks me about—what she saw."

Here, of course, was one of the unpleasant consequences, the first and most obvious one. "Tell her you were as surprised as she was."

"She will know I am lying," Anthony said with certainty. "I can spin tales quite happily to armed thugs; I cannot be so plausible when I am speaking to someone I respect."

Meyer made a helpless gesture of frustration. "Tell her something. Anything. Be vague. Look unhappy if she presses you."

"Why not simply let me tell her the truth?"

It would almost be a relief to have it over with. He wavered.

"I know some in the family are embarrassed by your activities, but I am not one of them," Roth said. "Trust me, I would not condemn you to her."

No, he thought. I am managing that quite nicely on my own.

"Do as you think best," Meyer said at last.

Abigail did not ask Roth about his uncle. She certainly wondered about Meyer's scars, and about the little arsenal which had emerged from various hidden pockets in his clothing, and about his sudden transformation into a Spaniard. But it seemed to her that Roth had been through quite enough in the past two days. More to the point, she was not certain he really knew the answers. Instead she waited until they stopped again to rest the horses and have some refreshments. After they were all seated indoors, and Meyer was busy forcing an increasingly pale and feverish Anthony to drink some tea, she slipped out and went to the stables.

"Mr. Santos," she called softly, stepping inside. The place seemed empty; the only sounds were the occasional thunk of a hoof against wood or the soft crunch of some animal eating its hay.

He appeared suddenly right next to her. "Did you call me, Mrs. Hart?"

Startled, she jumped. "Ah. Yes. Do you have a moment?"

He nodded. It didn't look like an answer to her question so much as it looked like a confirmation to himself of something he had suspected. "If you would come this way?" He ushered her into a small tack room. Most of it was taken up with a table, strewn with various bits of harness and awls and nails and scraps of leather. He pulled out the lone chair and held it for her.

Sitting down was a mistake. She realized that as soon as she did it. Now she was looking up at him. And she could not be as firm, as insistent, when she was sitting down. But it would look rather odd to get up again. She compromised on looking around for another seat for Rodrigo, and spotted a bench with a saddle on it. "Please sit," she said, indicating the bench. "And pull it closer to the table. I wish to speak with you in confidence."

He gave that same unsurprised nod, and dragged the bench over.

After he had been sitting in front of her for a full minute, she realized that he was not going to help her by providing any helpful prompts, such as "How may I help you?" or "What did you wish to ask?" On the other hand, he had not refused to speak to her, and he would have been well within his rights to do so. He was no servant of hers. She decided to start with something neutral and work her way up to the questions he would not want to answer.

"How long have you been with Mr. Meyer, Mr. Santos?"

"I do not use my surname unless absolutely necessary," he said, almost apologetically. "For personal reasons."

"Oh." Well, not surprisingly, the mysterious Nathan Meyer had an equally mysterious servant.

"Ten years." When she looked confused, he clarified his response. "The answer to your question, señora. I have been with him for ten years."

"Did you meet in Spain?"

"Yes."

"Was Mr. Meyer there on business?"

"Señora," he said gently, "why not ask what you really want to know? Someone might come in here at any moment."

She looked at him warily. "Will you answer me?"

"Perhaps. It depends on what you ask."

She was beginning to feel as though she were in an ancient temple, consulting an oracle that answered only in monosyllables, or worse, in riddles.

What did she really want to know? Did she want to know how Meyer had come by those scars? Why he had a knife in his boot? How he had made his face look like someone else's, just by changing his expression? She blurted out the first question she could think of. "Does he have any children?"

Rodrigo looked surprised. "He has a daughter and a son, both recently married."

The daughter was the one who had married a

Christian. As far as Abigail was concerned, she no longer existed. "Is the son a banker as well?"

The servant shook his head. "He is a captain in the army."

She frowned. Surely Jews could not hold commissions? The son, too, must have converted. She thought of Diana, lighting the candles at the wayside shrine as though it were some quaint local custom. How big was the gap between the sentimental gesture of a tourist and conversion? If Diana married outside the faith, would Abigail renounce her?

Suddenly she knew the real question she wanted to ask. "Does he see his children often? His daughter? Are they—are they still fond of each other?"

"Of course." The Spaniard looked surprised.

That offhand "of course" was very, very painful. She got up abruptly. "This is very wrong of me. I should not be asking you questions about your employer. It places you in an impossible position. Please forgive me. I do not know what I was thinking."

After she had gone, Rodrigo sat back down on the bench and waited, frowning. That conversation had not gone at all as he had expected. He began sorting the bits of harness into neat piles. He had barely started the first pile ("needs new buckle") when a shadow fell onto the table.

"Well?" asked Meyer impatiently. "Did you tell her?"

Rodrigo shook his head. "She did not ask. I think she meant to, at first, but then she changed her mind for some reason." He looked at Meyer, exasperated. "Señor, why do you not go to her yourself?

She will hardly be surprised, after what she saw this morning. Go now, before something else happens."

"Impossible."

"What do you think she will do? Denounce you to the next group of vigilantes? Shoot you? Scream and run away? She seems to be a very sensible woman."

"Sensible, yes. But also principled."

"True," Rodrigo conceded. "She did not leave just now because she heard you coming, for example. She decided that it was wrong of her to question me about my own master."

"I know." Meyer leaned against the wall. "I heard that part. I was eavesdropping, of course, as I so often do. Here I was, listening to a conversation she thought was private. And she, with ample evidence that I was at the very least a liar and likely something far worse, had scruples about questioning my servant. The contrast between her principles and my lack thereof struck me forcibly."

"Señor," he said, exasperated, "you should go to her yourself and explain."

He set his jaw. "No. It would do no good now. If I had confessed before she suspected anything, it would be different. But after this morning she will think I am simply making the best of a bad situation."

Rodrigo gave up. "Am I driving again?"

Meyer nodded. "Anthony by all rights should be in bed, but the gig is the best we can offer at the moment." He thought of something else that was worrying him. "Did they search it, by the way?"

"Search the vehicle? At the roadblock? Yes. Ruffled through a few bags."

Well, obviously they had not found anything, or Rodrigo would not be here. He told himself not to

be so nervous. But then, he did not usually have secrets from Rodrigo as well as from the French. If his
servant ever found that jar of sulphur, there would
be hell to pay. There would still be hell to pay, eventually, but Meyer was hoping to postpone it until
the jar was empty.

11

The Auberge du Marchand consisted of two century-old town houses on one of the principal streets of Gap. The houses had been acquired and then remodeled piecemeal, and the interior of the hotel thus resembled a three-dimensional maze. Staircases went up half a flight and ended abruptly at a single door; corridors turned and ran into a wall. Doors five yards apart proved to open into the same apartment; single doors gave access to three smaller doors. The stables were in an alley four buildings away and were impossible to find unless one of the hotel clerks led the way in person.

Meyer was not happy with the situation. He had ridden ahead to book rooms there on the recommendation of the host of a pleasant roadside tavern they had passed a few hours back. It might be "a very superior hostelry, very congenial to the ladies," as the tavern keeper had promised, but as Meyer looked around with a professional eye he thought he had never seen any place better suited to an assassination—if, of course, the assassin could find his victim. From the point of view of a man determined to protect someone, it was a nightmare. There were no adjoining rooms big enough to house a party of five, and after the experience in Sisteron he was unwilling to lodge the Harts in any room more than three steps from his own bedchamber. In the end he settled for two rooms, one of which was quite large and included a sitting area. The two shared a small hallway, and there were no other guest chambers anywhere nearby. The doors were even two different sizes: the larger room had double doors, and the smaller room, which the men were sharing, a single one. Meyer was determined not to stumble into the wrong room this time.

The two other men did not like the place much either. Anthony, who had climbed immediately into bed the moment they arrived, would have very much preferred his own room. Until he fell asleep he complained petulantly each time the door was opened. Meyer suspected very strongly that Anthony was coming down with a fever. As for Rodrigo, when he discovered that the easiest route to the stables involved traversing three courtyards, two of which were locked promptly at sundown, he informed Meyer that he would sleep in the stable loft with the grooms. Meyer felt sorry for him, but he was in no mood to let anyone lock up a possible means of escape from Gap. If Rodrigo was to take his turn riding south tonight there was really no choice in the matter. And of course, that also meant one fewer person in the already-crowded smaller room.

The ladies, on the other hand, did find the Auberge du Marchand congenial. Or at least, the younger lady did. When Meyer escorted the two women upstairs, Diana exclaimed rapturously. The room was so large! So elegantly furnished! It seemed more like part of a private home than a hired room at an inn! (Here Abigail had glanced at Meyer and raised her eyebrows expressively. Both the sleeping area and the sitting area were relentlessly decorated in high imperial style: gold eagles and red-velvet upholstery juxtaposed with Egyptian-style pieces—the most hideous of which, an ebony table in the shape of a crocodile, had actually made both adults wince when they saw it.) In addition, the hotel had several dining rooms, and Diana was looking forward to what she called "a proper meal, for once," meaning at least six courses and more waiters than diners. As Meyer left, she was shaking out her only evening frock and lighting all eight candles in the sconces attached to the mirror.

It was only when Meyer returned to his own room down the hall that he discovered the most serious disadvantage of the Auberge du Marchand. Certain rooms had unusual acoustical properties—unbeknownst to the guests being overheard—eerily projecting conversations to another room next door, or around the corner, or upstairs. Diana and Abigail Hart, for example, had no idea that their voices were emerging from Meyer's fireplace. The voices were so loud that he glanced over at the bed to see if Anthony had been awakened again. Apparently not. Meyer was just about to go next door and warn the two women to speak more softly when he heard his own name.

"Mama, how old do you suppose Mr. Meyer might be?"

"I don't know." There was a pause. "He must be over forty; he has two grown children. But he certainly doesn't look it."

"Did you peek . . . when he took his shirt off?"

"That is a *very* ill-mannered question." Abigail's voice was tart.

"Well, I did. I admit it. How do you suppose he came by all those scars?"

The reply did not come through as clearly; Abigail must have moved to a different spot in the room. He could hear only the word "affair," which he suspected had been preceded by the phrase "none of our."

"Do you think he is a criminal? A bandit? His servant is Spanish, you know, and they say Spain is full of bandits."

Spain was not full of bandits, he wanted to shout. Spain was full of men who had lost their land when Napoleon invaded and had never gotten it back, even after the Allied victory. Men like the character he had played today at the roadblock. They hired themselves out as fighters. What else could they do?

He didn't hear her next reply at all.

"Did you see he had a knife hidden in his *boot*?" Diana's voice rose so high on the last word that it was almost a shriek.

Now he could hear Abigail again: "Yes, I saw that."

"And where did he get those papers, the ones that said he was Spanish?"

"Perhaps experienced travelers furnish themselves with that sort of thing." She sounded hesitant.

"Mother! Don't be absurd! It is all very suspicious. Suppose he is not Mr. Meyer at all? Suppose he murdered the real Mr. Meyer and took his place?"

"And hired an actor to impersonate his nephew as well? Or do you believe Mr. Roth is also a bandit?"

"No." Grudgingly. "But Mama, something is very odd. You must see that. You must ask him to explain."

"I suppose you are right. I will speak with him tonight. After dinner." She sounded very reluctant.

"He is never to be found after dinner. Or sometimes even during dinner. That is another odd thing. I think you should find him now. Or I will, if you don't dare."

"Diana!"

He heard a door open.

Panic-stricken, his first impulse was to hide. He quenched the lamp and headed for the armoire, hoping it was big enough to conceal him. Then he reminded himself that they would knock. All he had to do was not answer.

Quick footsteps came down the hall, followed by an imperious tattoo on the door. "Diana, for goodness' sake, you need not beat the door down!" Abigail sounded exasperated. "Obviously there is no one there."

"I will just look."

Had he locked the door? He was not sure. He dove under the bed just as the answer became clear: no.

"You see?" The voice came from the doorway. He could see Abigail's feet in the block of lamplight spilling in from the hall. "It's dark. There is no one here."

But there was someone there. Meyer heard the bed creak suddenly above him.

Then sheets and covers flew over the side of the bed, and Anthony's voice roared, "Damn it, Rodrigo, I told you to stop leaving the door open!"

There was an appalled silence. Meyer saw Abigail's feet stepping back.

"Oh God." There was another whirlwind of sheets, this time back up off the floor. "I do apologize. I thought—I was asleep—"

"We—we were looking for your uncle," stammered Diana.

The feet were retreating rapidly. "I beg your pardon, Mr. Roth, most sincerely. We did not mean to disturb you." That was Abigail, a bit breathless. "Please go back to sleep. You do not look very well."

Meyer waited at least a minute after the door closed to slide out from under the bed. Anthony gave a choked cry and nearly dropped the lamp he had just rekindled.

"What the devil were you doing under my bed?" he demanded. His cheeks were flushed and his eyes very bright.

Fever, thought Meyer. Another complication. "Hiding."

"What?"

"Shhh." Meyer pointed to the fireplace. Sure enough, two female voices were once again floating out of it.

"Mother, why didn't you stop me?" moaned Diana. "I have never been so mortified! Poor Mr. Roth! He will never speak to me again."

"He looked ill." That was Abigail, sounding worried. "I will ring for someone; Mr. Meyer must be found. I think we should call a doctor."

Anthony was sitting up in bed, his mouth open, staring at the fireplace. Only now did Meyer notice that he was not wearing anything except a pair of drawers and the tape over his ribs. His bruises had turned green around the edges.

"Do me a favor," said Meyer. "Wrap yourself in a blanket, and go to their room at once. Tell them it is your turn to beg their pardon, but their voices are coming through our fireplace and you thought they might wish to know."

Anthony gave a dazed nod, heaved himself out of bed, and disappeared, trailing half the bedclothes behind him.

So, thought Meyer, at least he was no longer the only one in the family who had been displayed half-naked today to a woman he admired.

Dinner was a very awkward affair. First, Meyer had to pretend that he knew nothing about the conversation he had overheard. There was a speculative light in Diana's eye when she looked at him which made it difficult to forget some of her remarks, however. Her gaze lingered several times on his torso, and once he even caught her peering at his shoes. Perhaps she thought he had a dagger in them. Abigail, on the other hand, did not look at him at all. She kept her eyes lowered during the entire meal. In fact, she kept her head down as well, which meant that he spent over an hour looking at the top of one of her accursed caps. He suspected that she was nervous about her plan to interrogate him. He was none too sanguine himself about that prospect.

He also had to pretend that he knew nothing of the encounter between the two women and his nephew. Every time Anthony's name was mentioned, Diana turned scarlet, which made that particular bit of acting very difficult. Finally he decided that it would be more suspicious to ignore such a blatant display than to acknowledge it, and at the next blush, he broke off his sentence and asked Diana politely if she was too warm. She turned even redder, looked at her mother in frantic embarrassment, and fled the table, murmuring some disjointed excuse.

Abigail raised her head for a moment. "Pray do not tease her, Mr. Meyer," she said in a low voice. "She is—she is very conscious of Mr. Roth's attentions." Then she looked down at the table again.

Meyer could not believe his ears. The self-possessed, morally upright Abigail Hart was lying to him. She was doing a terrible job, too. He frowned. This was very interesting. Why would she lie to him? He knew her well enough by now to feel sure that she would not normally hesitate, once Diana was gone, to reveal what had happened with Anthony. She would even see the humor in it. He certainly did. If only he had hidden in the armoire; then he could have seen Diana's face when Anthony erupted bare-chested from under the covers.

Let us consider this logically, he said to himself. The only reason to lie about such a delicious story would be to conceal her visit to his and Anthony's bedchamber. And the only reason to conceal the visit would be to avoid answering the question he would probably ask: why did you come to my room?

He leaned back, studying tonight's cap. It was amber-colored silk, matching her gown, and nearly the same color as the tiny bit of hair at the edges. From what he had overheard, from what he had seen just now, it appeared that Abigail was even more reluctant to interrogate him than he was to be interrogated. Why not put her on the defensive? Why not take the initiative?

"Mrs. Hart," he said.

She looked up, alarmed at something in his tone.

"I would like to speak with you in private."

Flustered, she looked around the dining room. It

was not crowded; the weather at this time of year in Gap did not attract visitors. There were no other guests within earshot. There were, however, several hovering waiters. It was that sort of establishment.

He signaled to the nearest hoverer.

The man snapped to attention as though he were a subaltern and Meyer his captain. "Monsieur?"

"Is there a small room nearby where madame and I might take a glass of wine?"

"Certainly, monsieur. If monsieur will have the goodness to wait for one moment?" He summoned a lower-level hoverer, who darted off at his whispered instructions and returned a minute or so later accompanied by a very superior gentleman in a powdered wig who escorted Meyer and Abigail to an alcove off of the hotel's music room, where a horn quartet was playing. There was a certain amount of additional hovering, involving wine and biscuits, but at length the various carriers of trays and openers of wine were dismissed, and he and Abigail were alone. The musicians did not count; in fact, they were excellent insurance in case this room resembled the Harts's bedchamber acoustically.

Attack first, he reminded himself. "It seems to me that you might have some questions about what you learned of me today. Well-justified questions. I wanted to give you an opportunity to ask them."

She twisted the wineglass in her fingers. "That is very kind of you, but—"

"Come, Mrs. Hart. Surely, even if you averted your eyes from my, ah, *déshabillé*, you cannot have failed to hear the guard's description of my scars?"

"I saw them," she said, almost inaudibly. "There were . . . quite a few."

"Yes," he said. "Unless I was attacked simultaneously by five footpads, each armed with a different weapon, I think we must conclude that I have been wounded on more than one occasion. Oh, and he missed one."

She looked up, startled.

He pointed to a spot just below his left shoulder. "Dog bites. He thought they were knife wounds."

"Dogs? You had dogs set on you?" Her eyes were enormous.

"I have been chased by dogs. I have been stabbed, shot at, sliced at, and imprisoned. I carry several sets of false papers. I travel very well armed, and have already replaced the knife in my boot that was confiscated this morning. I am an excellent liar. These are not the usual credentials of the 'family friends' recommended to you by your cousin. You are owed an explanation."

She frowned. "I am not sure that I am. Let us not forget that I began our acquaintance by dismissing you very rudely after you had traveled quite a distance out of your way to do us a service. Then, the moment I needed help, I suddenly came running back to you, disrupting any plans you might have made. I am not blind, Mr. Meyer. It was perfectly obvious to me that whatever your intentions that first day in Digne might have been, by the time you saw us again in Barrême, Diana and I were an encumbrance."

It was true. It was only later that he had begun to perceive the advantages of having two women— genteel, attractive women—in his party.

She set down her wine cup and smoothed her skirt. "You are right that I was perturbed by what I saw this morning. I meant to ask you about it earlier, but I lost my nerve." She smiled briefly. "It is not easy to confront someone who carries a knife in their boot."

"I would never, *never* harm you or Diana," he said, horrified. "You must believe that."

"Oh, I do," she assured him, "now. Because once I was calmer, and had thought about everything carefully, it occurred to me that the explanation was really very simple."

"It did? It is?"

She nodded. "The first thing was the pigeons."

He had prayed she would not connect them with his other activities. He had already admitted to himself that he would have to tell her about the past. There was no avoiding it. It was the present he wanted to conceal. Apparently he was going to have to confess everything. Or, more accurately, listen to her formulate his confession for him.

"This afternoon, when we stopped to give Mr. Roth a hot drink, I—" She stopped, then continued determinedly, "I went to find Mr. Santos. Rodrigo. I began to ask him questions about you."

What did this have to do with pigeons? "He mentioned something of the sort."

"I am very ashamed of myself," she confessed. "But I was upset—to see Diana in the hands of that rabble! And then, when they searched you, and found all those terrifying, inexplicable things! I was angry; I thought you had deceived us."

"I *did* deceive you. You were right to be angry."

She ignored him. "When I left, I walked by the gig, and Mr. Roth's pigeons were cooing. That reminded me of what he had said about the bank's courier system. That was the first piece."

She still thought the pigeons were Anthony's. He gave a little sigh of relief.

"And then, just before dinner, I remembered the second piece. The most famous loan your family bank has ever made: the Roth-Meyer Bank smuggled gold through France, right under Napoleon's nose, to pay Lord Wellington's troops in Spain. Is that not correct?"

Puzzled, he nodded.

"A very dangerous, very difficult undertaking. Surely the bank did not entrust an operation of such magnitude, of such delicacy, to ordinary employees."

Right again. Meyer's brother, Jacob, had coordinated the entire affair from his house in Paris, and the shipments were escorted by two trusted subordinates.

"You never looked to me like a gentleman of leisure," she said vehemently. "The moment I met you I should have been suspicious of Joshua's description. You were not retired from the bank at all; you were their chief courier in France, supervising the currency smuggling. Naturally you would need to carry false papers, need to learn to handle weapons."

He sat back against the satin cushions of the sofa, stunned. Her reasoning was perfectly logical. Her conclusion was utterly false.

"I admire you," she said. "I want you to know that. I disapprove of war, as many women do. I think it is immoral; I think it corrupts those who practice it. Not all wounds are physical. But I do admire you. Your bank made a pledge to England, and honored that pledge under nearly impossible conditions. You risked your life to make certain that your family stood by their word." There were tears in her eyes.

"Mrs. Hart." He took a deep breath. "I do not know what to say." He looked down at his shoes. No dagger, alas. Perhaps he could stab himself with the buckle.

"I apologize for my rudeness to you, for my suspicions, for everything. I was mortified at dinner, to think how I had misjudged you. I could not even look you in the face. You were willing to let that dreadful French guard humiliate you this morning to protect my daughter, and I repaid you by deciding you were the lowest sort of criminal. Please forgive me."

Now it was his turn to explain that he was, in fact, the lowest sort of criminal. But, as was natural for a criminal, he thought better of it. If she wanted to take all that damning evidence and turn him into a hero, who was he to contradict her? "You exaggerate my contribution," he said finally, raising his eyes to meet hers.

There was a long silence. At some point, without his noticing, the horn quartet had stopped playing. The music room was empty. Neither one of them moved, or looked away. A few renegade strands of hair had, by some miracle, escaped from her cap; they fluttered slightly at her temples. Her face was open, unguarded. He knew, knew with total certainty, that he could kiss her. That he wanted to kiss her.

He also knew she would eventually hate him, and herself, even more if he did. Perhaps he wasn't the very lowest sort of criminal after all, because instead of kissing her, he got up, offered her his arm, and escorted her back to the safety of the hotel's well-staffed reception room.

12

"How is he?" asked Rodrigo before even dismounting. Meyer had intercepted him in the alley leading to the stable.

"Anthony? Not well. He is still asleep, but very restless and feverish." He glanced at the sky. "It is what, half-past six? He has been sleeping for twelve straight hours."

Rodrigo swung off the horse. "Did you send for a doctor? Mrs. Hart seemed to think he needed one."

"She may be right," he admitted. "He is in no shape to cross the Col Bayard, that is obvious. Perhaps we should stay here in Gap another day."

"That might not be wise." They had come up to the stable door. Rodrigo handed the horse to a sleepy ostler, and the two men headed around the side of the building to the enclosed yard where guests' vehicles were stored.

"Why? What did you find out? Wait, have some of this first."

His servant took a long drink from the bottle Meyer handed him. "Well, first I went south, and nearly ran into Bonaparte's advance force. They will arrive here late this morning at their present rate. It is even possible—not likely, but possible—that Napoleon and the rest of the troops could reach Gap by midnight tonight. They are moving very quickly. That is why I say it might be imprudent to remain here." He took another swallow. "On the other hand, there is the pass. I went north for a few miles to see what conditions were like."

"And?"

"Poor. Snow at the top, more snow likely today, by the look of things." He handed back the flask.

Meyer took another look at the sky and frowned. "Scylla and Charybdis. What do you think we should do?"

"Why consult me?" Rodrigo pulled the pigeon crates out from under the seat of the gig and began tipping grain from a little sack into the feeding box. "Surely the decision should be left to Mrs. Hart. Especially if you want to persuade her to trust you again, now that she knows the truth."

Meyer said nothing.

Rodrigo straightened up, grain dripping unheeded onto the dirt. He looked hard at Meyer and then swore softly in Spanish. "You told me you were going to speak with her last night." He stabbed one finger at Meyer's chest. "Right before I left, right here, in this very spot, you promised that you would explain everything to her. That you would not leave her wondering about what she saw at that roadblock yesterday morning."

"Oh, I talked to her." He laughed shortly. "Or rather, she talked to me. She is very clever—perhaps you have already realized that. She was suspicious long before yesterday morning. She even noticed the pigeons, and drew her own conclusions. We have come to an excellent understanding."

"You have?" The servant suddenly noticed the little pile of grain at his feet and righted the sack. "She— she was not angry?"

"Quite the reverse," Meyer assured him. "She admires me. She despises soldiers, of course, and war, but she thought it was very noble of me to help smuggle gold to Wellington in order to honor the contract signed by the Roth-Meyer Bank."

"What?" The sack dropped onto the floor of the gig. "You told her that you were covered with scars because you had been delivering *loan monies?*"

"No, no. *She* told *me.* I was getting ready to confess the truth, and she interrupted and started begging my pardon for misjudging me. She saw the pigeons—which, by the way, she still believes to be Anthony's—and that reminded her somehow of the bank's role in funding the British troops in Spain, and she put two and two together and came up with seven."

"What happens when she recalculates and comes up with four?" Rodrigo asked.

Meyer shrugged. "We will never see each other again after this week. What does it matter?" He looked down at the crates. "If those pigeons eat any more, they won't be able to fly," he observed.

Rodrigo hastily brushed the spilled grain out of reach of the birds.

"Get some sleep," Meyer said. "I will consult Mrs. Hart—I can do that in my capacity as former hero of the banking world—and if she agrees, we will stay here another day. I do not fancy the thought of dragging my feverish nephew over the top of that mountain."

He was badly out of practice, or perhaps distracted by his concern for Anthony and the women. Why else would he have returned from the stables by the back way, instead of going around on the street, where he would have seen the soldiers and the sweating horses? Why, for that matter, had he selected the largest, most ornate hotel in Gap, a place which would be the obvious choice to lodge a former emperor, should he happen to come to town? But he had chosen the Auberge du Marchand. He had returned through the courtyard. He had not paid attention to the noises he heard, noises suggesting the arrival of a large party of guests. He had not asked himself who would be arriving at a hotel in Gap before seven in the morning. He therefore entered the hotel through the back hallway and emerged into the main reception area just as a hawk-faced man in the uniform of the Old Guard came in from the opposite direction, followed by three mud-spattered officers and a very disdainful young man dressed in evening clothes.

Too late, old habits reasserted themselves. He allowed his glance to pass in an unhurried way over the new arrivals, gave a puzzled nod to the hawk-faced man, who looked as though he was trying to remember something, and walked purposefully, but not hastily, to the nearest staircase. The minute he was out of sight Meyer began frantically searching for a way to get out of the hotel unseen. The staircase he had chosen ended half a flight up at two locked doors; he cursed under his breath and debated. Right or left? He chose left, and picked the lock. The room was empty, thank God. He opened the shutters. Wrong side of the hotel; he was looking down on the street, where twenty more soldiers were stationed. Back out into the hall. The second room, too, was empty. It was a drop of ten feet to the courtyard; he swung out over the ledge and let go, hoping no one in the building opposite had been looking out their window at that moment. Then he headed back to the stables.

Rodrigo was still out in the stable yard, cleaning the pigeon crates. "What happened?" he asked, dropping the crate. The pigeons, crammed into the other container, gave an angry squawk as it landed on top of them.

"I ran into an old friend," said Meyer grimly. "You underestimated Cambronne's pace. He is in the reception hall of the hotel at this very moment, no doubt bespeaking rooms for two thousand men."

"Did he see you?"

"I am afraid so. And Raoul Doucet was with him. They only glanced at me, and I did nothing to attract their attention, but the odds that neither one of them will remember me eventually are very small. If I were Doucet—and he is, after all, one of my counterparts in Napoleon's old intelligence service—I would, sooner or later, think to look at the hotel's list of guests. I am registered under my own name."

"Do they know your real name?"

"Doucet does."

"We are leaving, I take it." Rodrigo closed up the crate.

"Yes, but we must not appear to be leaving,"

Meyer said. "Take the birds and whatever else you must have with you, but make sure there is still a crate here in the gig and clothing on your bed. Order a carriage and two horses for tomorrow morning, to travel south. Then find some other stable, one as far from here as you can, hire two mules and four horses, and meet me half a mile north of the edge of town in one hour. I will get Anthony and the ladies; we will go for a morning walk."

"Can Master Anthony walk half a mile?" the servant asked, worried.

"I devoutly hope so. Otherwise, we will have to leave him behind."

Abigail was a very light sleeper, especially when she was worried about something. When the door to her room opened, therefore, she woke almost instantly, and sat straight up. It was Meyer, and he had one finger on his lips in an imperative gesture for quiet.

She slid out of bed and went over to the door, which he closed behind him very, very carefully. She was going to say something clever—"Wrong room again, Mr. Meyer?"—but the expression on his face stopped her.

"Speak as quietly as you can," he told her, in a voice which provided an admirable model. She could barely hear him, and she was standing right next to him. "Remember, sound from this room goes to at least one other bedchamber."

"Why are you here?" she whispered.

"Napoleon's advance guard arrived ten minutes ago. They are here, in this hotel. You must be prepared to leave in twenty minutes. You must dress for a long, difficult day outdoors, riding and walking, possibly in snow. We will be pretending to go for a constitutional; therefore, you may bring only what a lady would carry on a morning stroll. Any spare clothing must either be worn or carried in some inconspicuous manner. You must behave as though you plan to return—order luncheon, send laundry out. I will come to fetch you. Once you leave this room, you must appear unconcerned, as though you know nothing about the troops." This was all delivered in a calm, barely audible monotone without any pause to allow questions or objections, and the next moment he turned, apparently intending to leave.

Abigail grabbed his arm and turned him around again. "Do you make a habit of bursting in on ladies at sunrise and giving them inexplicable commands to abandon all their possessions?" she hissed angrily.

There was a strange glint in his dark eyes. "Only when I believe them intelligent enough to understand that I would not do so without a very good reason." He glanced at the chair next to Diana's side of the bed, buried under a confused heap of stockings, shawls, gloves, and underthings. "I will of course replace the items you cannot bring with you at my own expense."

"Mr. Meyer, I am not complaining about the cost of a few frocks! We already lost the majority of our luggage when we joined you in Barrême. This is not about money." She was finding it very difficult to be angry and whisper at the same time, and anger was winning.

He sighed. "No. But money is what I can offer you."

"I want more than that. I want to be treated like a reasonable adult, someone who is entitled to be informed about risks and choices. I want to know what made you walk in here and order me and my daughter to behave like fleeing assassins."

"I *was* going to consult you," he said, leaning wearily against the closed door. "My nephew is very ill. When I spotted the troops I was on my way to your room, in fact. I intended to ask you whether you would be willing to stay in Gap today, in spite of the likelihood that Napoleon's army would be here by midnight tonight. Anthony should not be traveling at all, even in the most luxurious carriage, let alone riding over an ice-covered mountain on the back of a mule."

"But you changed your mind." She folded her arms. "You were prepared to remain here, in the face of Napoleon and his entire army, but at the sight of a few soldiers from the advance party you panicked?"

"Two particular soldiers. Officers. They recognized me from . . . an earlier encounter." He pushed his hair back from his forehead. "I would go on alone, but it would not do any good at this point. You have all been traveling with me; our party was registered here at the hotel under my name. None of you will be safe."

She opened her mouth to tell him that officers would not threaten a sick man, or two innocent women. Then she remembered the roadblock. The man with the helmet had been some sort of officer.

"What sort of officers? How do they know you?"

"Twenty minutes," he said, opening the door. "I must see to Anthony."

* * *

Before they had been on the road two hours, Abigail knew that something must have frightened Nathan Meyer very badly indeed to have convinced him that it was safer for Roth to go than to stay. "Very ill" had been no exaggeration, and today's journey might well change very ill into deathly ill.

After washing his face with cold water and gulping some extremely strong coffee, Roth had managed to walk out of the hotel on his own two feet. The minute they were out of sight of the soldiers, however, his legs had started to buckle, and Meyer had been forced to support him on one side. Sweat had glistened on Roth's face as he staggered determinedly on, and Meyer had ended by half-carrying him the last quarter mile. Once mounted, Roth had barely managed to keep his seat, even on the placid white mule. Every few minutes he had been slumping forward, then jerking himself back upright, and just now, at the first halt, he had collapsed into Meyer's arms upon being lifted out of the saddle.

"I'm not much better on a mule than I am on a horse, am I?" he said, with a faint smile. Meyer had propped him up against the massive remains of a fallen tree. "Sorry to be such a nuisance."

"Don't be an idiot." Meyer handed him a flask. Abigail suspected it was brandy, which was not an ideal drink for someone in Roth's condition, but they could hardly brew him tea halfway up a mountain. He did look a bit better after taking a few sips.

"It will be very steep for the next mile or so," Meyer told him. "If you faint, or even sway over to one side, it could be disastrous."

"Tie me on, then."

The other two men cut some branches to make a

small frame and lashed it to the saddle of the mule. It took them nearly fifteen minutes, and Abigail could not help glancing back down the road, as though soldiers might be galloping after them.

"Mother?" Diana had come over to her. "Do you think I should offer them my pelisse, to use for padding?" she asked, keeping her voice low. "It is ruined in any case, and I am quite warm."

Diana had had the clever notion of augmenting Abigail's postflight wardrobe by wearing one of her mother's gowns over her own riding habit. Once her tightly cut pelisse was added to the ensemble, she looked a bit like a fabric sausage, and had not been able to get into the saddle until Abigail had cut open the side seam of the coat.

It was chilly and overcast, but the snow Meyer had predicted had not arrived . . . at least, not yet. Abigail nodded in agreement. When they set off again, with Roth braced against his makeshift backrest, Diana rode alongside him, chatting determinedly. Abigail could not help remembering that first day in the carriage, when Roth had been the one bravely trying to make conversation, and Diana had been the one who had barely spoken. Roth had a much better excuse, of course. And he was trying. Every once in a while he would give Diana a shaky grin, or even a monosyllabic response.

Meyer dropped back from his position at the head of the cavalcade to ride next to Abigail. "Do you know," he said thoughtfully, "when I first saw your daughter, I thought she was nothing but an empty-headed flirt. She was holding court at your hotel in Digne, and she had every mannerism polished to a high gloss: the simper, the lowered eyelashes, the brittle laugh, the toss of the head. I would never have suspected she could outface five armed bullies, or would understand that my nephew will do better if someone stays by him and talks to keep him awake." He shook his head, bemused. "Last night we had to change the hour of our seating for dinner twice because of—what was it?"

"Her hair." Abigail gave a wry smile. "It would not curl properly. I make a very poor lady's maid, as she has told me repeatedly since our own ran off."

"Well then, last night she refuses to eat until her hair is arranged just so, and today she watches you slice open a fur-lined pelisse without even blinking, and then stuffs it onto the back of a mule to make my nephew more comfortable. I must retract what I said yesterday."

"What was that?" She twisted in the saddle to look at him.

"I believe I said that you were too sensible to have produced such a daughter."

"And I said she had many excellent qualities."

He gave a little half bow. "As seems to be the case whenever we disagree lately, you were right and I was wrong."

"We disagreed this morning," she reminded him. "About whether to leave."

"We did not disagree. I stormed in and behaved like an arrogant fool, insisting that we leave at once without explaining myself, and you were sensible enough to overlook my rudeness."

"Eventually."

He smiled. "Eventually, yes."

The track narrowed, and they were forced to ride single file again for some distance. It was very steep, as Meyer had predicted, and the horses were struggling in places. He jumped off, and began leading both his mount and hers; Rodrigo was doing the same for Diana. The mules were in their element now, and would have passed Abigail's horse easily if there had been any room to go by. After twenty minutes of this slow, uphill work, the ground suddenly leveled off. The road widened. It could easily hold six abreast, Abigail thought. And ahead of them, under high, sullen clouds, an enormous valley appeared. It was surrounded on every side by mountains—not the tree-covered peaks Abigail had seen in Italy, or even the sculpted rock gorges farther south here in France. These mountains were so tall that they disappeared right into the clouds. To the west, where the clouds were thinner, an occasional spire was visible, impossibly high, sparkling with snow even in the gray light.

She drew in her breath. Her horse had stopped, as though it, too, was stunned.

"You have never seen the Alps before? The true Alps, as they say in Grenoble?"

She shook her head.

"This is nothing," he said. "You must go to Switzerland one day."

"How tall are they?" she asked, gesturing towards the wall of rock ahead of them.

"These? Twelve, thirteen thousand feet. To the east of here, some of the higher peaks are more than fifteen thousand."

Almost three miles high. It was incredible.

"I am glad I saw this," she said, more to herself than to him. "I will always remember it."

"They are very beautiful," he agreed. "They are

also very dangerous." She looked at his face, outlined against the snow-covered rocks, at the fierce exhilaration she saw there, and an unwelcome but inescapable conclusion presented itself.

"You find it attractive," she said slowly. "The danger, that is. Perhaps even more attractive than the beauty."

"Yes." He looked at her. "I am afraid that is true."

"You must be having a wonderful time at the moment, then," she said bitterly.

"I would be," he admitted. "If I were by myself." He began to lead her horse forward again. "It narrows again ahead; I will stay on foot and keep hold of your bridle until we have descended a bit."

Abigail was not as competent on horseback as Diana was, but she still found it unsettling to have someone else leading an animal she was riding. It occurred to her, as they started down the mountain, that she had been experiencing that same unsettled feeling remarkably frequently of late. Since she had met Nathan Meyer, in fact.

13

Just before noon, in the middle of a meeting with the mayor and deputies of Gap, General Pierre Cambronne was interrupted by an aide. Monsieur Doucet wished to speak with him urgently. Cambronne excused himself, and stepped out into the hall. He did not like Doucet. The man was calculating and ruthless, and he did not behave like a soldier. But he was useful. He noticed things: Officials who were too nervous, or not nervous enough. Documents that looked real but were not. Apparently he had just noticed something important.

Doucet was pacing impatiently. "General! There you are. I have a question for you. Do you remember the man we saw at the hotel this morning, just after we came in—tall, dark-haired, aquiline features?" When Cambronne looked blank, he prompted him: "He came in from the opposite side of the room, from some back entrance. He nodded to you."

"Ah, that man. Yes, he looked vaguely familiar. Why?"

"He looked familiar to me also. I have an uneasy feeling about him."

Cambronne searched his memory for a minute, then gave up. "My dear Doucet, I am afraid there is nothing save the notion that I knew the face. My own associations were quite the opposite of yours, very positive ones; if I had to guess I would say he must be some local man loyal to the emperor, someone who came to Paris perhaps on government business and saw us there."

"Perhaps," muttered Doucet. "But then why not greet us?" He began pacing again.

"Monsieur Doucet, the deputies of Gap?" Cambronne indicated the half-open door to the council chamber.

"I beg your pardon. By all means, continue. But if you should remember anything further, please inform me at once."

An hour later, Cambronne was just sitting down to an excellent lunch with the deputies when he was interrupted again. With a sigh, he pushed back his chair and went out into an anteroom.

"He is British," said Doucet, not bothering with a greeting. "I somehow have remembered that much."

"Who?"

"The man at the hotel."

"Really, monsieur, I cannot think why you are so concerned about one man whose face we barely glimpsed," snapped Cambronne. "One would think the fellow had an entire battalion of royalists concealed in the cellars of the hotel." He returned to his lunch.

Fifteen minutes later, Cambronne remembered where he had seen that face. He put down his fork, stared blindly at his plate, and then left the table without a word to his fellow diners. "Where is Doucet?" he asked his astonished escort.

"He has returned to the hotel, my general," stammered one of the junior lieutenants.

"I will go there and find him. Make my excuses to the deputies."

He nearly ran down the hill to the Auberge du Marchand.

Doucet was in the reception room, slumped in a chair, staring at the doorway the mystery man had emerged from as if he could will the stranger to reappear.

"Doucet? I remembered. Not his name, but enough to concern me."

The younger man jumped to his feet.

"You were right," Cambronne said, breathing hard. "He *is* British. A Jew. Loosely connected to their intelligence service. He was the one who warned me last April, at Orgon."

The younger man closed his eyes. "Meyer," he whispered. He swore profusely. Then he jumped up and rang the bell at the desk, tapping his hand on the wood impatiently until the innkeeper's wife appeared. "Madame," he said, "is there by any chance an English gentleman staying here? A Monsieur Meyer?"

She beamed. "Why, yes. With another gentleman, and a very lovely young lady, and the young lady's mother, who—"

"Have they left?" Cambronne interrupted.

She looked puzzled. "I do not believe so. Just one moment." She returned a few minutes later. Doucet was gripping the edge of the desk so tightly his knuckles were white. "They are still here, monsieur.

The chambermaid has just returned from changing the beds."

Doucet looked at Cambronne. "We will have to detain him. He is very dangerous."

"I am under a considerable obligation to him," Cambronne objected. "As is His Imperial Majesty."

"I am under a personal obligation to him as well. We can both shower him with gratitude. After we lock him up." He turned to Madame Marchand. "This man is an enemy of France, madame. I must request permission to take some soldiers up to his room and arrest him."

She looked horrified. "Arrest him? In our hotel? Could you not wait outside, in the street, and detain him as he returns?"

"Returns?" asked Cambronne sharply. "Returns from what?"

"Merely a walk, General," she assured him hastily. "The ladies went as well. Right after breakfast."

"He's gone," said Doucet slowly.

"Oh, no, monsieur. There are bags and clothing in both rooms. Jeanette has just brought down two dresses to be pressed before dinner."

"He saw us. He's gone." Doucet slammed his fist down on the desk. "*Sacré con!*"

Even Cambronne flinched at hearing that particular oath in the presence of a respectable woman.

"I'll find him," Doucet said through his teeth. "He cannot travel very quickly, not with two women. Give me ten men, *mon général*, and two dispatch riders."

"I need those men here," Cambronne objected. "What harm can Meyer do us now? If he sends reports to London, what of it? We will be in Grenoble in two days, three at the most."

"Not if he blows up the bridge at Pont-Haut," said Doucet grimly. "Nathan Meyer single-handedly destroyed more bridges in Spain than the entire British engineering corps. It is one of his specialties." He waited for this to sink in. "Now, may I have my ten men?"

Cambronne nodded.

By the time the party was approaching Corps, the first town of any size in the valley beyond the pass, they had been traveling for over nine hours. It had been drizzling off and on for the last three of those hours; they were damp and cold and exhausted. Meyer wanted desperately to get Anthony into a bed somewhere, but he was fairly certain Doucet would be coming after him. Better, he decided, to get his nephew to a safe bed, one he could hope to stay in for the night. There was still some daylight left; he should be thankful for the chance that gave him. He therefore called a halt before beginning the ascent to Corps, and led the party away from the road until trees and thickets concealed them from anyone who might ride by.

"That is Corps," he said, pointing up the hill to the rooftops just visible through the mist. "Napoleon will almost certainly be staying there tomorrow night, which means that his advance guard will be here tonight."

"We cannot stop there, then," said Diana, disappointed. She had shadows under her eyes, but it was obvious from the worried glance she gave his nephew that her concern was not for herself.

"I believe we should try to get beyond the town,

perhaps find a secluded farmhouse." He looked at Abigail. If she said no he was not sure what he would do, but he was tired of playing tyrant.

Luckily, she seemed to agree with him. "How far beyond the town? How much longer must we ride?"

He shrugged. "Perhaps another forty minutes."

She, too, looked at Anthony. "We can do that. But not much more."

Meyer turned to Rodrigo. "Can you lead them around the base of the hill, rejoin the road from the other side?"

His servant scanned the wooded valley and nodded. "You will go through town?"

"Yes, give me your coat. I will be you." They made the exchange without dismounting. "I will engage rooms at every hotel in town for Mr. Meyer and his party, arriving later tonight; that should slow Doucet up a bit when he gets here. With luck, he will decide that he missed us somewhere and double back." He eyed Diana's pelisse, now supporting a very haggard-looking Anthony. "If possible, I will also purchase some more clothing for us."

"But it is Sunday," said Abigail, shocked. "No shops will be open."

"Perhaps someone will take pity on me when I explain that we lost all our baggage when the horses bolted and dragged our carriage into a ravine," he said solemnly.

"If you tell them you tried to take a carriage over that road, they will take pity on you, all right," she said tartly. "They will think you are the servant of a madman."

"Do you have a better story?" he asked, amused.

"Certainly," she said. "Your, er, master's nephew is

very ill, and as a precaution, your master burned all his clothing. Oh, and ours as well."

He laughed; he could not help it. She really was a terrible liar, but her attempt was oddly endearing. "Would you give a room in your hotel to someone so full of contagion that his uncle has burned all the baggage for the entire party? I suspect not. You would bar the gates of the town and stone any travelers who tried to come through."

"Oh." She blushed.

"I shall think of something," he said. In fact, his main goal in Corps, apart from laying a false trail at the hotels, was an item he would have to steal. He might as well steal a few pieces of clothing as well.

"Shall I leave the usual mark for you to follow?" Rodrigo asked him.

He nodded.

"And when should we expect you?"

"Within a few hours."

The servant looked relieved.

Meyer suspected Rodrigo would not be so relieved when his master disappeared after supper. He would try to slip off without attracting attention. The answer to "When should we expect you?" this evening would be a bit more dramatic: "possibly never" or "just before dawn, with a dozen troopers after me."

Of course, if the drizzle did not lift, his self-assigned mission would be impossible to carry out. Instead of defying the former French emperor, he would be spending the evening in the farmhouse, sitting by the hearth and watching the few visible strands of Abigail's hair turn different colors in the firelight.

* * *

"Where is my uncle?" Anthony asked Diana.

He was propped up against a mound of down-filled pillows, sipping a clear golden broth which most chefs in London would cut off their arms to produce. Towards the end of the day, he had been finding everything more and more confusing, so he was not quite sure why they were in this farmhouse in the middle of nowhere instead of at an inn, or why he was in what looked to be the bedchamber of the farmer and his wife, with its starched print curtains and old-fashioned furniture. He was certainly not complaining—after sleeping for several hours in the Durrys's luxuriously overstuffed featherbed he was feeling almost human again. And when he had finally been awake enough to understand what was being said as various people gave him medicines and plumped up pillows, he had realized, to his astonishment, that he was something of a hero. He had resigned himself to figuring in Diana's memories of this week as a clumsy weakling: too saddle-sore to walk one day, beaten by yokels the next, feverish the day after that. He would never have dreamed that she would look at him with obvious admiration while she held his soup for him. Or that his uncle would embrace him and tell him he was a credit to the family.

She frowned. "I am not sure. He went out again a few minutes ago. Perhaps he is back now."

The door opened, and Diana's mother came in.

"Have you seen Mr. Meyer?" Diana asked her.

"I believe he went out to the stables again." She came over to the bed. "You look much, much better," she said approvingly. "I am glad I let Madame Durry persuade me to try her tisane. It seems to have worked wonders. Do you think you could eat some toast?"

He considered this, and decided that the answer was yes.

"I'll go." Diana jumped up from her chair beside the bed.

"Thank you, dear," said her mother absently, taking her place. "There are kittens in the kitchen," she explained apologetically to Anthony.

"I know." He smiled crookedly. "Miss Hart has described them to me in great detail."

She picked up the bowl of broth. "I must confess that this is far more comfortable than many of the inns we have patronized. Madame Durry is the most cheerful, warmhearted woman I could hope to meet. Her daughter idolizes Diana and has already brushed and pressed her dress for her *and* helped her put up her hair. The two sons groomed and fed all of our animals, so that Rodrigo could come in and eat. I am sure that your uncle is paying them a great deal of money, of course. Nevertheless, at the moment I am almost happy that those officers frightened your uncle. Otherwise we would be staying at one of the hotels in Corps, and I cannot imagine you would have been tended so well there."

Anthony tried to remember his uncle saying something about officers, or about being frightened, and failed. His only memories of this morning involved cold water and a large mug of very dark coffee.

"It takes quite a bit to frighten my uncle," he said, worried. "Did he say what had happened?"

"Your uncle does not seem to be the communicative sort," she said dryly. "All he said was that two officers had recognized him, and we were all in danger. Which, I assure you, certainly frightened *me*. I assume they must have encountered him when he was smuggling the gold a few years ago."

"Smuggling the gold?" Anthony asked, bewildered.

"He told me all about it," she assured him. "I suppose it is some sort of trade secret, isn't it? I promise I will not say anything to any of the Harts in London."

"He told you he had smuggled gold? Where? When?"

"For Wellington's troops," she said impatiently. "In Spain. The gold your bank loaned the army."

"My uncle had nothing to do with that! I have no idea why everyone seems to think that loan was so complicated! Yes, we shipped the gold through France, but it simply went south through our regular convoy system for transferring bullion. The only difficult part was getting the wagons over the border. And even then the real problem was the Pyrenees, not the French."

She set the bowl back down on the night table. "But . . . your uncle . . . those scars . . . the knives," she stammered.

Too late he realized that his uncle had presumably used the undeservedly celebrated story of the loan to explain the damning evidence the two women had seen at the roadblock. He racked his brain to come up with a substitute for the gold-smuggling story. His brain was not responding very well. And of course, his uncle had already used the most plausible cover story, which he, Anthony, had just ruined. Abigail Hart was looking very upset. As well she might.

"Why," she asked, in a dangerously quiet voice, "would your uncle allow me to believe that he had incurred those injuries working for the bank if that was not the case?"

"He was—ashamed," said Anthony, desperate. "Embarrassed." His mind, reeling through the conundrum Spain-knives-scars, seized on the plot of his mother's favorite opera. "There were, ah, ladies involved."

Diana's reappearance saved him. "Here is the toast," she said breathlessly. "And Madame Durry sent some plum compote up as well. Oh, and your uncle has apparently gone off again; her oldest boy just helped him saddle up a few minutes ago."

"Would you mind running back down, Diana? And finding Mr. Meyer's servant? Could you tell him I would like to speak with Mr. Meyer the moment he returns, no matter how late it may be?"

She nodded and disappeared again.

"You won't say anything to him, will you?" said Anthony, a bit uneasy. "About the scars? He is a reformed character now, you know."

"He is not riding off to an illicit tryst in Corps, then?" she asked. There was an angry glitter in her eyes.

He was now very uneasy. "Of course not!"

"What a shame those two officers who are pursuing us do not know that he is such an upright citizen these days," she said.

14

"What do you mean, they cannot be found?" Doucet glared at the adjutant. "Five people and six animals cannot simply disappear between the last village and a town the size of this one!"

The adjutant, a middle-aged man with thinning hair, spread his arms helplessly. "Monsieur, up until now it has been a very plain trail. A party traveling in haste, with no baggage, including a young man who is clearly ill—everyone remembers them. The servant came here and inquired at all three hotels for rooms, but they were full, and he left. There is no trace of them in the next village along the road; no one has seen them pass northwards. Perhaps when there were no rooms available they turned back."

"Had they turned back," Doucet reminded him in a dangerously soft voice, "we would have met them."

"Ah. Of course." The older man cleared his throat. "*Eh bien*, I am at your service, monsieur. What shall I do now?"

Doucet flung himself into a chair and thought hard. "Fetch me the innkeeper again," he said.

Take A Trip Into A Timeless World of Passion and Adventure with Kensington Choice Historical Romances!

—Absolutely FREE!

Enjoy the passion and adventure of another time with Kensington Choice Historical Romances. They are the finest novels of their kind, written by today's best-selling romance authors. Each Kensington Choice Historical Romance transports you to distant lands in a bygone age. Experience the adventure and share the delight as proud men and spirited women discover the wonder and passion of true love.

Get 4 FREE Books!

We created our convenient Home Subscription Service so you'll be sure to have the hottest new romances delivered each month right to your doorstep—usually before they are available in book stores. Just to show you how convenient the Zebra Home Subscription Service is, we would like to send you 4 FREE Kensington Choice Historical Romances. The books are worth up to $24.96, but you only pay $1.99 for shipping and handling. There's no obligation to buy additional books—ever!

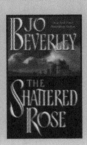

Save Up To 30% With Home Delivery!

Accept your FREE books and each month we'll deliver 4 brand new titles as soon as they are published. They'll be yours to examine FREE for 10 days. Then if you decide to keep the books, you'll pay the preferred subscriber's price (up to 30% off the cover price!), plus shipping and handling. Remember, you are under no obligation to buy any of these books at any time! If you are not delighted with them, simply return them and owe nothing. But if you enjoy Kensington Choice Historical Romances as much as we think you will, pay the special preferred subscriber rate and save over $8.00 off the cover price!

We have 4 FREE BOOKS for you as your introduction to
KENSINGTON CHOICE!
To get your FREE BOOKS, worth up to $24.96, mail
the card below or call TOLL-FREE 1-800-770-1963.
Visit our website at www.kensingtonbooks.com.

Get 4 FREE Kensington Choice Historical Romances!

♥ *YES!* Please send me my 4 FREE KENSINGTON CHOICE HISTORICAL ROMANCES (without obligation to purchase other books). I only pay $1.99 for shipping and handling. Unless you hear from me after I receive my 4 FREE BOOKS, you may send me 4 new novels—as soon as they are published—to preview each month FREE for 10 days. If I am not satisfied, I may return them and owe nothing. Otherwise, I will pay the money-saving preferred subscriber's price (over $8.00 off the cover price), plus shipping and handling. I may return any shipment within 10 days and owe nothing, and I may cancel any time I wish. In any case, the 4 FREE books will be mine to keep.

NAME _____

ADDRESS _____ APT. _____

CITY _____ STATE _____ ZIP _____

TELEPHONE (___) _____

E-MAIL (OPTIONAL) _____

SIGNATURE _____

(If under 18, parent or guardian must sign)

KN026A

Offer limited to one per household and not to current subscribers. Terms, offer and prices subject to change. Orders subject to acceptance by Kensington Choice Book Club. Offer Valid in the U.S. only.

lll..l..lll...ll.l.l..l.l.l..l.ll.l.l..ll.l.l..lll..l

KENSINGTON CHOICE
Zebra Home Subscription Service, Inc.
P.O. Box 5214
Clifton NJ 07015-5214

PLACE
STAMP
HERE

"Which one?"

"The one from this inn, fool. He is probably listening outside the door, in fact."

A moment later the adjutant came back into the dining room with both the innkeeper and his son.

"You wish something else, monsieur?" the father asked politely. "More wine perhaps?"

No. No more wine. He needed a clear head.

"This man, this servant who was looking for rooms for his master. Which of you spoke with him?"

The son bowed awkwardly. "I did, monsieur."

"What did he look like?"

The boy frowned. "Tall, stoops slightly. A Spaniard, from the sound of his French. Dark hair."

That was Meyer's servant, sure enough. Or Meyer himself, they were very much alike. Could their party possibly have separated? Was there another road that led to the bridge? He fought off a momentary surge of panic. He had sent five men and a dispatch rider onward to the bridge, and the messenger had already returned to report that it was secure.

"Your pardon, Monsieur Doucet." It was one of the soldiers, hovering in the open doorway. "I thought you might wish to speak to this man. He reports a theft from his shop."

Doucet raised one eyebrow. "Do I look like the prefect of police?"

The soldier said apologetically, "No, monsieur, of course not. But—is it not true that we hunt for a saboteur?"

"Yes. What of it?"

"Monsieur Roussier is a sausage-maker. The missing item is half a barrel of saltpeter."

Doucet sat up very straight. "And when did this

happen?" he asked the sausage-maker, who was twisting his hat nervously in his hands.

"I am not certain, monsieur. Madame Roussier heard a small noise while we were eating supper—I did not hear it, but she insisted, and you know how it is, monsieur, with women, when we were preparing to retire she became very nervous about this noise, and occasionally animals have managed to get into the shop; they do a great deal of damage—"

"Yes, yes, so you went downstairs, and your barrel was missing. When was this?"

"An hour ago, monsieur. But madame my wife remembered that Your Excellency had asked us to report anything suspicious . . ."

Thank God for the Madame Roussiers of this world, thought Doucet. At least when you were hunting spies. "And what time was it when you—or rather, your wife—heard the noise?"

"Perhaps six o'clock, your honor."

More than five hours ago. Had it rained since then? He could not remember. All he had been doing for the past six days was riding on terrible roads and interrogating people. Here in the mountains when it wasn't raining it was about to rain or it had just stopped raining. He turned to the adjutant. "Take the rest of the men. Borrow every lantern in Corps. Go to this man's shop and see if you can find any traces—footprints, hoofprints, anything—which might tell us where he has gone. Barrels of saltpeter are heavy; even Meyer can't carry one himself. If you do find something, follow it as though it were leading to the Holy Grail. Do you understand?"

"Perfectly, monsieur."

"Show this officer your shop," Doucet told the

sausage-maker. "And take this to replace your loss." He handed the man a small purse. If he could find Meyer before the Englishman blew up that bridge, he would buy every sausage the man had.

Meyer hoped this would be his last sleepless night; they were taking a toll. As he led his horse and the mule out of the barn he sent a quick glance back towards the farmhouse. Rodrigo had taken him at his word when he had requested a secluded refuge. The place was so secluded that even with Rodrigo's blaze cut on the trees by the road it had taken him three tries to find it. It was ideal for his purposes. There was even a stream at the foot of the hill, with a small waterfall that would mask most of the noise he would be making. Presumably everyone in the farmhouse would be asleep by the time he tested the mixture, though, and the small explosion should not be loud enough to awaken anyone. Unless he made a mistake, in which case he would not be around to worry about who had heard him.

When he reached the waterfall, he heaved the barrel off the mule's back and tethered the animals securely a little distance away. Then he cleared enough dead foliage away to form a small, flat working space and laid out his equipment. A large square of oilcloth, which he spread on the ground. The barrel on top of that. A sack of crumbled charcoal, also on the oilcloth. A mallet—he had borrowed it (without asking) from his host at the farmhouse. He hoped it was heavy enough. The paddle from a butter churn. That was another borrowed item. Madame Durry's butter was going to have an odd flavor for the next few weeks. A small wooden cup, taken from the barn. And finally, emerging from its concealment in the tin box, his precious jar of sulphur.

Pounding the charcoal into powder was easy, and the sack muffled the noise. He scooped up the grains which had spilled onto the oilcloth, and pushed them carefully back into the sack. Then he tipped over the barrel and dumped the saltpeter slowly onto the oilcloth. It formed a white, flaky mound that covered nearly the entire cloth. Odd, that gunpowder was so black when there was so much saltpeter in it and so little charcoal. He picked up the bucket and started scooping the saltpeter back into the barrel, adding small amounts of the charcoal and sulphur after every fifteen scoops of saltpeter, and stirring very gently with the paddle. It took quite some time; everything had to be done very precisely, very gently. Even in the cold he was sweating with tension. He ran out of sulphur after the third mixing. It was just as well; he should be on his way as soon as possible.

Now for his test. He mixed once more, took the broken stem of a clay pipe from his pocket, and poured a thin stream of the glittering dark powder into one end, stopping the other with his fingers. Then he pressed the tube upright into the ground, pushed a thin twist of paper into the top, and struck a light.

The result was very satisfactory, although perhaps louder than he would have liked. He glanced up at the moon. No time to clean up. He left the oilcloth, with its pile of unused saltpeter, and hoisted the barrel back onto the mule. It was reassuringly heavy. There was enough here to bring down most bridges, placed properly.

The moment he had stumbled downstairs in Barrême to find the news of Napoleon's escape sweeping up from the coast, he had thought of Pont-Haut and realized its importance. If he had not been hampered by Anthony and the Harts, he would have been here days ago. He would have packed the central pier with powder and blasted it apart as soon as Napoleon had moved north of Sisteron. Every day, the bridge was the first thing he thought of when he woke up and the last thing he thought of before he went to sleep—on the few nights he had slept. What was the safest way to get the saltpeter? How fast was Bonaparte marching? Where were his advance troops? How quickly—or slowly—could Meyer move his own party so as to stay ahead, but not too far ahead? Practical questions, questions whose answers usually required spending the entire night in the saddle, leaving him (conveniently) too exhausted to consider impractical questions. Ethical questions.

Only now, as he led the mule closer and closer to the ravine, did he realize that he had never thought beyond the moment when the bridge would collapse, tumbling in shards of blackened stone down into the river below. Suppose he did manage to evade the guards—Cambronne had surely posted some by now—and set off his homemade gunpowder. What then? Ride casually back to the farmhouse and tell three innocent people that they were now trapped between a bridgeless ravine and two thousand frustrated, angry soldiers? He had not asked for their company; he had not wanted their company. But he could not pretend they did not exist.

He would face that problem when it arose, he told himself firmly. His more immediate concern was the task ahead.

He stopped half a mile short of the hill that ran up to the cliffs and led the animals into the woods until he found a clearing where he could tie them up. There was some kind of path running up the slope, a goat track, perhaps. It was certainly safer than the road. He made his way up to the edge of the ravine and began moving cautiously west. The moon was right overhead, giving plenty of light through the thin clouds. He could see the top level of the bridge, the modern, three-arch structure, and after a moment the older Roman bridge below came into view as well. As expected, there were guards at both ends. He would have to bring the mule up here, then rope the barrel, and himself, down into the ravine. If he wanted to be done before dawn, he had better hurry. He went back down the hill much faster than he had come up and was panting by the time he reached the clearing.

Only at the very last minute did he see that there were three animals tied up, not two.

"Do you need any assistance?" asked Rodrigo in a cold voice, stepping out from behind a tree. "Or should I rejoin the other dupes back at the farmhouse?" He was still wearing Meyer's coat. In the moonlit shadows it was eerily like seeing his own reflection come to life.

"What are you doing here?" demanded Meyer, horrified. "How could you leave Anthony and the women alone, with Doucet likely searching for us at this very moment?"

"I am your servant, remember? You chose the

bridge over your nephew, over Señora Hart and her daughter. I concluded that the bridge was more important. So here I am."

"I trusted you," said Meyer, breathing hard. "I trusted you to be there while I was absent."

"You did *not* trust me. You never told me anything. I guessed, of course. But since you were never willing to explain what you were doing, you could never quite bring yourself to ask. To say, out loud, 'Rodrigo, please stay behind and stand guard while I go off and stop Napoleon single-handedly. And then I will come back—or not come back. And in either case all hell will break loose.'"

"I am asking you now. You can lecture me about my morals some other time. Just get back to that farmhouse."

Rodrigo gestured towards the cliff. "That is not a one-man job. You will need help."

"Get back to the farmhouse," Meyer said again.

"You want both," said the servant, hoisting himself back into the saddle. "You want the bridge . . . and the woman."

Meyer did not ask what Rodrigo meant by that. He knew perfectly well which woman.

"But sometimes, señor, you have to make choices. You cannot have both." He looked down at his master. "At this rate, you will have neither."

Abigail heard the explosion very clearly. She would have heard it even if she had still been in the farmhouse, but she was actually pacing back and forth outside the barn, rehearsing the fourth version of an impassioned speech she planned to deliver as

soon as the perfidious, lying, arrogant, ruthless
Nathan Meyer returned from whatever criminal mission had taken him away this time. She did not know
who was more despicable: Meyer, for using her and
deceiving her, or herself, for being so gullible. She
had *known* there was something odd going on right
from the start, from that first meeting at the inn in
Barrême, when he had pretended to defer to her
preferences and had pushed her—she could see that
now clearly—into choosing this northern route. But
she had ignored her own intuition.

Every day had witnessed some new act of folly on
her part. Why had she let him keep her papers? How
could she have failed to see that he was staggering
with fatigue nearly every morning, that he had been
out all night? He had even stumbled into her room
and she had still failed to comprehend the obvious.
And then he had let her make a complete fool of
herself, with her dramatic little story of the smuggled
gold. She remembered his face, during that sudden,
fraught silence in the alcove. He had been about to
kiss her, and she had been about to let him do it—
her own daughter's suitor! His feelings had seemed
so genuine—the mixture of confusion, desire, and
tenderness in his dark eyes so plausible to someone
who was feeling all those things herself. But it was a
sham, a fraud, like the mask of the Spanish partisan
he had put on at the blockade.

The explosion was the last straw. It had come
from the woods below the farmhouse, and she
would wager her entire fortune that Meyer was involved. She would not go to her bedchamber like
a dutiful female and wait for the next lie. She
wanted answers, right now.

The brush was very thick once she left the farm-yard, and after untangling her skirts twice she conceded reluctantly that even in the moonlight she would need a lantern. She returned to the barn and took one that was hanging inside the door already lit. With a sense of deep resentment, she saw that not only was Meyer's horse gone, but the servant's as well. She had thought Rodrigo was her friend.

Even with the lantern, it was slow going. She could hear a stream below. She wondered what she would do if she reached the stream and had not found him. Would she wade across? Give up? She stopped, and almost turned back, but then caught—faint but unmistakable—a thread of scent. Sulphur. She closed her eyes and breathed. It was coming from the bottom of the hill.

Two minutes later she found unmistakable signs of the recent presence of at least two horses. And one minute after that, she found the flattened brush, the oilcloth, and the blackened stump of clay pipe. It was still smoking gently in the ground. Setting the lantern down, she tried to make sense of what she saw. A pile of salt. An empty burlap sack with traces of charcoal. An empty jar. The paddle from a butter churn. It was like a riddle in a nightmare.

There were more hoofprints here, first a jumbled trampling around the oilcloth and then a clear trail along the side of the stream below the waterfall. Pulling her skirts closer, she followed. After a quar-ter mile or so, the trail widened and angled up steeply. She found herself standing on the road. It was completely deserted. To her left, barely visible, a few distant lights shone from the windows of wakeful citizens in the town of Corps. To her right the road was climbing another hill. Common sense told her to stop right now, to go back, before she became irretrievably lost. But the tracks led up the hill, away from Corps. Perhaps she would be able to see something from the crest. She promised herself that she would go only that far. No farther.

By the time she had climbed the hill, the distinctive tracks were gone, merged on this drier section of the road with the wear and tear of hundreds of other travelers. And at the top she saw nothing, save a few lights on a ridge some miles away. She turned slowly in a circle, holding the lantern close to the ground. No hints, no clues emerged from the pebbles and crushed fragments of straw at her feet.

Then, faintly, she heard the hoofbeats. They were coming from the direction of the farmhouse. Could she have been mistaken, followed the wrong tracks? The sound was getting closer. She stepped out into the middle of the road and raised the lantern.

There were six horses. Too many. The lead rider, clearly visible in the moonlight, was a complete stranger.

"Halt!" he called in French. Then, to the men behind him, "Lower your weapons! Await my orders."

It did not even occur to her to drop the lantern and run away.

He cantered slowly up to her and studied her for a moment, noting her damp cloak, her mud-spattered skirts and boots. A slender young man, in very rumpled, once-elegant clothing. Then he dismounted in one easy movement and bowed gracefully. "Raoul Doucet, madame, at your service." He spoke in English.

"I presume you are Mrs. Meyer? I am seeking your husband."

"I am not Mrs. Meyer," she informed him coldly. "And I, too, am seeking Mr. Meyer." Presumably this was one of Meyer's criminal associates.

"But how unfortunate that I have missed him," he said. He raised his voice. "Marcel! À moi!" Another man came riding up, then halted in puzzled dismay at the unexpected sight of a genteel female on foot, alone, in the middle of the road.

"Where is the rest of your party?" the slender man asked Abigail.

For the first time it occurred to her that perhaps this man was not a friend of Meyer's. He was handsome, in a delicate, languid way. He spoke English. He knew of their party. But Marcel, the new arrival, was in uniform. It looked like a more complete version of one of the uniforms she had seen at the roadblock. Hadn't Meyer told her that some of the officers in Napoleon's border police spoke English?

"I don't know," she said. Her voice was shaking. "I am lost."

He seemed to accept that. Presumably her voice would also shake if she were lost, instead of lying. He turned to the trooper, speaking in French. "You will conduct this lady—" He paused and looked inquiringly at Abigail. "It is mademoiselle? Madame?"

"Madame. Mrs. Hart."

"Ah. Yes, how stupid of me. I believe I knew that." Then he resumed his instructions to the soldier. "You will conduct Madame Hart to the guard's station in Pont-Haut."

"Yes, monsieur."

"She is to be treated with every courtesy." He

switched back to English. "I regret the necessity of confining you temporarily, madame, but as you see . . ." He gave a classic and very elegant French shrug.

"You will release me?"

"Naturally." He bowed. "As soon as I find Mr. Meyer. And I have a very good idea of where he is. Please consider this a momentary inconvenience. It would be unthinkable in any case to allow a lady to risk herself at night on this road with so many soldiers about." He took away the lantern. "Allow me."

It was all so absurd. The polite phrases, the courtly gestures, on a deserted hillside at midnight.

He escorted her, with that same terrifying courtesy, to a horse, assisting her to mount behind the trooper. He arranged her cloak. He asked politely whether she had further need of the lantern. But when he turned to go, the polished surface disappeared for a moment, and he said gently, "Do not worry. Your lover will come to no harm so long as he is prepared to be reasonable. We are civilized men."

He thought she was Meyer's mistress. For a moment, she was simply incredulous. Then she said, enunciating each word very clearly, "Mr. Meyer is not my lover."

Doucet's smile was absolutely enchanting. He swept her the most magnificent bow yet. "I would say, then, madame, that he is either blind or foolish." The smile faded. "How did you come to be traveling with him, in that case? If I may be so bold?"

Of course he could be so bold. She was his prisoner. "He is a friend of the family."

"Then he does care for you? He will be concerned for your safety?"

"If so," she said bitterly, "it will be the first time,

to my knowledge, that he has cared about anything or anyone except himself and his schemes."

He looked grave. "Let us hope that you are mistaken. For both your sake and his."

15

Everything always took longer than you thought
it would; that was one of the first rules of engineering, and it was true whether you were building
something or knocking it down. The uncooperative
moon had set by the time Meyer had managed to
maneuver both himself and the barrel onto the
Roman level of the bridge. Without a dark lantern,
he had worked by feel, testing cracks with thin sliv-
ers of wood to check for dampness. It had taken
quite a while to find a reasonably dry fissure that ran
near the base of one of the upper piers. At that
point he had been forced to light his candle briefly
to make sure that the crack was not too large for his
small supply of powder. But the guards on the bank
above him had not seemed aware of the momentary
flicker by the water. They were watching the road.

He was scooping the powder in—an agonizingly
slow operation—when he became aware of a light
moving in the darkness behind him. He turned,
squinting up at the cliff. Someone was waving a
lantern. It was not Rodrigo; his servant would have

used their prearranged code. The lantern stopped waving. It was moving towards the southern end of the bridge. For a few moments it disappeared, but then it emerged again directly overhead, dangling over the water. Now, bizarrely, it was descending. The mysterious signaler was lowering it over the side from above. He watched, fascinated, as the lantern came down to his level in a series of jerky movements.

He wasn't fool enough to stay anywhere where the light would reveal him to a sharpshooter; he ducked deep into the arch. Something else was coming down now. No, someone. A man. He could see boots gleaming. He took out his pistol. What kind of fool would expose himself like that, suspended and helpless, lit from below?

"Meyer, it's Doucet," shouted the owner of the boots in English. His voice was barely audible over the noise of the water. "I'm coming down. Don't shoot."

Not a fool, then. Someone who knew Meyer well enough to be sure that he would hesitate before killing. He put away the pistol and got out his tinderbox.

A minute later, Raoul Doucet bumped down the side of the bridge next to the lantern and swung himself onto the platform. "Meyer?" he called again. "We know you are here; we found your ropes on the cliff. We saw your light."

Without answering, Meyer lit the tinderbox, and then his candle.

Doucet came forward, very slowly, hands held out to show he held no weapon. When he was close enough to speak without shouting, he stopped, and peered uncertainly at the shadows beneath the candle Meyer was holding over the fissure. "I take it there is powder in that hole at your feet?"

"Yes. Not as much as I would like, but quite a bit."

"You don't strike me as the martyr type," the Frenchman observed.

"I thought perhaps I could use a little leverage in this situation. If one of your troopers shoots me, I would at least like to take the bridge with me as I go."

"No one is going to shoot you," said Doucet irritably. "I left very strict orders. Taking potshots at a man who is standing on half a barrel of gunpowder in the middle of the only bridge over the Bonne River strikes me as remarkably counterproductive."

"Well. We seem to be at an impasse. Although I believe I am holding the trumps at the moment." They were very warm trumps; the hand shielding the candle was uncomfortably close to the flame.

"That depends," said Doucet. His tone was oddly apologetic. "I met someone on the road on my way here. A Mrs. Hart. She claims she was searching for you and lost her way. She is presently enjoying my hospitality nearby."

Abigail. His hand shook slightly, and the candle dipped suddenly towards the lip of the fissure. Alarmed, he jerked it up again. That would be the crowning jest, to blow up the bridge by accident because he panicked at the mere thought of her in captivity. Where was Rodrigo? he wondered. Surely he should be here, to witness his predictions coming true. The pawn had been captured, and the king was in check.

Behind Doucet the lantern sputtered and went out. The younger man's voice came out of the darkness, remarkably calm for someone who had just been an inch from being blown to pieces. "Perhaps it would be more prudent to continue our discussion with the candle on the ground. You can always knock it in if I make any sudden movements."

He found another large crack and wedged the candle in, crouching behind it to block the wind. "What are we discussing?"

Doucet lowered himself to a sitting position on the other side of the flame. "Facts. Three simple facts. Item one: Mrs. Hart is in a house we have commandeered in the village, with several of my guards. She is being treated with great consideration. It is my hope that you will soon be taking her back to join the rest of your party. You, at least, presumably know where they are."

Another threat. Doucet would have no trouble finding the farmhouse once he questioned Abigail more closely. Anthony was there, perhaps feverish again. Rodrigo. Diana Hart. The gruff farmer and his family. It didn't matter. Abigail was more than enough leverage, to use his own term.

"Item two: This bridge is important but not essential. If it is destroyed, it will delay us by at most two days. Is it really worth the price we would all have to pay, to buy forty-eight hours?"

"There is a royalist regiment chasing you up this road," Meyer said. "The delay would allow them to catch you. You would be pinned against the ravine. So far you have had everything your own way. The loss of morale might well be the tipping point between a successful and unsuccessful attempt to retake France."

"That is true," acknowledged the other man. "But there is also a royalist regiment waiting for us on the other side of the bridge, halfway between here and Grenoble. Why not let us go and meet it?"

"What is your third fact?"

"You saved my career last year, perhaps even my life, when you warned me that my mistress was framing me for treason. Cambronne is grateful to you as well, for protecting the emperor on his way to Elba. We are not yet the official government of France. There is nothing that compels me to shoot you as a spy. We are therefore prepared to be very generous. If you will agree to certain conditions, we will release Mrs. Hart. We will escort your party towards Grenoble as our honored guests and will guarantee your safety. Once we reach the city, you will all be at liberty."

"And what are those conditions?"

"The first is the bridge, of course. You will make no further attempt to destroy it, and will disarm any devices you may have set to hinder our progress."

That condition was an obvious one. "And the second?"

"You will return immediately to England. During the voyage home you will do nothing that might endanger our campaign. No pigeons, no messengers, not even a verbal report afterwards to your superiors in London. If you wish to be a private gentleman, escorting your countrywomen away from a war zone, then you must conduct yourself as one, from this moment on."

That was more difficult.

"So I am to be, in effect, blind and deaf for the rest of this journey."

Doucet shrugged. "Surely you would not wish to

endanger the ladies in your party by inviting unwanted military attention?"

"Why don't you just lock me up?"

"We've tried that," Doucet pointed out. "You've
escaped every time. The last time you were running
a messenger service from your cell, remember?
Cambronne and I believe your parole is a more effective cage than a jail cell."

The younger man waited, an oddly sympathetic
expression on his face.

"I suppose I should be flattered," Meyer said at last.
He would have to accept, of course. He would have
to watch Napoleon march on to Grenoble, where the
not-so-former emperor would receive a hero's welcome.

Slowly, he reached over and pinched out the
candle.

"You could have waited until I lit the lantern
again," said Doucet dryly.

"I thought it best to remove temptation," he said.
He tilted his face up and felt the breeze circling
through the arches.

Marcel, if that was his name, apparently took the
command to treat Abigail "with every courtesy"
very seriously. She was taken to a small house at one
end of the street—the single narrow street which
comprised Pont-Haut. A sitting room was instantly
cleared for her private use, with only a few empty
wineglasses and crumpled tally sheets remaining to
indicate that it had been full of a dozen soldiers
playing dice when she arrived. From somewhere, a
sleepy village girl was produced to serve her. She

was offered tea, wine, cakes, a very smelly cheese wrapped in leaves, and some pickled fruit. The earnest young trooper came in at regular intervals to make announcements, bowing and removing his hat each time.

These bulletins were meant to reassure her, but they had the opposite effect. The first announcement came after she had refused all the offered refreshment save the tea. Marcel knocked, entered, removed his hat, bowed, and said, "Madame will be pleased to be informed that this house is at a safe distance from the bridge."

"I beg your pardon?" she asked, bewildered.

His round face flushed slightly. "In case of an explosion, that is." He looked acutely embarrassed, as though the mention of exploding bridges was inexcusably vulgar.

"The bridge is in danger of exploding? The bridge at the end of this street?" She had caught only a glimpse of it before Marcel had detached her from the rest of the troop and brought her down to this house.

"We hope not, madame. But if by some unfortunate chance something were to occur, madame is not to be alarmed, no matter how loud the noise." He bowed again, and withdrew.

The next interruption told her to be pleased to be informed that the general would be here shortly. More prudent this time, he bowed himself away before she could ask him who the general was and why she should be pleased that he was coming.

Five minutes later, Marcel advised her that the additional troops who would arrive shortly would not dream of invading her private sitting room. Next, that the general did not stand on ceremony and she was to have no fear that he would expect to be treated with any great formality. Abigail was tempted to tell the young soldier that it would serve the general right if she smothered him with impersonal periphrases in imitation of his own behavior to her, but he was gone again before she could marshal enough French to deliver her witticism.

Five minutes later, by the clock, the door opened again. Marcel entered, removed his hat, bowed. "Madame is pleased to be informed that General Cambronne wishes to speak with her." He stepped aside, and a thin, hawk-faced man with curly graying hair strode into the room. He, too, bowed. At least he did not remove his hat. Someone had obviously taken it, along with his coat and gloves; he was carrying a sheaf of papers in one hand and looked at them now as though only just realizing he was still carrying them. He gave them to the ubiquitous Marcel and waved the boy away.

"Pierre Cambronne, madame. Your most obedient servant."

"General Cambronne." She curtsied.

"You are free to go." Cambronne's speech was considerably more concise than Marcel's. "You may wait for Monsieur Meyer, or I will send one of my own men to take you back to Corps." He added after a moment, "I must tell you that I have the most sincere admiration for your *ami*."

"Monsieur Meyer is merely a family friend," said Abigail, gritting her teeth.

Cambronne raised his eyebrows and shrugged. *You Englishwomen! So prudish!* said that shrug. "As you wish. But he is a very fine gentleman, even if he is a

Jew. I am relieved this incident has ended so happily. I am too much in his debt to wish otherwise."

What incident? she wanted to ask. What do you mean, happily? Marcel-happy, as in "the explosion will not reach this section of the street"? Why are you in his debt? She had been constructing wilder and wilder theories in her head ever since her conversation with Roth. She had known perfectly well that his tale of Meyer's seductions was a desperate fiction. Meyer was certainly attractive enough, but there was a reserve there which was incompatible with the picture of a dashing Lothario. No, Nathan Meyer was no Doucet. But her own theories were hardly more plausible. He was a bandit. A gun-runner. An assassin. Now it appeared he might be working for the French. But then why would they be holding her hostage?

Doucet came in now, without knocking. He looked even more strained and disheveled than he had an hour ago. There was another round of bowing, and Doucet repeated Cambronne's assurance that she was free to go.

"Where is Monsieur Meyer?"

Cambronne seemed to want the answer to that question as well, and Doucet addressed himself to him. "He is making certain that the powder is thoroughly soaked. He will be here shortly. You were told, were you not, that he agreed to all our terms?"

"Excuse me, General," she interrupted.

Their expressions changed; the serious, military air disappeared and the courtly gallantry returned. They were, she decided, simply more polished versions of Marcel.

"Yes, madame?"

She did not think he would answer her question, but the increasingly tangled assortment of half-explained allusions to explosions and bridges and powder was maddening. "What is Monsieur Meyer's connection with the possibility of an explosion at the bridge? The powder is gunpowder, is it not?"

"He did not take you into his confidence?"

"No," she said bitterly.

Cambronne gave her a paternal smile. If she had been a little girl, Abigail thought, he would have patted her on the head. "It is just as well. These matters are not suitable for the tender ears of ladies."

It was at this unfortunate moment that Meyer appeared in the doorway. His gaze sought her out at once, and she saw, with a queer pang, that he was wearing an expression she knew well. She had last seen that combination of exhaustion and guilt on the face of Paul's doctor the night her first husband had died. That initial sympathetic impulse might have prevailed; she might not have lost her composure so completely—if only he had not bowed.

"Mrs. Hart," he said.

She was sick of gallantry. She was sick of lies. She was sick of being terrified and ignorant. She walked over to Meyer and slapped him across the face so hard that her hand stung. "You despicable, cowardly sneak!" she said contemptuously.

There were cries of horror from both of the Frenchmen, exclamations, calls for brandy and smelling salts and handkerchiefs, because, of course, she had collapsed, sobbing onto the nearest chair. Madame was overwrought. It was perfectly understandable. Madame should calm herself, all was well.

Madame calmed herself. But all was not well. They

found, from heaven knows where, a carriage. She rode in lonely splendor back towards Corps, with an honor guard of three French soldiers. Meyer rode in front, to lead the way. At the top of the lane which led to the farmhouse, one of the soldiers helped her out. They escorted her, very solemnly, to the gate of the farmyard, and then huddled in low-voiced conversation with Meyer for a few minutes. She looked longingly at the house. Diana was in there. She wanted to see her daughter. It seemed incredible that everyone here had been asleep, while she had been bowed to and madamed by half of Napoleon's advance force.

Now the soldiers were leaving, and Meyer was leading his horse into the barn. There was a mule as well; she had not even noticed it before. His shoulders were set in a rigid line, as though he were holding himself straight by sheer force of will. He turned in the doorway. "I will sleep in the barn," he said. "I am sure you would prefer that."

She nodded.

Rodrigo came hurrying out with a lantern. When he saw her standing there he nearly dropped it. "You were not in the house?" he said, horrified. He turned to Meyer. "She was with you? Señor, are you mad?"

"Monsieur Doucet invited her to a soirée in Pont-Haut," said Meyer. He was looking off into the distance. Whatever he saw did not seem to appeal to him. He grimaced and continued through the doorway.

The servant turned to her. "Did he blow up the bridge?"

"He soaked the powder," she said. "I think that means the answer is no."

"What it means," he said, "is that the answer was going to be yes, but someone or something changed it to no."

She suspected that someone was the elegant, charming Raoul Doucet. Perhaps he was only charming to ladies. And the something was her. No wonder they had all been so deferential in Pont-Haut.

16

After an hour Meyer gave up on sleeping. After another half hour he found that the contented snuffles and grunts of the animals in the barn were inspiring him with bitter reflections on the happiness he might have found as, say, an ox. So he got up, put on his coat, and went outside.

The sky had cleared, and it was much colder, the air so still that every tiny sound rang out sharply. There would be frost on the ground in the morning. He went over to the stone wall which separated the sheepfold from the rest of the fields behind the barn and sat down. After a few minutes his eyes grew accustomed to the darkness, and the stars overhead began to assemble themselves into familiar patterns. To the east, the jagged edges of the mountains were blocking off the bottom sections of late-rising constellations. Between the mountains and the stars and his conscience he was feeling very, very small.

When he heard footsteps heading towards the barn he assumed it was Rodrigo.

"Over here," he called in Spanish.

The footsteps turned, shuffled in his direction. Those were not Rodrigo's footsteps.

"I cannot see very well," she said hesitantly. She was a dark form, only barely distinguishable from the silent house behind her.

For the second time that night, he took out his tinderbox, lit his candle from it, and jammed it into a crack in a rock. He suspected that this interview was going to be almost as painful as the one the candle had witnessed under the bridge.

"Oh." She came closer. "It is you. I thought perhaps it was your servant."

He got up. "I will go back to the barn."

"No, I came to find you. I need to speak with you." She sat down, carefully pulling her cloak away from the candle.

"I cannot imagine why you would ever want to see me again, let alone speak to me."

"Curiosity," she said. "Frustration. There are so many unanswered questions. And I owe you an apology."

He gave a short laugh. "If you owe me one, I owe you fifty. Unless you want to be here until dawn, I suggest we pass over the apologies and proceed to the questions."

"I am apologizing not only for your sake, but for mine. I am ashamed that I struck you. I do not approve of violence."

"Then you most assuredly will not approve of me."

"What *are* you?" she burst out. "What were you doing at that bridge? Where do you go every night? Why do you lie to everyone? You are such an accomplished liar that last night you even persuaded me to do it for you! You let me tell my story of the smuggled gold and never said one word to contradict me! If your nephew had not accidentally revealed the true story, I would have gone on believing my own fabrication for years!"

So that was why she had been looking for him last night. She had wanted a second round of explanations.

"Have you no respect for the truth? Don't you trust anyone?"

"Trust does not pay in my line of work," he said. "I am a spy. Your smuggling theory was not so far off. I smuggle information rather than gold, that is all. Occasionally I also sabotage enemy communications. Blow up bridges, for example."

"And which side do you—spy for?" She said the word as though it was a disease. "Or are you for hire, like a mercenary soldier?"

His jaw tightened. "I take no pay for my work. And I report to Lord Wellington. Or, more precisely, to two colonels who supervise his intelligence officers. One based in London, one in the field."

"Did they order you to blow up the bridge, then?"

That would be an easy way to excuse himself. She had approved of his violent ways, after all, when he was supposedly honoring a commitment from the bank. He could tell her he had pledged himself to Wellington's service, had tried to obey orders without revealing himself to his innocent traveling companions.

"No," he said after a long pause. "It was my decision to try to stay with Napoleon's forces, even after I became responsible for you and your daughter and my nephew. I was angry at first that you had arrived to complicate my self-appointed mission. But I was perfectly ready to make use of you. I deliberately goaded you into choosing what I thought—correctly—would be Bonaparte's route. I rode out every night and sent off dispatches noting the enemy's position and troop strength, knowing that I was far less conspicuous with women in my party. I risked your lives, as well as mine, by attacking the bridge. I lied to you, to all of you—even to my nephew, even to Rodrigo. I cannot blame any of it on my colonel, or on Wellington. I can communicate with them, but they cannot reach me until I arrive in a large city."

"The pigeons," she said slowly. "You let your nephew tell that lie for you."

"Well, I did let him use one of the birds," he said. "There was a price."

"And what was the price you paid for my convenient tale of smuggled gold?"

"I didn't kiss you," he said in a low voice. "That was the price."

"Yes, and that is another thing," she said, outraged. "How can you suppose I would ever let you marry Diana when you looked at me in such a—a disrespectful fashion?"

He stood up and jerked her to her feet. "And how can *you* suppose that I want to marry your daughter?" He was suddenly furious. "Are you blind? Was your husband a stick? Can you not recognize desire when you see it? If I didn't kiss you last night, it was because I *do* respect you." He seized her chin and tilted it up. "Look at me." He stared down at her, holding her eyes with his own. The candle lit her from below and sent shadows racing up into the hood of her cloak. "Look at my face, and tell me I want to marry Diana. Look at my face and tell me I have some frivolous habit of kissing every female who sits next to me on a sofa after dinner." He pushed off her hood, and her hair spilled out over her shoulders. "Don't you realize that every time you come out with one of those damned caps on I want to tear it off?"

She put her hand up and touched her bare head. Her mouth made a small *O*, as if the world had suddenly tilted slightly, and she was no longer sure which direction was up.

And somehow one moment he was telling himself that he should let her go, should step back, and the next moment he had pulled her straight up against his body and was kissing her so fiercely that he thought he might never breathe again. They were hot, scorching kisses; he was in a fever, he branded her mouth, her throat, her shoulder; he was desperate to take as much as he could in these few minutes. He had thought she would push him away, or at least stiffen. Instead, after the first stunned instant she yielded. Her body softened, sank towards him; her face tilted upward. He found himself sitting on the wall; she had tumbled down into his arms, and he was pulling her dress off her shoulder, sliding his hand down the side of her breast. She was not going to stop him, he realized, incredulous. He would have to find a small remnant of sanity somewhere all on his own.

Training yourself to be ruthless had its disadvantages. You could not tell yourself that you had no self-control. He drew back, breathing hard. She was still on his lap.

"Was that disrespectful enough for you?" he said harshly. "Have I thoroughly disqualified myself as a candidate for your daughter's hand? Or should I take you into the barn right now and continue?"

She gave a choked cry and pushed herself off his lap.

"Do you know why I didn't kiss you last night?" he said. "Because I knew that later, when you found out how I had tricked you, you would hate me. But after what happened in Pont-Haut, of course, I have nothing further to lose."

With shaking hands she pushed her hair back under her hood. She sat for a moment, struggling to calm her breathing. "I suppose now you will tell me you want to marry me."

"I would not insult you by pretending that I have any hopes in that direction at all. Depraved as I am, I draw the line at asking women to marry me when they find me morally repugnant. When they despise me and everything I stand for."

She stood up, eyes flashing. "You expect me to protest, to say that of course I do not *despise* you. That is a very strong word, after all. But it is the right one. I do not dislike you. You are in fact a very attractive man; what just happened proves that I am not indifferent to you. But I find you unethical. Unscrupulous. It is all a game to you, isn't it? To all of you! General Cambronne, who admires you profoundly! Monsieur Doucet, the so-charming, so-elegant courtier, who bows to me while he is taking me hostage! You send off your reports, in some cipher, I am sure, attached to your pigeons. And then there is a battle, and thousands of people die, or have their legs shot off, or go deaf from cannon fire. You killed those men, as surely as if you shot them down with your own rifle! And then you go off and play more games, and congratulate yourself on how clever you are, and when you meet the other players, like Cambronne, you bow and smile and tell each other that it was 'very well contrived' and your opponent is 'a fine gentleman' and 'we are civilized people.' I suppose I will be obliged to put up with your company until we reach Grenoble. If you have any sense of decency whatsoever, you will keep your hypocritical courtesies to yourself. I want no compliments from a man with so much blood on his hands."

He had risen as well. He felt hollow. It *was* almost a game to him. He was no innocent—he knew what the reports he wrote would mean. He had made choices to save these ten people, and sacrifice those eight. He had blown up bridges with dozens of men on them. He had spiked guns so that they exploded in some youngster's face the next time they were fired.

He had told himself that in the long run, he was saving lives. That he hated killing and did it only when necessary and even then with extreme reluctance. That England was right and France was wrong. That he deserved to play God, because he was willing to risk his own life, over and over again. What he rarely admitted, even to himself, was that he enjoyed his work far more than any man with a conscience should. "Game" might be the wrong word—addiction would be closer—but she was right. It was not patriotism that motivated him.

He walked away from her and leaned against the wall. "Do you know how I became a spy?" he asked over his shoulder. "No, of course not. Until today you thought I was a very dedicated banker."

He didn't wait for her to answer. "My wife died. We had married very young, so that even though she was barely thirty when she died, we had been together for over a dozen years. I had been working for the bank, as you know. I traveled frequently. I had a gift for languages; I already spoke German and English and Portuguese, I then acquired French and Italian and some Spanish as well. I only had to hear them spoken and I could reproduce the accents and phrases of the native speakers as though I had been living in the country for years. We were happy, or so I believed—Miriam with me and the children, I with her and my work. And then I came home one day from one of my business trips, and Miriam was ill, and within a week she was dead. Four months later, Spain invaded Portugal at Napoleon's instigation, and I quit the bank and went to work as an unofficial British intelligence courier in Portugal.

"My family was horrified. They were even more horrified when I took my two young children with me to Spain a few years later. They told everyone I had gone mad with grief, that I was courting death, hoping to join my wife. But do you know what had really happened?" He turned around.

She had moved quite close to him. She gave a tiny shake of her head.

No, she didn't know. No one knew. He had let his family tell this lie for him.

"I did grieve for my wife. I loved her. I missed her. But the reason I became a spy was not grief. It was fear. I watched a healthy, beautiful woman die of a fever in the space of six days, and I told myself it could happen to me. I did not want to die a banker. I loved traveling. I loved being in strange places, speaking new languages, seeing if I could fool people into thinking I was one of them. I loved the idea of pretending, and wearing disguises, and learning to move silently, and carrying knives in my boot. I was a banker who wanted to be a pirate, and the war gave me my chance. So you see, you are right to condemn me. I am a chess player. And the pieces on my board are armies and fleets and bands of partisans. They die, and somehow I survive. I survive, and I go on to the next match and play again. You said it yourself. I find danger attractive."

"Perhaps I do, too," she said in a low voice.

He remembered her face, alive and eager, as she took in the view of the mountains from the top of the Col Bayard. If he could go back, if he could take her aside there, with the mountains as his witnesses, and explain it all, would things have been different?

Probably not. Even the Alps could not excuse him to Abigail Hart. She had standards, and he did not meet them.

He straightened up. "Do you have any more questions?"

"No." Then, "Wait. Yes. One more. General Cambronne said that he owed you a great debt. What did he mean?"

He shuddered. Orgon was not a pleasant memory. The screaming mob, seeded with hired cutthroats; the dazed former emperor, hustled away in disguise. "Last April, when Napoleon was on his way to Elba, I learned of a French royalist plot to assassinate him. I warned Cambronne and helped him get Napoleon away safely."

"But—I don't understand. Why would you do that?"

He used her terms. "The rules of the game. He was under British protection. We were responsible for his safety. We had signed a treaty."

"You were responsible for *our* safety," she said. Her face was bleak. "Mine and Diana's. But I had not signed a treaty, had I?" She lifted her chin. "Good night, Mr. Meyer. Thank you for answering my questions."

He watched her disappear back into the house. Then he walked slowly back to the barn. The candle still burned in its rocky holder; he left it there. In another hour it would be nothing but a melted puddle of wax, a puzzle for Durry or one of his sons the next time they repaired the wall.

17

What was the proper behavior the next day for a sensible woman of high moral standards who had disgraced herself the night before? She had no idea. The travelers were, for all intents and purposes, confined to the farmhouse. It would have been far less awkward had they been able to continue on their way. Abigail and Diana would have been in a carriage again, isolated from Meyer except for the brief halts, and the journey would have offered some distraction from her situation. But everyone except the patient himself had agreed that Roth should rest for at least another day.

She tried for Diana's sake to pretend that nothing had happened, but she understood now what Anthony Roth must have felt like the day after the beating. Her bruises were not physical, but they were numerous and painful, and the effect was very similar. She moved stiffly; she had no appetite; she could not focus on anything for more than a few minutes at a time. For someone who liked pretending and disguises Meyer did not seem to be making much of an effort either. He barely spoke to anyone and when he smiled in response to something the younger Durry boy said there was a bleak twist at the side of his mouth. By the end of the day Diana was giving Abigail constant, worried glances; and when Abigail and Meyer were in the same room Diana and Anthony took on the frightened, too-cheerful manner of children whose parents have been quarreling.

To his credit, Meyer did his best to avoid Abigail, and she was grateful. Every time she caught even a glimpse of him (which, admittedly, was as infrequently as both could manage it) she would feel her heart begin to pound, and a jellylike quiver would lodge itself in her stomach. She was not sure whether these were symptoms of embarrassment, or terror, or desire. Or all of them combined.

Even in his absence she found it difficult to maintain her equilibrium. The smallest incident would precipitate another round of memory and self-recrimination. In the morning, for example, she had put on her cap as usual. But when she glanced in the mirror her face had looked so wistful and vulnerable that she had hastily tucked every single strand of hair out of sight. A minute later she had pulled them out again, furious at herself. At the midday meal Madame Durry triumphantly produced a plate of the same pungent, leaf-wrapped cheeses Abigail had been offered in Pont-Haut. Evidently they were a local specialty. The smell immediately took her back to the terrifying wait in the guard station; she managed one taste, then choked out some feeble excuse and fled. Two hours later she ventured outdoors for some fresh air only to see Meyer over by the infamous stone wall, releasing two pigeons. She hastily retreated before he could see her.

Towards sunset she was beginning to feel a little calmer, but then Meyer came in and asked his nephew if he could have a word with him in private. Roth had been so much better by lunchtime that he had been allowed to get up, and as he went off with Meyer he smiled cheerfully. When he came back, he looked sick again, and he avoided Abigail's eye all during supper. She could guess what had happened: Meyer had decided Roth was finally well enough to be told about the events of last night. Meyer himself did not reappear. Since the house was not very large, she could only conclude that he had once again taken refuge in the barn.

Very late in the evening, Rodrigo brought her a note—or rather two notes: a terse one from Meyer and a much longer one from Raoul Doucet. The Frenchman sent his most profound respects to M. Meyer and his eternal devotion to Mme. Hart. In view of the illness of M. Roth he had been obliged to forego the pleasure of escorting them to Grenoble himself this morning. Instead he had made arrangements for them to travel tomorrow with the rear guard of the emperor's army. They should be prepared to leave at a very early hour. Meyer's note was one sentence: *I forward the enclosed from M. Doucet.*

Was this Meyer's idea of a joke? She thrust the note into Rodrigo's hands. "Have you read this?" she demanded.

"No, señora."

"Please do so. And tell me whether he is serious."

Expressionless, he scanned it; then handed it back. "I believe he is quite in earnest."

"Is he in the barn?"

He looked alarmed. "Yes, but—"

Without even bothering to fetch her cloak, she strode out of the house and burst into the barn.

He was sitting on a bench, his dark head bowed, studying his clasped hands. On the floor by his feet sat the empty crate which had held the pigeons; there were a few feathers caught in the slats on one side. "*¿Lo ha leído? ¿Qué dijo?*" he asked without looking up.

"I do not speak Spanish," she said.

He straightened up, shocked, and slowly got to his feet. His eyes were very dark, and for a minute she thought he had been drinking. But no, they were clear. At least she was not the only one still feeling awkward about what had happened last night; he was obviously ill at ease.

She held up Doucet's letter. "What is the meaning of this?"

"I am afraid that it means exactly what it says."

"You are seriously proposing that Diana and I should travel with Napoleon's army? The very army we have been fleeing for the past five days? Or rather," she amended bitterly, "the army I *believed* we were fleeing, while you, in fact, did everything in your power to keep us nearby."

"I am not proposing anything," he said. "Monsieur Doucet is proposing. It is only for one day; once you reach Grenoble, you will be at liberty to continue on in any direction you please."

"This is because of you," she said, her voice shaking. "Because of you and that bridge. Isn't it?"

"Yes," he said. He looked away.

"And if I refuse?"

His voice was very quiet. "I do not advise it. You

will, in fact, be safer under the army's protection than you would be on your own. Masséna is racing up from the south with a corps of royalist volunteers. They will be here by tomorrow afternoon."

She sank down onto the bench. "So we are trapped between Napoleon's army and an opposing army?"

"No," he corrected. "You are trapped between Napoleon's army and a loosely organized gang of Bonaparte-haters. The former are disciplined veterans under the command of men like Cambronne—who, by the way, has personally guaranteed your safety. The latter are little better than an armed mob."

"We could not stay here for a few days? In the farmhouse?" She heard a pleading note in her own voice and forced herself back to a cold tone. "By we, of course, I mean Diana and myself. You and Mr. Roth are welcome to do as you see fit."

"I have no options. I gave Doucet my word that I would remain under military supervision until we reach Grenoble. You and Miss Hart, however, could choose to ignore that letter. As could my nephew."

"But you do not advise it." She mimicked his phrasing savagely.

"No."

"You will forgive me if I am inclined to seek another opinion."

She stalked off to find Madame Durry. But her hostess only endorsed Meyer's recommendation emphatically. Abigail could not tell whether her expressions of confidence in Napoleon's officers were genuine or whether the Frenchwoman spoke from fear of what might happen to her farm if Abigail failed to cooperate with the soldiers.

Roth was equally unhelpful, although from a different point of view. Anthony raged against his uncle; the man was a ruthless, cold-blooded plotter, no more to be trusted than a snake. He would lie to his own mother. Family loyalty, chivalry, responsibility meant nothing to him. Whatever Meyer proposed was sure to be the worst possible course of action. When she hesitantly mentioned the advancing royalist volunteers, he brushed his uncle's warning aside. He did, however, promise to accompany Diana and Abigail, no matter what Abigail decided to do. It was the least he could do to make up for Meyer's villainy.

In the end, she went back to Rodrigo. She found him cleaning and loading two pairs of pistols. The sight of four guns next to the pan of bread dough on Madame Durry's enormous kitchen table did not seem a good omen.

"Mr. Santos?" He looked up, frowning, and she remembered that he did not use his surname. This flustered her so much that she stammered as she continued. "May I—may I—could I ask you a question?"

He rose, setting down the gun he was holding. "Certainly, señora."

But she could not even put into words what she wanted to say. *Why did you betray me? Why did he betray me? How can I tell my daughter that the man I believed to be her protector has handed her over to fifteen hundred soldiers?*

He understood at least part of what she wanted to ask. "It is only one day," he said. His olive-skinned face held an expression that looked suspiciously like pity. "You and your daughter will be safe; I am sure of it. By tomorrow night we will be in Grenoble. The

Roth-Meyer Bank has an exchange office there; they will provide everything we need."

"The Hart brokerage has an agent in Grenoble as well," she said. "And you may tell Mr. Meyer that I will be seeking their assistance in returning to England the minute we arrive in the city."

"You will accept the offer of Señor Doucet, then?"

She hesitated, then nodded, watching his face in spite of herself to see what his reaction to her decision would be. He seemed relieved.

"Please do not worry, señora. You will be under the protection of General Cambronne. He is an honorable man."

She gave a bitter smile. "That will be a pleasant change from my current circumstances," she said.

Rodrigo watched her leave. She was holding herself so stiffly he wondered how she could breathe properly. He went back to cleaning one of the pistols, but after a few minutes he sighed, put it down, and went out to the barn. It was empty. So was the farmyard. But as he was scanning the other outbuildings, he caught a flash of light from the trees at the foot of the slope behind the barn. It bobbed gently up and down intermittantly, and as Rodrigo drew closer he saw that the light came from a lantern that had been suspended from a low-hanging tree branch next to a stream.

Beneath the lantern Meyer was kneeling, scooping white crystals from a heap on a piece of oilcloth into a burlap sack. At the edges of the heap, where the damp had reached the crystals, large sections were crusted together in sharp-edged chunks. His hands were bleeding slightly.

"Saltpeter?" Rodrigo asked.

Meyer did not answer or even look up.

"Señora Hart has agreed to accept the escort of Napoleon's guard."

That elicited a slight nod.

Rodrigo edged nervously around the side of the oilcloth. "I could have done this, señor."

Meyer turned then. "Sometimes a man has to tidy up after himself. Even a wealthy man with loyal and well-trained servants." He went back to shoveling the saltpeter into the bag. When the heap was nothing more than scattered flecks on the oilcloth, he carefully swept the last remnants into the center of the cloth and then folded it into a neat square. "You can take the lantern. And the butter paddle and mallet," he told Rodrigo as he picked up the sack and cloth. Rodrigo saw the wooden implements propped against a nearby tree. They were damp, and the flat blade of the paddle looked as though it had been scoured with something abrasive.

They walked back up the hill in silence.

Meyer stowed the oilcloth in the saddlebag of his horse and set the sack in the corner of the barn. He grimaced when he looked at the stained paddle in Rodrigo's hands. "Best leave a silver coin with it when you put it back in the churn. Madame Durry may require a new one."

"Yes, some things are not so easy to clean," Rodrigo said, eyeing the yellow and black grime in the cracks of the wood.

"True of more than that paddle." Meyer hung the lantern back on its hook. "Do you remember what you told me last night? That because I was unable to choose between the bridge and Mrs. Hart I would likely end up with neither?"

Rodrigo remembered. He had hoped Meyer would not. "Perhaps the situation is not hopeless, señor," he said. "At the moment Señora Hart is very upset, of course, but in time—"

Meyer cut him off. "She came out to speak with me last night," he said. "She let me kiss her. More than let me, in fact. Then she told me she despised me."

"Well then," Rodrigo said, brightening, "if she kissed you—"

He was interrupted again. "Wrong order," his employer informed him. "Denunciation first, embrace second is the one you want. Embrace followed by denunciation is a very bad sign. I will wager a large sum that Mrs. Hart will not even speak to me tomorrow. And that the minute we reach Grenoble she will seek out some means of returning to England that does not involve me or anyone remotely connected to me. Unless, like my nephew, they have renounced me and all my evil works."

Rodrigo thought this a very safe bet. It was time for a change of subject. "Speaking of Master Anthony— he seems much better," he offered tentatively.

"Yes." Meyer said. "He also despises me, of course. But since he didn't kiss me first his scorn is not quite as damning."

18

The journey to Grenoble was accomplished in the most luxurious manner imaginable. Abigail, Diana, and Roth were first conveyed in a gig from the farm out to the main road. There a large barouche awaited them, fitted with every convenience: rugs, lanterns, heated footrests, cushions, a basketful of things to eat and drink, even a small bottle of cologne. The vehicle had two coachmen and a footman, all in livery, and was escorted by a troop of twenty men. Abigail gathered that the entire ensemble—coach, servants, and fittings—had been appropriated from a local count by Doucet and sequestered for their use. Diana had looked around wide-eyed after they had been settled in the carriage and whispered to her mother, "What do you suppose people will think when they see us go by?" Abigail knew perfectly well what they would think. They would think the women inside were the mistresses of some high-ranking officers. As a result, Abigail decreed that Diana was to sit in the middle, between Roth and herself. At least that way the speculation would be directed at her rather than at her innocent daughter. At every village crossroads, it seemed, there were people gathered to watch them pass, many waving *tricouleurs,* and Abigail felt as though all the females over the age of sixteen were eyeing her with the same disapproving, speculative stare. It was ironic that after nine years of conducting herself with rigid propriety, now, within a space of forty-eight hours, she had first been taken for the mistress of a British spy and then a French general.

Among the soldiers accompanying them was a very handsome version of her friend Marcel from Pont-Haut, a Lieutenant Franconnin, who rode up to the carriage every so often to announce some new cause for the ladies not to be alarmed. Diana thought he was amusing and flirted with him outrageously. Abigail, who found the bulletins increasingly ominous ("the ladies should not be alarmed if they hear cannon fire"), was not entertained. The carriage stopped frequently for no apparent reason, and although Franconnin explained this as due to the slow progress of the foot soldiers in front of them, Abigail could see that he was growing more and more nervous as the day went on.

At around two in the afternoon, they stopped for the sixth or seventh time—Abigail had lost count—and she waited impatiently for the lieutenant to appear and offer his usual excuses. This time she would tell him that she knew perfectly well how fast Napoleon's troops could march; she had been traveling ahead of them for nearly a week. And if she, a female, could be walking twice as fast as this carriage was traveling right now, then surely troops who had marched over the Col Bayard in one day could not be the cause of the delay. After ten minutes, she decided that she would also insist that Franconnin permit the three passengers to leave the carriage and walk around. So far that had been expressly forbidden at all the stops save one. After twenty minutes, she opened the door herself, in spite of the lieutenant's prohibition. A young trooper stationed outside quickly closed it again, with a hoarse request for the ladies to wait patiently inside, where they would be safe. Safe from what? She looked out her window. All she could see were trees.

"Mr. Roth?"

He turned away from his own window. He, too, was growing impatient and worried, she saw.

"Would you mind seeing if you can discover why we have stopped?"

"Not at all," he said courteously. He opened the door on his side and stepped out quickly before one of the guards could close it. A heated argument immediately ensued; three or four soldiers converged on Roth and did everything short of lifting him bodily back into the carriage. She could not follow the beginning of the exchange, but Roth's voice grew louder and sharper as the discussion continued. When he shouted, "I demand to see Monsieur Meyer!" she had no trouble hearing him at all. A minute later he climbed back into the carriage, looking very angry.

"What is it?" asked Diana, scrambling hastily away from the window back into the center of the seat.

"They won't tell me a thing," said Roth. "And when I tried to move to the side so that I could see what was in front of us, they blocked my path. All I can tell you is that we are quite alone here; there are no soldiers at all nearby save those who are guarding our carriage. The rest of the column seems to have disappeared entirely."

Earlier Abigail had seen the troops formed up ahead of them, on the one occasion when they had been allowed to leave the vehicle. They were marching in ranks of four in deference to the narrow width of the road, and the line of men stretched out for at least half a mile.

"I sent for my uncle," Roth added after a minute. He looked uncomfortable.

"Yes, I heard you." Her voice sounded very far away in her own ears.

"I asked for the lieutenant first, of course, but he did not seem to be available."

Diana was anxiously looking back and forth from Roth to Abigail. Having failed to persuade her mother to confide in her last night, she had made several attempts to get answers from Roth this morning. But for once even Diana's persuasive charm had failed. Roth had merely turned red and stammered something about a misunderstanding.

Now Abigail saw a familiar tall figure striding through the trees. To her disgust, the troopers seemed in awe of Meyer; one approached timidly and after a brief exchange escorted him over to the carriage. At Meyer's gesture, the door was opened and Roth was permitted to get out. The two men moved away; Abigail could not see their faces or hear anything that was said, but she saw Roth stiffen. After a few minutes he returned to the carriage.

"You may get out, if you wish," he said.

Diana was scrambling over to the door as he spoke. Abigail followed more slowly, glancing nervously at the troopers. But they seemed to be taking their cue from Meyer. She felt a surge of bitter resentment at the sight of the cowed soldiers. She and Diana had been virtual prisoners in their carriage for eight hours, while Meyer, an enemy spy, was giving orders to men who should have been his captors.

"Why have we stopped here? What did you learn?" Abigail asked anxiously as Roth handed her out.

"There are royalist troops blocking the road about a mile ahead," he answered. "But my uncle says there is no cause for alarm." He added this last very hastily when he saw Abigail's horrified expression.

"No cause for alarm," she repeated in a flat voice. It seemed lately that everyone in France was eager to assure her there was no cause for alarm.

Diana, who knew that particular tone very well, seized her arm. "Mother!" she cried. "Don't! Just wait here!"

Abigail shook her off. "Where is Mr. Meyer?" She walked away from the coach and turned, scanning her surroundings. They were on a large hill, she saw. The carriage had been driven slightly off the road, at a level spot shaded by pines. Just ahead, the road sloped down through the thinning trees and disappeared, and at the very edge of the trees a group of soldiers was standing. She thought she recognized several members of the patrol that had been escorting the carriage. She definitely recognized the figure standing to one side. He was holding a field glass and scanning something farther down the hill.

She started running down the road; when one of the soldiers hurried after her, protesting, he shrank back at the fierce expression on her face. The sound of trumpets echoed faintly upwards from the valley below, and she ran even faster. By the time she reached Meyer she was panting and had one hand pressed to her side.

He turned slightly as she came up beside him. "Mrs. Hart." He touched his hat and then went back to studying the scene below. After a minute, as though he had only then understood why she might be there, he said, "You need not be frightened. You are perfectly safe." His voice was oddly distant and impersonal, like the trumpets.

She looked down into the valley. Where the road passed into a narrow plain between a hill and a lake, two masses of men were confronting each other. One group stood across the road facing south, their ranks forming a solid wall between the hillside and the water's edge. The other group, Napoleon's men, was marching forward in their groups of four and forming up into new lines of twenty. After three lines of twenty had formed, they would shift to the side, moving so precisely that it looked as though the square was a single organism. Mounted men rode up and down in front of both armies, calling out orders.

"How can you tell me not to be frightened?" she demanded wildly. "They are about to fight!"

"No." He smiled briefly, as though something had amused him. "There will be no battle. You and Miss Hart need not worry."

Pointing down at the valley, she asked, still breathing hard, "What is that, then?"

"Theater," he said, adding after a moment, "I am not sure whether it is tragedy or comedy."

"Who are the soldiers across the road, then? Are they not the king's troops?"

"In theory, yes. That is a battalion from an old and distinguished infantry regiment, however. They are very different from the royalist volunteers Masséna is bringing up from the south. At least half of the men down there—and virtually all of their sergeants and corporals—are veterans."

"You mean that they fought previously under Napoleon," she said slowly. "That they are loyal to him rather than to their present commander."

"Watch," he said, handing her the glass.

But she did not need the glass. There was no doubt who the small figure was who had detached himself from the neatly formed squares of the advancing army. There was no doubt what it meant when he marched forward alone and stood facing his enemies with arms spread wide, inviting them to fire straight at his chest.

"My God," Meyer breathed beside her. "He is magnificent. A magnificent monster."

A great roar swelled up from the plain below; the opposing troops had fallen to their knees, stretching out their hands to their former general. The roar solidified into a chant, the chant of thousands of men, beating rhythmically against the hillside. Now both armies were chanting, and men were breaking ranks and embracing each other in the middle of the plain.

"What are they shouting?" she asked.

"Vive l'Empereur."

"Surely it is somewhat premature to hail him once again as emperor?"

"Is it?" He gestured towards the mingled armies. "Your escort has just doubled in size. There is another royalist battalion waiting for us closer to Grenoble. They, too, will defect and join him. By the time we reach the city his army will be four thousand strong.

When news of this encounter spreads, more regiments will defect. Six days ago he had fifteen hundred men. By tomorrow night he may have fifteen thousand. By the end of the month, one hundred fifty thousand."

No wonder Meyer had been willing to risk so much to destroy the bridge at Pont-Haut. For the first time she wondered uneasily whether there might not in fact be two sides to the story of Nathan Meyer, ruthless betrayer of innocent females.

The tiny human figures below were beginning to reassemble themselves into marching units. With an imperious lift of his hand Meyer summoned one of the French troopers still hovering nearby. "We will be getting under way again any moment," he said to her. "You should return to the carriage." He did not offer to accompany her himself.

"Will I see you in Grenoble?" she found herself asking.

"I think not."

She nodded slowly, then turned and left. She looked back only once. He was still standing in the same spot, staring down at the valley and the long line of men that had been, only a few minutes ago, two opposing armies.

For the next six hours, as they bumped towards Grenoble, she looked out the window at the boisterous soldiers and cheering crowds of villagers and saw instead the solitary figure on the hillside. *How he must hate me*, she thought.

Meyer left Grenoble that same night, but not without exercising his authority as a part owner of the

Roth-Meyer Bank to drag the head of their affiliated office out of his house at eleven at night to take care of certain practical matters. Then he summoned Rodrigo. "I am dismissing you," he said curtly.

The Spaniard did not seem surprised.

"You will go immediately and find Mr. Roth. Inform him that you have left my service. You will accompany him—and any companions—to London." He handed Rodrigo a purse and a sealed packet. "A draft on the bank; two sets of false papers, plus your real papers."

"Master Anthony will be very suspicious," his servant objected.

"If you do not remember to call him Mr. Roth, he will sack you immediately," Meyer pointed out. He tossed the two clean shirts he had commandeered from his fellow banker an hour earlier into his saddlebags. "He might be suspicious, but he will be too grateful to ask many questions. If he refuses to employ you—although I doubt that he will—you will follow him unobtrusively and make certain that all goes smoothly."

"And where will you be?"

"Riding as fast as I can towards the coast." He checked his pistols and slipped them into his coat pocket. "Every hour I am in France is another hour's worth of information I am not allowed to pass on to Whitehall."

Rodrigo raised his eyebrows. "Another one of Doucet's ideas? Ransoming Señora Hart seems to have been very expensive. Although I am sure she was very grateful to be rescued."

"She slapped me across the face and called me a coward," Meyer said. Oddly, it did not trouble him to remember that. What still made him wince was the next part, where she had collapsed in tears. He felt as though he had inadvertently seen her naked.

"As you know, the señora has been very friendly to me," Rodrigo said cautiously. "Perhaps I could ask her whether she still finds you—"

"If you say *one word* to her about me, you will regret it," Meyer promised savagely. "Leave Mrs. Hart in peace. I've interfered quite enough in her affairs."

"And this is not interference?" Rodrigo asked scornfully, indicating the purse and the packet of papers. "Do you think I really believe that you are sending me to help Master Anthony? You know perfectly well he had promised the señora he would stay with her and her daughter until they reached England."

"Interference," said Meyer, "was when I tricked her into doing what I wanted. Choosing the northern route from Digne-les-Bains. Staying in a farmhouse near the bridge at Pont-Haut. This"—he waved at the papers—"is compensation."

"She has not asked for compensation," the servant told him, exasperated. "And if she had asked, she would not wish for it in this form. This is simply another round of deception and manipulation. Only now your goal is to make yourself feel better rather than to blow up a bridge."

Meyer had not been very successful with the bridge. He suspected he was not going to do much better with this attempt to salve his conscience. But at least if he foisted Rodrigo onto Abigail Hart he would not have to listen to moralizing lectures in Spanish all the way back to London.

19

London, May 1815

Louisa Roth looked up in surprise as her husband tapped lightly on the open door of her sitting room. It was the middle of the afternoon, the heart of the working day. In fact, because of the chaotic state of things in Europe since Bonaparte's return to France, everyone at the bank had been working longer hours than usual for the past few weeks. She had not expected to see him for hours.

"May I come in?"

She put her sewing back in the drawer of her worktable. "Of course."

"Are you expecting any callers?"

"No, but if you like I shall ring for Sweelinck and tell him we are not to be disturbed."

Roth performed this office himself, and closed the door firmly behind the retreating figure of their butler. "I have just had a most interesting conversation," he told her as he pulled up a chair next to her. "A conversation I was enjoined to hold in strictest confidence. Since it concerned Nathan, I requested permission to consult you, and that permission was granted. But you must speak of this to no one else."

She was intrigued. "Who was it who came to see you?"

"Colonel White."

"Nathan's colonel?"

"Indeed."

Her brother-in-law had no official standing in the British army. Unofficially, however, he reported to the irascible White, and for all intents and purposes was the most senior of the colonel's intelligence officers. Meyer and White had been working together for over ten years, and never before, to Louisa's knowledge, had the colonel sought a private interview with her husband.

"What did he want?"

Roth gave her a wry look. "He wanted to know if we had noticed anything peculiar about Nathan since his return from France."

She gave an exasperated sigh. "Anything peculiar? I could give him a list. A long list. And that in spite of Nathan's determined and largely successful efforts to confine his presence in this house to hours when I am either out or asleep."

"He is not avoiding you, my dear," Roth reminded her. "Or even me. He is avoiding Anthony."

That was the first peculiar thing. Even though they had originally been traveling together, Nathan and her nephew had arrived separately from France. The second peculiar thing was that Rodrigo had been with Anthony instead of with his own employer. The third was that the servant and Anthony had clearly been very angry with Meyer. Louisa had been unable to persuade any of them to explain the cause of the hostility. After a few weeks Rodrigo had seemed more like his normal self, but just as Louisa was scheming to make a second attempt to suborn him, he had disappeared. Which was the fourth peculiar thing, because usually her brother-in-law and his servant were inseparable. Thus, Rodrigo was away and Nathan was here in London—yet another oddity. She would have expected Meyer to be abroad at a time like this. Her nephew James, for example— Meyer's son—was the most junior courier in White's service and he had barely been in England three days out of the last sixty. And then there was Nathan's strange, abstracted mood. As expected, he had thrown himself into a frenzy of activity, reading reports and papers, conferring repeatedly with her husband, sending queries out through the bank's messenger service. But there was something almost mechanical about his actions. He would ask a question and ignore the answer, or comment twice on the same story in the newspaper. He seemed withdrawn and tense.

"Why did the colonel want your opinion of Nathan's behavior?" she asked, frowning.

Roth sat back in his chair. "First of all, when Nathan came back, you may remember that he refused to give the bank any further information about Bonaparte's forces and their projected rate of progress towards Paris. He said that he had been asked not to do so, and I thought that for some reason the War Office had forbidden him to discuss his report with civilians. In fact, however, he also refused to report to White, claiming that he had personal reasons for the omission. The colonel accepted that, although he thought it rather strange. But then last week Nathan was asked to go to Belgium. Twice. And both times he said he would rather not leave London."

She was taken aback. "He was not willing to go to Belgium? I have never known him to refuse a request from Whitehall before. Have you?"

"No. In fact, before his trip to France, he had been to Vienna several times to maintain a clandestine watch over the Allied military leaders—at his own suggestion. The very same role Wellington was asking him to play in Belgium. Finally White summoned Nathan to his office and asked him point-blank why he would not go. And Nathan had no reasonable answer. He simply said that he thought others could do a better job."

Louisa frowned. False modesty was not one of Meyer's attributes. "You would think he could at least have produced something more convincing."

"Colonel White was not very happy with that answer either," Roth said. "He confessed to me that he lost his temper a bit. He asked Nathan what the—er, what Nathan thought he was doing behaving like a coy maiden when Europe was going up in flames and he was needed in Brussels. Nathan replied that in his judgment he was no longer fit for confidential surveillance work. That he would be better employed as he was now, decoding ciphers and monitoring reports. At which point the colonel lost his temper *more* than a bit and let fly a few rather choice oaths—his own phrase, Louisa—before informing Nathan that Whitehall, not individual couriers, made decisions of that sort. And then Nathan lost *his* temper and swore right back, reminding White that he held no commission, that he accepted no pay, and that he was free at any moment to walk out of White's office. Which he proceeded to do."

"Nathan lost his temper?" she said, incredulous. "That is odder than everything else put together."

"Yes, White was rather stunned as well. Hence his visit to me. And hence my visit to you."

Louisa sighed. "I don't see how I can be of any help. I see Nathan even less frequently than you do. You at least catch occasional glimpses of him in the morning."

Her husband brooded for a minute. "Do you remember what you said when he first came back to London? About my little scheme?"

A week after Nathan's return, Eli had dragged her into the bookroom one morning and confessed everything: how he had sent Meyer off to Digne-les-Bains with Diana Hart as a decoy, and Diana's mother as the real candidate. "Go on," he had said, "you have been dying to say 'I told you so' ever since Nathan stalked in here looking as though he wanted to strangle me. I surrender. I will leave Nathan to go his own way from now on. You were right. My attempt was a complete, unmitigated disaster." But Louisa, to his surprise, had been unwilling to gloat.

"Yes, I remember," she said now. "I told you that I had heard some rather strange rumors about Abigail Hart and that it might be just as well if nothing came of your plan." Luckily, Eli had never pressed her for details of those rumors.

"No, not that. The other thing you told me."

"Oh. Yes." She had pointed out that it might well be too soon to label the result a disaster, that Nathan's anger was not at all the same thing as the amused scorn which had followed all of Eli's earlier attempts.

"I believe we have been proceeding from a false assumption," he said. "We believed Nathan's distress, his preoccupied air, must be related to the news from abroad. At least, I did."

Louisa nodded. Her brother-in-law's unhappiness was easily explained by the increasingly grim quality of that news: Marshal Ney defecting to Bonaparte; King Louis fleeing to Belgium; Napoleon's triumphant entry into Paris and his call for all Frenchmen to return to armed service.

"Well, we may have been wrong. Perhaps something happened in March when Nathan was in France," Roth said. "Something connected with the Harts. Look at how Anthony and Rodrigo have been behaving. I will make another attempt to question Nathan myself, but if that fails there is only one thing to do. You must go and see Mrs. Hart."

She blinked. "I beg your pardon?"

"Abigail Hart," he said impatiently. "You must call on her. Cultivate her acquaintance."

"And how, pray, am I to do that? We have never met. Will she not think it rather odd when I suddenly appear on her doorstep asking questions about Nathan?"

"She did nurse Anthony," Roth reminded her. "He told us he was quite ill for a few days. You could call to thank her."

"Eli, that was two months ago! And Anthony himself visited, quite properly, the week after he arrived here."

Her husband coughed. "Apparently he is still calling on Mrs. Hart occasionally. Or, more accurately, on Miss Hart. At least according to Battista."

Anthony's servant had arrived in London several weeks ago and had promptly quarreled bitterly with

Rodrigo. Meyer had seized upon the quarrel as an excuse to send the Spaniard away.

"You are suggesting that I go and insinuate myself into Mrs. Hart's confidence on the pretext that I am concerned for Anthony's welfare?" She wished she could sound more indignant. Between her curiosity and her concern for her brother-in-law, Eli's proposal was dangerously appealing.

"Anthony is my brother's only son," Roth said piously. "And he has not been looking very well of late."

Privately Louisa thought the thinner, sterner version of her nephew had a certain appeal. At least to females. And Nathan was not the only one who had been spending many unexplained hours away from the house. If Anthony was dangling after Diana Hart, it behooved her to investigate further. "Very well," she said. "If your talk with Nathan does not produce satisfactory results I will call on Mrs. Hart. Although why a woman I have never met should wish to confide her opinions about Nathan to me I am sure I do not know."

Roth waved his hand airily. "All women enjoy gossip."

No, thought Louisa. All women did *not* enjoy gossip. Especially a woman who had herself been the victim of gossip for many, many years.

"Now push the ramrod down the barrel. Hard." Mark Davis illustrated the movement on his own weapon in one smooth thrust.

Anthony jammed the brass rod up against the wadded mass of ball, powder, and paper in the barrel of his musket and shoved. As usual, the rod got stuck halfway down.

His instructor sighed. "Try banging the butt on the ground."

Obediently, Anthony slammed the butt a few times onto the hard-packed surface of Walworth Fields. There had been grass here earlier in the spring, but now that militias were drilling here every evening it was long gone. This time the ramrod slid properly to the end of the barrel.

"Level your weapon."

His shoulder aching, Anthony hoisted the gun up and sighted.

"Fire!"

The bullet buried itself near the center of the straw target.

"Nothing wrong with your aim," Davis said sourly. "But if you can't load faster, my sergeant won't have you. Try again. A round a minute, minimum, is what you need, and most of our lads could do twice that."

After weeks of sweaty, backbreaking practice every Tuesday and Thursday, Anthony had progressed from two rounds every ten minutes to two rounds every four minutes. Doggedly he pulled out the cartridge, bit off the end, poured in powder, tipped the ball into the muzzle, and picked up the ramrod for the twentieth time.

"Push," ordered Davis.

Anthony shoved. The rod jammed, and he swore fluently. His stock of oaths had tripled since beginning his training at Walworth.

"Try twisting the rod a bit as you go," suggested a grizzled veteran, peering at Anthony's weapon. A crowd always collected around him during practice, curious as to why a well-dressed young man who spoke in educated accents should be in one of the worst districts in London wrestling with a Brown Bess. The answer was simple: Mark Davis was the only Jew Anthony knew who had served as an enlisted man under Wellington. Davis lived in Walworth; Anthony, therefore, crossed the river twice a week to train and put up with comments about his clothing, hairstyle, vocabulary, posture, and, inevitably, religion. Davis's advice on how to ignore these sallies had been far more effective than his instruction with the musket; Anthony was rapidly becoming totally impervious to insults.

Gritting his teeth, Anthony tried the rod again, this time twisting slightly. There it was, the smooth, efficient movement he had been trying to master for nearly a month. Simultaneously annoyed and elated, he rounded on Davis. "Why didn't you tell me to twist it?"

Davis fired his own gun, reloaded, and tamped. Now that he knew what to look for, Anthony could see the slight rotation of his wrist.

"I'll be!" Davis said, abashed. "Didn't know as I was doing any twisting, Mr. Roth. It's been many years since I learned to load this old girl. Try another round now."

Anthony fired, reloaded, fired, and reloaded. It was still a struggle, but the ramrod was behaving itself. "How long?" he asked.

"Just under three minutes, sir," said Noah, Davis's eight-year-old son. He was holding Anthony's watch as though it were made of eggshells.

Anthony grinned. "Another go?" he asked Davis.

The older man shrugged. "Your powder and shot, sir."

Cartridge, ball, wadding, rod, aim, fire. And

again. His shoulder felt as though it had been kicked by a horse. He looked at Noah.

"Just under three minutes."

Anthony sighed.

"But more under," Noah added hastily. "Closer to two and a half, really."

"It's tearing open the cartridge is slowing you down now, sir," Davis said critically. "And you could practice that at home."

Anthony pictured Battista finding little half-chewed bits of paper smeared with gunpowder in Anthony's room. His servant would go straight to Eli Roth, and that would be the end of Anthony's plan.

It was a simple plan: Anthony had decided to enlist and go fight Bonaparte. He was very clear about it. He knew that part of what was driving him was the humiliating beating he had taken at Sisteron, but he knew, too, that he had other, better reasons. The perfumers of Grasse, hoping for the first time in over ten years to be able to export their wares, were a reason. His uncle Jacob, who had been isolated from the rest of the family for the simple reason that he lived in Paris, was another. And although Italy was not as closed off as France, Anthony had felt the strain of doing business in French-controlled territory more and more. When Bonaparte had abdicated last spring, it was as though a giant weight had been lifted from every Englishman in Europe.

His uncle was another reason. Anthony was still furious with Meyer. To hoodwink innocent companions and place their lives at risk seemed to him inexcusable, no matter what military advantage might be at stake. Enlisting was his way of showing his uncle that there were honorable ways of fighting Napoleon.

When he had first approached Davis, who was the brother of a clerk at the bank, the older man had assumed Anthony wanted a berth as an officer. It had taken quite some time to convince him that a wealthy young man was prepared to become a private.

"The pay is only a shilling," Davis had warned him. "We sleep on the ground, most nights. The food is full of weevils, if there is any at all. And enlisted men can be flogged."

But Roth had refused to consider purchasing a commission. Not only was he quite certain that he would be a danger to his men if he held a command, but he was also unwilling to take a false name and pretend to be Christian, as his cousin James had done. No lies, he told himself. He conveniently ignored the deception involved in concealing from everyone in Eli Roth's household both his outings to Walworth and his larger purpose.

"Once more," Anthony said now. "Last two rounds."

Noah, who had closed up the watch, brightened and flipped up the lid again.

"Ready?" he asked the boy.

Noah nodded.

Concentrating fiercely, Anthony loaded and fired twice. The bullets went nowhere near the center of the target, but he didn't care. "Time?" he asked, panting and leaning on the musket.

"Two and one-half minutes," announced Noah, peering at the watch in the fading light.

It would have to do for tonight. He was exhausted, and his mouth was acrid with the taste of gunpowder. He had not imagined how physically intimate the process of loading a musket was. Every shot was preceded by the horrifying act of putting a packetful of explosives in your mouth and ripping it open with your back teeth. Davis had told him that men who wanted to avoid conscription would sometimes knock out their molars to make themselves unfit for service.

The evening ended as it always did. Under Davis's strict supervision, he cleaned his gun, handed it to Noah in exchange for his watch, and then shook hands solemnly with his teacher.

"Thank you, Mr. Davis."

"You are making very good progress, sir."

For once Anthony actually believed him.

20

Abigail was seriously contemplating hiring a butler. Her house was not large, and up until recently she would not have imagined that she could need any more staff, but the vision of someone imposing who would tell callers that she was not at home was more appealing every day. Her downstairs maid had an exasperating tendency to admit visitors even after explicit instructions to the contrary, explaining afterwards that "it was just this once, ma'am, and Mrs. Herron did say that she was expected."

Last year, the possession of a very marriageable daughter had transformed Abigail from an involuntary hermit into a semirespectable member of her community. There were still glances and whispers, but she no longer hesitated to appear in public or accept the invitations which began to arrive within a few weeks of Diana's taking up residence. She had regarded her new status as something temporary, a phantom that would vanish as soon as Diana accepted an offer; and had tried to be grateful, for her daughter's sake, as matrons who had ignored

her for years suddenly included her in luncheons
or teas. If she occasionally wanted to stand up and
remind the circle of women placidly eating sweet-
meats that she was still Abigail Hart, divorced
adulteress, she suppressed the impulse.

Since her return from France the number of visitors
had only increased. First, there was the predictable
interest in her encounter (or near-encounter) with
The Corsican Monster. Acquaintances stopped her on
the street and begged for the story; complete
strangers came to her little house in Goodman's
Fields presenting their calling cards, with a few lines
on the back citing the recommendation of a friend of
a friend. Even her mother, through Leah, had demanded an account. Eventually the tale became old
news, but in the meantime Diana had been acquiring
a circle of admirers. There were three round-faced
brothers, some connection of Joshua's, who called en
masse and presented Diana with three exactly identical posies. A young man visiting from Amsterdam had
prolonged his stay in London for Diana's sake—or so
he told her. Anthony Roth called at least twice a week.
There were also female visitors; her daughter had
made the acquaintance of several girls her own age.
When the knocker sounded these days it was usually
Miss Hart who was requested.

Today was no exception. Rosie had just come up
to tell her that Diana was entertaining some friends.
"No need for you to go down, ma'am, for Mrs.
Asher is with them," she added. But Abigail, with an
inward sigh, set down her half-finished letter and
headed downstairs.

The voices came clearly up the staircase as she
hurried down: girls' voices, one loud and confident,

the other low and hesitant. She stopped, reconsidering her decision to join Diana. She knew those voices; Martha Woodley and her cousin Eleanor were here. Reminding herself sternly that these were her daughter's guests, Abigail summoned her best company smile and opened the door.

Fanny was embroidering over by the window, trying not to interfere with what she called "the young people." The two visitors were on the sofa with Diana, all three girls in pastel muslins much more appropriate for the warm weather than Abigail's long-sleeved cambric gown. Martha bounced up at once as Abigail came in and gave her a cheerful smile; Eleanor, who was quite shy, got up more slowly. Abigail wished it had been Eleanor, and not the boisterous Martha, who had become Diana's friend. No, that was unfair, she told herself firmly. Martha Woodley was a polite, warmhearted girl. It was not her fault that she had a father, two brothers, and a brother-in-law in the army and had spent several years in Portugal and Spain with her father's regiment—a circumstance that had attracted Diana instantly. It was Diana's fascination with all things military that made Abigail uncomfortable, not Martha herself. And Abigail did not object in principle to Diana's having Christian friends, although in the back of her mind she could not quite dispel the image of the little shrine in the mountains where Diana had lit candles.

She could not precisely recall who had introduced Martha and Diana—it had happened at a concert— but the girls had discovered that they shared the same voice teacher, and then that they had both been pursued by Napoleon's troops; after that first conversation in Hanover Square their families had nearly been compelled to use force to separate them. Abigail suspected that Martha's mother, a vicar's daughter from an old Lincolnshire family, did not entirely approve of the friendship either. And yet when the two women had met they had liked each other nearly as much as their daughters had. Henrietta Woodley was a down-to-earth woman whose years of traveling with the army had given her a brusque manner leavened by a wry sense of humor. She had bluntly told Abigail that Diana was far too pretty and that she would be obliged if Abigail could keep Diana away from Martha's two unmarried brothers. "For you must know," she had said, "that one of my boys is in the same regiment as Lord Alcroft's son, and if a peer's son—and a major!— could marry Eli Roth's niece, it will be no use my telling Charles that it is not to be thought of." Only late that night had Abigail realized who the niece was: Meyer's daughter, of course. Another black mark against poor Martha.

"Mama, may I go to Hatchard's with Martha and Eleanor?" Diana asked as soon as Abigail came in. "A new book by Captain Clarke is out, and they have come express to tell me."

"Good morning, Mrs. Hart," said Martha politely as her cousin offered a quick curtsey. "I hope this is not too early to call, but there is already a queue in front of the shop, and his last book sold out on the first day."

"They have their carriage," Diana added. "And will bring me back."

Martha nodded in confirmation.

"I suppose you may," Abigail said. "Be sure to be home by three. Your aunt is coming to take you to see your grandmother."

The three girls went happily off to help Diana select a bonnet and shawl, abandoning Diana's latest project—a patchwork needle case—on the sofa.

"Other young ladies rush to buy Byron's latest," Abigail said to Fanny, resigned. "But not Diana. Ever since our adventure in France, my daughter buys every publication about Wellington's campaigns that she can find."

Fanny took another stitch. "I believe Clarke's writings are said to be quite unexceptionable," she offered. She blushed a little. "Unlike—that other book."

Fanny referred to *Leisure Moments in the Camp and in the Guard Room,* authored by "A Veteran Officer." This work had boasted that it revealed the true life of a soldier, and Abigail, finding that the true life of a soldier apparently consisted of drinking, gambling, and flirting, had promptly confiscated the volume. She did not consider killing (presumably the ideal activity for a soldier) much better, but she could hardly forbid Diana to read about events which were published in every newspaper in the country.

There was a knock at the door, and one of the maids peered in. "Mr. Roth is below, ma'am," she announced. "Shall I show him up?"

"Yes, but after that I am not at home," Abigail said firmly. "Miss Hart is going out, and I have letters to finish."

The maid, however, had disappeared the moment she had heard the word *yes.*

"I need a butler," Abigail told Fanny, exasperated.

"So you keep saying," her friend answered absently, holding up two different skeins of blue thread to the light from the window. "Although it would be a bit odd to have a butler when there is only one footman."

"It would be worth hiring another footman *and* a butler to be able to have some privacy from unwanted guests in my own home." She stalked angrily over to the sofa and scooped up the bits of cloth Diana had left there.

From behind her she heard an embarrassed cough. It was Anthony Roth, standing in the doorway. Yet another reason for a butler. Her maid did not always announce visitors properly.

"I beg your pardon," Roth said. "I just stopped by for a moment, to give you this." He held out a small parcel.

"Oh dear." Abigail hastily stuffed the little pieces of cloth into her pocket and accepted the package. "I don't suppose there is any way to pretend you did not hear that? I assure you it does not apply to you, Anthony." She deliberately used his first name. "Please do stay for a little while. Diana is on her way out with friends, but she will wish to greet you first."

He glanced nervously at the hallway but consented to sit down. She was not certain what his thoughts were about her daughter these days. In France he had gone from infatuation to disillusionment to bewilderment, and so far as she could tell, he was still mired firmly in the last of the three. When he called, he always looked as though he was not quite sure why he found himself once again in the Harts's drawing room. He rarely smiled, and the informal banter she had seen between him and her daughter during their journey had completely vanished. Nor could she blame him for his confusion and hesitation. Diana was just as awkward and inconsistent in her treatment of him.

Now, for example, as she came back into the room, chattering and laughing with Martha, she stopped dead at the sight of Roth. "Oh!" she said, startled, as he rose to greet her. "Mr. Roth. How—how nice to see you." Then, recollecting her companions, "May I present my friends, Misses Martha and Eleanor Woodley?"

Stiff nods were exchanged on both sides.

"We are off to the bookstore," Diana told him with artificial brightness. "Perhaps you would care to accompany us?"

This offer was politely declined.

All four young people stood in uncertain silence for a moment, and then, forgetting to maintain her worldly pose, Diana suddenly frowned. "What have you done to your hand?" she asked in her normal voice. "It looks as though it is bleeding." Martha, next to her, leaned forward to see better.

Roth hastily put both hands behind his back, which gave Abigail an excellent view of them. The tips of two fingers on his right hand were indeed bleeding slightly. "It is nothing. A scrape." He had some small scratches on one side of his face as well, Abigail noticed. Perhaps Roth was one of those young men who somehow attracted illness and injury. Paul, her first husband, had been like that.

Martha whispered something to Diana, and her daughter reverted to doll mode. "We must be off, I am afraid," she announced, very grande dame. "The Woodley's carriage is waiting." The girls took their leave of Abigail and Fanny but forgot to close the door, so that Martha's loud "Who was that, Diana? A suitor?" was easily audible.

Roth flushed and picked up his hat and gloves. "I must go as well."

"But your gift," Abigail objected. "I have not even opened it, or thanked you." She began to unwrap it, wondering for the first time why Roth had brought something for her rather than for Diana. It was a book: Byron's latest, in fact, his *Hebrew Melodies*, a disconcerting choice.

"It is not from me," he confessed. "It is from my uncle. There is a note inside." He saw her expression and sat down again. "He came to find me two days ago. We had a long talk. He feels very badly about . . . everything."

"I see." Abigail's voice was tight.

Roth added, "I believe he is no longer working with the army."

"So, he is 'a reformed character,' as you told me once before." She was not sure if Roth remembered his ill-fated attempt to explain his uncle's scars as relics of a career as a seducer. Apparently he did; he flushed.

"You need not keep the book," he said. "My uncle thought you would not, in fact. He told me to give it in that case to the library at the Chelsea Hospital."

Torn between curiosity and indignation, Abigail hesitated. If she opened the book to read the note, she would have to keep it. She glanced uncertainly at Fanny, hoping for a cue, but her friend was concentrating with implausible dedication on her embroidery and clearly wanted no part of this conversation.

Curiosity won. She lifted the cover and peered at the flyleaf. To her disappointment the inscription said merely: *I saw this and thought it might interest you. I hope you will forgive the presumption.* It was unsigned.

What had she expected? A passionate declaration?

She told herself that he must have felt constrained to keep his statement impersonal, knowing that the volume was likely to end up in the hands of an elderly pensioner.

"Thank you for bringing it," she said. "I am sure I shall enjoy reading it." That was a suitably ambiguous response.

But Roth was not willing to leave it there. He twisted his hat in his hands. "If my uncle were to call here, would you be willing to see him?"

She was not ready for that question, and her face must have shown it.

"Never mind," he said, rising hastily. "He said nothing of any plans to visit; I am merely engaging in a long-standing Roth family pastime."

"And what is that?" she asked.

"Meddling." He gave her a crooked smile. "I am not very good at it, am I?"

"I don't know about that," she muttered as he left. She had accepted the book of poems, hadn't she? And when Roth had asked his question, she had not said yes, but she had not said no either. A butler would not be much use if she could not make up her mind about whether she wanted to see her visitor or not.

After two unsuccessful attempts to catch his brother-in-law before he left the house, Eli Roth abandoned his original "casual encounter at breakfast" plan and turned to the other end of the day, instructing the night porter to come and fetch him the minute Meyer returned. He thus had the satisfaction of shocking the normally imperturbable Nathan by appearing in that gentleman's study at just past one in the morning.

"My God, what is it?" Meyer exclaimed, rising in alarm from his stool by the fire. "Is it James?"

Meyer's son was in Belgium with Wellington. So far as Roth could tell, the Allied army was spending its time attending balls and musicales and quarreling over who would command which sections of the four-nation force. It was no wonder Wellington wanted someone to keep an eye on the Dutch and the Prussians. "Last I heard, James is perfectly well, if a bit bored," he said. Without being invited, he took a seat across from Meyer in a large armchair beside the desk. "And if you had not abandoned Whitehall in a fit of pique, you would be seeing regular reports from him and would not frighten yourself needlessly because I have paid you a late-night visit."

His brother-in-law subsided back onto his stool. "Is this a scolding, then?" he asked in a resigned tone.

"More of an interrogation." Roth helped himself to a pear from the tray of food sitting on the desk. "Your colonel came by two days ago," he said, slicing the pear in half. "He informed me that you did not seem to be yourself and asked me whether I had noticed anything unusual about you since your return from France."

Meyer's face settled into a stony mask. "And what did you say?"

Roth took a bite of pear, chewed, and swallowed. "I said that you had not been home much, but that you seemed abstracted. As though you were contemplating some difficult question."

"I have been contemplating something," said Meyer. "I have been contemplating the pitfalls of matchmaking. From the bottom of the pit." His tone was nicely shaded between annoyance and irony. "Miss Hart was not one of your better candidates, Eli."

"Yes. Well." It was Roth's turn to be on the defensive. He took another bite of pear. "I admit my fault. I have already promised Louisa I will make no further attempts on your celibacy." Then, at the ironic lift of Meyer's eyebrows, he corrected himself. "Perhaps celibacy is the wrong word. On your unmarried state, then." Meyer had kept a mistress in Spain for some years, and lately there had been rumors of someone in the south of France.

There was an uncomfortable silence, which Roth filled by eating more pear, followed by a bit of bread and cheese. Then, feeling as though he might as well earn the cool stare he was getting, he asked bluntly, "Are you, er, keeping company with anyone at the moment?"

The stare went from cool to cold. "You know perfectly well I would never do so in London. Louisa would be mortified. I had thought you would be as well, but perhaps, given the tenor of this conversation, I was mistaken."

No, he was not mistaken. Roth had always been grateful that his brother-in-law's illicit activities—both military and amatory—took place under assumed names in far-away places. Feeling more and more as though he was pushing against an immovable wall, Roth nevertheless returned to his inquest. "But in all seriousness, Nathan, is there any particular reason why you do not wish to accept assignments from White any longer?"

Now the stare was positively arctic. "What possible concern is that of yours?"

Roth refused to be intimidated. "The natural concern of anyone for a kinsman. Allow me at least the virtue of consistency. I questioned you when you resigned from the bank. I questioned you when you moved to Spain. I actively tried to prevent you from taking Rachel and James there a few years later. If, at a crucial time for the British army, you suddenly withdraw from your unofficial government position, you cannot be surprised that I am curious and even a bit troubled."

Meyer shrugged. "There is no great mystery. I felt that I would not be of much use."

"Colonel White tells me that he disagrees with your evaluation."

"White will say anything that he finds expedient at the time. He needs someone in Brussels at the moment; he therefore assures you—and me—that I am perfectly capable." There was a bitterness in his voice that Roth did not quite understand.

"So you think his visit to me was simply motivated by irritation? He finds himself short-staffed, and comes to see me to ask if I can try to persuade you to return? He has worked with you, and with James, for years, and his only thought, when you abruptly resign, is for his own inconvenience? If that is your judgment of the man I can only say that I am astonished you were willing to work with him for as long as you did."

The dark eyes fell, and Roth pressed his advantage. "What happened in France, Nathan? Did something there cause this change?"

"Nothing happened." Meyer made an impatient gesture. "Compared to most of my visits to France, I assure you that it was very tame." He rose. "You must excuse me; I have an early appointment tomorrow."

"Yes, I have noticed that all your appointments seem to be early these days," Roth retorted. "Early enough to make certain that you avoid seeing me."

Meyer sighed. "If you wish to play the concerned kinsman, you might ask Anthony where he got those blisters on his face."

"Anthony is almost as hard to track down as you are," Roth said irritably. "And just as touchy. It's a good thing he is going back to Italy soon."

"He is?" Meyer looked relieved. Roth still did not know what had caused the rift between uncle and nephew, but in Meyer's present mood he was clearly not going to get any answers.

"Yes, his man is leaving tomorrow, and Anthony himself follows at the end of next week." Roth leaned back in his chair. "You can recall Rodrigo now from whatever artificial exile you concocted for him. That was why you sent him away, was it not? Because of his quarrel with Battista?"

"No," Meyer said, "I sent him away because he sometimes answers questions I do not wish to have answered. Questions from overanxious relatives, for example." The door shut behind him with a gentle click.

Roth belatedly realized that he was sitting in Meyer's favorite chair in Meyer's own study having just eaten most of what must have been his brother-in-law's supper. With a sigh, he got up, banked the fire, and snuffed the candles. His total profit for the evening was one pear and two ounces of cheese. Louisa was going to have to see if she could do better with Abigail Hart.

21

The day after his visit to Abigail Hart, Anthony reluctantly decided that unless he wanted to be just as dishonorable as his uncle, he would have to tell his family—at least the London branch of it—that he was planning to enlist. And although he saw his aunt Louisa twice within the hour after this decision, and knew quite well that Eli Roth was in his office at the bank, he was determined that he would tell Meyer first. The prospect was terrifying, but there was no point in signing on to fight the French if he could not even face his own uncle.

It took him quite some time to track Meyer down. His uncle was not in his study at the back of the Roths's town house, nor at the desk reserved for his occasional use at the bank. Anthony knew better than to go over to Colonel White's headquarters at the Tower, but he did try several of the coffeehouses near the Horse Guards. He finally did what he should have done first: he consulted the Roths's butler, who directed him to the Traveller's Club, where Anthony found his uncle leafing through the latest newspapers from Brussels. Meyer did not seem very interested in what he was reading, which was understandable, since the papers were all at least three weeks old. He did not seem interested in his surroundings either, however; he did not even look up as Anthony approached.

Anthony sat down quietly in an adjacent chair. "We have more current reports from Belgium at the bank," he observed after a moment.

Meyer put down the papers, startled. "Anthony! How did you get in?"

Jews were not normally welcome at the Traveller's, but Castlereagh, who had founded the club, had insisted that all White's couriers should have access to the place. Meyer's membership listed his status as international guest and his residence as Frankfurt.

"I told them I needed to see you on army business. It even happens to be true."

Meyer eyed the faint red lines on Anthony's cheek. "Is this army business by any chance connected to the powder burns on your face? Or your torn fingers? If I did not know better, I would say you had been firing a rifle. Repeatedly. Or perhaps a musket."

"Musket." He slumped back, disgusted. "I might have realized that you would notice."

"I take a personal interest in your bruises, these days," his uncle said. "Having caused so many of them myself during our recent adventure. Why are you training with a musket? Are you joining the militia?"

Several of Anthony's colleagues at the bank were active in their local militias, which had been drilling regularly for ten years in case Bonaparte ever invaded England. It was a relatively safe method of demonstrating patriotism. He said, watching his uncle's face, "No, not the militia. An infantry regiment. The 44th Foot."

Meyer lost his faintly bored look. He sat up with a jerk. "An infantry regiment? You are joking, surely."

Anthony set his jaw. "James is in the Rifles," he pointed out. "At least, he serves in the 95th when he isn't doing something even more dangerous, like sneaking into French fortresses. No one suggests he is joking when he goes off with his battalion."

"Yes, and a fine model for prudence he is!" Meyer snapped. He left unspoken what they both knew: James had been studying to be a spy since he was eight. Anthony could barely fire a gun. His uncle took a deep breath. In the patient tones of a man trying to reason with a child, he said, "Forgive me, but you cannot have thought this through. You have no idea what the life of an enlisted man is like."

"Do not tell me about floggings and weevils and seventy-pound haversacks," Anthony said, his jaw set. "I have already heard it all. Mr. Davis, my unofficial trainer, insisted that I walk from Battersea to Walworth carrying all my gear on the hottest day last week. I still have the blisters."

"And you are prepared to sign on for seven years of these delights?"

"No, but it will not be seven years, no matter what the enlistment papers may say. Everyone believes there will be one great battle. In mid-July, most likely. That is less than two months from now. I want to fight in that battle."

"What if everyone is wrong? What if it takes years of slow, grinding, dreary work to push Bonaparte back again? As it did in Spain?"

"Then I will ask you to buy me out." He gave his

uncle a level stare. "Don't tell me you would not be able to do it."

"What I would like to do is to *talk* you out. Before you are in." Meyer sat back in his chair and brooded. "This is because of that beating you took in Sisteron," he muttered, half to himself. "In front of Miss Hart. You asked me to teach you how to shoot a gun right afterwards; I should have seen this coming."

"That is not the reason. At least, not entirely." Anthony shifted uncomfortably. Here was his cue for a fiery speech denouncing Meyer's devious ways and justifying his own decision, but he no longer wanted to deliver the speech. To his surprise, he found himself reaching for a very different explanation. "I was in Grasse, you know, meeting with perfumers, when the news of Bonaparte's escape arrived," he said slowly.

Meyer frowned, but waited for him to continue.

Anthony made a frustrated gesture. "Do you know how long it has been since those poor men could export their goods legally? Over ten years! How much of a local market for fine perfume do they have in the hills of southern France?"

"So you are going to war for the lavender growers of Provence."

"Yes, I am," said Anthony fiercely. "I am sick of being a smuggler instead of a businessman. You and James enjoy breaking the rules. I don't. If the only way to stop Napoleon from bringing another decade of war and embargos and blockades to Europe is to stand there with a musket in some field in Belgium, then so be it."

There was a long silence. His uncle studied him

carefully, then said at last, "When are you meeting the recruiter?"

He had been holding his breath. Now he let it out. "Friday."

"They will have you on a boat to Antwerp twenty-four hours after you sign on, you know. Wellington is desperately short of men."

"So I have been told."

There was another silence. "Have you shared this news with anyone else?"

Anthony shook his head. "I wanted to tell you first."

"Hoping I would talk you out of it, perhaps?"

"Hoping that I could resist when you tried," Anthony admitted. "I thought you would be the toughest. With the exception of my mother, of course, but she is in Italy." He asked after a moment, "What do you think her reaction will be?"

"Apoplexy," said Meyer succinctly. "Followed by death threats against me for failing to stop you."

"I'll write to her tonight," Anthony said, dreading the thought. "And what of Aunt Louisa and Uncle Eli? I suppose I must tell them as well."

"You must do more than that. You must persuade them, as you did me. Unless you fancy being abducted from your regiment by bank hirelings."

"Uncle Eli would never do anything of the sort!" Anthony was shocked.

His voice dry, Meyer said, "You think not? I assure you that in his own way he is just as ruthless as you accuse me of being."

That gave Anthony pause. What if Meyer had only been pretending to accept his decision to enlist? What if Anthony woke up tomorrow to find himself drugged and bound in the hold of a ship headed for the Antipodes? He shot his uncle an uneasy glance.

"I have renounced ruthlessness," Meyer reminded him. "You are safe from me, if not from the French army." He stood up. "Are you going to the bank? Now that I will have you to worry about as well as James, I think I would like to see those reports you mentioned. On our way we can stop by the house and you can tell your aunt Louisa what you have told me."

Anthony swallowed. "This morning?"

"Do you want her to hear it from someone else? I have already hinted to your uncle Eli that he might want to investigate those powder burns on your face."

"May I observe," said Anthony bitterly, "that in Italy I only have *one* parent?" But he stood up and put on his hat and gloves.

They were walking out together when Anthony suddenly remembered his other piece of news. "Oh, I stopped by the Harts's yesterday. Mrs. Hart accepted your gift."

Meyer stopped and turned around. "She did?" he said, looking both relieved and apprehensive.

"Yes, and I took the liberty of asking her whether you might call on her at some point."

Now his uncle looked even more apprehensive. "What did she say?"

"Nothing. But if I had to interpret her silence, I would translate it as 'not yet.'"

"Well," said Meyer, "that is better than the 'Over my dead body' silence, which is what I was expecting."

It was not until the morning after Anthony Roth's visit that Abigail finally got up her courage to look carefully at the book Meyer had sent. The note on the flyleaf had been so brief that she had begun to wonder whether there was not some other message inside—a loose sheet of paper folded between two pages, perhaps. Or something in the margin of one of the poems. She brought the volume down to breakfast with her, and made herself wait until she had looked at all of the post, including the bills. Only then did she pick it up and shake it. Nothing fell out. She flipped the pages. No pieces of paper appeared. No marginalia either. Perhaps the poems themselves were meant to be the message. Glancing up quickly to make sure that Fanny was still absorbed in the newspaper, she began to read.

The first poem, "She Walks in Beauty," was a love poem. It made her a bit uncomfortable, especially when it described the flowing hair of the beloved. The second poem, "The Harp the Monarch Minstrel Swept," was incomprehensible. The third seemed to be another love poem, in an almost sacrilegious vein. She stopped reading and began skimming. Then, increasingly uneasy, she turned back to the beginning and read every word on every page. It was not a long book.

An hour later she was on her way to find Meyer.

Sweelinck came to find Louisa in the kitchen, where she was consulting the cook about a new pastry recipe her niece Rachel had sent her. "I beg your pardon, madam," he said, "but there is a caller for Mr. Meyer."

"He has gone out," Louisa said. "I heard him tell you so myself. He is at his club and may not be back until this afternoon. If it is someone from Whitehall, send them on to the Traveller's, or ask them to leave a note." She turned back to the recipe, which seemed to be missing some key ingredient. She and the cook had both tried to roll out the dough, and it crumbled apart each time.

"The caller is a lady," Sweelinck said. "A Mrs. Hart."

Louisa turned around. "Mrs. Hart? Not Miss Hart?"

The butler's injured look told her that he did not make errors of that sort.

"I will be right up," she said, hastily looking around for something she could use to clean off the flour from her hands and bodice. "Put her in the bookroom. No, that is full of Eli's papers. The drawing room, then."

Sweelinck bowed and withdrew.

"Offer her some refreshments as well," Louisa called after him. One of the kitchen maids brought her a basin of water and she repaired the damage to her gown as best she could. But she felt harried and untidy as she arrived to greet her unexpected guest, and the sight of Abigail Hart did not make her feel any better.

Neat. That was how Louisa would describe her. Everything about her was neat. Her features were regular; her clothing impeccable; her hair smooth beneath a starched cap. She was sitting very carefully on the edge of a gold silk armchair, with her hands folded in her lap. Under her hands, centered precisely, was a small book. Then she looked up, and Louisa saw her eyes. They were wide and green and did not belong to the person who had chosen that modest gown and folded her hands over the book.

Abigail rose, setting the volume on an adjacent chair.

"Mrs. Hart?" Louisa hurried over. "Louisa Roth. My brother-in-law is from home, but I have been wanting to meet you; my nephew Anthony speaks of you often."

"I am sorry, I cannot stay." She looked nervous. "I only came by to return this book. Mr. Meyer gave it to me by mistake."

Louisa wisely did not ask why the book had not been sent with a footman. "Please do sit down, if only for a minute or so," she said. "I should have called weeks ago to thank you for your care of Anthony; you must at least allow me to do that much now."

Abigail sank back onto her chair.

"Were you offered anything? Would you care for some tea?"

"Yes." Then she corrected herself. "That is, yes, I was asked if I wished for anything. I am quite content as I am." A blatant lie, her folded hands were trembling slightly.

"Anthony tells me that you had quite a time of it in France," Louisa said. "What with his illness, and the soldiers, and the snow." Her phrasing was deliberately constructed to suggest that she knew many more details; in fact, those three words—illness, soldiers, snow—had been acquired only through patient sifting of Anthony's occasional offhand references combined with judicious consultation of newspaper reports.

"It was not very pleasant," her visitor admitted. "But it was certainly memorable."

"You had your daughter with you as well. That must have made you even more anxious."

The first hint of a smile softened Abigail Hart's face. "That is an understatement. When I saw Diana being held at gunpoint at that roadblock, I thought I would faint. Luckily Mr. Meyer remained calm, even when they stripped him and found all of his weapons."

Louisa tried in vain to think of some way to obtain the full story of this incident. No wonder none of the travelers had been willing to answer questions about what had happened. She gave the other woman an encouraging smile.

There was a pause. "Perhaps you are wondering about Diana," said her visitor. "In connection with your nephew, that is. He does call quite often, but I cannot say that I have seen any signs of a serious attachment. If something does come of it, it might reassure you to know that the Harts acknowledge Diana as a full member of the family, and have been very courteous to me as well. You need not fear that my divorce will harm her prospects in any way, in spite of the unusual circumstances."

Another tantalizingly incomplete piece of information. "What unusual circumstances?" Louisa wanted to ask. But her question was never spoken, because at that moment the door opened and Meyer came in, closely followed by her nephew Anthony.

"I beg your pardon, Louisa," Meyer said. "I know you have company, but when you have a moment Anthony has something rather urgent to tell you."

Then he saw who was with her.

It was hard to say who was more shaken. Abigail turned pale and half-rose from her seat. Meyer stopped so quickly that Anthony nearly ran into him. Glancing back and forth between her visitor and her brother-in-law, Louisa sighed. Something had indeed happened in France. She was looking at it. For once, Eli's matchmaking had produced some results; they were, unfortunately, not happy results.

Meyer recovered first. He gave the smallest possible inclination of his head, as though he were afraid to move more than a fraction of an inch.

Abigail answered with an equally restrained nod. "I stopped by to return the book," she said. Louisa could see her swallow. "It—it was very kind of you to think of me, but perhaps you should offer it to someone who will enjoy it more."

Louisa glanced down at the volume on the chair and recognized it at once. As clumsy as her husband was at matchmaking, her brother-in-law was evidently even clumsier at the rituals of courtship. What had he been thinking, to give such a gift to a woman like Abigail Hart? But then she suddenly realized what must have happened.

"Nathan," she said. "Did you *read* those poems before you gave Mrs. Hart the book?"

"No," he confessed. Alarmed, he asked, "Are they—unseemly? I thought Byron was very widely read. The bookseller assured me that the ladies who patronized his shop admired him greatly. And I was told that everything in this collection is based on the Bible."

"The poems are not improper, or not very much so." Louisa was groping for words to describe what happened when scripture and Byron were mixed. "It is just that the allusions to the Bible are very free. And it is all quite morbid; doomed love and battles and exile and death." Typical Byron, in other words. Obviously Meyer had never read him. "It might not be to everyone's taste," she added diplomatically.

"You found it offensive." Meyer addressed Abigail.

She hesitated. "Perhaps I did. I do not read very much poetry. I suppose I took Lord Byron's sentiments as representing yours. After what happened at Pont-Haut, to read about pure maidens and armies and dead patriots was not pleasant."

"Obviously I do not read much poetry either." His eyes caught hers. "I meant no insult," he said. "Please forgive me."

The silence that followed was so charged that Louisa almost expected Abigail to be drawn across the room to Meyer, like a piece of iron caught by a magnet.

Instead she wrenched her gaze away, turned, almost blindly, and picked up the book. "I am unused to modern verse," she said. "Fanny was right; I should not have been so quick to condemn what I did not understand. That is a far greater fault than offering someone an ill-chosen gift. Thank you for your hospitality, Mrs. Roth." And before anyone realized what she was doing, she was already at the door.

"Abigail, wait," Meyer said in a low voice, catching her arm. "The book is nothing. I should have sent you a note, but I was afraid you would not read it."

"I must go," she said faintly. She looked down at his hand on her sleeve as if not quite understanding what it was doing there.

He released her at once. "At least tell me that you are well."

"Yes, quite well." She did not, Louisa noticed, ask Meyer how he was.

"If I can do anything—if you need anything—"

"Thank you. You are very kind."

"Allow me to see you out," he said.

"No, please—" Her voice was trembling slightly.

He stepped back and held the door for her. After she had left he closed it again and stood leaning against it, his expression unreadable.

Louisa glanced at Anthony. He, too, was wearing the implausibly bland face males use to signal that questions on a certain topic are not welcome. She sighed inwardly and made a mental note to add "roadblock" and "Pont-Haut" to her list of items to be investigated. Then she turned her attention to her nephew. "You had something to tell me, Anthony?"

He shot a worried look at Meyer.

"Go ahead," said her brother-in-law. "I am not endorsing your decision—Miss Hart still looms a bit too large in the background for my comfort—but I do not oppose it either.

Frowning, she looked at Anthony. "What decision?"

"I am enlisting," Anthony said with an odd mixture of embarrassment and defiance. "In an infantry regiment." He added, half under his breath, "And it is *not* because of Diana."

Louisa was beginning to wish that Eli had never heard of Joshua Hart's beautiful cousin and her daughter. Abigail Hart was making Nathan so unhappy that he had resigned from the army, and now her daughter had provoked Anthony into joining. At least, she thought, this latest news would cure her husband of interfering in Nathan Meyer's love life. Permanently.

22

The sky on this sixth day of June arched in a cloudless blue band over the parade ground behind the Horse Guards, and the assembled soldiers looked very impressive as they stood at attention under the midday sun. Their trousers were pristine white, their boots and tall hats gleaming black. Weapons, carefully polished, were held at precisely the same angle by doll-like men in neat rows.

"They are nearly all recruits," said Martha to Diana in an undertone. She sounded disappointed. Diana had learned more about the British army in the half hour they had stood here than in her entire lifetime. As they had watched the latest batch of troops muster for transport to Belgium, Martha had issued a series of pronouncements. Veterans were good; recruits were bad. Infantry were good; cavalry were bad (this in spite of Martha's brother Charles, who was in the Light Dragoons and was the family black sheep as a result). Officers promoted on the field were good; spoiled aristocrats who bought commissions were bad.

"How can you tell?" Diana thought the men looked magnificent. They looked, in fact, exactly as she thought soldiers *should* look. Orderly. Disciplined. Nothing like the patrol of Frenchmen who had stopped their party on the road to Gap: unshaven and dirty, wearing bits of old uniforms.

"All their gear is new." Martha nodded towards a sergeant standing to one side. "That man is a veteran. Look at his uniform."

Diana had not even realized the man was in uniform. His red jacket had faded to a rusty brown; his trousers were gray with dirt, and his hat was a different shape from the tall shakos of the men beside him. "Where is your brother, then?" Charles Woodley was most definitely a veteran.

"He's just come in, at the back, with the cavalry." Martha pointed to a line of horsemen at the far end of the parade ground. "Second to last on the left. He's hoping to make captain this time. He was almost promoted last spring, but then Bonaparte abdicated and they put everyone on half pay."

"He does look a bit shabby," Diana conceded, accepting her friend's strangely inverted notions of proper military appearance. "Why is he blue instead of red?"

"He is a Light Dragoon," explained Martha. "They wear blue. The regular Dragoons wear red. And the infantry. You can tell which regiment by the trim. Charles is in the 19th; they have yellow trim."

"Are those men in your brother's regiment, then?" Diana indicated a group of foot soldiers in red coats with yellow trim standing nearly opposite them.

"No, no, those are infantry," Martha said, very patient with her new pupil. "Infantry and cavalry are never in the same regiment. It is just a coincidence that—" She stopped, peered more closely at the line of men, then turned to Diana. "Isn't that your friend Mr. Roth?" She was pointing to a soldier in the second row. He was difficult to see clearly, because the man in front of him was taller.

Diana looked, more out of curiosity than out of any real belief that Anthony Roth would suddenly appear in a scarlet jacket in the middle of a battalion on parade. "It does look like Anthony," she admitted. "But of course it cannot be him."

Her friend raised one eyebrow. "So, it is Anthony now? Does he call you Diana?"

"Sometimes," Diana said, adjusting her parasol to give Martha more shade. The parasol was, in fact, a gift from Roth. He had given one to both her mother and Fanny at the same time.

Martha frowned. "Are you sure it is not him? He is looking at you as though he recognizes you."

It was an absurd notion, that Roth could be here in that mass of soldiers. But as the line of men shifted slightly, she caught a glimpse of the fine-boned face beneath the shako. For a moment shocked blue eyes met hers, and she suddenly understood with a sick lurch of her stomach that however absurd the notion might be, Anthony Roth was in fact standing in front of her and was about to be shipped off to Belgium.

Panicking, she clutched her friend's shoulder. "Martha! It *is* him! What shall I do?"

"What do you mean?"

"He's going to Belgium! You said they were sailing this evening!" Her imagination immediately presented her with a picture of Anthony lying on a

battlefield, breathing her name as he expired in a
pool of blood. "He called yesterday and I wasn't
even *home*," she said frantically. "Can we not stop
him from going? I am sure he should not go!"

"He is an enlisted man," Martha pointed out. "He
can't leave now; that would be desertion. Besides,
he must want to go, or he would not have signed
on." She gave Diana a sympathetic look. "It is hard
to watch them march away, though. My mother
stopped going for a while; she said that if anything
happened she wanted to remember my father at
home and not in the middle of a line of men in uniforms. But then she decided she was being morbid."

The men were wheeling in crisp, angled movements. A band had started playing. In a moment
the troops would be marching off through the
archway. "What if we wanted to say good-bye? Can
we go and find them somewhere before they leave
London?"

Martha looked over at the elderly manservant
who had accompanied them. "Samuel, is there
someplace Miss Hart might be able to go to speak
with one of the enlisted men?"

He shook his head. "They're being taken off by
barge, Miss Martha. I reckon most of the women-
folk said their farewells this morning outside the
barracks."

"Can I write, then?" Diana was a terrible corre-
spondent, but it suddenly seemed very important
to her to say something—anything—to Roth before
he met the doom she was sure awaited him. Even
if it had to be in writing rather than in person.

"You can if you know how to direct your letter,"
Martha said. "What regiment is that?" she asked

the servant as the long lines of scarlet-coated men filed past.

"Those first two ranks? The 44th." He eyed the lines disapprovingly. "Not a very promising lot, as your pa would say, miss."

"The 44th," Diana muttered, trying to memorize it. Two fours. That was not hard to remember. She had no idea how one sent a letter to a soldier serving abroad, but evidently the regiment number was important. Then she realized that she had the means to get Anthony at least one letter right away. "Martha!" She tugged on her arm. "Will you take a letter with you? When you go to Belgium next week?" Mrs. Woodley, like many army wives, had hired a house in Brussels for a month. No one expected Napoleon to attack before the middle of July, and Martha's mother had decided that it was worth the inconvenience of moving the household across the Channel and back to maintain some semblance of family life for another four weeks.

"Of course I will," Martha said warmly. "Even if Mr. Roth's regiment is not billeted in Brussels, it will be far easier to send it on from headquarters there than from here." The last columns were filing off the ground now, and the two girls started to walk back towards the park. Martha paused as another possibility occurred to her. "Eleanor is coming with us," she said hesitantly. "You don't suppose your mother would let you come as well? Just for a few weeks?"

At once Diana knew that the dearest wish of her heart was to go to Brussels with Martha Woodley. Abigail, of course, would chain Diana in her room if she so much as mentioned the idea of stepping on the same continent as French troops. But Diana did not say anything of the sort. "Oh, I am sure she would agree," she said promptly. "She has always wanted me to travel." That, at least was true. Or had been true, until their ill-fated stay in France. "But do you think your mother would be willing to invite me?"

"I don't know." Martha frowned. "Perhaps if I told her about Mr. Roth. She followed my father to India, you know, when they were first married, even though both her parents and my father's parents had told her not to go."

"You mustn't tell anyone this, but Anthony and I had hoped to be engaged," Diana said, allowing a small tear to form in the corner of one eye. Another lie. She had sometimes, it was true, wondered whether Anthony Roth would make a good husband. She had also wondered whether he even liked her any longer.

"Oh my," breathed Martha, completely swept away by this image of doomed romance. She seized Diana's hand. "I will ask her," she promised. "Tonight. And if she says yes, I will come and tell you tomorrow morning."

"Not tomorrow," said Diana quickly. "We will not be at home. Come Thursday." Thursday morning, as it happened, her mother was going with Fanny to call on an elderly relative of Fanny's late husband. Abigail did not even bother to ask Diana to accompany her to Miss Asher's any longer; she disliked her quite as much as Diana did and only went out of affection for her longtime companion.

If Abigail could have seen Diana now, could have seen the narrowing of her eyes and the slight jut of her chin, she would have known that her daughter was planning mischief. But Martha, walking beside her friend, saw only what Diana wanted her to see: the patient, wistful face of a girl hoping to embrace her beloved one more time before he went into battle.

Louisa Roth had also gone to see the troops assemble for departure, with very mixed feelings. Her husband was still furious about the whole enlistment affair, and alternated between blaming Anthony, Meyer, and himself. She had not even ventured to suggest that he escort her; instead, she asked Meyer, who seemed to think she was imposing this duty as some sort of penance. He stood at her side through the entire ceremony, answering her questions courteously but making no conversation otherwise. The only time he showed any sign of real interest was at the very end, when he suddenly turned to stare after two girls who were walking away in the opposite direction, arms linked.

"I might have known," he muttered.

Louisa squinted at the receding figures. "Who are they?"

"I don't know who the taller one is, but the shorter one is Diana Hart."

At that distance, in the glare of the open field, Louisa could form only a vague impression of a slender, fashionably dressed young woman. "What is she like?"

"Very pretty, but otherwise not at all like her mother," he said dryly. "Capricious, theatrical, well aware of her own beauty and its effect on men of all ages." He paused, then added, "No, I must amend that. She is a bit vain and spoiled, but she is also fearless and she is surprisingly capable of sympathy for someone as indulged and sheltered as she has been. On the worst day of our journey, when we were crossing the Col Bayard, Anthony would not have made it over the pass if not for her."

The two girls were almost out of sight now. "Do you suppose she was here to see Anthony off?" Louisa asked.

"I am sure of it. And if you are about to ask me what her feelings are for Anthony, or his for her, I can only say that I believe they are no more capable of answering that question than I am, at least at the moment."

"He has been calling to see her quite often," Louisa observed.

"So he told me."

"And what of you? Have you seen Mrs. Hart recently?"

"No, not recently." He offered her his arm. "Shall we go and find the carriage?"

The first part of the ride was accomplished in silence, but Meyer was clearly holding some sort of internal debate. He kept glancing at Louisa, then looking away. Finally, when they were nearly home, he said abruptly, "Louisa, may I ask your advice on something?"

She had been lost in her own reflections, but now she looked up. "What sort of advice?"

He frowned down at his hands, which were clenched in his lap. "On etiquette."

She did not think he wanted to know about the correct forms for place settings at a formal dinner. "General advice? Or advice about a particular problem?"

"Both. Neither. Perhaps etiquette is the wrong word." He was now examining the door handle. "You saw how Mrs. Hart reacted to my imprudent attempt at a gift."

She made a small, neutral noise.

"I have made a mess of things, Louisa," he said, his eyes still fixed on the door handle. "And I don't know how to go back and start over."

She remembered his face when he had caught Abigail Hart's arm. She remembered Abigail's desperate reaction. She asked herself whether she wanted to encourage her brother-in-law to pursue a woman like Abigail Hart and found, to her surprise, that the answer was yes. "Nathan, you cannot start over," she said gently. "You have to go on from where you are."

"I don't *know* where I am."

Louisa asked the question that no one, so far, had been willing to answer. "What happened? What happened after you met the Harts in France?"

He gave a small, unhappy smile. "Would you like the long version or the short version?"

"Short." She sat back so that she could look at him more easily. His dark head was bent in profile against the window. She noted with detachment that a haggard, confused Nathan was just as good-looking as the self-possessed version more normally on display.

"I followed my usual program of lies and manipulation, and Mrs. Hart took exception."

"That was a bit too short," she said, her voice dry. "I suspect your answer needs to be at least detailed enough to contain the name Pont-Haut, for example."

Startled, he looked up. "You know about that?"

"Only what Mrs. Hart said."

He sighed. "Pont-Haut is the site of an important bridge south of Grenoble. I tried to blow it up ahead of Bonaparte's troops, although doing so would have placed Mrs. Hart and her daughter at considerable risk. Even before that, I had been using the two women as camouflage while I reconnoitered and sent off dispatches. At any rate, when the French caught me at the bridge, they forced me—and everyone in my party—to proceed under military escort the rest of the way to Grenoble. Picture Mrs. Hart traveling with her eighteen-year-old daughter in the midst of fifteen hundred soldiers, and you will have some idea of the consequences of my actions."

His answer dismayed her, and it must have shown in her face, because he returned to his contemplation of the door handle. "There is no going on from that particular place on the map, is there?" he said in a low voice. "I burned the proverbial bridge instead of the real one."

"I don't think Mrs. Hart is indifferent to you," she said cautiously. "From what I saw last week."

"Oh, she told me herself that she finds me attractive and engaging." His eyes glittered. "Also that I am unscrupulous, immoral, and personally responsible for the death of every soldier whose commander makes use of the information I supply to the army."

There was no use telling Meyer that a self-contained woman like Abigail Hart would never have said half of those things if she had not been afraid of her own feelings for the villain of her speech. He would not believe it, and in any case, it would not solve his problem.

"I do not have much in the way of advice to offer you," she said. "I do think that if you try to court her openly, she will reject you. For one thing, she is very reserved. For another, you violated her trust, and pursuit will seem like a threat rather than a compliment."

"You recommend patience, then."

"Yes, you must let her come to you."

He shook his head. "She will never do so."

"Nathan," she said, exasperated, "she already *did* do so. She accepted the book from Anthony, did she not? When she decided to return it, she came in person rather than sending it with a footman. And in the end she changed her mind and kept it! You can hardly expect more, at this stage. In time she will understand why you acted as you did."

"No, I don't believe she will ever understand. Her principles are too rigid to accommodate a suitor of dubious virtue—spies falling decidedly on the dubious end of the scale."

She said sharply, "Abigail Hart is hardly in a position to criticize the virtue of others."

He stiffened. "What do you mean by that?"

So, he had not known. Eli had not known either. The Harts kept their family secrets very well guarded. The divorce had been obtained as quickly as possible, and Abigail had retired to live in seclusion with a companion. "Mrs. Hart comes by that title not once, but twice. She was married first to the older brother, Paul. When he died within a year or so of their wedding, she begged Aaron Hart to follow the ancient practice in the case of childless widows and offer her marriage."

"But no one observes that practice any longer!"

he said, startled. "Not for centuries! The brother always refuses to make the offer, and the widow goes through the ceremony of spitting on him, and both are free."

"She went to her rabbi. She argued that Paul was a pious and wealthy man and deserved to have an heir. If she married Aaron, rather than someone else, our law would deem any son to be Paul's, and the boy could inherit. Somehow she persuaded him. I believe the Harts supported her request, and they are a powerful family."

"And then her second husband died? Diana's father?" He clearly did not understand how this story supported her accusation. Levirate marriage was frowned upon, but if the rabbi gave permission it could hardly be called immoral. "No, I remember now. There was a divorce. But I cannot think Mrs. Hart was at fault there."

"You may judge for yourself who was at fault," she said. "Aaron Hart found her in their bedroom with another man."

23

Anthony had been in Belgium for a week and had never been so bored, or so exhausted. The new troops were being drilled for hours every day, often under the amused eyes of loafing veterans. If you were bone-weary, it only made it worse to look up from your seventh attempt to form square and see a half dozen old soldiers sitting nearby, smoking pipes and making acerbic comments in voices just soft enough to pass for conversation rather than shouted insult. And on top of the drills, Anthony was serving as a messenger. His colonel had discovered that Anthony spoke German and sent him regularly to the German-speaking officers of the Duke of Brunswick with queries. He had even been dispatched with messages to the Prussians, who were fifteen miles away. After thirty miles on horseback Anthony was barely able to walk before finally collapsing onto his bedroll.

It was tiring, too, to feel constantly as though he did not belong. His fellow soldiers were suspicious of both his religion and his wealth. He had thought

that the latter, at least, would not be all that notice-
able, but the first time he put on his glasses, one of
the corporals had peered at him and said incredulously, "Are those gold?" Which, of course, they
were. The corporal had proceeded to empty out Anthony's entire kit, commenting on the luxurious
nature of all the personal items, and ridiculing him
in particular for bringing several books with him,
which, as the corporal correctly pointed out, were
adding at least five pounds to the weight he carried.
The one thing that saved him from complete os-
tracism was the story of his journey through France.
The other men in his battalion boasted of him to
less-fortunate regiments. How many English soldiers
could claim to have been a mere seven miles from
Bonaparte when he had landed again in France? Or
to have crossed the Alps ahead of his army?

When Anthony walked through the streets of
Brussels, on the other hand, he suffered from the
opposite problem. The city was full of English visitors. He had expected that some officers and
diplomats would have their families with them; he
had not expected that hundreds of wealthy aristocrats would have moved their entire households to
Brussels for the summer. After six years of working
in Italy and London, he had a fairly broad circle of
acquaintances: clients from the bank, patrons of
charities the Roth family supported. He learned
quickly not to bother nodding to any of them if he
spotted them in the Upper Town. Enlisted men
were, like children, meant to be seen and not heard.
Also like children, they were generally assumed to
be nearly illiterate, and whenever he spoke German

or French the reaction was astonishment or even ir-ritation, as if some unwritten law had been violated.

It seemed likely that he had many more weeks of boredom and fatigue waiting for him. Napoleon was gathering troops on the northern border of France, but no one believed he would be ready to move before the middle of July. Anthony was not unhappy, however. He was beginning to under-stand that he had never truly ventured out on his own before. Growing up in London, he had been with his family constantly. He had been tutored at home, since the better schools did not accept Jewish pupils; subsequently, his father and his uncle Eli had supervised him at the bank. Even after the establishment of a branch in Italy had required An-thony to travel back and forth between London and Naples, he had always been accompanied by Battista, who was in essence a Catholic, male exten-sion of Anthony's mother. When Anthony had sent the servant off ten days ago he had felt like a pris-oner released from jail.

At the moment Anthony himself was playing ser-vant. The Duchess of Richmond was giving a ball in her rented house near the Botanical Gardens, and Anthony's colonel, recollecting his talents as a trans-lator, had suggested him for sentry duty: a glorified term for acting as an unpaid footman. He had now been standing at attention for three hours, watch-ing a procession of officers in full-dress regimentals parade into the house. The music had started right after Anthony had taken up his post, but he was not sure how much dancing there would be. From what he had seen, there were ten men for every woman in the ballroom at the back of the house.

After several days of relentless drilling, it was quite pleasant to form one of the Duchess's human ornaments at the entrance to her ball. He entertained himself and his companions by guessing the nationalities of the guests before they were announced. Unlike his fellow sentries, he was hopelessly ignorant about the various uniforms; he could barely even remember, in his own regiment, which piece of braid on a jacket indicated which rank. But he astonished the others with his ability to identify the women by their clothing and hairstyle. He won several bets before his comrades realized that the odds were against them and stopped wagering. Unfortunately, once Wellington arrived, the flow of guests slowed to a trickle, and Anthony began to grow restless, wondering when he was due to be relieved.

The first hint that there was anything wrong came when a group of officers clattered up on horseback. They were not dressed for a ball. Two of them, in fact, were filthy, and their horses were stumbling with exhaustion.

"Is the Duke inside?" asked the lead rider, without dismounting.

"Yes, sir," said the corporal in charge of the sentries.

The rider nodded to another man, who swung off his horse and handed the reins to Anthony.

"Sir! You can't go in like that!" protested the corporal belatedly as the grimy officer headed into the house. "You haven't an invitation!"

The man turned and held up a sweat-soaked packet of paper. "Urgent dispatches," he said. "That's my invitation." He vanished through the door.

"Why do you suppose they are here?" Anthony asked another sentry in a low voice, jerking his head at the riders. They still had not dismounted.

"God knows," said his informant. "Could be the real thing, could be a false alarm. Before you lot came we had a message the French were going to steal around our right flank and cut off our supplies from Ostend; there was a right panic at that one."

But the sentries closest to the street were breaking ranks and murmuring to each other, and one of the riders, overhearing Anthony's companion, leaned over and said quietly, "This is the real thing, all right. Boney crossed the border twelve hours ago. We'll be marching before dawn."

The horse Anthony was holding sidled and backed a few paces. "Here, you!" said another mounted officer to Anthony. "Mind what you're about; he's trampling the Duchess's shrubbery." Then he caught his breath and leaned forward in the saddle. "Anthony?" he asked incredulously.

It was Anthony's cousin James.

Anthony had known, as an abstract notion, that he might encounter his cousin. Their regiments were in the same division. But an abstract notion was one thing; James looming over him on his horse at the very moment he had learned that he was to fight tomorrow was something else. He was miserably aware that James was mounted and he was on foot, that James was an officer and he was a private, and that James had been in countless battles while he had never fired a shot at a living creature in his life.

"What are you doing here?" demanded his cousin.

"Sentry duty. Sir."

"Don't 'sir' me," snapped James. He dismounted in one quick leap and handed both his horse and the one Anthony had been holding to another sentry. Then he hauled Anthony into the partially mauled shrubbery bed. "I thought you were going back to Italy," he said.

"I changed my mind."

His cousin raised one eyebrow. "From banker to infantryman. A dramatic transformation."

"At least I kept my own name," Anthony said coldly. "And my religion."

That produced a scowl. "Does my father know about this?"

Anthony lost his temper. "What business is it of yours what I do or who knows of it?" he asked, nearly shouting. "In case you had forgotten, I'm two years older than you are and have double your shares in the bank! I don't care if you are a goddamned captain; I don't have to answer to you—or my uncle—for my actions. Now get out of my way; I'm on duty. You have no authority to relieve me." Shoving past his cousin, he resumed his stance by the door, still shaking slightly with the force of his anger. When his unit was hastily dismissed and sent back to quarters to prepare to move south, he did not even look to see if James was still there.

Nothing could have endeared Anthony more to his fellow soldiers than that defiant confrontation. Their meek little banker had routed an officer— not just any officer, but a captain from their hated rivals in the 95th. The catcalls and cheerful congratulations enlivened the tedious business of packing and checking weapons and lining up for ammunition, and persisted as the company began to march south. Even Pack, the brigade's general, somehow got wind of the affair and came by to warn Anthony's lieutenant with mock solemnity that one of his men appeared to have a dangerous tendency to insubordination.

Only at the first halt did Anthony suddenly realize what was happening. He was on his way to battle.

For several days Meyer felt uncomfortable every time he saw his sister-in-law. He was unaccustomed to asking advice from anyone, at least on personal matters. On the few occasions when he had done so, it had been his daughter, Rachel, who had been his confidante. But Rachel was currently in Portsmouth waiting for her husband's regiment to return from Louisiana, and even if she had been nearby, he doubted whether he would have been willing to consult her about her potential step-mother. It had been a momentary impulse to confide in Louisa during the carriage ride, and more than once he wished the words unspoken. In his more rational moments he trusted her to keep his confidence from everyone except her husband, and he suspected that the sharp-eyed Eli would not be very surprised by what she reported. In his irrational moments, however, he pictured Louisa and Eli sharing the story with everyone in the family: the arrogant Nathan Meyer humbled at last, reduced to begging his sister-in-law for help with his wooing.

Since he had paid a high price in embarrassment for Louisa's advice, he was determined to follow it. He scrupulously avoided the neighborhood of

Goodman's Fields. He no longer wandered into jewelers just in case he might see something tasteful set with emeralds. He had sent Rodrigo away in part because of his infuriatingly correct predictions; now he wrote to him in Amsterdam and recalled him from his trumped-up assignment. His servant believed Louisa to be the wisest woman in England; he would endorse her recommendation wholeheartedly and would stop Meyer from doing anything rash if his resolution faltered.

He resumed his work at the Tower. There was an uneasy truce between him and White. Both men were civil, but there was a tension there. Meyer knew the colonel well; it would be a long time before White would even consider apologizing. It might be simpler if Meyer did it first, but he delayed. If he apologized the next logical step would be to volunteer to go to Brussels. It was one thing to comply with Louisa's suggestion and wait for Abigail to soften towards him. It was another thing to be in Belgium if she finally did soften.

Late one Friday evening he was sitting in his study. For once he was at his desk instead of on the stool by the fireplace; he was reading the latest report sent by the bank couriers from Brussels. These usually arrived several days ahead of the official army reports and often included information omitted from the latter; this one, for example, reported that friction between Wellington and some of the other Allied commanders continued to create minor problems in the disposition of the forces. He felt a small twinge of guilt. Had he accepted White's assignment, he might have prevented the latest incident, which involved one of the Prussian generals.

When he heard a knock he assumed it was Eli. No one else would disturb him at this hour. He grunted a command to come in and when the door did not open he got up, exasperated, and opened it himself.

The Roths's night porter, a stout older man named Bullin, hovered uncertainly in the doorway. It must be later than Meyer had thought; Sweelinck usually stayed on duty until eleven or so. "Yes, what is it, Bullin?" he asked curtly.

"A lady to see you, Mr. Meyer," said the porter. He looked very unhappy. Couriers arrived at the Roth house at all hours; ladies were another matter. "Says to beg your pardon, but it is very urgent."

He knew at once who it was. At this hour, on the Sabbath, something terrible must have happened to bring her here.

"Where is she?" he demanded. Without waiting for the answer he was already headed towards the front of the house. He rounded the corner at a near-run and saw Abigail standing in the front hall, twisting her hands nervously in the folds of her pelisse. Her face was so pale he thought she was about to faint.

When she saw him, she gave a little cry, started forward, and then stopped. "Please forgive me," she said. "I didn't know what to do—you said to ask you if I needed help—I don't know how to find her—"

He forgot all about Louisa's advice to be cautious, to take things slowly. In two strides he had caught her in his arms.

* * *

Abigail had not suspected that anything was wrong until dinnertime. At this time of year, sunset (and therefore the Sabbath meal) was quite late. As a result it had been nine o'clock before Abigail and Fanny realized that Diana was not in the house, and even then, since it was still light out, they were not very concerned at first. Rosie was summoned; she had not seen Diana since just after luncheon. Perhaps she had gone for a walk.

Abigail questioned the other servants. If Diana had gone walking, she had gone unaccompanied. None of the servants reported being asked to escort her. No one had seen her leave. No invitations had arrived; no callers had stopped in after lunch.

"She has stayed late at a friend's house and has forgotten to send word," Fanny suggested. She was beginning to sound anxious.

Abigail turned to the maid. "Rosie, did you see anything odd when you looked in her room just now?"

"It was a bit untidy," Rosie said hesitatingly. "And her wardrobe was open."

Untidy might not mean much, given Diana's habits. Until an exasperated Abigail had limited her daughter to one round of maid service every morning, the staff had sometimes felt compelled to clean her bedchamber and parlor every few hours. The open wardrobe was another story, however. She ran up the two flights to Diana's suite with her heart pounding against her ribs like a giant mallet.

She could tell at once that the chaos had an urgent quality to it very different from Diana's usual carelessness. It was not as easy as it had been in France to determine what was missing—her daughter had a very ample wardrobe—but after a preliminary inventory it became clear that Diana had not simply ventured out for a walk. In addition to the dress she had been wearing two others were gone; she had also taken half boots, two pairs of slippers, and a nightgown. All her chemises and pairs of drawers remained, however—incontrovertible proof that Diana herself had done the packing. Wherever she had gone, she would not have any clean linens when she got there.

Abigail sank down onto the bed and put her head in her hands. "Couldn't she even leave a note?" she asked, despairing.

The practical Fanny was looking at the scraps of paper in Diana's grate to see if the note had been discarded by mistake. She did not find a letter, but she did find a packing list in Diana's handwriting: *new bonnet, two prs shoes, ostrich fan, nightclths, pink muslin, perhps yellow, shawl, gloves, jwlry.* This last prompted Rosie to search Diana's trinket box, which proved to be virtually empty. Diana's father had been very generous; Abigail realized unhappily that her daughter was probably carrying enough money in jewels to run away to the other side of the world, if she chose.

By this time it was almost ten o'clock. Abigail went back downstairs and sent out the footman to make enquiries in the neighborhood. Then she paced back and forth in the front hall until he returned. He had very little to report. The kitchen maid at Number Fifteen *might* have seen a young lady carrying a bandbox walking briskly west just after noon. But she could not be sure.

Abigail sent him out again, this time accompanied by the coachman, with instructions to proceed towards Cornhill and see if they could find any traces of her. They left with a list of possibilities that would have daunted a Bow Street runner: taverns, hackney stands, stagecoach inns, shipping agents, and jewelers. The last was Fanny's suggestion; presumably Diana would need to sell some of her treasures to obtain cash.

The letter arrived at half-past ten, delivered by a postboy. Her first reaction was relief to have news—any news. Then she read the letter more carefully.

Dearest Mother,

I hope this finds you well and Fanny also. I discovered last week that Mr. Roth has enlisted in the army and I must go to Belgium now to be with him in case there is a battle. You need not worry, because I am very well chaperoned (the word very was heavily underlined) *and will be back within a few weeks. I forgot to pack clean linens and my tooth-powder has accidentally become soaked with cologne, but it will be far easier to buy new things than to send anything after me, so pray do not trouble yourself. I will write again from Brussels and I remain*

Your loving daughter,

Diana

Abigail closed her eyes. Not content with the fifteen hundred soldiers who had escorted them to Grenoble, Diana was now headed, alone and unprotected, for a city that currently housed eighty thousand soldiers. She opened her eyes just in time to see the postboy collecting his fee from Fanny and heading for the door. "Wait!" she cried, hurrying after him. She asked the poor messenger so many questions so quickly that he began to look dizzy, but a pint of ale and a few coins remedied her error. After that she let Fanny ask the questions.

His name was Will and he was a postboy at the Crown and Eagle, on the Dover road. The message had been given him by a young lady at about six this evening. Fanny asked him what the young lady looked like; he gave an accurate (and very admiring) description of Diana. Was she traveling alone? He couldn't say; the coffee room at the inn had been very crowded. Did she look unhappy, or frightened? (This was Abigail's question.) No indeed, she had been very cheerful and had told him her mother would pay him very well for the message. Abigail more than fulfilled this prophecy and then, reluctantly, let the person who had seen her daughter last leave the house.

Nothing Fanny said could convince her that some immediate action was not necessary. Yes, the runaway had an eight hours' start; that made it all the more imperative to leave at once. Yes, Diana might send a second letter with more information. Fanny would please forward it on to her at once, for Fanny, of course, must stay at home in case Diana returned. There was no point urging Abigail to rest or to wait for morning; Diana was in danger every minute Abigail delayed. Her daughter's idea of a chaperone was likely some woman she met on the stagecoach who was not even going to Brussels, and the idea of Diana alone in a foreign city on the brink of war was insupportable.

Fanny tried one last time. Surely Abigail was not planning to travel by herself to Belgium? That was as foolish as what Diana had done. What would she do when she arrived? How would she find Anthony Roth—the only clue to Diana's location in Brussels—among the thousands of soldiers assembled there?

That was when Abigail had realized that there was someone who could help her, someone who knew how to travel quickly at night, someone who could find one soldier—or one runaway girl—in a foreign city. Her coachman and footman had not yet returned, but it was less than a mile to the Roths's house. She had run up to her room, snatched her pelisse and bonnet, and paused only to tell the horrified Rosie where she was going before running back downstairs and out into the night.

Fifteen minutes later she was at the door of the Roths's town house, trembling and out of breath. The servant who admitted her surveyed her very dubiously before agreeing to fetch Mr. Meyer. Some part of her knew that she should have sent a messenger rather than coming herself, should have at least brought a maid. She did not care. The only thing she wanted was to be in Brussels as quickly as possible.

She heard a murmur of voices; heard quick footsteps coming into the hall; saw a tall, familiar figure, blurred through a film of unshed tears. She started to explain why she was there, but her sentences were broken and disjointed; she could barely speak without choking. And then two strong arms were around her; her head was resting on something reassuringly solid and warm; a deep voice was repeating her name gently, telling her that everything would be all right.

For years she had been the responsible one, had been careful and sensible, always calm and correct, as if she could prove by her behavior that she was not as fragile and uncertain as she felt inside. Now she was tired of pretending. She let him hold her. She let the tears fall. She let herself imagine that she was not alone.

24

Henrietta Woodley was clearly suspicious of her daughter's friend, and Diana, in all fairness, could hardly blame her. Diana had been afraid to attempt an extended letter in her mother's handwriting, so the forged reply to the Woodleys invitation was almost insulting in its brevity. The tale of the broken carriage pole, which she used to justify her arrival at the Woodley's in a hackney cab—and her lack of a portmanteau—had not stretched to explain why no maid or footman had accompanied her across London. And the small bag she had brought with her horrified the practical Mrs. Woodley by its contents or, rather, lack of contents. Diana had assured her hostess that her trunk would find them at Dover, but to her secret relief Martha had been ordered to provide a spare set of linens "just in case" Diana's own luggage failed to appear.

If there had been more time for questions, Diana's brittle network of lies might have collapsed then and there, but fortunately for Diana there was no time. Within an hour of her arrival, the Woodleys had set out for Dover in two coaches; they had made only the briefest of halts on the road and instead of staying overnight at the port, as Diana had expected, they had embarked at once to take advantage of favorable wind and tide. By then it was so late that everyone had retired immediately to their cabins and attempted to sleep. As a result, Mrs. Woodley was not able to act on her suspicions until the following morning, as the ship was coming into port.

When Martha appeared, looking rather nervous, and stammered that her mother wanted to see Diana in her cabin, Diana did feel a twinge of anxiety. She told herself firmly that it would be far too much trouble now for Mrs. Woodley to send her home, that the worst she could expect was a scolding. So she stepped into the adjacent cabin, hoping her fears were unjustified but resolved to take her chastisement meekly if necessary. A little voice at the back of her head was warning her that what she had done was far more serious than a schoolgirl prank, and that this would be no ordinary scolding. She tried to ignore that voice.

Mrs. Woodley was seated on her berth, frowning down at a letter. Diana had an uneasy feeling that she recognized it.

"Good morning, ma'am," she said. "Martha said you wished to see me?"

"There is one," muttered Mrs. Woodley, peering at the letter. She looked up. "Miss Roth, how do you spell 'obliged'?"

Flustered, Diana did her best to produce the correct spelling. She was not sure if the word had one *d* or two. Evidently it had only one, because Mrs. Woodley winced when she inserted one after the *i*.

"I cannot think how I came to insult your mother so dreadfully," was Mrs. Woodley's comment as Diana fell silent. She held up the forged letter. "I had met her several times, and I was still prepared to believe that she was both discourteous and illiterate. She did not write this, did she?"

Diana dropped her eyes. The enormity of what she had done was becoming clearer every moment.

"Does she even know you are here? Did you leave her a note?"

"I sent her a letter from the inn yesterday," Diana said in a small voice.

"Have you any notion of what she must have suffered when she found you gone?"

No response was expected, but Diana for some reason found herself remembering the old days— they were not so very long ago—when she had been allowed to see her mother only twice a year. In particular she was remembering the tight, frozen look on her mother's face whenever it was time to say good-bye.

Mrs. Woodley sighed. "I should have trusted my own judgment more. Do you know what I thought when I first met you?"

Diana bit her lip. "No."

"I thought you were too pretty for your own good, and I was right. You are not much used to hearing the word 'no,' are you? You wanted to come to Brussels, and your mother said no, and so you have made me and my daughter accomplices in fraud."

"She didn't say no," said Diana fiercely. She blinked back tears. "I did not ask her, because I *knew* she would never agree. She hates soldiers and she hates war and after what happened in France she hates them even more, and she doesn't care that Anthony enlisted and I was not even able to say good-bye."

"So that part, at least, was not a lie," Mrs. Woodley said. "There is actually an Anthony."

"He is a private." Her voice wobbled only very slightly. "In an infantry regiment."

The older woman looked at her sternly and held up the forged letter. "Did Martha know about this?"

"No! No!" Diana willed her to believe it. "I swear it!"

"Well, that is something, at any rate." She sighed and put it down. "I must send you home, of course, and it will be very inconvenient. We have only the two servants with us. I suppose we will have to hire someone in Ostend to escort you back. Or perhaps one of the wives I know from the regiment will be traveling home."

Diana was stunned. "You are going to send me home?" she said, half-disbelieving. It had never occurred to her that Martha's mother would share most of Abigail's views on proper behavior. Diana had thought that her mother was unusually strict. She was beginning to understand that the opposite was true: her father had been unusually permissive.

"Of course." Mrs. Woodley looked stern. "Apart from my obligation to return you to your family as quickly as possible, I do not care to have you keep company with my daughter and my niece."

As painful as the thought of her mother's anxiety had been, this was even more painful. Guilt was familiar to Diana. Shame was not.

"For the moment," Mrs. Woodley went on, "I am

afraid I must lock you in my cabin. We are just coming into Ostend now, and I cannot take the chance that you would run off and find the Belgian version of a hackney cab. I will return as soon as I can discover what arrangements can be made for you."

Diana wanted to object, to argue, to promise to behave, to beg for a reprieve. But before she could say anything, Mrs. Woodley had gone. She heard the lock protest as it was forced home, and then, to add to her humiliation, Mrs. Woodley's voice giving orders to a seaman that no one was to let Miss Hart out of her cabin for any reason whatsoever until she returned.

She sat in the cabin for what seemed like hours. At first she got up eagerly whenever she heard footsteps or voices, but after a while she realized that on a small packet like this one she would hear every sailor or passenger who walked anywhere nearby. As the ship was warped in to the dock, those noises were added to the confusion. She gave up and lay down on the bed, feeling wretched. Somehow her own picture of this voyage as a heroic adventure was impossible to recapture after Mrs. Woodley's pointed questions. Indeed, her own conscience was asking her other, equally disturbing questions about her penchant for excitement and her willingness to stoop to practices such as forgery.

When the door was finally unlocked, she struggled up onto her feet. It was Mrs. Woodley, followed by a rather frightened-looking Martha.

"It appears that we will not be able to send you home," said Martha's mother. Her face was taut. "Our forces met the French yesterday afternoon near Brussels, and the British civilians in the city, as civilians are wont to do, are panicking and spreading rumors of disaster. Consequently the docks are swarming with foolish people clamoring to be taken off at once. It is simply not possible to get you safe passage on a boat at the moment."

Diana, who did not share her mother's distrust of the military, saw no contradiction at all in the notion that it was safer to proceed towards a battlefield than to travel home with hysterical Londoners who were fleeing in terror.

Mrs. Woodley looked at her daughter. "Martha has engaged to be personally responsible for your good behavior until I can return you to your mother. That means that consequences for your actions will fall not only on you, but on her."

Diana looked at her friend. "Thank you," she said faintly.

"You will write a letter to your mother right now, to be sent with the captain of this packet. You will explain to her that Martha and I were not aware of the true situation. You will give her our address in Brussels and will tell her that unless I hear from her I will send you home as soon as I can find a safe means of doing so."

Diana nodded.

"Do you have any questions?"

Yes, she had a question. A very urgent question. "Please—forgive me if I sound ignorant. But you said our forces met the French. Does that mean that they fought?"

"Yes," said Mrs. Woodley, her expression almost kindly. "Not all of our men, of course. Just a few regiments."

"Do you know which regiments were there? Were any of the soldiers killed?" She strained to remember the suddenly elusive, all-important number. "Anthony—Mr. Roth—is in the 44th Foot."

"I am afraid that division was involved, yes," said the older woman gently. "And there were quite a few casualties on both sides."

Diana had seen the word "casualties" in the newspapers. It had seemed very impersonal and abstract until now. She swallowed. "I am very good at nursing," she offered. "Truly. And I know how to set bones, if they are only broken a little."

"Do you?" Mrs. Woodley looked at her thoughtfully. "In that case I may not be in such a hurry to send you home after all."

Under a gray, threatening sky the remnants of the second battalion of the 44th Foot were huddled around a small fire making tea. It seemed very strange to Anthony that they should be having tea, as though this were an ordinary morning. A few miles away eight thousand corpses were lying scattered around a little rural crossroads, and the men here could not really explain why they were alive while their comrades were dead.

Yesterday afternoon Anthony had finally understood the purpose of drills. Drills were boring and exhausting; battle was boring and exhausting and terrifying. If you had drilled enough, the similarities (boredom and exhaustion) outweighed the differences (terror) and when the sergeant screamed "fix bayonets!" you moved quickly enough so that the charging enemy met a wall of blades instead of a helpless man with an unloaded musket. Anthony had not drilled enough. He knew that it was sheer luck that he was not dead.

"Here," said a freckled soldier, handing him a tin mug. He took it gratefully. It tasted foul, but it was hot, and it was liquid. Since yesterday afternoon he had been constantly, fiercely thirsty. Between the smoke and the sun and the residue of gunpowder in his mouth, Anthony had thought at times that he would be willing to kill simply for a drink of water.

"That was your first battle, wasn't it?" the other man asked, watching Anthony drink.

"Yes." Anthony handed back the empty mug. "And you?"

"My tenth. I've been in since '09. Been wounded twice."

"What did you think of yesterday?" Anthony asked cautiously.

He himself had absolutely no idea why they had fought at that particular place. The crossroads seemed to him a perfectly ordinary one, indistinguishable from countless others they had passed on their hurried march to relieve the Dutch forces. When they had arrived, things had become even more incomprehensible. So far as he could tell, his company had done nothing but stand there and get shot at by French cannon. Occasionally some French infantry would attack; then they were allowed to shoot back. Even more occasionally, the French cavalry would attack. That was a break in the monotony: everyone would scramble into a tightly packed square facing out. The horses would shy away from the wall of bayonets, the 44th would send a volley of musket fire after them, and the excitement was over until the next cavalry charge. But most of the time they stood there in the smoke and waited for cannon balls to smash into their ranks.

Evidently the battle had not made much sense even to the veterans; his companion spat in disgust and then growled: "It was a bloody mess, that was what it was. Half a division wiped out, and then we abandon the damned crossroads anyway and come north."

As the morning wore on, the phrase "bloody mess" seemed to be the general consensus about Quatre Bras. The supply wagons had never caught up to the troops. So there was no food, no spare gear, and, most importantly, no grog. When the dark clouds finally split open and disgorged a brutal, soaking rain, the men began complaining even more bitterly. Why were they marching out in the open, when in the nearby woods they could at least find some shelter? Where were the supplies? Where, for that matter, was the rest of their division? They continued north, going more and more slowly as the roads and fields turned to mud. In places it was ankle-deep, and several men had to stop and retrieve boots that had been sucked off their feet. Eventually the rain slowed to a drizzle, but the mud persisted.

In the middle of the afternoon, a rider in the blue coat of a staff officer pulled up to the weary troop. He was met with catcalls. "Where are the damn wagons?" several men yelled. "Where are our mates?"

He ignored them and addressed the nearest officer. "Lieutenant Tomkins?"

"No, sir. I'm Willoughby. Tomkins was killed yesterday."

"Sorry to hear it." The rider looked grim. "Do

you still have a trooper named Roth? Or was he killed as well?"

"He's here, sir." Willoughby turned and bellowed "Roth!"—then blushed furiously when he saw Anthony standing a few feet away.

The man danced his horse sideways so that he was facing Anthony. "You're the one who speaks German?"

"Yes, sir."

"Can you ride? Nothing fancy, we're not recruiting you for the cavalry."

Anthony hesitated. "Yes, sir."

"You're to report to headquarters, then. They're forming a messenger corps for the next round. Requisition a horse when you get to the next village." He turned back to the lieutenant. "Tell your colonel this man has been seconded to Major Barnes." Then he wheeled his horse and rode away.

"You lucky dog," said the man next to Anthony, giving him an envious look. "Swanning around headquarters nice and dry while we slog through the mud. The ladies are very partial to a man just returned from battle, you know." There was a chorus of agreement, and some suggestions as to what Anthony might do with the ladies.

Anthony merely grunted and kept walking.

"Do you have a girl in Brussels?" his companion asked, curious.

"No."

There was a gigantic crack of lightning as he spoke, and rain began again, harder than before.

25

The storm finally subsided around midnight. Abigail, venturing out of her tiny cabin, saw that the boat was under way again, and the terrible sense of frustration eased somewhat. Five hours, the ship's master had said. Five hours more to Ostend, and then seventy miles to Brussels. What was the road like? she had asked. How long would it take to cover that seventy miles? He had shrugged. He was a sailor, he told her. He never went more than two miles inland if he could help it.

She knew how long it had taken to drive from London to Ramsgate: eight hours. Meyer had arranged everything. He had sent to her house for a change of clothing and her maid; he had arranged for money; he had even made sure that any letters Diana might send would be intercepted at the coast and forwarded on. Then he had commandeered one of the bank's fastest coaches and they had sped away south. A boat had been waiting for them in Ramsgate. Unlike the luxurious coach, it was a rather small and suspicious-looking craft, and Abigail had been forcibly reminded that

her escort had made many illegal trips to France. The
boat was seaworthy, however, and that was all she cared
about. They had set sail at around nine in the morning
and Meyer had told her they would be in Ostend by late
afternoon. Master Cooper's boat was very fast, as were
the bank's teams of horses; Abigail might well find herself only five or six hours behind Diana when they
reached Belgium.

That was before the storm. It had come up from
the west very suddenly at noon. At first they had
been able to run before it, heading straight for
Calais instead of angling northeast. But as the
squalls grew stronger, the ship's master had reluctantly reefed all but a few sails, and they had limped
into a sheltered cove to sit it out. The waiting nearly
drove Abigail mad, especially when the winds died
down towards early evening. She had demanded to
know why they were not putting out to sea again,
and when Cooper had pointed to a second line of
black clouds scudding towards them she had retreated to her cabin (more accurately, *the* cabin)
in despair.

Now it was as though the storm had never been.
The winds were gentle and steady. The sky was overcast, but the moon created a luminous glow behind
the thinner clouds, and in a few places far to the
west you could even see the occasional star. After
hours in the close, dark cabin it felt wonderful to
be outside. She took a deep breath of salt and pitch
and damp wood. In the cabin, all she had been able
to do was fret. Now they were moving. The clock
had started again: so many hours to Ostend, so
many to Brussels.

A dark figure detached itself from the group at

the stern of the boat and made its way over to her. "How is your maid?" Meyer asked.

"Better, thank you." Rosie had been very seasick during the storm. She had also been sick in the carriage. So far Abigail had been waiting on her rather than the other way around, but she knew that the reason Meyer had insisted on fetching Rosie had very little to do with hairdressing or with bringing cups of chocolate in the morning.

"We will be in the way here," Meyer said. "Would you like to go forward?" He helped her to climb around the block that supported the mast. In front of the block was a sort of hollow, filled with casks and crates and neat coils of rope. The last made surprisingly comfortable seats, Abigail discovered. Meyer handed her down and then lowered himself onto an adjacent coil.

"Do you think Diana is all right?" Abigail asked, for the hundredth time since they had left London.

He made the same answer he always did. "Yes." This time he elaborated a bit. "She is not as reckless as she seems. Recollect that when she ran off after Anthony in France, she took a groom with her. I think it very likely that she is with this friend you told me of, this Miss Woodley. It cannot be coincidence that she ran away the same week the Woodleys were leaving for Brussels."

That made her feel better. She had recalled Martha's existence only when they reached Dover.

"Be thankful you are not responsible for my daughter," he added. "Rachel once went over to France in boy's clothing and managed to get herself taken prisoner by the *Sûreté*. Since at the time I myself was masquerading as chief inspector of that very same branch of the *Sûreté* the situation was rather awkward. Luckily her brother and some of his fellow officers managed to rescue her."

That did not make Abigail feel better. She knew the ending of that story. Rachel Meyer had married one of those officers. She stiffened and shifted slightly on her coil of rope so as to put more distance between herself and Meyer.

"What is it? What is wrong?"

She shook her head.

"My scandalous past, I suppose." He was only half-joking.

The question came rushing out before she could stop herself. "How could you? How could you let her become a Christian? And your son?"

"Ah." He hunched forward, clasping his knees. He said, almost to himself, "So that is the problem."

"I beg your pardon," she said, drawing herself even farther away. "It is none of my business, of course."

He ignored this last. "Rachel has not converted. Neither has James. It is true, however, that they have both been compelled to pretend briefly that they were Christian: my son to obtain his commission and my daughter to obtain a marriage license. As far as my mother is concerned, there is no difference between the pretense and the reality. She will not let their names be spoken in her house. They are dead to her."

"And what of you?" she asked, her mouth dry. "Did she disown you as well?"

"No." He leaned back against the gunwale. "She graciously informed me that she would not hold me responsible for the sins of my children. I, however, found myself unwilling to pretend that James and Rachel were dead. I have not seen her in three years."

"I have not seen my mother in ten years," she confessed, her head bowed. "Since the divorce. She sends messages to me through my sister."

He was silent for a moment. "Do you know why Rodrigo avoids using his surname?" he asked abruptly. "Because his father disowned him. Formally disowned him, taking a public oath in front of witnesses."

She shivered. "For what reason?"

"Rodrigo opposed the French regime in Spain. His father supported it."

"Politics?" she asked, incredulous. "Rodrigo's father disowned him because of *politics*?"

"Señor Santos called it treason, not politics. But yes, he did. I myself see very little difference between his actions and my mother's." He sat up and looked at her intently. "What of you? Do you believe I should have disowned James and Rachel? Do you disapprove of me because I still consider them my children?"

There was a long pause. "Perhaps," she said in a low voice.

"And if Diana were to convert, would you renounce her? Would you forbid her name to be spoken in your presence? Destroy every picture of her? Walk by her on the street as though she did not exist?"

There was an even longer pause. "No," she confessed. "I could not do it. I paid a terrible price to bear her, and another almost as terrible to get her back. Even if she did something truly dreadful, she would still be my child."

"Running away to Belgium, I take it, does not count as truly dreadful."

"No." She gave a painful smile. "Although I beg you not to tell Diana that."

The wind freshened, and the boat began to pitch slightly, sending the occasional spray of water over the bow. "You will wish to go below again," he said, standing and offering her his hand.

The thought of the cramped, musty cabin made her shudder. "I would rather not," she said.

"Take my coat, then," he said, pulling it off and draping it over her shoulders. He sat down again.

They sat for a long time without speaking. It was growing lighter; she could see the coast now, low hills and dunes just visible above the rail of the boat. She knew that she should go and see if Rosie needed something, but a strange lassitude possessed her. Her limbs felt heavy. She did not know if she could move. After a while she leaned back against the gunwale and closed her eyes.

"Abigail?" He sounded hesitant.

She did not correct his over-familiar address. She did not answer at all; she was in some sort of trance.

"Asleep," he muttered. She felt him tucking the coat more closely around her and then, tentatively, reaching out to brush some windblown strands of hair away from her forehead. His hand hovered for a moment at her temple and then traced a slow line downward to her jaw, barely grazing her skin.

"God," he whispered. He moved abruptly away from her and there was a small thump as he settled back against the side of the boat.

With an immense effort, she forced her eyes open. He was sitting a few feet away, staring off into the distance. The expression on his face made something twist painfully inside of her.

She must have moved, or made some small noise. His eyes met hers. "You were not asleep just now."

"No," she said. She wanted to tell him that she did not mind, did not mind at all. But her voice was frozen.

He mistook her silence for condemnation. "Put it on my account," he said savagely. "Item, one attempted embrace of sleeping mother while searching for missing daughter. Add it to Pont-Haut." He stood up. "We will be coming into port soon. You should see if your maid is ready to disembark." He beckoned a sailor to assist her back into the stern. By the time she had climbed aft he had disappeared into the bowels of the boat.

She returned to the cabin, still moving very slowly, as though the air was water. Rosie was sitting up on the edge of her berth, looking rather wan.

"We will be landing soon," Abigail said.

Rosie brightened at this news.

"I hope you are feeling a bit better."

"Yes, ma'am, I am." She peered at Abigail. "Is everything all right? You look a bit pale."

No, she wanted to say. Everything is not all right. My daughter has run off to a city that is about to be invaded, and I have fallen in love with a spy. But instead she handed Rosie a damp towel. "Everything is fine," she said. "Do you think you could keep down some tea?"

Even exempting personal affairs from consideration, everything was not fine. Napoleon had not waited until mid-July to attack. From Ostend in a continuous line stretching back to Brussels the road was packed with fugitives, and their stories grew more and more ominous: there had been a great battle. Tens of thousands of soldiers had been killed. Wellington was dead; the Allied army had broken and fled.

After the first garbled reports at the dock, Meyer hired a young Belgian to ride crosscountry into the city and return with some reliable news. In the meantime, he made sure that Abigail and her maid were bundled into a carriage, and set on their way as quickly as possible. At every halt he brought refreshments to them himself, and escorted them personally when they stopped for longer rests. He could not prevent her from overhearing the conversations of others, however, and Abigail huddled in the carriage, more and more terrified as they crawled along. She wished that she did not understand French. Even the normally placid Rosie heard enough from the numerous English-speaking fugitives to make her round-eyed with anxiety.

At the fourth halt, Abigail opened the carriage door. "Can we not go any faster?" she pleaded as Meyer came over to assist her.

"We would have to ride through the fields. They are a sea of mud, and in any case I do not think it would be safe for you and your maid; not with deserting soldiers between us and the city."

"I hate this," she said, her voice shaking. "We are going so slowly, and every new rumor is worse than the last." She looked back at the highway. Coaches clogged the road, the frantic passengers shouting and cursing as slower vehicles in front of them blocked their progress. Alongside the carriages and wagons and gigs groups of refugees trudged northwards on foot, moving hardly more slowly than the vehicles. Women were sobbing as they walked along, and the wails of hungry infants could be heard everywhere. It was as though the world was coming to an end.

"This?" he said, gesturing towards the wretched crowd of fugitives. "It happens every time armies engage near a large city. You cannot trust anything these people tell you."

"If you tell me there is no cause for alarm," Abigail said in a tight voice, "I will never speak to you again."

"There is certainly cause for alarm. There has been a battle. That much I believe. For the rest, there is no evidence whatsoever. Look at those people. We have been driving past them, hundreds of them, for hours. Have you seen a single British soldier?"

"No," she admitted.

"And do you hear that noise? Almost like a very low drum?"

She nodded.

"Those are cannon," he told her. "No one fires cannon after a battle. Therefore, the battle is not over. The Allies may or may not win, but they have not lost. Not yet. And that means that the armies are not yet in Brussels."

She was unconvinced.

With a sigh, he handed her into the carriage and climbed back onto his own horse. He and a groom had been riding ahead of the carriage, trying to clear a path; the road was wide and well drained but even when the northbound vehicles kept to their side the pedestrians oozed out around them and made the road impassable.

Four hours later, she saw a messenger pull up next to the carriage, sweating and breathless. She recognized him only by his jacket: it was the young man Meyer had hired at Ostend. He was now hatless and covered from the waist down in a layer of mud. She was already out the door before Meyer had even dismounted, and she stood clenching and unclenching her hands as he came over to her.

"I have news from someone I know in the city," Meyer said, holding up a folded piece of paper.

"Someone in the army?"

"I am afraid the only person whose address in Brussels I could recall is an informant for the British foreign office," he said apologetically. "But I believe him to be an honest man." He broke the seal and scanned the closely written page. "DeCoster reports that as of four o'clock this afternoon, the two armies were heavily engaged about ten miles south of the city. And as you can hear, they are still fighting now, two hours later." The sound of the cannon had grown louder and louder as they drew farther south.

"So the city has not been invaded?"

"No." His eyes ran down the rest of the page. "The rumors of Wellington's death date from Friday, when there was a preliminary engagement, and those rumors are false." He turned the sheet over and drew in his breath sharply. After a moment he said, "Diana is safe. She is with Mrs. Woodley, as we suspected."

"Thank God," she said, closing her eyes for a moment in relief. "Thank God." Rosie was peering out of the carriage window. "They have found her," Abigail called. "She is safe; she is with the Woodleys."

She turned back to Meyer. "May I see the letter?" Not waiting for an answer, she plucked it from his hand, searching for Diana's name, as though the sight of it was proof that she was indeed unharmed.

It took her a minute to realize that she would not see the word *Diana*, another minute to grasp that the letter was in French. *Mademoiselle Hart*. There it was. She savored the entire sentence. *As to Mademoiselle Hart, as monsieur had foreseen, she is situated with the Woodley family, who have taken a house on the Rue de la Madeleine*. She felt suddenly alive for the first time in days, full of eager questions. Where was this Rue de la Madeleine? How long would it take them to reach the city from here? The battle and its potential outcome had receded into the back of her mind, and she looked at the plodding ranks of fugitives on the road with bemused pity.

She was about to hand the letter back when she caught sight of another name: Roth. And then, lower down, James. She had forgotten that she was not the only parent with a child in Brussels. Numbly, she read the rest of the page.

> *The 44th, the regiment of Monsieur Roth, took part in the engagement Friday afternoon and lost many men. I know nothing further. Your son James I saw here in the city yesterday, but the runners arriving at the Namur Gate say that his battalion is in the middle of the fighting today, in a very exposed position between the French artillery and the Allied lines. I will await you at the city gate with further news.*

So that quick, stifled gasp had not been a reaction to the good news about her daughter. It had been a reaction to the unsettling news about his nephew and his son. Very subdued, she handed back the piece of paper. Meyer accepted it without comment, folded it neatly, and tucked it into a pocket.

"I am sorry," she said. The words sounded ridiculous.

"James has not managed to get himself killed yet," he said. "And not for want of trying, I assure you. I am more concerned about Anthony." He surveyed the jammed road. A grim smile appeared. "At least we will not have any trouble finding a hotel room in Brussels."

26

News of Anthony had arrived piecemeal, a bewildering jumble of contradictory items, alternately terrifying and reassuring. Mrs. Woodley, who seemed to know half the military wives in Brussels, had been able to confirm within a few hours of their arrival last night that the 44th had indeed taken part in Friday's engagement at Quatre Bras, and that there had been a significant number of men killed on both sides. Although an entire day had gone by, however, there did not seem to be an official casualty list. Only very late last night had a boy arrived, dripping wet, with a note from one of her acquaintances. It contained not only the welcome news that Major Woodley had been posted north to reorganize the coastal garrisons but also an eyewitness report: Anthony Roth, the banker-infantryman, had survived Friday's battle unharmed.

"Your Mr. Roth appears to have become something of a celebrity," Mrs. Woodley had commented as she read the note. "Apparently he dressed down an officer in the Rifles in front of half of Brussels.

We will not have trouble getting news of him." And she was right. The trouble was, the news seemed always to be half a day behind. On Saturday morning at Ostend, the news was of Friday's battle. On Saturday evening, it was of the survivors mustered that morning.

Things had become even more confusing today. For one thing, Diana had thought that everything was over. It had never occurred to her—especially after she saw the scores of wounded men lying in the streets—that there could be two such horrible events within the space of forty-eight hours. She had assumed that the casual references to "the battle" made by Mrs. Woodley and the other wives were references to Friday's affair, and only gradually had she realized her mistake.

"They are going to fight again?" Diana had asked in horror, looking up at her friend from yet another half-conscious patient. Martha, Diana, and Mrs. Woodley had been working nearly around the clock tending the wounded since they had arrived the previous evening.

"No one won," explained her friend. "And it has stopped raining now. Of course they will fight again."

"When?"

Martha poured more water into the cup Diana was holding. "This morning, most likely. I am surprised they have not started already."

"On a Sunday?"

"They have prayers first."

Realizing suddenly what this meant, she almost dropped the cup. "Anthony might be fighting right now!"

"No, not until you hear the cannon."

Diana had moved along the rows of men in a state of terror for over an hour, convinced that every loud noise was the guns starting up again. A chance remark by one of her patients had relieved her anxiety: Anthony's regiment was not fighting today. They were stationed as reserves north of the city.

When the guns had begun firing just before noon, she had felt very thankful that she did not have to think about Anthony and picture the balls crashing into his company. She was worried on Martha's behalf, of course. Her friend's father was safe for the moment, and Charles Woodley was posted in London, but Christopher Woodley was in an infantry regiment which had marched out last night to take their places in today's conflict. As the other wives and daughters and sisters who were helping tend the wounded looked up at the sound of the first shot, Diana felt almost guilty to be spared.

That happy state had lasted for only a few hours. In the middle of the afternoon a very cheerful man had come along, wearing a tattered uniform that Diana could barely recognize as the one from the parade ground at Horse Guards.

"My wife tells me there's a pretty girl paying for news of the 44th," he said, grinning at Martha. She pointed at Diana. "Is it you, then, love?" he asked, turning with an equally wide smile to Diana. "I'm bound for camp now, who's the lucky fellow? I'll tell him I've seen you."

"Mr. Roth," she said.

"Ah, the little banker." He shook his head. "Headquarters nabbed him yesterday."

"Where is he, then?" she asked.

"No idea. They took him off for messenger duty. He's some sort of foreigner, speaks German."

She paid him well anyway, but afterwards she had asked Martha what messenger duty would mean. "Perhaps he has been sent away, like your father," she said hopefully.

Martha had not been certain; Mrs. Woodley, when consulted, had murmured vague, reassuring generalities about couriers and dispatches. But Diana, mulling over the likely needs of a multinational army composed of thousands of men, was becoming more and more convinced that Anthony was at the battle. He was not even with his company, who could offer some protection. No, he was galloping around on the field unarmed and unaccompanied—a perfect target. And he was not a very good rider even under ideal conditions. She had tended enough men in the past twenty-four hours who had been crushed by horses to be under no illusions about the possible penalties for poor horsemanship on a battlefield. Ever since the grinning man had arrived all she could think of to do was to pray for night to fall. And as if to torment her—and the thousands of combatants—the sun seemed to be inching across the sky with provocative slowness.

Diana had no idea who was winning or losing. She could hear the cannon and see the pall of smoke hanging over the fields, but early reports of a catastrophic Allied defeat had proved false, and Mrs. Woodley had advised the girls not to listen to any more rumors. Otherwise they would end up prostrated with hysterics, like Eleanor. Martha's cousin was currently in bed attempting to roll

bandages and bursting into tears every fifteen minutes for no apparent reason. Martha and Diana,
meanwhile, were bringing another load of medical
supplies from the Woodleys's rented house to the
impromptu hospital in the streets around the
Namur Gate. The victims of Friday's battle were
now a distant memory; since the middle of the afternoon, ever-increasing numbers of men were
staggering or being carried into the city from
today's action.

She put down the jars she was carrying and wiped
her face with her sleeve. It had been getting hotter
and hotter; she did not know how the men could
bear it in their wool jackets. "I haven't any handkerchiefs," she explained to Martha apologetically. "I
used both of them last night for the man with the
hole in his elbow." Then she looked up at the sun.
"It is lower, isn't it?" she asked anxiously.

"It is," Martha assured her. "It will set within the
hour."

"If only it were not June. The days are endless at
this time of year." She picked up the jars again.

As they came up to the church of St. Jacques,
Diana saw that the rows of men waiting for help
had now reached the church steps, all the way at
the top of the street leading down to the gate.
Some of the other women were there, assisting the
newcomers, and one of them hurried over to take
the heavy jars from Diana.

Suddenly a murmur ran through the ranks of the
wounded men. A voice called out sharply, "Quiet,
you lot! Listen for it!"

Diana had not realized how much noise the men
were making until they stopped. The calls for water,

the curses, the encouraging speeches, even the groans—all silenced, for one long moment. Then the cheering began, rolling down the street in waves.

"What is it?" asked Diana, bewildered.

"The cannon," Martha said slowly. "They've stopped. The cannons have stopped." She gave a little sob. "It's over." Thrusting her bandages into the arms of an older woman she began to run towards the gate, with Diana right behind her. At the end of the street a huge crowd was gathered, some already streaming out towards the site of the battle, eager to see for themselves. Women were shouting, jostling each other, calling out names. Diana realized they were asking for news. There were eighty thousand Allied soldiers, eighty thousand Anthonies whose mothers or sisters or sweethearts were waiting, here or in London or in a village in Yorkshire, for someone to tell them whether the name represented a living man or a dead one.

When she heard someone call her own name, she thought it was a hallucination. They called again, more urgently. It was more than one someone now, and it was coming from behind her. She turned. Mrs. Woodley was hurrying down the hill. Next to her was Anthony's uncle. And next to him, picking up her skirts and beginning to run towards her, was her mother, with an expression on her face that told Diana exactly what those women wanted to happen when they called out the name of their missing soldier.

A miracle, that was what they wanted. It was a bit terrifying to be someone else's miracle.

"Are you all right?" asked her mother, gripping her shoulders so hard that they hurt.

She nodded.

"And Mr. Roth? Did you find him?"

"No." She turned to Meyer, who was standing off to one side, as if afraid of intruding. "He was on messenger duty, and no one has seen him since this morning."

"I will find him," said Meyer. "That seems to be my specialty lately. Finding lost children."

He had been searching for hours. It was very dark now; the moon had set. He had a lantern, but he kept it shielded. He did not want to attract attention. The looters were out in force, and he was alone. He moved carefully in little squares, crossing off pieces of an imaginary map, looking at the easiest clues: jackets and weapons. Blue, no. Black facings, no. Sabre, no.

He had started out on the road. It had still been light then, although just barely; it had taken some time to make sure that Abigail and Diana were safely settled and to persuade them to wait there for his return instead of hovering by the city gate. It was light enough, however, to make him decide that the road was a bad idea. Men were still pouring towards the city; it was nearly impossible to walk against the flow, and if James or Anthony were on this road they would not need his help. He had cut through the woods instead.

There were more corpses here than he had expected. Most were lone men who must have staggered instinctively into the trees to die, but occasionally he would come across a small cluster in a clearing. He had to go carefully in the dark. It was distasteful to step on corpses; it could be fatal to step on a pike, or onto the trigger of a loaded musket.

Not all the bodies in the woods were dead either. He had stumbled—literally—onto several wounded men, and had heard many more, thrashing and breathing raggedly in some thicket as he picked his way through the trees. He had gritted his teeth and walked by when they called for help. He would never even have made it through Brussels to find Diana Hart if he had stopped for every man who needed him. On the steps of the church alone there must have been two hundred. So he had a routine: every man in the woods, alive or dead, got the same quick glance. If they were not wearing the right jacket—green, or red with yellow facings—he moved on.

At the farmhouse just beyond the woods, which had been converted into a hospital, he had been able to work more quickly. The bodies were all laid out neatly in one place for him. He felt like a monster holding his lantern up over one bloodless face after another, but there were others doing the same thing. The men outside were not so neatly arranged, but they were less serious cases; they could answer questions. No one had seen Anthony. No one had seen James. There were several men from the Rifles, however, and they had been able to describe their position on the field fairly accurately, so that was where he had started his search. A shallow pit, they told him, just over the brow of the hill. He had spent over two hours in the sandy depression. There were hundreds of bodies, and they were all wearing green jackets. Some of the bodies were piled three and four deep, and he had to lift one corpse to see another. He had stopped looking at faces; there were so many men to examine that he searched only for the telltale epaulette which marked the officers. There were plenty of those, too. He began hauling the bodies he had already checked to one side so that he would not look at them again, an endless round of blood-stained green. The neatly laid-out rows attracted a looter eager to save himself some work; Meyer looked up from the pit, startled, as a voice came out of the darkness in French: "Mind if we share? There are plenty." A lantern bloomed, and Meyer saw a square, unshaven man with a haversack over his shoulder. Looped around his waist were five silver-trimmed sword belts, and in the lapel of his coat he had pinned several pairs of gold spectacles.

"Where did you get those?" Meyer asked, his eyes locked on the spectacles. He was trying to remember precisely what Anthony's pince-nez looked like. His nephew had not been wearing it much lately; he used it only for reading and accounts. Perhaps he had not even brought the damn thing with him. But Meyer couldn't stop looking.

The man shrugged. "Here and there. Most of them don't wear them in battle, and they hide them away in strange places like their boots so they won't get broken, but if you find them alive you can tickle them a bit with a knife and they'll tell you fast enough where they are."

Without even thinking about it Meyer pulled out his pistol and shot the man in the head. Then, his hands shaking, he pulled the spectacles off the man's coat. Two were proper spectacles, with ear pieces. Two were like Anthony's. He held them up. They didn't look familiar, but what did, in this hellish pit full of dead men? Carefully tucking both pairs away, he had gone back to work.

When he heard footsteps he grabbed his gun again, certain that it was another looter. The voice that emerged out of the darkness spoke English, though.

"Looking for me?"

He held up the lantern and saw the haggard, unshaven, and unutterably wonderful face of his son.

"Yes," he said. "And for Anthony."

"I wouldn't mind finding him myself," said James. "He gave me a blistering setdown in front of half of the officers in my regiment. I've been thinking of clever responses ever since." He stared somberly into the pit. "Of course, there are not many witnesses left."

Meyer climbed up to the rim of the depression and stood next to his son. Even in the small circle of light from his lantern there were over a dozen bodies.

"Did you go through all of them?" James asked.

"Nearly all."

"How many are there?"

That was the problem with training as a spy. Your powers of observation did not shut off, even when you would have strongly preferred them to do so. "I would estimate around three hundred enlisted men and two dozen officers."

"There are dozens more of both at the hospital. Most won't last the day." James gave a short laugh. "I am a rare species. Nearly extinct."

They began walking back towards the farmhouse-hospital. "How did you know I was out there?" asked Meyer.

"The walking wounded over there told me." He nodded towards the men clustered around the farmhouse door. "You were very conspicuous, not being covered with mud. You look much more like the rest of us now, of course."

"Any notion of how I might find Anthony?"

"He was one of the messengers." James gestured helplessly. "He could have been anywhere."

Meyer stopped. "Let us consider this logically," he said. "Anthony was seconded to the messenger corps because he speaks German. That means he would most likely have been sent either to the German legions or to the Prussians. The Prussians arrived late, on the right flank of the French. Where were the Germans?"

"Back there," said James, pointing. "With the reserves. And in the woods."

"I've done the woods. The parts nearest the road, at any rate."

"In that case, I'll try over where the reserves were stationed," James had proposed. "It's on my way back to what's left of my company in any case. You look over by the Prussians."

It had seemed like a reasonable plan. Meyer had walked back towards the hillock which had served as Wellington's command post and had begun working his way methodically across the field with his little squares, angling towards the southeast.

Waterloo was not a big battlefield. There was perhaps a mile between the ridge where the French had placed their cannon and the ridge where Wellington had stood. When you took the diagonal, as he did, it was a mile and a half. He moved one square at a time: pace off the distance, circle with the lantern, turn over prone bodies. The looters were out in force now; he saw parties hauling away cartloads and heard quarrels and threats in the gradually ebbing darkness around him. It was almost dawn; the most dangerous time, when the robbers became hasty and reckless. He reloaded his pistol, and felt automatically for the knife in his boot every time he bent over.

He found Anthony just after two looters did. His nephew was curled in a ball on his side, covered with mud. Meyer might have missed him if the looters had not rolled him over, exposing the relatively clean side of his distinctive jacket.

"That's my nephew," he said in French.

"Bugger off," said one of the looters in the same language. "We found him first." He stepped on Anthony's shoulder to push him flat on his back for easy stripping, and Meyer heard a faint moan.

He raised his gun. "He's my nephew," Meyer repeated. There was a soft click as he cocked the trigger.

"You can have him after we strip him, then." The man bent over to pull off Anthony's boots.

If he had thought about it at all, he would have let them have their booty. Or offered them some money. But some primitive force rose up in him, as it had in the sandpit. He kicked the man in the ribs, hard, and pulled his big knife out of his waistband, not wanting to shoot unless forced. A pistol, once fired, was useless. The second man lunged at him; Meyer sidestepped and slashed him with the knife. Then the first man was on him again, holding his side with one hand but brandishing a gun of his own in the other. A high kick knocked the gun to the ground, and the man dove after it, swearing, but Meyer kneed him in the neck. His companion was up again; Meyer turned and hit him in the side of the head with the butt of the pistol. The man fell to his knees, then toppled sideways. Meyer glanced over at his other opponent. He, too, was on the ground, motionless.

Meyer flung himself down by Anthony, running his hands over him to see where he was hurt. He didn't feel any large, sticky patches on the clothing; that was a good sign. And Anthony was breathing, breathing steadily. Meyer lifted the lantern higher and moved it slowly up his nephew's body. One arm was lying at an odd angle; it was probably broken. There were no other visible wounds until he eased off Anthony's shako. On the right side of his face, just at the temple, was a huge bruise. The scalp behind the bruise was split, and the fair hair was caked with blood. He lifted the head, bracing his arm behind his nephew's shoulders. That produced another moan. He would have to hope Anthony's neck wasn't broken.

The second looter, the one with the gun, was stirring. Meyer looked at him, then walked over and knelt by his side. "You don't deserve this," he said, "but I'm offering you the chance to earn some money."

The man struggled up onto one elbow, wincing. "How much?"

Meyer held up a gold coin. "Three of these. Help me lift him. I don't want to jostle his head much; he may have a broken skull."

After a minute the man nodded grudgingly.

Clutching his injured ribs, he got to his feet and hauled Meyer up once he had Anthony balanced on his arms.

Meyer gave him four coins. The man grinned, backed away, picked up his gun from the ground and aimed it at Meyer, almost contemptuously.

Meyer froze. If he put Anthony down, the man would have an easy shot. If he held on to him, the man might well aim for his nephew. He stooped slowly, as though setting down his burden.

The man was enjoying himself; he grinned again and raised the gun.

In one quick movement Meyer let Anthony's legs slide to the ground as he pulled the knife out of his boot. It hit the looter in the chest just as he pulled the trigger.

The force of the shot knocked Meyer backwards; he fell clumsily, trying to protect Anthony's head. Upper arm, he thought. Not fatal. He felt no pain, but he knew that would change within seconds. Desperately he dragged Anthony over his shoulder and got to his feet, first kneeling, then on one knee, then pushing off with the other foot.

He started back across the valley. His five seconds of numbness were over; his arm began to throb after the first step. One mile to the other side. Five thousand two hundred eighty steps.

He began to count.

27

"Mother, why aren't they back yet?"

Abigail looked up from the sheet she was tearing into strips. She thought Diana's phrasing was overly optimistic. It was nine o'clock in the morning, and already some civilians had driven out to the battlefield and returned with tales of unimaginable horror: three solid miles of corpses, wounded men stripped and killed by looters, field hospitals with piles of amputated limbs outside the door. It would take a long time to search through an entire valley full of bodies. She was not surprised that Meyer had not returned, and she had the unhappy premonition that when he did return, it would be alone. She had been trying to shield Diana from the more grisly reports, however, so she merely said, "There is always a great deal of confusion after a battle."

Diana abandoned the window with a sigh and came back to the table. "May I go and see Mrs. Woodley? Very quickly? Perhaps she has heard something."

"She has promised to send a message if she does."
Abigail handed her daughter a sheet of her own to
tear up. "Start it with the scissors, otherwise it goes
sideways," she reminded her, before returning to
the topic of Mrs. Woodley. "Her son was wounded;
I am sure she is very busy."

"Christopher was not badly wounded." Diana gave
the sheet a savage rip.

"*Lieutenant Woodley* took a ball in the elbow and
will be lucky not to lose the arm," Abigail corrected.

"I know. I am sorry." She sighed. "I waited all day
Saturday, while we were driving here from Ostend,
because they told us when we docked that there
had been a battle the day before, but they didn't
really know what had happened. And then I waited
all day yesterday, and the cannon didn't stop firing
for one minute the whole day, and after what happened at the first battle I thought about people
getting their heads taken off every time I heard
one, and then I waited all last night, and I even
tried to go to sleep, but I couldn't. I don't know
how Mrs. Woodley can bear it, being a soldier's
wife."

While not the most eloquent speech, this was a
fair reflection of Abigail's own state of mind, so she
merely said, "I already told you, if no word has
come by noon we will go out together. Perhaps
Rosie will have heard something at the market. But
you promised last night that you would not go out
on your own, and I will hold you to it."

That promise had been the result of a mother-
daughter conversation which had surprised Abigail.
She had expected Diana's usual extravagant re-
morse and even more extravagant pledges of

eternal good behavior, but after Meyer had left, Diana had said nothing except, "You must tell me what you wish me to do." And Abigail had extracted the promise. Even more surprising was Diana's halting description, late last night, of the revelation she had experienced yesterday at the gate when Abigail had found her. "And I cannot marry Anthony," Diana had added. "At least not yet. Because I knew when I saw your face that I would not feel like that about him. I am fond of him, and worried about him, and I will be very anxious until we find him, but he is not my miracle." The room had been dark; they were both trying to sleep. Abigail suspected the confession would never have happened otherwise.

Diana sighed and went back to her sheet.

A few minutes later there was a light knock at the door. Diana jumped up so quickly that the scissors flew halfway across the room from her lap. It was only a chambermaid, however, come to change the bed linens. She was scandalized to find them tearing up sheets, but after Abigail had reassured her that they did not belong to the hotel, she became very sympathetic and promised to see if she could find some older, torn ones that the innkeeper might be willing to discard.

After she left, Diana went over to the window again and perched on the broad sill, peering down into the street below. "I wish we were nearer the Namur Gate," she said. "We are halfway across the city."

"It is not that large a city," said Abigail. The same light knock came at the door. "I'll get it," said Abigail, rising. "It's the chambermaid with the spare sheets."

She opened the door. The chambermaid was there, looking rather frightened. Behind her stood Meyer. Anthony was draped over his uncle's shoulder; his eyes were closed and there was blood all down Meyer's side.

Abigail gave a little cry of horror and backed into the middle of the room.

"I'm sorry," Meyer said. He sounded as though he was speaking from a great distance. "I should have taken him to the hospital. There are so many men there, though, I thought—" he staggered slightly. "I thought he might do better here."

Diana, her eyes enormous, was standing by the window clutching a piece of sheet.

"Of course he should be here," Abigail said fiercely. She held the door open and helped Meyer set his burden down on the bed.

"I believe his arm is broken," Meyer said. "And he has taken a nasty blow on the head."

Her daughter was issuing low-voiced instructions to the chambermaid. Now she came over and stood looking down at the slight figure on the bed. "He needs a doctor," she said, worried.

"They are in very short supply." Meyer turned back towards the door, stumbling a little. "I will see if I can find one."

Diana was already cutting off Roth's jacket, easing it carefully away from the injured arm. "There is a great deal of blood," she observed. "Not dried blood either. He must have a wound here that is still bleeding."

Abigail, staring after Meyer, did not really hear

her at first. She returned to the bed to find her
daughter frowning down at Roth's body, which was
naked from the waist up. She was too exhausted
even to be shocked.

"Do you suppose all that blood could be from his
head?" Diana asked. Then she answered her own
question. "No, for that is all dry now."

"What blood?" said Abigail, emerging from her
daze.

"Look." Diana stooped and picked up the ruined
jacket, which she had tossed onto the floor. The
lower portion was sodden with blood. "He should
have a wound here"—pointing to the stomach—
"but there is nothing." She covered her patient with
a shawl and began sponging the sticky mess at his
temples.

At this point the chambermaid returned with hot
water and towels, which the two women accepted
gratefully.

"Shall I mop up the floor, then?" asked the maid.

Abigail looked down. There were little splotches
of blood leading to the bed—and back. She went to
the door and opened it. Little splotches in the hall.
One set to the door, one set away from the door.

"Diana," she said, feeling faint. "It's not Anthony's blood."

Her daughter looked up, startled.

"Stay here," Abigail told her. "Do not leave. I am
going to find Mr. Meyer." She picked up the nearest
roll of bandages, grabbed her reticule, and ran out
the door, nearly knocking over the chambermaid,
who was mopping the hall. Down the stairs. Through
the front room. There were little splotches everywhere. When she reached the street she stopped,

suddenly at a loss. It was a short, narrow street, with several alleys and cross streets angling off of it. The cobbles, unlike the floors of the hotel, did not show bloodstains. And she did not see Meyer anywhere. There were too many people, people hurrying past on foolish errands that did not involve someone dripping blood onto the floor. As she ran from one alley to the next, hoping to catch a glimpse of him, she began to understand what he must have gone through last night. She was searching for a wounded man in the daylight, in a small street full of healthy, ordinary people. He had been searching in the dark, in an enormous field full of corpses, not knowing whether he would find his son and his nephew alive or dead.

After a minute she gave up trying to spot him. She would have to guess where he might have gone. And since the only place in Brussels she knew, besides Mrs. Woodley's house, was the Namur Gate, she began walking in that direction.

Meyer had actually passed through the gate before he realized where he was going and stopped. He closed his eyes. "No," he whispered. Whatever monstrous undertow was dragging him back to the woods and fields of Waterloo, he would not give in to it. He turned around and walked back inside the walls. He knew he was not thinking very clearly. He had had no sleep at all; he had rummaged through piles of corpses; had shot a looter in the head; had been shot in turn; had walked for more than a mile carrying an unconscious man. There were holes in his memory, too. For instance, he could remember arriving in the city with Anthony in the supply wagon, but he could not remember getting into the wagon. And he knew he had promised to do something when he left Abigail's room, but now he could no longer remember what it was. He wished that some of his other memories would also disappear. Unfortunately, they refused to leave.

He looked around, seeking a place for a man with ugly memories and a fogged intellect to rest and take stock. His arm ached fiercely, but he ignored it. His intellect was not that badly fogged; he knew he needed a doctor. He also knew his chance of finding one today in Brussels was virtually nonexistent. There were others who needed a doctor far more than he did, and most of them would not get one. For one moment he recalled his promise to Abigail. Doctor. Anthony. The next moment it was gone again.

A few yards down from the gate was a staircase leading up to a platform on the wall. It had been built to allow defenders to haul cauldrons of pitch up to the edge of the wall and it was now considered a charming relic of more barbarous times. Somehow that platform, with its gruesome past, seemed entirely appropriate to him as a retreat. He made his way over to the base of the stairs and started to climb. After a few minutes he realized that he had stopped partway up. He looked down. The staircase seemed very narrow and steep. Better to go up. He clutched the wall with his good hand and resumed climbing.

There was a magnificent view from the top. Facing in, he could see all the way across the city to the walls on the lower side. He could see the cathedral, and, nearly below him, the palace. In the other direction he could see the road to Waterloo, with its litter of bodies and abandoned artillery pieces. He could see the forest. He could not see the battlefield itself, but the wheeling birds told him where it was. Then he began to feel dizzy—or rather, even more dizzy. He sat down on the stone floor and leaned his right shoulder against the parapet. The day was already warm; the cool stone felt good, and now that he was seated he was in the shade. Not only that, he could no longer see the battlefield, only the city.

When the small, green-garbed figure carrying a sausage began to climb the stairs he paid no attention at first. He couldn't imagine why anyone else would want to climb up ninety-six steps. They would become discouraged and go back down.

The figure kept climbing.

It occurred to him that he had seen that green dress before. Earlier this morning, in fact. That the cap—which was all he could see of her head from above—was also familiar. The sausage was a puzzle, but there was no doubt who it was. He watched her come closer and closer. She was climbing steadily—not fast, but at an even, disciplined pace. Every twenty steps she would pause, catch her breath, and then continue.

It occurred to him that he was trapped.

When she finally reached the platform, she glared at him. "Don't bother to get up," she said, dropping down beside him. "I suppose you think it is a great joke to drip blood all over my bedchamber and then come up here to hide like a wounded bird."

She was angry. He didn't understand that. He

stole a quick glance at her profile, at her beautiful, perfectly modeled profile. He realized that she was not so much angry as frightened.

"It is just a flesh wound," he said.

She was opening her reticule, which was the tube-like shape he had mistaken for a sausage. It was crammed with rolls of bandages. "Can you get your jacket off without hurting the wound more?" The answer was no, but he suspected that anyone who had brought bandages up to the top of the Namur Gate would also have scissors, and he did not want her cutting his clothing off in front of half the population of Brussels. With her assistance he managed to get his left arm out of the sleeve.

She sucked in her breath at the sight of his shirt. The scissors duly appeared. "Lean forward," she said.

Obediently, he leaned forward.

"No wonder there was so much blood. The bullet went all the way through." She began to bind on folded pads of bandaging, first on the front of his arm, then on the back. She tied the pads very tightly; his arm began to throb. "Good," she said, standing up. "Let's go."

He began to laugh.

"What is so funny?" she snapped.

"Abigail, there is no possible way that I can go down those stairs. I am sleepless, injured, starving, and dizzy. I will kill myself, and if you try to help me I will kill you, too. I am doomed to stay here until I rot." The word *rot* made him shudder slightly, remembering the pit. At least up here there was no mud.

"Why did you come up, then?"

"I don't know." But he did know.

"How am I going to get you down?" She sounded frantic.

"Why would you want me down?" He picked up the remnants of the blood-soaked shirt and held them up. "Would you want to wear this?"

She stared, bewildered.

"Last night," he said, "I spent the whole night looking for my son and my nephew. And I found both of them. I even found them alive. I should be grateful, don't you think? I found your daughter, too. Three in one day!"

He paused, then said thoughtfully, "Do you know what I had planned to do, after I found Diana? What I fantasized about, on the way to Ramsgate and Ostend? I was going to present her to you, like a trophy from a contest, and ask you to marry me. I was too much of a gentleman to ask you while you were so distraught, you see. But my plans went wrong. Anthony went missing, and James. I needed more trophies."

Her eyes were wide with shock. He wondered if he seemed mad to her.

"I spent hours on that battlefield," he continued. "It was dark, and I went from body to body with my lantern, looking at the regimental markings on the jackets—that was the quickest way, you know, because a lot of them didn't have faces any longer. But the lantern can only show you one little spot. Two bodies. Three bodies. Maybe five or six. And I was still there when dawn came." He shuddered. "I looked—I couldn't help myself—I looked at the whole thing, at the miles and miles of corpses, and I thought of the tiny fraction I had been able to see as I searched, and I remembered what you had said."

"What I had said?"

"That I send off reports, and thousands of people die. That I play games, and boys wake up without an arm, or a leg, or an eye."

"No!" she cried, horrified. "You cannot blame yourself for this! You cannot believe I meant my words so literally!"

"It looked quite literal to me," he said. "The thousands of people dying, in particular. Don't misunderstand me. I am not accepting sole responsibility for that slaughterhouse. But even if I only accept a fraction—and I think I must—a fraction of that horror is too much. When I brought Anthony to you this morning, I felt unclean. I could not be in the same room with myself. I could not even be in the same building with myself. So I came up here." He gestured. "No roof."

"What if I accept a fraction?" she asked fiercely. "Shall I throw myself off the city walls as well?"

He stared at her. "You?"

"What if I had never interfered that night at Pont-Haut? What if you had been able to blow up the bridge? Would Napoleon have retaken France? Would all this have happened?" She waved towards the forest beyond the walls. "Perhaps not."

He frowned. "That is different."

"Well then, let us consider a much smaller, less complex problem. If you starve yourself to death over the Namur Gate because of some misguided, self-righteous remarks I made in a fit of temper, what is my responsibility for your death?"

"I am not going to starve myself to death." He was beginning to feel a little calmer.

"Then you are coming down with me?"

He sighed. "Abigail, I am filthy. In every sense of the word. I will come down, yes. But not with you."

"Because I am a woman of principle, and you are an unprincipled scoundrel?"

"Something like that."

She sat up very straight, her hands clasping her knees. "Let me tell you about my principles," she said. "Let me tell you about how pure and virtuous I am."

"Abigail, don't," he said. He knew what she was going to say, or thought he knew.

"I let you make your confession," she said. "And I assure you mine is infinitely more modest. I don't claim to have destroyed the entire British army. Just my good name."

He sighed.

"Did you know that I was married to two different Harts?"

"Yes," he said. "It is very unusual, these days."

"Paul, my first husband, died very young. And I had loved him, and I had wanted his child. I begged Aaron to marry me." She paused. "Don't imagine I was an innocent. I knew what he was; Paul used to worry about him constantly. Aaron was never sober after four in the afternoon. I didn't care. I wrote to the rabbi of the Sephardic synagogue and asked him to send my family records of other cases where it had been permitted. I got my wish. I married Aaron, and I had a child. But Diana was not a boy. She could not be Paul's child, as I had hoped. And after she was born I was told I could never have any more children. I had married a drunkard to have a child for a dead man, and I had failed."

"You had Diana."

"Yes, I had Diana. I tried to stay for her sake, but

I couldn't. Aaron loved Diana, loved her passionately; I knew he would never harm her except perhaps through overindulgence. He hated me, though. I had tricked him, as he saw it. I was to produce Paul's son, and bring us Paul's money. I did not keep my part of the bargain. But he would not divorce me; I was too wealthy."

He put his good arm around her. "Abigail, stop."

"No. No. You are the only one besides Fanny I have ever told." She wiped her eyes. "I hired a man," she said defiantly. "I suppose you would have to call him a prostitute. And I could not take a chance that Aaron would claim it was a fraud, so I—I went to bed with the man. And Rosie, poor Rosie, made sure that Aaron and Stephen would come in and find me."

She looked up at him, her green eyes glittering with tears. "So you see, when I lectured you in France about deception and manipulation and playing games I was only condemning in you what I hated in myself. I lied to make Aaron marry me, and I lied to make him divorce me, and in the process I degraded myself in every possible way."

"You did what you had to do," he said helplessly. "Sometimes circumstances don't allow us to be moral. Sometimes we have to choose between different ways of being immoral."

"So you think I should forgive myself?"

He was weak from loss of blood, and a bit feverish, but he was not stupid. "This is a trap, isn't it?" he asked. "You've argued me into a corner. I've fallen in love with the Spinoza of Goodman's Fields."

"Are you coming down?" she asked, very gently this time.

"Yes. I don't know how we will manage it, though. Who will come up ninety-six stairs and help me down?"

"Don't be ridiculous," she said. "This is Belgium." And she stood up and waved her white cap in the air until some people began peering up at the top of the wall from the street below. "Good citizens of Brussels!" she called, in clear, carrying French. "Who will earn four gold pieces helping me carry my husband the banker down the stairs?"

Six men began running towards the stairs before she even finished.

"You got more value for your four gold pieces than I did," Meyer told her as they climbed back up to her rooms. On the way up the hill he had told her the story of the looters. "Your hireling helped me down *and* fetched a carriage for us."

"Also, he did not shoot us," she reminded him.

She opened the door.

"Mother!" Diana jumped up. "I did *not* go out, even though you were gone a very long time, and the doctor is here, and Anthony has just woken up this minute!"

The doctor was there. He looked at the mountain of bandages on Meyer's arm and raised his eyebrows.

Meyer went over to the bed. Anthony was looking up at him. "Did we win?" he croaked.

Meyer nodded.

"Good." Anthony closed his eyes. "You can buy me out now," he said.

EPILOGUE

London, July 1815

The Harts were lined up in Abigail's drawing room like a panel of judges facing a prisoner. The women were on the left: Danielle Hart and Abigail's sister, Leah, who was an honorary member of the family—a replacement for Abigail, who had been demoted. The men were on the right: Joshua and Stephen. They sat stiffly, with a look of sorrow on their faces. They would do their duty, but they did not have to enjoy it.

Danielle, as usual, was the spokeswoman. "We have come to see you, Abigail, because Leah has heard a rather disturbing rumor. It is being said that you are planning to remarry."

"I am," said Abigail.

"We do not approve." Stephen crossed his arms. "This was not part of our bargain when we agreed to allow Diana to reside with you."

She had expected this, but that did not make it any easier. "I made no promise not to remarry.

Surely there is nothing improper about marriage? And Diana will benefit from some male guidance."

"We do not object to marriage *per se*," Danielle said. Joshua muttered something, clearly in disagreement, and she glared at him. "We object to your choice of husband."

"And why is that? 'He is a gentleman of means and leisure, received by notables such as the Duke of Wellington.'" It was childish, but she couldn't help herself.

Joshua winced as she recited the words of his own letter. "I was deceived," he said. "I admit it freely. I did not know that his daughter had abandoned her faith to further her worldly interests. We cannot permit you to bring someone of such unsteady principles into the family as Diana's half sister."

"His daughter is grown," said Abigail. "She is married, with a household of her own." It infuriated her that they were using Rachel Drayton as a weapon against her father. Only distantly did she remember that at one time she had condemned him for the same reason.

Stephen cleared his throat. "There is another difficulty." He looked at Joshua, who nodded. "It pains me to speak of this, but apparently Mr. Meyer's son committed perjury. With his father's full endorsement."

"You are forgetting the duels," said a voice from the doorway. "Let us by all means be complete in our indictment. James has fought at least a dozen. Every one of them illegal, under English law."

She had not seen him in a week. How had he known to come today, right now? She wondered if he had been having her house watched. The thought should have horrified her. It didn't. She was profoundly thankful that he was here.

Meyer was duly presented to her sister and the three Harts. They barely acknowledged the introduction and sat staring at him as though he were a poisonous snake.

"You were saying, before I came in?" Meyer prompted, taking a seat near Abigail.

"We were having a family council," Joshua said. "About private matters."

"As I shall soon be joining the family, I would be delighted to assist you in your deliberations."

Danielle at least had the courage of her convictions. She glared at him. "If you must know, we were telling Abigail that if she marries you, we will feel obliged to remove Diana from her care."

"Because I am a bad influence."

"Yes," she said defiantly.

"My son, for example. Serving as an officer under a false name." His eyelids were drooping; he looked half-asleep. "Patriotism carried too far, you would say."

"He is infamous," Danielle snapped.

"Oh, hardly infamous. Notorious, perhaps. Since his marriage he has renounced all ambitions towards infamy." He narrowed his gaze, focusing on Joshua. "You did hear that he married last year, did you not? His wife has been a remarkably steadying influence on his character. Perhaps you should reconsider your judgment of James. Samuel Bernal might take offense at the notion that his son-in-law is unacceptable to one of his principal business partners."

Stephen turned in alarm to Joshua. "Is this true? Is Meyer's son married to Bernal's daughter?"

Joshua muttered that perhaps he had heard something of the sort.

"It was a quiet wedding," Meyer said. "Illness in the bride's family. You could hardly be blamed for failing to note the event."

Abigail watched Joshua squirm. It was one thing for Joshua to insult the Roth-Meyer family, who had no connection with the Harts's cargo brokerage. It was quite another to insult Samuel Bernal, who controlled half the shipping in England. Her stomach felt hollow. She knew she should intervene; should reassure Joshua that of course Meyer would not ruin his brokerage in retaliation for a dispute about Diana, that she would never permit anything of the sort.

She said nothing.

Five minutes later, the four visitors were being ushered out by Abigail's new butler.

Meyer stood leaning against the door of the drawing room, studying her with a faintly anxious look on his face. "That was extortion," he pointed out, as though she would not have noticed. "I believe it is illegal." He added scrupulously, "I feel obliged to tell you that I enjoyed every minute of it."

"I didn't," she admitted. "But I wanted to." She crossed her arms over her chest and shivered. "Sometimes I feel as though I have forgotten how to laugh."

"Perhaps you should strive to break the rules more, and I should strive to break them less."

"Perhaps." She looked down.

He had a terrifying ability to move very quickly without making any noise. Somehow he was now right next to her.

"These caps, for example." He tugged hers off. "If you are going to look down every time I mention anything dangerous, I would prefer to look at your hair."

"Only when we are alone," she said, feeling suddenly as though there was no air to breathe.

"We are alone." He added, after a moment. "You are not *required* to look down."

Some minutes later, Diana opened the drawing room door without knocking and burst in. "Mother, Anthony is back from Edinburgh," she said happily. "He sent me a note. May I go to a concert with him?" Then she gasped, turned bright scarlet, and backed out, forgetting to close the door behind her.

Meyer sighed, crossed the room, and latched the door. "While I was waiting to make my grand entrance I believe I heard you say that Diana would benefit from some male guidance. Knocking on doors will be the first lesson."

HISTORICAL NOTE

Many novelists, including authors of historical romance, have written about Waterloo. Although that epic battle does figure in the conclusion of this story, I wanted to concentrate instead on the beginning of the story of Waterloo—on Napoleon's return from Elba. The former emperor landed near what is now Cannes on the evening of March 1, 1815, accompanied by some fifteen hundred troops of his personal guard, a courtesy force assigned to him for his residence in exile on Elba. That small army marched on foot over two hundred miles—through some of the most mountainous terrain in France—in seven days, reaching Grenoble in triumph on the evening of March 7. This feat is memorialized by the modern French highway called the *Route Napoléon* (N85), which follows the emperor's march and commemorates with historic markers everything from the dramatic confrontation at Laffrey, narrated in this book, to little inns where Napoleon ate an omelet. I have tried to be as accurate as possible in depicting travel conditions and landscapes as my hero and heroine precede Napoleon over the mountains, but true Napoleon buffs may find a few slips.

Readers are invited to find photos of my own trip from Cannes to Grenoble, as well as further information about Wellington's intelligence service and the Jewish community of Regency London, at my web site (www.nitaabrams.com). There is also a mail link; I always enjoy hearing from readers.

Many thanks to my research assistants on the N85, Rachel and MK, and to my many wonderful readers, who write me about everything from Jewish marriage law to Regency architecture.

BARRON'S BOOK NOTES

ALDOUS HUXLEY'S

Brave New World

BY

Anthony Astrachan

SERIES EDITOR

Michael Spring
Editor, *Literary Cavalcade*
Scholastic Inc.

BARRON'S EDUCATIONAL SERIES, INC.
Woodbury, New York / London / Toronto / Sydney

ACKNOWLEDGMENTS

We would like to acknowledge the many painstaking hours of work Holly Hughes and Thomas F. Hirsch have devoted to making the *Book Notes* series a success.

© Copyright 1984 by Barron's Educational Series, Inc.

All rights reserved.
No part of this book may be reproduced in any form,
by photostat, microfilm, xerography, or any other
means, or incorporated into any information retrieval
system, electronic or mechanical, without the written
permission of the copyright owner.

All inquiries should be addressed to:
Barron's Educational Series, Inc.
113 Crossways Park Drive
Woodbury, New York 11797

Library of Congress Catalog Card No. 84-18429

International Standard Book No. 0-8120-3405-8

Library of Congress Cataloging in Publication Data
Astrachan, Anthony.
   Aldous Huxley's Brave new world.

   (Barron's book notes)
   Bibliography: p. 80
   Summary: A guide to reading "Brave New World" with
a critical and appreciative mind encouraging analysis
of plot, style, form, and structure. Also includes
background on the author's life and times, sample tests,
term paper suggestions, and a reading list.
   1. Huxley, Aldous, 1894–1963. Brave new world.
[1. Huxley, Aldous, 1894–1963. Brave New World.
2. English literature—History and criticism]
I. Title.   II. Series.
PR6015.U9B6723   1984   823'.912   84-18429
ISBN 0-8120-3405-8 (pbk.)

PRINTED IN THE UNITED STATES OF AMERICA

456   550   98765432

CONTENTS

HOW TO USE THIS BOOK

You have to know how to approach literature in order to get the most out of it. This *Barron's Book Notes* volume follows a plan based on methods used by some of the best students to read a work of literature.

Begin with the guide's section on the author's life and times. As you read, try to form a clear picture of the author's personality, circumstances, and motives for writing the work. This background usually will make it easier for you to hear the author's tone of voice, and follow where the author is heading.

Then go over the rest of the introductory material—such sections as those on the plot, characters, setting, themes, and style of the work. Underline, or write down in your notebook, particular things to watch for, such as contrasts between characters and repeated literary devices. At this point, you may want to develop a system of symbols to use in marking your text as you read. (Of course, you should only mark up a book you own, not one that belongs to another person or a school.) Perhaps you will want to use a different letter for each character's name, a different number for each major theme of the book, a different color for each important symbol or literary device. Be prepared to mark up the pages of your book as you read. Put your marks in the margins so you can find them again easily.

Now comes the moment you've been waiting for—the time to start reading the work of literature. You may want to put aside your *Barron's Book Notes* volume until you've read the work all the way through. Or you may want to alternate, reading the *Book Notes* analysis of each section as soon as you have finished reading the corresponding part of the original. Before you move on, reread crucial passages you don't fully understand. (Don't take this guide's analysis for granted—make up your own mind as to what the work means.)

Once you've finished the whole work of literature, you may want to review it right away, so you can firm up your ideas about what it means. You may want to leaf through the book concentrating on passages you marked in reference to one character or one theme. This is also a good time to reread the *Book Notes* introductory material, which pulls together insights on specific topics.

When it comes time to prepare for a test or to write a paper, you'll already have formed ideas about the work. You'll be able to go back through it, refreshing your memory as to the author's exact words and perspective, so that you can support your opinions with evidence drawn straight from the work. Patterns will emerge, and ideas will fall into place; your essay question or term paper will almost write itself. Give yourself a dry run with one of the sample tests in the guide. These tests present both multiple-choice and essay questions. An accompanying section gives answers to the multiple-choice questions as well as suggestions for writing the essays. If you have to select a term paper topic, you may choose one from the list of suggestions in this book. This guide also provides you with a reading list, to help you when you start research for a term paper, and a selection of provocative comments by critics, to spark your thinking before you write.

THE AUTHOR AND HIS TIMES

Aldous Leonard Huxley was born on July 26, 1894, into a family that included some of the most distinguished members of that part of the English ruling class made up of the intellectual elite. Aldous' father was the son of Thomas Henry Huxley, a great biologist who helped develop the theory of evolution. His mother was the sister of Mrs. Humphrey Ward, the novelist; the niece of Matthew Arnold, the poet; and the granddaughter of Thomas Arnold, a famous educator and the real-life headmaster of Rugby School who became a character in the novel *Tom Brown's Schooldays*.

Undoubtedly, Huxley's heritage and upbringing had an effect on his work. Gerald Heard, a longtime friend, said that Huxley's ancestry "brought down on him a weight of intellectual authority and a momentum of moral obligations." Throughout *Brave New World* you can see evidence of an ambivalent attitude toward such authority assumed by a ruling class.

Like the England of his day, Huxley's Utopia possesses a rigid class structure, one even stronger than England's because it is biologically and chemically engineered and psychologically conditioned. And the members of *Brave New World*'s ruling class certainly believe they possess the right to make everyone happy by denying them love and freedom.

Huxley's own experiences made him stand apart from the class into which he was born. Even as a small child he was considered different, showing an alertness, an intelligence, what his brother called a superiority. He was respected and loved—not hated—for these abilities, but he drew on that feeling of separateness in writing *Brave New World*. Bernard Marx and Helmholtz Watson, both members of the elite class, have problems because they're different from their peers. Huxley felt that heredity made each individual unique, and the uniqueness of the individual was essential to freedom. Like his family, and like the Alphas of *Brave New World*, Huxley felt a moral obligation—but it was the obligation to fight the idea that happiness could be achieved through class-instituted slavery of even the most benevolent kind.

Another event that marked Huxley was his mother's death from cancer when he was 14. This, he said later, gave him a sense of the transience of human happiness. Perhaps you can also see the influence of his loss in *Brave New World*. The Utopians go to great lengths to deny the unpleasantness of death, and to find perpetual happiness. But the cost is very great. By denying themselves unpleasant emotions they deny themselves deeply joyous ones as well. Their happiness can be continued endlessly by taking the drug *soma*, by making love, or by playing Obstacle Golf, but this happiness is essentially shallow. Standing in contrast to the Utopians are the Savages on the Reservation in New Mexico: poor, dirty, subject to the ills of old age and painful death, but, Huxley seems to believe, blessed with a happiness that while still transient is deeper and more real than that enjoyed by the inhabitants of London and the rest of the World State.

When Huxley was 16 and a student at the prestigious school Eton, an eye illness made him nearly blind. He recovered enough vision to go on to Oxford

University and graduate with honors, but not enough to fight in World War I, an important experience for many of his friends, or to do the scientific work he had dreamed of. Scientific ideas remained with him, however, and he used them in many of his books, particularly *Brave New World*. The idea of vision also remained important to him; his early novels contain scenes that seem ideal for motion pictures, and he later became a screenwriter.

He entered the literary world while he was at Oxford, meeting writers like Lytton Strachey and Bertrand Russell and becoming close friends with D.H. Lawrence, with whom you might think he had almost nothing in common.

Huxley published his first book, a collection of poems, in 1916. He married Maria Nys, a Belgian, in 1919. Their only child, Matthew Huxley, was born in 1920. The family divided their time between London and Europe, mostly Italy, in the 1920s, and traveled around the world in 1925 and 1926, seeing India and making a first visit to the United States.

Huxley liked the confidence, vitality, and "generous extravagance" he found in American life. But he wasn't so sure he liked the way vitality was expressed "in places of public amusement, in dancing and motoring . . . Nowhere, perhaps, is there so little conversation . . . It is all movement and noise, like the water gurgling out of a bath—down the waste. Yes, down the waste." Those thoughts of the actual world, from the book *Jesting Pilate*, were to color his picture of the perpetual happiness attempted in *Brave New World*.

His experiences in fascist Italy, where Benito Mussolini led an authoritarian government that fought against birth control in order to produce enough manpower for the next war, also provided materials for Huxley's bad Utopia, as did his reading of books critical of the Soviet Union.

Huxley wrote *Brave New World* in four months in 1931. It appeared three years after the publication of his best-seller, the novel *Point Counter Point*. During those three years, he had produced six books of stories, essays, poems, and plays, but nothing major. His biographer, Sybille Bedford, says, "It was time to produce some full-length fiction—he still felt like holding back from another straight novel—juggling in fiction form with the scientific possibilities of the future might be a new line."

Because *Brave New World* describes a bad Utopia, it is often compared with George Orwell's *1984*, another novel you may want to read, which also describes a possible horrible world of the future. The world of *1984* is one of tyranny, terror, and perpetual warfare. Orwell wrote it in 1948, shortly after the Allies had defeated Nazi Germany in World War II and just as the West was discovering the full dimensions of the evils of Soviet totalitarianism.

It's important to remember that Huxley wrote *Brave New World* in 1931, before Adolf Hitler came to power in Germany and before Joseph Stalin started the purges that killed millions of people in the Soviet Union. He therefore had no immediate real-life reason to make tyranny and terror major elements of his story. In 1958 Huxley himself said, "The future dictatorship of my imaginary world was a good deal less brutal than the future dictatorship so brilliantly portrayed by Orwell."

In 1937, the Huxleys came to the United States; in 1938 they went to Hollywood, where he became a screenwriter (among his films was an adaptation of Jane Austen's *Pride and Prejudice*, which starred the young Laurence Olivier). He remained for most of his life in California, and one of his novels caricatures what he saw as the strange life there: *After Many a Summer Dies the Swan*. In it the tycoon Jo Stoyte tries to achieve immortality through scientific experimentation, even if it means giving up humanity and returning to the completely animal state—an echo of *Brave New World*.

In 1946 Huxley wrote a Foreword to *Brave New World* in which he said he no longer wanted to make social sanity an impossibility, as he had in the novel. Though World War II had caused the deaths of some 20 million inhabitants of the Soviet Union, six million Jews, and millions of others, and the newly developed atomic bomb held the threat of even more extensive destruction, Huxley had become convinced that while still "rather rare," sanity could be achieved and said that he would like to see more of it. In the same year, he published *The Perennial Philosophy*, an anthology of texts with his own commentaries on mystical and religious approaches to a sane life in a sane society.

He also worried about the dangers that threatened sanity. In 1958, he published *Brave New World Revisited*, a set of essays on real-life problems and ideas you'll find in the novel—overpopulation, overorganization, and psychological techniques from salesmanship to hypnopaedia, or sleep-teaching. They're all tools that a government can abuse to deprive people of freedom, an abuse that Huxley wanted people to fight. If you want to further relate his bad new world to the real world, read *Brave New World Revisited*.

In the 1950s Huxley became famous for his interest in psychedelic or mind-expanding drugs like mescaline and LSD, which he apparently took a dozen times over ten years. Sybille Bedford says he was looking for a drug that would allow an escape from the self and that if taken with caution would be physically and socially harmless.

He put his beliefs in such a drug and in sanity into several books. Two, based on his experiences taking mescaline under supervision, were nonfiction: *Doors of Perception* (1954) and *Heaven and Hell* (1956). Some readers have read those books as encouragements to experiment freely with drugs, but Huxley warned of the dangers of such experiments in an appendix he wrote to *The Devils of Loudun* (1952), a psychological study of an episode in French history.

Another work centering on drugs and sanity was *Island* (1962), a novel that required 20 years of thought and five years of writing. Among other things, *Island* was an antidote to *Brave New World,* a good Utopia. Huxley deplored the drug he called *soma* in *Brave New World*—half tranquilizer, half intoxicant—which produces an artificial happiness that makes people content with their lack of freedom. He approved of the perfected version of LSD that the people of *Island* use in a religious way.

Huxley produced 47 books in his long career as a writer. The English critic Anthony Burgess has said that he equipped the novel with a brain. Other critics objected that he was a better essayist than novelist precisely because he cared more about his ideas than about plot or characters, and his novels' ideas often get in the way of the story.

But Huxley's emphasis on ideas and his skill as an essayist cannot hide one important fact: The books he wrote that are most read and best remembered today are all novels—*Crome Yellow, Antic Hay,* and *Point Counter Point* from the 1920s, *Brave New World* and *After Many a Summer Dies the Swan* from the 1930s. In

1959 the American Academy of Arts and Letters gave him the Award of Merit for the Novel, a prize given every five years; earlier recipients had been Ernest Hemingway, Thomas Mann, and Theodore Dreiser.

The range of Huxley's interests can be seen from his note that his "preliminary research" for *Island* included "Greek history, Polynesian anthropology, translations from Sanskrit and Chinese of Buddhist texts, scientific papers on pharmacology, neurophysiology, psychology and education, together with novels, poems, critical essays, travel books, political commentaries and conversations with all kinds of people, from philosophers to actresses, from patients in mental hospitals to tycoons in Rolls-Royces. . . ." He used similar, though probably fewer, sources for *Brave New World*.

This list gives you some perspective on the wide range of ideas that Huxley studied. He also wrote an early essay on ecology that helped inspire today's environmental movement. And he was a pacifist. This belief prevented him from becoming an American citizen because he would not say his pacifism was a matter of his religion, which might have made him an acceptable conscientious objector.

Huxley remained nearly blind all his life. Maria Huxley died in 1955, and Huxley married Laura Archera a year later. He died November 22, 1963, the same day that President John F. Kennedy was assassinated. He was cremated, and his ashes were buried in his parents' grave in England.

THE NOVEL

The Plot

Brave New World is partly a statement of ideas (expressed by characters with no more depth than cartoon characters) and only partly a story with a plot.

The first three chapters present most of the important ideas or themes of the novel. The Director of Hatcheries and Conditioning explains that this Utopia breeds people to order, artificially fertilizing a mother's eggs to create babies that grow in bottles. They are not born, but decanted. Everyone belongs to one of five classes, from the Alphas, the most intelligent, to the Epsilons, morons bred to do the dirty jobs that nobody else wants to do. The lower classes are multiplied by a budding process that can create up to 96 identical clones and produce over 15,000 brothers and sisters from a single ovary.

All the babies are conditioned, physically and chemically in the bottle, and psychologically after birth, to make them happy citizens of the society with both a liking and an aptitude for the work they will do. One psychological conditioning technique is hypnopaedia, or teaching people while they sleep—not teaching facts or analysis, but planting suggestions that will make people behave in certain ways. The Director also makes plain that sex is a source of happiness, a game people play with anyone who pleases them.

The Controller, one of the ten men who run the world, explains some of the more profound principles on which the Utopia is based. One is that "history is bunk"; the society limits people's knowledge of the past so they will not be able to compare the present with anything that might make them want to change the present. Another principle is that people should have no emotions, particularly no painful emotions; blind happiness is necessary for stability. One of the things that guarantees happiness is a drug called *soma*, which calms you down and gets you high but never gives you a hangover. Another is the "feelies," movies that reach your sense of touch as well as your sight and hearing.

After Huxley presents these themes in the first three chapters, the story begins. Bernard Marx, an Alpha of the top class, is on the verge of falling in love with Lenina Crowne, a woman who works in the Embryo Room of the Hatchery. Lenina has been dating Henry Foster, a Hatchery scientist; her friend Fanny nags her because she hasn't seen any other man for four months. Lenina likes Bernard but doesn't fall in love with him. Falling in love is a sin in this world in which one has sex with everyone else, and she is a happy, conforming citizen of the Utopia.

Bernard is neither happy nor conforming. He's a bit odd; for one thing, he's small for an Alpha, in a world where every member of the same caste is alike. He likes to treasure his differences from his fellows, but he lacks the courage to fight for his right to be an individual. In contrast is his friend Helmholtz Watson, successful in sports, sex, and community activities, but openly dissatisfied because instead of writing something beautiful and powerful, his job is to turn out propaganda.

Bernard attends a solidarity service of the Fordian religion, a parody of Christianity as practiced in England in the 1920s. It culminates in a sexual orgy, but he doesn't feel the true rapture experienced by the other 11 members of his group.

Bernard then takes Lenina to visit a Savage Reservation in North America. While signing his permit to go, the Director tells Bernard how he visited the same Reservation as a young man, taking a young woman from London who disappeared and was presumed dead. He then threatens Bernard with exile to Iceland because Bernard is a nonconformist: he doesn't gobble up pleasure in his leisure time like an infant.

At the Reservation, Bernard and Lenina meet John, a handsome young Savage who, Bernard soon realizes, is the son of the Director. Clearly, the woman the Director had taken to the Reservation long ago had become pregnant as the result of an accident that the citizens of Utopia would consider obscene. John has a fantasy picture of the Utopia from his mother's tales and a knowledge of Shakespeare that he mistakes for a guide to reality.

Bernard gets permission from the Controller to bring John and Linda, his mother, back to London. The Director had called a public meeting to announce Bernard's exile, but by greeting the Director as lover and father, respectively, Linda and John turn him into an obscene joke. Bernard stays and becomes the center of attention of all London because he is, in effect, John's guardian, and everybody wants to meet the Savage. Linda goes into a permanent *soma* trance after her years of exile on the Reservation. John is taken to see all the attractions of new world society and doesn't like them. But he enjoys arguing with Helmholtz about them, and about Shakespeare.

Lenina has become popular because she is thought to be sleeping with the Savage. Everyone envies her and wants to know what it's like. But, in fact, while she wants to sleep with John, he refuses because he, too, has fallen in love with her—and he has taken from Shakespeare the old-fashioned idea that lovers should be pure. Not understanding this, she finally comes to his apartment and takes her clothes off. He throws her out, calling her a prostitute because he thinks she's immoral, even though he wants her desperately.

John then learns that his mother is dying. The hospital illustrates the Utopia's approach to death, which includes trying to completely eliminate grief and pain. When John goes to visit Linda he is devastated; his display of grief frightens children being taught that death is a pleasant and natural process. John grows so angry that he tries to bring the Utopia back to what he considers sanity and morality by disrupting the daily distribution of *soma* to lower-caste Delta workers. That leads to a riot; John, Bernard, and Helmholtz are arrested.

The three then confront the Controller, who explains more of the Utopia's principles. Their conversation reveals that the Utopia achieves its happiness by giving up science, art, religion, and other things that we prize in the real world. The Controller sends Bernard to Iceland, after all, and Helmholtz to the Falkland Islands. He keeps John in England, but John finds a place where he can lead a hermit's life, complete with suffering. His solitude is invaded by Utopians who want to see him suffer, as though it were a sideshow spectacle; when Lenina joins the mob, he kills himself.

The Characters

Because this is a Utopian novel of ideas, few of the characters are three-dimensional people who come alive on the page. Most exist to voice ideas in words or to embody them in their behavior. John, Bernard, Helmholtz, and the Controller express ideas through real personalities, but you will enjoy most of the others more if you see them as cartoon characters rather than as full portraits that may seem so poorly drawn that they will disappoint you.

The Director of Hatcheries and Conditioning

The Director opens the novel by explaining the reproductive system of the brave new world, with genetically engineered babies growing in bottles. He loves to throw "scientific data" at his listeners so quickly that they can't understand them; he is a know-it-all impressed with his own importance. In fact, he knows less and is less important than the Controller, as you see when he is surprised that the Controller dares to talk about two forbidden topics—history and biological parents.

The Director comes alive only when he confesses to Bernard Marx that as a young man he went to a Savage Reservation, taking along a woman who disappeared there. She was pregnant with his baby, as a result of what the Utopia considers an obscene accident. The baby grows up to be John; his return to London leads to the total humiliation of the Director.

The Director's name is Thomas, but you learn this only because Linda, his onetime lover and John's mother, keeps referring to him as Tomakin.

Henry Foster

Henry is a scientist in the London Hatchery, an ideal citizen of the world state: efficient and intelligent at work, filling his leisure time with sports and casual sex. He is not an important character but helps Huxley explain the workings of the Hatchery, show Lenina's passionless sex life, and explore the gulf between Bernard and the "normal" citizens of Utopia.

Lenina Crowne

Lenina is young and pretty despite having lupus, an illness that causes reddish-brown blotches to appear on her skin. She is, like Henry Foster, a happy, shallow citizen, her one idiosyncrasy is the fact that she sometimes spends more time than society approves dating one man exclusively.

Like all well-conditioned citizens of the World State, Lenina believes in having sex when she wants it. She can't understand that John avoids sex with her because he loves her and does not want to do something that he thinks—in his old-fashioned, part-Indian, part-Christian, part-Shakespearean way—will dishonor her. She embodies the conflict he feels between body and spirit, between love and lust.

Lenina is more a cartoon character than a real person, but she triggers John's emotional violence and provides the occasion for his suicide when she comes to see him whip himself.

The Controller, Mustapha Mond

Mond is one of the ten people who control the World State. He is good-natured and dedicated to his work, and extremely intelligent; he understands people and ideas that are different, which most Utopians cannot do. He has read such forbidden books as the works of Shakespeare and the Bible, and knows history and philosophy. Indeed, he resembles the Oxford professors that Huxley knew, and his discussion of happiness with the Savage resembles a tutorial between an Oxford don and his most challenging student.

Once a gifted scientist, the Controller made a conscious choice as a young man to become one of the rulers instead of a troublesome dissident. He is one of the few Utopians who can choose, who has free will, and this makes him more rounded and more attractive than most of the characters you'll meet in the book. It also makes him concerned with morality, but he uses his moral force and his sanity for the immoral and insane goals of the Utopia. You may decide that he is the most dangerous person in *Brave New World*.

Bernard Marx

A specialist in sleep-teaching, Bernard does not fit the uniformity that usually characterizes all members of the same caste. He is an Alpha of high intelligence and therefore a member of the elite, but he is small and therefore regarded as deformed. Other people speculate that too much alcohol was put into his bottle when he was still an embryo. He dislikes sports and likes to be alone, two very unusual traits among Utopians. When he first appears, he seems to dislike casual sex, another departure from the norm. He is unhappy in a world where everyone else is happy.

At first Bernard seems to take pleasure in his differentness, to like being a nonconformist and a rebel. Later, he reveals that his rebellion is less a matter of belief than of his own failure to be accepted. When he returns from the Savage Reservation with John, he is suddenly popular with important people and successful with women, and he loves it. Underneath, he has always wanted to be a happy member of the ruling class. In the end, he is exiled to Iceland and protests bitterly.

Helmholtz Watson

Helmholtz, like Bernard, is different from the average Alpha-plus intellectual. A mental giant who is also successful in sports and sex, he's almost too good to be true. But he is a nonconformist who knows that the world is capable of greater literature than the propaganda he writes so well—and that he is capable of producing it. When John the Savage introduces him to Shakespeare, Helmholtz only appreciates half of it; despite his genius, he's still limited by his Utopian upbringing. He remains willing to challenge society even if he can't change it, and accepts exile to the bleak Falkland Islands in the hope that physical discomfort and the company of other dissidents will stimulate his writing.

John the Savage

John is the son of two members of Utopia, but has grown up on a Savage Reservation. He is the only character who can really compare the two different worlds, and it is through him that Huxley shows that his Utopia is a bad one.

John's mother, Linda, became pregnant accidentally, a very unusual event in the brave new world. While she was pregnant, she visited a Savage Reservation, hurt herself in a fall, and got lost, missing her return trip to London. The Indians of the Reservation saved her life and she gave birth to John. The boy grew up absorbing three cultures: the Utopia he heard about from his mother; the Indian culture in which he lived, but which rejected him as an outsider; and the plays of Shakespeare, which he read in a book that survived from pre-Utopian days.

John, in short, is different from the other Savages and from the Utopians. He is tall and handsome, but much more of an alien in either world than Bernard is. John looks at both worlds through the lenses of the religion he acquired on the Reservation—a mixture of Christianity and American Indian beliefs—and the old-fashioned morality he learned from reading Shakespeare. His beliefs contradict those of the brave new world, as he shows in his struggle over sex with Lenina and his fight with the system after his mother dies. Eventually, the conflict is too much for him and he kills himself.

Linda

Linda is John's mother, a Beta minus who sleeps with the Director and becomes pregnant accidentally, 20 years before the action of the book begins. She falls while visiting a Savage Reservation, becomes unconscious, and remains lost until the Director has to leave. She is then rescued by Indians, gives birth to John, and lives for 20 years in the squalor of the Reservation, where she grows old, sick, and fat without the medical care that keeps people physically young in the Utopia. Behaving according to Utopian principles, she sleeps with many of the Indians on the Reservation and never understands why the women despise her or why the community makes John an outcast. When she returns to London, she takes ever-increasing doses of *soma* and stays perpetually high—until the drug kills her.

Other Elements

SETTING

Setting plays a particularly important role in *Brave New World*. Huxley's novel is a novel of Utopia, and a science-fiction novel. In both kinds of books the portrayal of individual characters tends to take a back seat to the portrayal of the society they live in. In some ways, the brave new world itself becomes the book's main character.

The story opens in London some 600 years in the future—632 A.F. (After Ford) in the calendar of the era. Centuries before, civilization as we know it was destroyed in the Nine Years' War. Out of the ruins grew the World State, an all-powerful government headed by ten World Controllers. Faith in Christ has been replaced by Faith in Ford, a mythologized version of Henry Ford, the auto pioneer who developed the mass production methods that have reached their zenith in the World State. Almost all traces of the past have been erased, for, as Henry Ford said, "History is bunk." Changing names show the changed society. Charing Cross, the London railroad station, is now Charing T Rocket Station: the cross has been supplanted by the T, from Henry Ford's Model T. Big Ben is now Big Henry. Westminster Abbey, one of England's most hallowed shrines, is now merely the site of a nightclub, the Westminster Abbey Cabaret.

The people of this world, born from test tubes and divided into five castes, are docile and happy, kept occupied by elaborate games like obstacle golf, entertainments like the "feelies," and sexual promiscuity. Disease is nonexistent, old age and death made as pleasant as possible so they can be ignored.

Some parts of the earth, however, are allowed to remain as they were before the World State came to power. With Bernard and Lenina, you visit one of these Savage Reservations, the New Mexican home of the Zuni Indians. It is a world away from civilized London: the Zunis are impoverished, dirty, ravaged by disease and old age, and still cling to their ancient religion.

The settings in *Brave New World*, then, seem to offer only the choice between civilized servitude and primitive ignorance and squalor. Are these the only choices available? One other is mentioned, the islands of exile—Iceland and the Falkland Islands—where malcontents like Bernard Marx and Helmholtz Watson are sent. But Huxley does not discuss these places in enough detail to let us know whether or not they provide any kind of alternative to the grim life he has presented in the rest of the book.

THEMES

This novel is about a Utopia, an ideal state—a bad ideal state. It is therefore a novel about ideas, and its themes are as important as its plot. They will be studied in depth in the chapter-by-chapter discussion of the book. Most are expressed as fundamental principles of the Utopia, the brave new world. Some come to light when one character, a Savage raised on an Indian reservation, confronts that world. As you find the themes, try to think not only about what they say about Huxley's Utopia, but also about Huxley's real world—and your own.

1. COMMUNITY, IDENTITY, STABILITY— VERSUS INDIVIDUAL FREEDOM

Community, Identity, Stability is the motto of the World State. It lists the Utopia's prime goals. Community is in part a result of identity and stability. It is also achieved through a religion that satirizes Christianity—a religion that encourages people to reach solidarity through sexual orgy. And it is achieved by organizing life so that a person is almost never alone.

Identity is in large part the result of genetic engineering. Society is divided into five classes or castes, hereditary social groups. In the lower three classes, people are cloned in order to produce up to 96 identical "twins." Identity is also achieved by teaching everyone to conform, so that someone who has or feels more than a minimum of individuality is made to feel different, odd, almost an outcast.

Stability is the third of the three goals, but it is the one the characters mention most often—the reason for designing society this way. The desire for stability, for instance, requires the production of large numbers of genetically identical "individuals," because people who are exactly the same are less likely to come into conflict. Stability means minimizing conflict, risk, and change.

2. SCIENCE AS A MEANS OF CONTROL

Brave New World is not only a Utopian book, it is also a science-fiction novel. But it does not predict much about science in general. Its theme "is the advancement of science as it affects human individuals," Huxley said in the Foreword he wrote in 1946, 15 years after he wrote the book. He did not focus on physical sciences like nuclear physics, though even in 1931 he knew that the production of nuclear energy (and weapons) was probable. He was more worried about dangers that appeared more obvious at that time— the possible misuse of biology, physiology, and psychology to achieve community, identity, and stability. Ironically, it becomes clear at the end of the book that the World State's complete control over human activity destroys even the scientific progress that gained it such control.

3. THE THREAT OF GENETIC ENGINEERING

Genetic engineering is a term that has come into use in recent years as scientists have learned to manipulate RNA and DNA, the proteins in every cell that determine the basic inherited characteristics of life. Huxley didn't use the phrase but he describes genetic engineering when he explains how his new world breeds prescribed numbers of humans artificially for specified qualities.

4. THE MISUSE OF PSYCHOLOGICAL CONDITIONING

Every human being in the new world is conditioned to fit society's needs—to like the work he will have to do. Human embryos do not grow inside their mothers' wombs but in bottles. Biological or physiological conditioning consists of adding chemicals or spinning the bottles to prepare the embryos for the levels of strength, intelligence, and aptitude required for given jobs. After they are "decanted" from the bottles, people are psychologically conditioned, mainly by hypnopaedia or sleep-teaching. You might say that at every stage the society brainwashes its citizens.

5. THE PURSUIT OF HAPPINESS CARRIED TO AN EXTREME

A society can achieve stability only when everyone is happy, and the brave new world tries hard to ensure that every person *is* happy. It does its best to eliminate any painful emotion, which means every deep feeling, every passion. It uses genetic engineering and conditioning to ensure that everyone is happy with his or her work.

6. THE CHEAPENING OF SEXUAL PLEASURE

Sex is a primary source of happiness. The brave new world makes promiscuity a virtue: you have sex with any partner you want, who wants you—and sooner or later every partner will want you. (As a child, you learn in your sleep that "everyone belongs to everyone else.") In this Utopia, what we think of as true love for one person would lead to neurotic passions and the establishment of family life, both of which would interfere with community and stability. Nobody is allowed to become pregnant because nobody is born, only decanted from a bottle. Many females are born sterile by design; those who are not are trained by "Malthusian drill" to use contraceptives properly.

7. THE PURSUIT OF HAPPINESS THROUGH DRUGS

Soma is a drug used by everyone in the brave new world. It calms people and gets them high at the same time, but without hangovers or nasty side effects. The rulers of the brave new world had put 2000 pharmacologists and biochemists to work long before the action of the novel begins; in six years they had perfected the drug. Huxley believed in the possibility of a drug that would enable people to escape from themselves and help them achieve knowledge of God, but he made *soma* a parody and degradation of that possibility.

8. THE THREAT OF MINDLESS CONSUMPTION AND MINDLESS DIVERSIONS

This society offers its members distractions that they must enjoy in common—never alone—because solitude breeds instability. Huxley mentions but never explains sports that use complex equipment

whose manufacture keeps the economy rolling—
sports called Obstacle Golf and Centrifugal Bumble-
puppy. But the chief emblem of *Brave New World* is the
Feelies—movies that feature not only sight and sound
but also the sensation of touch, so that when people
watch a couple making love on a bearskin rug, they
can feel every hair of the bear on their own bodies.

9. THE DESTRUCTION OF THE FAMILY
The combination of genetic engineering, bottle-
birth, and sexual promiscuity means there is no monogamy, marriage, or family. "Mother" and "father"
are obscene words that may be used scientifically on
rare, carefully chosen occasions to label ancient
sources of psychological problems.

10. THE DENIAL OF DEATH
The brave new world insists that death is a natural
and not unpleasant process. There is no old age or
visible senility. Children are conditioned at hospitals
for the dying and given sweets to eat when they hear
of death occurring. This conditioning does not—as it
might—prepare people to cope with the death of a
loved one or with their own mortality. It eliminates
the painful emotions of grief and loss, and the spiritual significance of death, which Huxley made increasingly important in his later novels.

11. THE OPPRESSION OF INDIVIDUAL
    DIFFERENCES
Some characters in *Brave New World* differ from the
norm. Bernard is small for an Alpha and fond of solitude; Helmholtz, though seemingly "every centimetre an Alpha-Plus," knows he is too intelligent for the
work he performs; John the Savage, genetically a
member of the World State, has never been properly
conditioned to become a citizen of it. Even the Con-

troller, Mustapha Mond, stands apart because of his leadership abilities. Yet in each case these differences are crushed: Bernard and Helmholtz are exiled; John commits suicide; and the Mond stifles his own individuality in exchange for the power he wields as Controller. What does this say about Huxley's Utopia?

11. WHAT DOES SUCH A SYSTEM COST?

This Utopia has a good side: there is no war or poverty, little disease or social unrest. But Huxley keeps asking, what does society have to pay for these benefits? The price, he makes clear, is high. The first clue is in the epigraph, the quotation at the front of the book. It is in French, but written by a Russian, Nicolas Berdiaeff. It says, "Utopias appear to be much easier to realize than one formerly believed. We currently face a question that would otherwise fill us with anguish: How to avoid their becoming definitively real?"

By the time you hear the conversation between the Controller, one of the men who runs the new world, and John, the Savage, you've learned that citizens of this Utopia must give up love, family, science, art, religion, and history. At the end of the book, John commits suicide and you see that the price of this brave new world is fatally high.

STYLE

Although Huxley's writing style makes him easy to read, his complex ideas make readers think. Even if you're not familiar with his vocabulary or philosophy, you can see that, as the critic Laurence Brander says, "The prose was witty and ran clearly and nimbly."

Huxley's witty, clear, nimble prose is very much an upper-class tradition. *Brave New World*—like all of Huxley's novels—is a novel of ideas, which means

that the characters must have ideas and must be able
to express them eloquently and cleverly. This de-
mands that the author have considerable knowledge.
In pre-World War II England such novels were more
likely to have been written by members of the upper
class, simply because they had much greater access to
good education. Huxley, we remember, attended
Eton and Oxford.

Huxley, like other upper-class Englishmen, was familiar with history and literature. He expected his
readers to know the plays of Shakespeare, to recognize names like Malthus and Marx, to be comfortable
with a word like "predestination." (Literally "predes-
tine" means only "to determine in advance," but it is
most importantly a word from Christian theology—
describing, in one version, the doctrine that God
knows in advance everything that will ever happen,
and thereby decides who will be saved and who will
be damned.)

Although Huxley was very serious about ideas, he
never stopped seeing their humorous possibilities.
His biographer, Sybille Bedford, says that in 1946 he
gave the commencement speech at a progressive
school in California, where he urged the students *not*
to imitate "the young man of that ancient limerick...
who

     . . . . said "Damn,
  It is borne in on me that I am
    A creature that moves
    In predestinate grooves;
  I'm not even a bus, I'm a tram!"

To appreciate this joke, you have to remember how
a tram or trolley car moves on its tracks. It's a reminder that you'll have much more fun with *Brave
New World* and get much more out of it if you don't let

the language scare or bore you. Use the glossary in this guide and your dictionary as tools. See how many of the words you know. See if you can guess what some words mean from their spelling and the context in which you find them. Look them up and see how close you are. Look up the ones whose meaning you can't guess. If you put even a few of the words you meet for the first time in *Brave New World* into your vocabulary, you'll be winning a great game.

Games were an important part of an upper-class English education in Huxley's day. Many elite students developed a readiness to make jokes with words and ideas. You may find some of Huxley's jokes funny, while you may think the humor has vanished from others. But you'll have more fun with the book if you try to spot the humor. You'll find big jokes like the Feelies, movies that you can feel, as well as see and hear. You'll also find little jokes like plays on words—as in calling the process for getting a baby out of its bottle "decanting," a word ordinarily used only for fine wine. There is humor in "orgy-porgy," a combination of religious ritual and group sex, a parody of a child's nursery rhyme.

In *Brave New World* Huxley plays many games with his characters' names. He turns *Our Lord* into *Our Ford*, for Henry Ford, the inventor of the modern assembly line and the cheap cars that embodied the machine age for the average man. He names one of his main characters for Karl Marx, the father of the ideas of Communism. His heroine is called Lenina, after the man who led the Russian Revolution. Benito Hoover, a minor character, has the first name of the dictator of fascist Italy and the last name of the President of the United States who led the nation into the Great Depression, but he is "notoriously good-natured." Look up any names you don't recognize.

POINT OF VIEW

Huxley's point of view in *Brave New World* is third person, omniscient (all-knowing). The narrator is not one of the characters and therefore has the ability to tell us what is going on within any of the characters' minds. This ability is particularly useful in showing us a cross section of this strange society of the future. We're able to be with the Director of Hatcheries and Conditioning in the Central London Conditioning and Hatchery Centre, with Lenina Crowne at the Westminster Abbey Cabaret, with Bernard Marx at the Fordson Community Singery. The technique reaches an extreme in Chapter Three, when we hear a babble of unidentified voices—Lenina's, Fanny Crowne's, Mustapha Mond's—that at first sound chaotic but soon give us a vivid understanding of this brave new world.

FORM AND STRUCTURE

Brave New World fits into a long tradition of books about Utopia, an ideal state where everything is done for the good of humanity as a whole, and evils like war and poverty cannot exist.

The word "Utopia" means "no place" in Greek. Sir Thomas More first used it in 1516 as the title of a book about such an ideal state. But the idea of a Utopia goes much further back. Many critics consider Plato's *Republic*, written in the fourth century B.C., a Utopian book.

"Utopia" came to have a second meaning soon after Sir Thomas More used it—"an impractical scheme for social improvement." The idea that Utopias are silly and impractical helped make them a subject for satire, a kind of literature that makes fun of something, exposing wickedness and foolishness through wit and irony. (Irony is the use of words to express an idea that is the direct opposite of the stated meaning, or an outcome of events contrary to what was expected.)

In this way two Utopian traditions developed in English literature. One was optimistic and idealistic—like More's, or Edward Bellamy's *Looking Backward* (1888), which foresaw a mildly socialist, perfect state. H.G. Wells, an important English writer, believed in progress through science and wrote both novels and nonfiction about social and scientific changes that could produce a Utopia.

The second tradition was satiric, like Jonathan Swift's *Gulliver's Travels* (1726), in which both tiny and gigantic residents of distant lands were used to satirize the England of Swift's day. Another satiric Utopia was Samuel Butler's *Erewhon* (1872; the title is an anagram of "nowhere"), which made crime a disease to be cured and disease a crime to be punished.

In *Brave New World*, Huxley clearly belongs in the satiric group. (Though toward the end of his career he wrote a nonsatiric novel of a good Utopia, *Island*.) He told a friend that he started to write *Brave New World* as a satire on the works of H.G. Wells. Soon he increased his targets, making fun not only of science but also of religion, using his idea of the future to attack the present.

As in most works about Utopia, *Brave New World* lacks the complexity of characterization that marks other kinds of great novels. The people tend to represent ideas the author likes or dislikes. Few are three-dimensional or true to life; most resemble cartoon characters. As do many writers of Utopian works, Huxley brings in an outsider (John the Savage) who can see the flaws of the society that are invisible to those who have grown up within it.

As Huxley worked on his book, his satire darkened. The book became a serious warning that if we use science as an instrument of power, we will probably apply it to human beings in the wrong way, producing a horrible society. *Brave New World* belongs firmly in the tradition of Utopian writing, but the Utopia it portrays is a bleak one, indeed.

The Story

CHAPTER ONE

The novel begins by plunging you into a world you can't quite recognize: it's familiar but there's something wrong, or at least different from what you're used to. For example, it starts like a movie, with a long shot of a building—but a "squat" building "only" thirty-four stories high. The building bears a name unlike any you've heard in real life—"Central London Hatchery and Conditioning Centre"—and the motto of a World State you know doesn't exist.

The camera's eye then moves through a north window into the cold Fertilizing Room, and focuses on someone you know is a very important person from the way he speaks. He is the Director of Hatcheries and Conditioning, and he's explaining things to a group of new students who still have only a very limited understanding of what goes on here.

You may find the Director and his Hatchery strange, but you probably know how the students feel as they try to note everything the Director says, even his opening remark, "Begin at the beginning." You know how anxious you can be to make sure you don't miss something a teacher says, something that will be important later on.

In fact, the functions of the Hatchery are hard to understand because Huxley has the Director throw large amounts of "scientific data" at you without giving you time to figure out their meaning. Huxley thereby undermines one of his intentions here—to use the Director as a cartoon character who expounds some of the scientific ideas that the author wants you to think about. He also wants to satirize a world that makes such a know-it-all important and powerful.

Sometimes the real world gives such people power, too. You may meet scientists like the Director in college or businesspeople like him at work.

The Director talks about incubators and fertilizing, about surgically removing the ovary from the female and keeping it alive artificially. He talks about bringing together ova (the unfertilized eggs of a female) and male gametes (the cells or spermatozoa containing the father's half of the genetic material needed to make a new being) in a glass container. He talks about a mysterious budding process that turns one egg into 96 embryos. The Director mentions all these things and more before Huxley tells you that the Hatchery hatches human beings.

The Director takes that fact for granted, but Huxley surprises you all the more by letting it sneak up on you. Do you think it's frightening or disgusting to breed human beings like chickens on a farm? In this Utopia, the price is worth paying to control the total population; it breeds as many or as few people as the world controllers decide are needed. Huxley's imaginary world is thus dealing with a real world problem—overpopulation. You've probably read or heard warnings about this, warnings that the world, or the United States, or a developing country like Kenya, has more people than it can feed. China is trying to reward families that have only one child and penalize those that have more, but no country has yet tried to do what Huxley's brave new world does.

The Director talks less about stemming overpopulation than he does about increasing population in the right way. In the real world, it's unusual for a woman to produce more than ten children, and the average American family has two or fewer. In Huxley's world, Bokanovsky's budding process and Podsnap's ripening technique can produce over 15,000 brothers and sisters from a single ovary. You may know this idea from the word "cloning," used in science fiction and to describe look-alike clothing styles. Identical clones will make a stable community, the Director says, one without conflict.

In the world of Bokanovsky and Podsnap, babies are not born. They develop in bottles and are "decanted"—a word that usually refers to pouring wine gently out of its bottle so that the sediment at the bottom is not disturbed.

The Director takes you and the students to the bottling room, where you learn that the clone-embryo grows inside the bottle on a bed of sow's peritoneum (the lining of the abdomen of an adult female pig). In the embryo room, the bottled embryos move slowly on belts that travel over three tiers of racks—a total of 2136 meters (about 1⅓ miles) during the 267 days before decanting. Huxley makes a point of the distance because each meter represents a point at which the embryo is given specific conditioning for its future life.

The 267 days are approximately equal to the nine months it takes a baby to develop inside its mother in the real world, but neither Director nor students mention that kind of birth. "Mother" is an unmentionable and obscene word in this brave new world, as you'll see in the next chapter. Although Huxley doesn't state it yet, if you think about it you'll see that bokanovskifying and bottling mean that nobody becomes pregnant. This gives you a hint of what will be said concerning sex and family life.

In this world, a person's class status is biologically and chemically engineered. The genes that determine brains and brawn are carefully selected. Then, a bottled embryo undergoes the initial conditioning that will determine its skills and strength, in keeping with its destiny as an Alpha, Beta, Gamma, Delta, or Epsilon.

These names are letters in the Greek alphabet, familiar to Huxley's original English readers because in English schools they are used as grades—like our As, Bs, etc.—with Alpha plus the best and Epsilon minus the worst. In *Brave New World*, each names a class or caste. Alphas and Betas remain individuals; only Gammas, Deltas, and Epsilons are bokanovski-fied. Alpha embryos receive the most oxygen in order to develop the best brains; Epsilons receive the least because they won't need intelligence for the work they'll do, like shoveling sewage.

Embryos predestined to be tropical workers are inoculated against typhoid and sleeping sickness. Bottles containing future astronauts are kept constantly in rotation to improve their sense of balance. There's a conditioning routine for every function in this society. Nobody complains about having to do hard, dirty, or boring work; everyone is conditioned to do·their job well and to like it.

In this chapter you meet two people besides the Director, though you hardly notice them in the barrage of scientific information, and you don't get to know them very well until later. One is Henry Foster, a Hatchery scientist, one of the cardboard characters that Huxley pushes to keep the plot moving. The other is Lenina Crowne, one of only two women who are important in the story. She is as close as *Brave New World* comes to having a heroine, but she is so completely a creature of the system that she barely has any personality. She is a technician in the embryo room, which like a photographic darkroom can be lit only with red light. Everybody who works in this room has purple eyes and lupus, a disease that causes large red or brown patches to appear on the skin. Huxley doesn't tell you whether this is a result of the red light or a way of matching the workers to the workplace, but neither purple eyes nor blotched skin prevents Lenina from being "uncommonly pretty." Thus, the author shows you that standards of beauty and sex appeal are different in this world of the future.

NOTE: *Brave New World* is a novel about a Utopia, an ideal state in which everything is done for the good of humanity, and evils like poverty and war cannot exist.

Perhaps you, too, have created stories about imaginary countries in which everything happens the way you think it should, countries that could be called ideal states if you looked at them closely. Or you may have seen the television program, "Fantasy Island," which is a modern, mass-audience twist on the theme of Utopia, a place that grants you your fondest wishes.

Some aspects of *Brave New World* may seem attractive to you. Everybody is happy, hygienic, and economically secure. There is little sickness and no old age, poverty, crime, or war. But notice how the Director emphasizes that bokanovskifying is "one of the major instruments of social stability," and how he reminds his students that the motto of the World State is "Community, Identity, Stability."

The most important events in this novel all center around conflicts between people like the Director, who want to maintain stability, and people whose actions might threaten this stability, even unintentionally. The Director never questions what people have to give up to achieve the World State's goals. Later in the book, other characters do ask this question, and they provide some answers. As you read *Brave New World*, keep asking yourself this question. What price would we have to pay to live in this Utopia?

CHAPTER TWO

This chapter takes you from the biological and chemical conditioning of embryos to the psychological conditioning of children in Huxley's world of the future. The Director shows the students how Delta infants, color-coded in khaki clothes, crawl naturally toward picture books and real flowers, only to be terrorized by the noises of explosions, bells, and sirens and then traumatized by electric shock. The babies learn to associate books and flowers with those painful experiences, and turn away from them.

NOTE: This section of the center is named the Neo-Pavlovian Conditioning Rooms for the Russian scientist, Ivan Petrovich Pavlov (1849–1936). In a classic experiment he trained dogs to salivate at the sound of a bell that was linked to memories of food, proving the theory of the conditioned reflex. You'll see how Pavlov's theories have been used—and misused—throughout the brave new world.

The reason for making the infants dislike books is psychological—if they read the wrong things, they might lose a bit of the conditioning that guarantees stability. The reason for making them dislike flowers is economic. If, as adults, they traveled to the country, they would "consume transport." Here Huxley

makes fun of the way some economists use the word
"consume." He means that when they travel to the
country, people use cars, trains, or helicopters. Thus,
"consuming transport" is good for an economy that
sells transport services and makes vehicles. But if they
only went to enjoy nature, they would "consume"
nothing else. Instead, they are conditioned to dislike
nature and love sports, which have been redesigned
to involve elaborate mechanical and electronic equipment. They therefore "consume" transport in traveling to the country to "consume" sports equipment.
This sounds as though they gobble it up, but in reality
they are using it and wearing it out, thereby doubling
the economic benefit.

In proceeding to the next kind of conditioning, the
Director gives you your first clue to this world's reli-
gion: the phrase "Our Ford," obviously used as reli-
gious people in the real world might say "Our Lord."
You learn that the calendar year is no longer A.D.
(Anno Domini, the year of our Lord) but A.F., After
Ford. Instead of making the sign of the cross, the
Director makes the sign of the T, from the Model T
Ford.

NOTE: This is a parody of Christianity—not so
much of its essential beliefs as of the way organized
religion can be used to control society. In 1931 it
seemed funnier and more daring than it does today,
especially in England, where the Anglican church is
established (linked to the state). Huxley made Ford
the new Jesus because Ford became the best-known
symbol of modern industry after he invented the
automobile assembly line that produced cheap, basi-
cally identical cars. Watch for further elaboration of
the Ford religion in later chapters.

The next conditioning technique is hypnopaedia, sleep-teaching. The Director tells the students it was discovered accidentally hundreds of years earlier by a little Polish boy who lived with his "father" and "mother," two words that hit the students' ears with much more force than obscene words hit your ears today. Would you be shocked if your high school principal, a middle-aged gentleman who spoke correct English with a proper accent, used a carefully enunciated obscene word during a school assembly? That's how the students feel when the Director utters those unmentionable words.

In the Director's story, little Reuben Rabinovitch discovered hypnopaedia by hearing in his sleep a broadcast by George Bernard Shaw, the British dramatist, and sleep-learning it by heart though he knew no English. Shaw thought himself a genius both as playwright and political thinker, as did many of his followers. Huxley makes a little joke at the expense of people who claim to recognize genius but really know no more about it than a sleeping child who can't speak the language it's expressed in.

The Director goes on to explain that hypnopaedia doesn't work for teaching facts or analysis. It works only for "moral education," which here means conditioning people's behavior by verbal suggestion when their psychological resistance is low—by repeated messages about what's good or bad, in words that require no intellectual activity but can be digested by a sleeping brain. (This is Huxley's own explanation in *Brave New World Revisited*, a book of essays written in 1958, a generation after the novel appeared. He also found that in the real world, sleep-teaching of both kinds shows mixed results.)

The Director gives you and the students an example of this kind of moral education, a sleep-lesson in class consciousness for Betas. They learn to love being Betas, to respect Alphas who "work much harder than we do, because they're so frightfully clever," and to be glad they're not Gammas, Deltas, or Epsilons, each more stupid than the preceding. "Oh no," the tape suggests to them, "I *don't* want to play with Delta children."

In other words, the Betas learn to love the system and their place in it. The lesson, repeated 120 times in each of three sessions a week for 30 months, seals them into that place. Huxley likens it to drops of liquid sealing wax, which the English upper classes used to seal envelopes, placing a drop of wax on the edge of the flap and pressing a design into it as the wax hardened. The envelope couldn't be opened without showing a break in the wax. Sealing wax is seen infrequently in the U.S. today, but if you imagine a candle dripping endlessly, you will understand the effect.

CHAPTER THREE

This chapter switches back and forth from place to place and from one set of characters to another in order to give you your first view of sex, love, and the nonexistent family in the brave new world.

In the first scene, the Director and some almost embarrassed students show you that sex is a game that children are encouraged to play. Later scenes make plain that for adults, sex is a wholesome source of happiness, rather like going to a health club. Nobody lives with or is married to one person at a time. In fact, there is no marriage. Everybody is expected to be promiscuous—to keep switching sexual partners without any important reason for distinguishing one partner from another.

Huxley expected his readers to be surprised or at least to giggle at the idea of promiscuity as a virtue. Some of them surely thought promiscuity meant happiness, as Huxley's characters do, but they had grown up with the idea that it was wicked. Today, many teachers and clergymen claim that high school and college students are promiscuous, but *Time* magazine says that Americans in general are becoming less so. "Promiscuous" is a word that can make you feel a connection between the real world and *Brave New World*, and help you decide if you would like the novel's world better than the one you live in.

In the first scene, the Director is upstaged by one of the ten men who run the world, the Resident Controller for Western Europe, Mustapha Mond. (Alfred Mond was a British chemist, economist, and cabinet minister; for Huxley's original readers the name probably had the same kind of ring that "Rashid Rockefeller" would for Americans.) He tells the students, "History is bunk." This is an anti-intellectual quotation from Henry Ford, who believed that a person who wasted time studying history would never create anything as revolutionary as an assembly line. But the Resident Controllers tell people that "history is bunk" for another reason: people who know history can compare the present with the past. They know the world can change, and that knowledge is a threat to stability. (George Orwell went a step further in *1984* and had the rulers of his state constantly rewrite history because they knew that if they controlled people's memories of the past, it would be easier to control the present.) This quote allows Huxley to list the glories of history, from the Bible to Beethoven, in a single paragraph, thus showing what his new world has whisked away like dust.

Also whisked away is the family. The Controller's description of traditional families links fathers with misery, mothers with perversion, brothers and sisters with madness and suicide.

Mond says this is the wisdom of Our Freud, as Our Ford chose "for some inscrutable reason . . . to call himself whenever he spoke of psychological matters." This is another of the intellectual and serious jokes that Huxley loves to make. Sigmund Freud revolutionized psychology and invented psychoanalysis, but people misuse his name and twist his ideas to fit their dogmas, just as they do Christ's.

Mond compares love to a pipe full of water that jets forth dangerously if you make just one hole in it. This is a metaphor for individual motherhood and monogamy, which he believes produces people who are mad (meaning "insane," not "angry"), wicked, and miserable. The water only makes safe, "piddling little fountains" if you put many holes in the pipe—a metaphor for the safety of growing up in a group and for being promiscuous.

After the Controller repeats the Director's lessons about the need for stability and population control, he adds something new—the elimination of emotions, particularly painful emotions. When he asks the students if they've ever experienced a painful feeling, one says it was "horrible" when a girl made him wait nearly four weeks before going to bed with him. Do you think that's real pain? Or is it part of Huxley's satire?

NOTE: Even as satire, this idea is very important in Huxley's book: the idea that people can live happily without emotional pain, and that the way to achieve this happiness is to eliminate as many emotions as possible, because even happy feelings carry the possibility of pain with them. Huxley's Utopia is built on this idea. Do you think it's true that human beings can live this way? Would it make you happy in the long run? Make a note of your answer so you can see if you change your mind after you finish the book.

The Controller makes these points as the "camera eye" of the novel switches back and forth from him to Lenina Crowne coming off work, changing clothes, and talking to her friend Fanny; from them to Henry Foster and other men, and back again. As the chapter continues, it becomes more and more difficult to tell which scene you're viewing because Huxley stops identifying the character who is speaking at any given moment, and you have to decide that from the nature of the remark.

Through Lenina and Fanny you learn more of the mechanics of feeling good, as they turn different taps for different perfumes and use a "vibro-vacuum" for toning up skin and muscles. In a world where no woman bears a child, women need periodic Pregnancy Substitutes—chemical pills and injections to give them the hormonal benefits that pregnancy would give their bodies. And one fashion item is a "Malthusian belt" loaded with contraceptives, rather like a soldier's bandolier with magazines of bullets. Thomas Malthus was a political economist who wrote in 1798 that population increases much more rapidly than does subsistence; later groups that wanted to limit population often invoked his name.

The two women also give you a closer look than the Controller's talk did at personal relations in a world that prizes promiscuity and makes monogamy impossible. Fanny reproaches Lenina for seeing nobody but

Henry Foster for four months. She calls Henry a "perfect gentleman" *because* he has other girlfriends at the same time.

After the scene switches to Henry, you meet another very important character: Bernard Marx, a specialist in hypnopaedia. He's unusual in this world because he likes to be alone, and he despises Foster for conforming to the culture of promiscuity, drugs, and "feelies"—movies that appeal not only to your eyes and ears but also to your sense of touch. (*Brave New World* was written only a few years after silent films gave way to "talkies," as the first films in which audiences could hear the actors speak were called.)

Bernard is on the verge of falling in love with Lenina, and he hates Foster for talking about her as though she were a piece of meat. Lenina is also interested in Bernard, if only because he is a bit *different* in a world in which everybody conforms. Bernard is physically small for an Alpha, and Fanny repeats a rumor that his small stature was caused by someone adding too much alcohol to his blood-surrogate when he was an embryo. Lenina says "What nonsense," but later she'll wonder if this is true.

NOTE: When Bernard becomes angry, Foster offers him a tablet of *soma*. Although this is one of the most important concepts in the book, Huxley doesn't signal it for you the first time he mentions it. A voice that can only be that of the Controller reviewing the history that produced the world state, says that five centuries earlier the rulers realized the need for the perfect drug. They put 2000 pharmacologists and biochemists to work, and in six years they produced the drug. The voice doesn't mention the name *soma*; Foster does that when he offers Bernard the tablet, and Foster's friend the Assistant Predestinator says, "One cubic centimetre cures ten gloomy sentiments." A bit later, the Controller says that half a gram of *soma* is the same as a half-holiday, a gram equals a weekend, "two grams for a trip to the gorgeous East, three for a dark eternity on the Moon." In other words, *soma* makes you high—like marijuana or LSD—but has none of the dangerous side effects those drugs can have. This world couldn't function without *soma*, because the world can't be kept free of pain without a drug that tranquilizes people and makes them high at the same time—and never leaves them with hangovers.

The word *soma*, which Huxley always puts in italics, is from the Sanskrit language of ancient India. It refers to both an intoxicating drink used in the Vedic religious rituals there and the plant from whose juice the drink was made—a plant whose true identity we don't know. *Soma* is also the Greek word for body, and can be found in the English word "somatic," an adjective meaning "of the body, as distinct from the mind." Huxley probably enjoyed his trilingual pun.

The Controller's description of *soma* is part of a scene scattered over several paragraphs in which he explains that in this Utopia there is no old age. People remain physiologically young until they reach their sixties and die. Would you like to stay young and healthy until you die, and know that you would die in your sixties? Many people would say "yes" at first. But what price would you have to pay for a lifetime of youth? Huxley wants you to answer that question, too. If you never grow old, you never feel the pains of aging—but you never feel the positive emotions of achievement or contentment with the life you've lived, either. You never know the wisdom that comes from changes in your body, mind, and life, from the knowledge that death is approaching.

CHAPTER FOUR

In this chapter, Huxley turns from building up his new-world technology to telling his story, which gives more vivid life to Lenina, Bernard, and a new character named Helmholtz Watson. Lenina is still little more than the typical hedonist of the new world. (A hedonist is someone who believes that pleasure is the highest good.) In the first scene, Lenina makes sexual advances toward Bernard in a crowded elevator and can't understand why he is embarrassed. Then she goes to a suburban park with Henry Foster to "consume" sports equipment. In some ways she is the book's heroine, but Huxley forces you to see how shallow she is.

In the second scene, Bernard reveals himself as someone you can understand more easily than most of the other characters you have met so far—because he's more of an individual, more like you or someone you know, and less like the instructional cartoon characters of the Director and Controller or the always cheerful conformists and clones.

By accident, Bernard is small for an Alpha. This makes it hard for him to deal with members of lower castes, who are as small as he is, but by design. He treats them in the arrogant but insecure way that some poor whites in the old South treated blacks, or that lower-class British people treated natives in Africa or India in the days of the British Empire. Huxley's original readers knew such people as friends or relations, or through the novels of Rudyard Kipling. Americans might know them best through the novels of William Faulkner.

Bernard goes to meet his friend Helmholtz, a writer and emotional engineer. Like Bernard, Helmholtz is unhappy in a world of people who are always happy.

Like Bernard, he is different from most Alphas. He is different not because he is short and feels inadequate, but because he is a mental giant. He is successful in sports, sex, and community activities—all the activities in which Bernard feels he is a failure. But Helmholtz is still not happy because he knows he is capable of writing something beautiful and powerful, rather than the nonsense that he has to write for the press or the feelies.

While the two friends are talking, Bernard suddenly suspects someone is spying on them, flings the door open, and finds nobody there. This is surprising, because while you've been told that the state runs everything in this new world, you haven't felt oppressed by the rulers. You find nothing like the Big Brother of George Orwell's novel *1984* or the secret police in books about Nazi Germany or the Soviet Union. The scene is a reminder that this world, too, is a dictatorship.

CHAPTER FIVE

This chapter gives more dimensions to the familiar pictures of Lenina as hedonist and well-trained citizen and Bernard as a malcontent among contented comrades. In scene one, Lenina and Henry return from their Obstacle Golf game. By now you know that Huxley has a reason, which will be revealed in a later chapter, for scattering bits of technological and ideological information along their path—like Henry's telling Lenina that the dead are all cremated so the new world can recover the phosphorus from their bodies. They have dinner and go to a nightclub in what was Westminster Abbey 600 years earlier. There they listen to a kind of electronic pop music that might describe what rock musicians play on Moog synthesizers 50 years after the book was written.

They get high on *soma* and go up to Henry's room for a night of sex. Lenina is so well conditioned that despite her high, she takes all the contraceptive precautions she learned in the Malthusian drill she performed three times a week, every week for six years of her teens. Huxley uses Lenina to underline the point that pregnancy is a sin, a crime, and a disgusting ailment in the world of Hatcheries, and that it almost never happens.

Scene two switches to Bernard, who attends a solidarity service, the equivalent of a religious service, where he reveals new dimensions of his difference from other brave new worldlings, and of his unhappiness. The new world version of a church is a Community Singery. The one Bernard attends is a skyscraper on the site a Londoner would know as St. Paul's Cathedral.

Every solidarity service takes place in a group of twelve people, six men and six women who sit in a circle, sing twelve-stanza hymns, and take a communion of solid and liquid *soma* instead of wafers and wine. The participants all go into a religious frenzy—except for Bernard, who doesn't really feel the ecstacy, but pretends to.

The frenzy takes the members of the group into a dance and the song that is one of the most remembered bits of this book, the parody of a nursery rhyme:

> *Orgy-porgy, Ford and fun,*
> *Kiss the girls and make them One.*
> *Boys at one with girls at peace;*
> *Orgy-porgy gives release.*

The group then does indeed fall "in partial disintegration" into a real orgy, though it seems to be by couples rather than group sex.

Even that doesn't give Bernard the experience of true rapture that his partners seem to feel. Huxley underlines that this rapture is not the same as excitement, because if you're excited, you're still not satisfied. This feeling is satisfying. Bernard is miserable that he has not achieved it, and thinks the failure must have been his own fault.

In this scene, Huxley satirizes both religion and sex, but still shows how both serve one of the goals of the brave new world, Community.

CHAPTER SIX

Lenina and Bernard get together in this chapter, and travel from England to North America to visit a Savage Reservation that is not unlike today's Indian reservations. Huxley signals that he is bringing you a step closer to a climax by stressing that he is taking you and his characters to a place with none of the endless, emotionless pleasures of this Utopia, a place with no running perfume, no television, "no hot water even."

Lenina is troubled because she thinks Bernard is odd, and she wonders if what she once called "Nonsense" might be true—that he was given too much alcohol while he was still an embryo in a bottle. He's odd because he hates crowds and wants to be alone with her even when they aren't making love. He's odd because he'd rather take a walk in England's beautiful Lake District than fly to Amsterdam and see the women's heavyweight wrestling championship. He's odd because he wants to look at a stormy sea without listening to sugary music on the radio. Most of all he's odd because he is capable of wishing he was free rather than enslaved by his conditioning.

But Bernard doesn't do many of the things he wants to do. He's odd in his desires but not in his behavior. In the end he does just what a brave new worldling should do: he leaves the choppy waters of the English channel, flies Lenina home in his helicopter, takes four tablets of *soma* at a gulp, and goes to bed with her.

The next day Bernard finds that even he, like Henry Foster, can think of Lenina as a piece of meat. He hates that, but he realizes that she likes thinking of herself that way. That doesn't stop him from returning to his odd desires: he tells her he wants to feel something strongly, passionately. He wants to be an adult, to be capable of waiting for pleasure, instead of an infant who must have his pleasure right now.

Lenina is disturbed by this, so disturbed that she thinks, "Perhaps he had found her too plump, after all." In this throw-away irony about her body weight, Huxley makes her shallowness plainer than ever.

But she still wants to go with Bernard to America to see the Savage Reservation, something that few people are allowed to do.

In the second scene, Bernard goes to get his permit for the trip initialed. The Director stops acting like a caricature of a bureaucrat and tells Bernard how he had gone to the same Reservation as a young man, 25 years before. Bernard, for all his desire to be different, is disturbed because the Director *is* being different: he is talking about something that happened a long time ago, which is very bad manners in this society.

The Director is obviously remembering events that affected him very deeply. The girlfriend he had taken to the Reservation wandered off and got lost while he was asleep. Search parties never found her, and the Director assumed she had died in some kind of accident. He still dreams about it, which means that even he has more individual feelings than the system thinks is good for you.

The Director suddenly realizes that he has revealed more about himself than is good for his reputation. He stops reminiscing and attacks Bernard, who has been unlucky enough to be his unintended audience. He scolds Bernard for *not* being infantile in his emotional life, and threatens him with transfer to Iceland as a punishment.

His status as a rebel makes Bernard feel pleased with himself. But when he goes to see Helmholtz, he doesn't get the praise he expects. Helmholtz doesn't like the way Bernard switches back and forth from boasting to self-pity, the way he knows what to do only after he should have done it, when it's too late.

The third scene takes Bernard and Lenina across the ocean to Santa Fe and into the Reservation, which resembles a real-world Navajo or Hopi reservation. The Warden of the Reservation is a replica of the cartoon-like Director, pumping an endless flow of unwanted information. Bernard remembers that he left the Eau de Cologne tap in his bathroom open, pumping an expensive flow of unwanted scent. He calls Helmholtz long distance to ask him to go up and turn it off, and Helmholtz tells him that the Director has announced that he is indeed transferring Bernard to Iceland. Despite Bernard's distrust of *soma*, he takes four tablets to survive the plane trip into the Reservation. Huxley is setting the stage for the coming confrontation.

CHAPTER SEVEN

From the moment they set foot on the Reservation, Bernard and Lenina are confronted with the differences between it and their familiar world. Huxley shows the comfortable mindlessness of his Utopia by contrasting it to the startling, often ugly reality of primitive life.

This life clearly lacks the new world's stability, friendliness, and cleanliness. The Indian guide is hostile, and he smells. The Reservation is dirty, full of rubbish, dust, dogs, and flies. An old man shows what aging does to the human body when it isn't protected by conditioning and chemicals; he is toothless, wrinkled, thin, bent.

Lenina has left her *soma* in the rest-house, so she is deprived of even that form of escape. She discovers that the Indians do have some kind of community; at first, a dance reassures her by reminding her of a solidarity service and orgy-porgy. The reassurance ends when she sees people dancing with snakes, effigies of an eagle and a man nailed to a cross, and a man whipping a boy until the blood runs. She can't understand the sense of community that runs through that kind of religion.

They then confront a man who will become the greatest threat to their world's stability. He steps into their rest-house and they see that, though raised an Indian, he has blond hair and white skin, and they hear that he speaks "faultless but peculiar English."

Bernard starts questioning the Savage and soon realizes that he is the son of the Director and the woman whom the Director had brought to the Reservation from what the stranger calls the "Other Place," the Utopia. The woman had not died. She had arrived pregnant with the Director's child by an accident, a defect in a Malthusian belt. During her visit she had fallen and hurt her head, but she survived to give birth, and she had reached middle age. Her son had grown up in the pueblo. Huxley tells you that the story excites Bernard.

The young man takes them to the little house where he lives with his mother, Linda. Lenina can barely stand to look at her, fat, sick, and stinking of alcohol. But the sight of Lenina brings out Linda's memories of the Other Place that is Huxley's new world, and of all the things she learned from her conditioning. She pours out what she remembers in a confused burst of woe.

NOTE: Linda's speech helps complete the portrait of the society Huxley wants you to compare to the brave new world. Linda reveals her shame at having given birth. She complains about the shortcomings of *mescal*, the drink the Indians make (in real life as in the novel) from the mescal plant, compared to *soma*, and about the Indians' filth, their compulsion to mend clothes instead of discarding them when they get worn, and worst of all, their monogamy. The Indian women have attacked her for what she had thought of as the virtue of being promiscuous. They were asserting their own values and showing that their ideas of community, identity, and stability were the opposite of the world controllers'. Huxley doesn't romanticize these values or ideas, though. The Savage Reservation may not suffer under the sophisticated oppression of London, but neither is it paradise.

CHAPTER EIGHT

In this chapter John, Linda's son, the young Savage, tells Bernard the story of his life. Huxley gives you broad hints that John will have a unique perspective on the brave new world because he inherited the genes and some of the culture of Utopia while growing up in the primitive culture of the Reservation.

As a boy, John witnessed his mother's painful shift from the happy sex life of Utopia to being the victim of both the Indian men who came to her bed and the Indian women who punished her for violating their laws. As her son, he, too, was an outsider—barred from marrying the Indian girl he loved and from being initiated into the tribe. He was denied the tribe's community and identity.

Instead, he went through the Indian initiation rituals of fasting and dreaming on his own, and learned something about suffering. He discovered time, death, and God—things about which the citizens of Utopia have only very limited knowledge. He discovered them not in the company of other boys his age, but *alone*. When Bernard hears this, he says he feels the same way because he's different. Huxley wants you to compare John's aloneness with Bernard's. Which do you think is more complete, more painful? Is it possible to be truly alone in the civilization of the Other Place?

John used Linda's stories of the Other Place as the first building blocks of his own mental world. He added the Indian stories he heard. And he crowned the mixture with what he found in a copy of Shakespeare that somehow made its way onto the Reservation. The book educated him in reading and in the English language. Shakespeare means no more to Bernard and Lenina than to the Indians, because he is part of the dust of history that the Controller whisked away in Chapter 3. But John finds a reference in Shakespeare for everything he feels.

NOTE: Here we see where Huxley found the title for his book. When Bernard comes up with a scheme to take John and Linda back to London, John loves the idea. He quotes lines from *The Tempest* that Huxley expects the reader to know even if Bernard doesn't. They are spoken by Miranda, the innocent daughter of Prospero, a deposed duke and functioning magician. She has grown up on a desert island where she has known only two spirits and one human being, her father. She falls in love with a handsome young nobleman who has been shipwrecked on their island, and then meets his equally gracious father and friends, and she says: "O, wonder! How many goodly creatures are there here! How beauteous mankind is! O brave new world, that has such people in it."

John doesn't intend to be ironic when he uses the lines as he contemplates plunging into his new world, but Huxley does. Bernard enables you to see the irony, and Huxley's true feelings about his bad Utopia, when he says to John, "Hadn't you better wait till you actually see the new world?"

CHAPTER NINE

This short chapter sets up the steps from confrontation to climax, the decisive point in the development of the story. Lenina goes on an 18-hour *soma* "trip" to escape from the horrors she encountered on the Reservation. Bernard helicopters to Sante Fe and puts in a long-distance call to Mustapha Mond, the Controller, back in London. He tells Mond the story of Linda and John—and presumably of the Director. Huxley doesn't spell that out, but you know it's true because you know that Bernard wants to protect himself from the Director's threat of exile in Iceland, and because Huxley told you in Chapter Eight that Bernard had been "secretly elaborating" a strategy from the moment he realized who John's father must be. Mond issues orders to bring them back to London.

Indeed Bernard is plotting his own advancement, as you can see from the way he shows off to the Warden about the orders to take John and Linda back with him. He likes to think he's different from his fellows, but he also wants to be accepted or, better, looked up to. Yet he *is* being different; most of the citizens of the brave new world wouldn't dare to do what he's now doing. In this world, being different may threaten community, identity, and stability. Do you think Bernard's actions threaten those goals? Do you think he intends to make such threats? He might endanger them without wanting to.

Meanwhile John observes Lenina asleep. He has fallen in love with her as quickly as Miranda with Ferdinand, or Romeo with Juliet, and he quotes *Romeo and Juliet* to her as she sleeps. This sublime emotion marks him as a Savage, in contrast to the civilized worldlings who believe in their commandment to be promiscuous: "Everyone belongs to everyone else." John believes instead in an idea he found among the Indians but knows better in Shakespearean language, the idea of "pure and vestal modesty." ("Vestal" is the name of ancient Roman priestesses who had to be virgins.) He does have sexual feelings: he thinks of unzipping Lenina and then hates himself for the mere thought. Do you think she would understand this if she woke up and heard him murmuring to himself?

John is aroused from his reverie by the return of Bernard's rather un-Shakespearean helicopter. Huxley had not yet written any film scripts when he wrote this book, but he is using a screenwriting technique, making the helicopter prepare you visually for a change of scene in the next chapter. Perhaps his poor vision made him more conscious of the need to see things happen, and to make the reader see things happen.

CHAPTER TEN

The scene indeed shifts abruptly—back to the London Hatchery and Conditioning Centre. The novel's first climax is about to occur: John and Linda's plunge into the brave new Utopia, the thrusting of unorthodox, emotional humans into the world of orthodox, emotionless clones.

The Director, as the chapter opens, is working to maintain orthodoxy. He is going to make a public announcement of Bernard's transfer to Iceland as punishment for the "scandalous unorthodoxy" of his sex life, his refusal to behave like a baby and seek instant gratification. As far as the Director is concerned, Bernard's emotional sins are all the greater because of his intellectual eminence.

The Director doesn't know he is about to be confronted with a much greater unorthodoxy from his own past. In the presence of all the high-caste workers of the Fertilizing Room, he announces the transfer and gives Bernard what is meant to be a purely formal opportunity to make a plea for himself. Bernard replies by bringing in Linda, "a strange and terrifying monster of middle-agedness," who recognizes the Director as her lover of a generation earlier and greets him with affection.

When he responds with disgust, her face twists "grotesquely into the grimace of extreme grief," an emotion that of course is completely foreign to civilized people in this world. She screams, "You made me have a baby," which fills the Director and all the others there with real horror.

Linda calls in John, who enters, falls on his knees in front of the Director, and says, "My father!" That turns the horror into a comic obscenity. The Director is humiliated. He puts his hands over his ears to protect them from the obscene word—"father"—and rushes out of the room. The listeners, almost hysterical, upset tube after tube of spermatozoa, another example of Huxley's grimly appropriate jokes.

CHAPTER ELEVEN

All the important characteristics of the brave new world and its people are visible in this chapter, though the action does not carry the plot much further forward. After you finish reading it, decide whether you regard the chapter as a peak or a plateau, an exciting vision or a restful summary.

Everybody who is important in London wants to see John, the true Savage. Nobody wants to see Linda, who had been decanted just as they had been, who committed the obscene act of becoming a mother, and who is fat and ugly. Linda doesn't care, however, because she has come back to civilization—which for her is a *soma* holiday that lasts longer and longer—and that will kill her, though she doesn't know it. Is Huxley really saying that everyone in this Utopia is in the same fix, but doesn't know it?

As John's guardian, Bernard Marx is suddenly popular and successful with women. Huxley shows you how hollow Bernard's success is in two ways: he lets you see that Bernard's friend Helmholtz is not impressed but only saddened because Bernard has revealed that he really is like everybody else; and he tells you that people still don't really like Bernard or the way he criticizes the established order.

Bernard takes the Savage to see all the high points of the World State, a literary trick from older, classical Utopias that enables Huxley to satirize both the real world and the brave new world. One of the simplest examples is the official who brags that a rocket travels 1,250 kilometers an hour—not unlike an airline ad in one of today's newspapers. John responds by remembering that Ariel, the good spirit of Shakespeare's *Tempest*, could travel around the world in 40 minutes.

Bernard and John also visit a coeducational Eton, where Bernard makes advances toward the Head Mistress. This is another joke that Huxley aims at his English readers. He attended Eton, probably the most elite school in England—then and now a school for boys only.

Huxley really wants you to notice the Eton students laughing at a movie showing Savages in pain as they whip themselves for their sins, and that with the help of toys and chocolate creams, the students are conditioned to lose any fear of death. The Head Mistress says death is "like any other physiological process." Huxley follows her comment by saying that she and Bernard have a date for eight that night at the Savoy. He does not have to actually say that they plan to experience a different physiological process. This is an example of Huxley's wit and elegance, the ability to say much in few words.

The satire on both real and Utopian worlds continues when the scene switches to Lenina and Fanny. Thanks to her new-found fame, Lenina has slept with many very important people, like the Ford Chief Justice (in England, the chief justice is a lord) and the Arch-Community Songster of Canterbury (the Archbishop of Canterbury is the chief clergyman in the Church of England). They all ask her what it's like to make love to a Savage, but she still doesn't know; John has maintained his purity against Utopia's promiscuity.

The highlight of this scene is the song that says, "Love's as good as *soma*." This is an important variation on a theme; the people of *Brave New World* use their promiscuity to escape dull routine, just the way they use the drug.

John's purity even survives a trip to the feelies with Lenina. Because she knows the celebrity Savage, Lenina has already been on the Feelytone news. Huxley mentions television as a feature of the brave new world, anticipating something that became available to the public over 15 years after he wrote this book. However, he didn't anticipate that television news programs would end movie newsreels. "Feelytone" is a parody on Movietone News, one of the leading newsreels of the 1930s.

The feely shows a black making love to a blonde, which reminds John of Shakespeare's *Othello*. Huxley reminds you in this chapter, as he does throughout the book, that the Utopian caste system resembles real-world racial discrimination, though he takes pains to show that Deltas and Epsilons, at the bottom of the pecking order, may be white *or* black.

John's feelings about the feelies are not happy. He thinks the erotic touch of the show is "ignoble," and he thinks he's noble for not making love to Lenina as she expects and wants him to.

CHAPTER TWELVE

The characters and their ideas come into conflict again in this chapter. First Bernard invites important guests to meet the Savage, but John refuses to leave his room. The guests immediately start to feel contempt for Bernard, whom they had pretended to like only to meet John. Bernard again becomes a victim of the system, and again suffers the feeling of being different that plagued him before.

John likes Bernard better that way, and so does Helmholtz, who has become John's friend. Helmholtz recites verses he wrote about solitude, a sin against the Utopian system; John responds with some of Shakespeare's verses on the self. Helmholtz is entranced, and is annoyed when Bernard equates a Shakespearean metaphor with orgy-porgy. But Helmholtz himself is a creature of Utopia. He thinks it absurdly comical that Juliet has a mother and that she wants to give herself to one man but not to another. He says a poet in the modern world must find some other pain, some other madness to write well. Actually, he says a "propaganda technician" must find these feelings, seeing no difference between that label and "poet." The chapter ends with his wondering what madness and violence he can find—a signal that Huxley wants you to wonder, too, and to suspect that the answer will soon become plain.

CHAPTER THIRTEEN

In this chapter the conflict between John and Lenina reaches its peak.

Lenina, distraught over John's failure to make love to her, goes to his apartment determined to make love to him. At first he is delighted to see her and tells her she means so much to him that he wanted to do something to show he was worthy of her. He wants to marry her. She can't understand either the Shakespearean or the ordinary words he uses because the idea of a lifelong, exclusive relationship is completely foreign to her. If she did understand it, it would be either a horror or an obscene joke, like Linda's motherhood.

She does finally understand, however, that John loves her. Her reaction is immediate: she strips off her clothes and presses up against him, ready for the enthusiastic sex that is as close as this system comes to love. John becomes furious, calls her a whore, and tells her to get out of his sight; when she goes into the bathroom, he begins to recite Shakespearean lines that say that sex is vulgar.

What do you think about this scene? Huxley has made plain throughout the book that he doesn't like the promiscuity of the brave new world. But is he taking John's side here? At one moment he seems to, but at others he suggests that John's attitude is madness, and he certainly brings John close to violence.

CHAPTER FOURTEEN

The book moves from sex and love in Chapter 13 to love and death in this chapter. John rushes to the Park Lane Hospital for the Dying, where his mother, Linda, has been taken. All the *soma* she has been using has put her into a state of "imbecile happiness." Those words seldom appear together; joining them creates a phrase of immense strength that tells us Huxleys' real attitude toward his Utopia. Seeing her makes John remember the Utopia she described to him when he was a child, the brave new world in his head that contrasts so painfully with the Utopia he now lives in.

A group of Delta children comes in for their weekly conditioning in seeing death as a natural process, and John is furious at their invasion of his grief. He is also furious when, in her delirium, his mother fails to recognize him and thinks he is Popé, her chief lover from the Reservation. Linda dies, and John collapses in tears. This threatens to destroy the conditioning the Deltas are receiving, and the nurse in charge has to give them chocolate éclairs to remind them that death is a natural and happy event.

NOTE: Huxley wants to show how monstrous it is to deny the emotions of grief and loss. He hates a process that conditions people not to feel those emotions, that sorrow can be erased with gooey pastry. He doesn't mention any way of learning to experience mourning without being destroyed by it, though. Perhaps he is reflecting here his grief over the death of his own mother when he was only 14.

CHAPTER FIFTEEN

John leaves Linda's deathbed and plunges into the midst of the daily distribution of *soma* to the Deltas who work in the hospital. He thinks again of Miranda's words—but mockingly this time—as he looks at the Deltas, and says, over and over again, "O brave new world." He feels a challenge in the words, a challenge to turn the nightmare into something noble, so he tries to stop the distribution of the *soma*, telling the Deltas that their precious drug is poison and imagining that he can urge them to freedom. John is still the Savage, and he has the savage idea that any person can be free; apparently he still can't imagine the real nature of conditioning.

Bernard and Helmholtz learn that John is going mad at the Hospital for the Dying. They rush to meet him and find they have to save him from the mob of Deltas, maddened and frustrated because he has thrown away their *soma*. The police restore order; although this new world is one in which everyone is happy and hardly anyone breaks the law, the police still come when they're needed. Like Bernard's suspicion of spies at the door in Chapter 4, this scene anticipates Orwell's *1984*, though with a much gentler police state. Helmholtz, Bernard, and John are arrested. In every stage of this scene, Bernard seems to be trying to escape the consequences of the difference between himself and other Utopians that in other moments he is proud of.

CHAPTER SIXTEEN

This chapter begins the final climax of *Brave New World*, which continues into Chapter 17. The friends who can't accept the system confront the man who speaks for the system—the Controller, Mustapha Mond. As usual, John and Helmholtz speak their minds, and so does the Controller; as usual, only Bernard worries about the "unpleasant realities of the situation."

The Controller knows Shakespeare, it turns out— knowledge forbidden to the ordinary elite. He who makes the laws is free to break the laws, he says. Huxley wants to remind you that many real-life rulers have taken the same attitude.

The Controller explains that Shakespeare is forbidden both because it's old and beautiful, qualities that might make people turn against the synthetic beauty of the brave new world, and because the people wouldn't understand it. In the new world, there can be no great art because it's impossible to have both happiness and high art at the same time; "you can't make tragedies without social instability." This returns the scene (and you) to the basic theme of the book, the need for stability.

The Controller acknowledges that stability has none of the glamour or picturesque quality of a fight against misfortune or a struggle against temptation. He says happiness and contentment are worth the loss. Do you think Huxley agrees? Or is he saying that that fight, that struggle, is necessary for a truly good life? The chapter doesn't tell you what he thinks; you have to decide the issue for yourself.

The Controller also explains why society cannot function with nothing but Alphas—they won't do the dirty work, the work Epsilons *like* doing. The Controllers once tried to create an experimental society composed only of Alphas, and it led to a civil war that killed 19,000 of the 22,000 discontented Alphas. The lower castes, he says, find happiness in their work, happiness that guarantees stability.

NOTE: Here you see that the brave new world has stifled not only art and religion but also the science that first gave it the tools of control and that it still pretends to worship. Keeping the populace stable prevents this society from using most of its scientific knowledge. If it did use this knowledge, science would produce inventions that would reduce the need for Delta and Epsilon labor; the lower castes would then become unhappy and threaten stability. Mustapha Mond knows the tragedy of this better than anyone else, because he was a first-class scientist who gave up science to be a ruler—a ruler of a society that constantly invokes the name of science. Huxley was making fun of English and American society; in 1931, he couldn't have known how well he was describing the future development of Nazi Germany and Soviet Russia, which pretended to worship science but actually crippled it.

The Controller has to deal with the three friends, who in his terms are dissidents, like the people in the Soviet Union whom the newspapers call dissidents—people who can't accept the wrongs they see in their society. He sends Bernard to Iceland and Helmholtz to the Falkland Islands. Bernard objects, pathetically; Helmholtz doesn't, because he accepts the Controller's notion that a small island, distant from the metropolis, is the right place for people who are too individual to fit into community life in this Utopia. England is an island, of course, but it's clearly too large, too central, and too highly populated to be a good place for unorthodox individuals. Huxley's love of and fantasy about islands, signaled here, later inspired his novel of a good Utopia, *Island*.

CHAPTER SEVENTEEN

After determining the fate of Bernard and Helmholtz, the Controller still has to deal with John, the Savage, in the climactic confrontation of the book. John insists the world has paid a high price for happiness by giving up art and science. The Controller adds religion to this list and quotes at length from two 19th-century religious figures in order to conclude that "God isn't compatible with machinery and scientific medicine and universal happiness."

NOTE: This is one of the fundamental principles of the brave new world, though only the controller knows that. Do you think it's true? Does Huxley think it's true? You should be able to figure out that he doesn't—by listening carefully for the tones of voice in which John and Mond speak, especially in their exchange of ideas about God.

John sees it as natural for people to believe in God when they are most alone. Mond says they have made it almost impossible to be alone. John knows he suffered equally from being shut out of the Indian community and from being unable to escape the civilized community. Do you feel that just by mentioning those two opposites, Huxley suggests a third, a compromise, is possible?

John also sees God as one who manages, punishes, and rewards. Huxley never says he agrees with John, and often he doesn't, but he keeps using the Savage to point up the hollow quality of the Controller's ideas, again using classic Utopian devices.

This is clear when Mond says that Edmund, one of the villains in Shakespeare's *King Lear*, would not be punished in the new world, only thrust into its "pleasant vices," and John says that that itself would be a punishment for Edmund. It becomes even clearer when the Controller tells John that passion means instability and instability means the end of civilization, that a properly organized society has no need of the noble or heroic. Huxley is telling you here as plainly as he can that this is a bad Utopia.

But the Controller knows that passion is part of the definition of humanity; even in the brave new world people take monthly treatments of Violent Passion Surrogate, which floods their bodies with the same hormone that would flow through them if they felt real fear and rage. The Savage rejects this idea and claims the right to be unhappy, the right to suffer illness, pain, and fear. The Controller tells John he can have them. In one sense, Mond understands why John wants them; in another, he can't really understand that anyone would make that choice. You can read both reactions in the shrug of the shoulders that ends the chapter.

CHAPTER EIGHTEEN

John opens this chapter by making himself throw up—a crude but brilliant metaphor for his claim to the right to be unhappy, and for his need to purify himself after "eating" civilization and what he sees as his own wickedness.

He tells Bernard and Helmholtz that he, too, asked to be sent to an island, and that the Controller refused because he wanted "to go on with the experiment." The Controller apparently didn't realize that John was capable of refusing to go on with it.

Instead, the Savage sets himself up as a hermit in an abandoned air-lighthouse once used to show helicopters their proper air route. He is discovered by accident while whipping himself in a penitential rite. Reporters soon descend on him and make a news story out of everything, even the kick he delivers to one reporter's coccyx. (Huxley wrote in a world and time when a civilized writer didn't put certain phrases in print.)

One of the things John punishes himself for is his sexual desire for Lenina. Huxley shows you that even an idealist can feel lust; John is learning the truth that the Controller recognized in the previous chapter, that passion is part of the definition of humanity.

A mob of tourists descends, much worse than the reporters. Worst of all, one of them is Lenina. Like fans at a boxing match or hockey game, they become crazed with fear and fascination when John starts to whip Lenina as well as himself. He chants "Kill it, kill it" (meaning "kill fleshy desire"), as Lenina writhes at his feet. An orgy of beating possesses the mob and becomes an orgy-porgy. When John wakes up the next morning, he hates himself with new intensity. Huxley never says that he actually has sex with Lenina or that he kills her, but it's not important; the thought that he might have done either one is enough to make John want to kill himself. When a new crowd arrives that evening, they find he has.

Why do you think John chooses death? Did he have to choose between death and the stable, mindless happiness of the brave new world? In the Foreword, Huxley says he gave John only two alternatives: what he saw as an insane life for the Savage in Utopia, and what he called the lunacy of a primitive life in an Indian village, "more human in some respects, but in others hardly less queer or abnormal." At the end of the novel, John could not tolerate either alternative and found a third choice: suicide.

In the 1946 Foreword, Huxley said he could see a third choice that would have made suicide unnecessary, a choice he hadn't seen when he first wrote the book—a compromise in which science would serve man, economics would be decentralized, and politics cooperative rather than coercive. Much later he wrote *Island*, a novel about a good Utopia, in which he developed some of those ideas.

A STEP BEYOND

Tests and Answers

TESTS

Test 1

1. The exposition of this novel is accomplished _____
   through the use of
   A. a separate introductory essay
   B. a tour for new students through the
      Central London Hatchery
   C. a question-and-answer dialogue between
      the Director and his new assistant

2. Children are taught morals in their sleep _____
   through a process called
   A. hypnopaedia
   B. decanting
   C. consumerism

3. For their holiday, Bernard and Lenina go to _____
   A. the moon
   B. London
   C. New Mexico

4. Bernard's idiosyncrasies are generally _____
   explained by
   A. a poor family life
   B. alcohol in his blood surrogate
   C. his infatuation with Lenina

5. The Solidarity Service which everyone must _____
   attend usually ends
   A. in an orgy
   B. with a deep religious revelation
   C. when the clocks strike thirteen

6. People are taught to hate nature because ____
  A. there are not enough trees left
  B. they would be allergic to natural substances
  C. it doesn't cost anything to enjoy nature

7. Each person's social rank is predetermined in order to ____
  A. insure an adequate number of workers for each function
  B. create a stable society
  C. both A and B

8. Ford occupies a position of reverence because ____
  A. he invented the assembly line
  B. everyone has a car
  C. both A and B

9. *Soma* is ____
  A. the day of rest
  B. a drug
  C. the major religion of this future world

10. A motto of this new world is ____
  A. Sex and Soma
  B. Alpha, Beta, Gamma, Delta, Epsilon
  C. Community, Identity, Stability

11. *Brave New World* is a novel of ideas. Discuss what this does to the characters and the plot, giving three examples of different ways that Huxley presents ideas.

12. *Brave New World* is a Utopia. Describe the goals of its ideal state and the state's general principles for achieving them, and give three examples of particular techniques that illustrate those principles.

13. How does *Brave New World* satirize the present day? Describe three particular vices and follies that are its targets.

14. *Brave New World* keeps asking how much it would cost to achieve the benefits of the new society. What are the benefits? Does Huxley think the price is high or low? Do you agree? Discuss in terms of three specific costs.

15. Discuss Huxley's attitude toward science. Does he think the brave new world uses it well? Does he think it's possible to use it well?

Test 2

1. The Indians made Linda an outcast because _____
   A. they considered her an immoral woman
   B. she was white
   C. she considered herself better than the Indians

2. Bernard brings Linda and John back to London because _____
   A. he thinks this will be an interesting experiment in cross-cultural studies
   B. he wants to embarrass the Director
   C. he is falling in love with Linda

3. John learned to read by reading the work of _____
   A. Ford
   B. Freud
   C. Shakespeare

4. "If one's different one's bound to be lonely. They're beastly to one. Do you know, they shut me out of absolutely everything?" This was said by _____
   A. Bernard
   B. Helmholtz
   C. John

5. As John's guardian, Bernard finds that he is suddenly _____
   A. jealous

   B. too busy to do his job
   C. popular

6. John falls in love with   _____
    A. Lenina
    B. a Delta minus
    C. the Director's wife

7. When Linda dies, John   _____
    A. is glad she's gone to a final rest
    B. decides to return to the Reservation
    C. starts a riot at the Hospital for the Dying

8. In his discussion with Mustapha Mond,   _____
    John claims
    A. he is willing to adapt to the customs of
        the new world
    B. the right to be unhappy
    C. he never really belonged on the
        Reservation

9. Bernard and Helmholtz are to be   _____
    A. executed
    B. reprogrammed
    C. sent to an island

10. John's final answer to the "brave new   _____
    world" is to
    A. start an underground anarchist group
    B. go back to the Reservation
    C. commit suicide

11. Analyze the personality of Bernard Marx, giving three
    examples of his thoughts, feelings, and actions at critical
    moments.

12. Discuss Lenina as a person, as a citizen, as a woman.
    What are her functions in this novel?

13. Discuss three ways that John the Savage differs from
    the citizens of the Other Place. What do his thoughts
    and feelings enable you to see about the Utopia?

14. Discuss *Brave New World* as a look at the future, analyzing the difference between prophecy and prediction.

15. Discuss sex, sports, and *soma*. What do they have in common and how do they differ from the point of view of the individual citizen and of the state?

ANSWERS

Test 1

1. B   **2.** A   **3.** C   **4.** B   **5.** A   **6.** C

7. C   **8.** A   **9.** B   **10.** C

    11. Every section of this guide can help you answer this question. Some characters exist only to express or embody a particular idea, and some have something close to three-dimensional, live personalities. Huxley expresses some ideas by putting them in the mouths of cartoon characters like the Director; some by making them part of serious dialogue, like the conversations between Bernard and Helmholtz and between the Controller and John; and some by actual behavior, like Lenina's sex life with Henry Foster and Bernard, and her attempt with John.

    Compare the different kinds of characters and say what you like and don't like about them. How do their ideas affect their actions and their personalities, and vice versa?

    Look for specific chapters where the plot stands still while ideas are expressed, and compare the "action" to a chapter in which the characters really do things and relate to each other. Which category does Chapter 17, in which the Controller and the Savage argue, belong in?

    12. The goals of the world state are mentioned in the first paragraph of the book and frequently thereafter, and they are mentioned also in this guide. They are community, identity, and stability. The general principle for achieving them is to use new scientific techniques to make people like to do what they *have* to do, as the Director says in Chapter 1, and to eliminate every painful emotion, as the Controller says in Chapter 3 and Chapter 17. Among the many specific techniques embodying those principles are the different kinds of conditioning; the use of *soma*, sex, and sports; the training about death; the elimination of history and literature. You should focus on three in detail.

13. This kind of satire is a matter of exaggerating behavior that Huxley saw around him and projecting it into the future. Look for vices and follies in the use of science, religion, the economic structure, and the attitude toward sex, in every theme and every chapter. Almost everything that the book satirizes existed either in the 1920s or today, but you may have to think about some or do research on others, like particular church practices. It would also be interesting to decide which is a vice and which a folly.

14. The benefits are the achievement of community, identity, and stability, if you prize them as the Controllers do, and the absence of war, poverty, disease, and social unrest. What do you think about them as benefits? What price would you be willing to pay for them?

Huxley thinks the cost in *Brave New World* is far too high. You can find some costs mentioned in the first three chapters and others in Chapters 16 and 17; they are summarized under Theme 11 in this guide. You can write an A (or alpha) paper if you think carefully about the value that *you* put on the benefits and the costs.

15. Huxley says in his 1946 Foreword that the theme of *Brave New World* is "the advancement of science as it affects human individuals." He had some scientific training before he lost his vision, and believed that scientific advances could and would be made, but he didn't trust scientists or rulers to use them properly. He foresaw danger in most scientific and technological discoveries—the danger that their use would turn into abuse and produce evil. The whole point of *Brave New World* is that it does not use science well. But as the guide tells you, Huxley never gave up on the possibility of using science well, and made that possibility a reality in his last novel, *Island*.

Test 2

1. A   **2.** B   **3.** C   **4.** C   **5.** C   **6.** A

7. C   **8.** B   **9.** C   **10.** C

11.   Bernard feels different because of his small size, and that sense of difference enables him to see what is wrong in the brave new world and to imagine alternatives. But he lacks courage and secretly wants to succeed on the society's own terms. You should have no trouble finding examples of either criticisms or failures in his first appearance, his trip to the Reservation, his relations with John and Helmholtz, his involvement with Lenina, or his distress at being exiled. You can write a better answer if you compare him to Helmholtz, who is different in another way.

12.   Lenina is an exemplary citizen except for one peculiarity that makes her more of an individual than most citizens: she will sometimes date or sleep with only one man at a time for as long as four months, violating the commandment to be promiscuous. As a female, she is particularly "pneumatic"—usually taken to mean that she has attractive breasts, but perhaps also meaning that she is especially exciting during intercourse. As a woman, her main function is to excite feelings in Bernard and John that show their respective differences from brave new worldlings. A feminist might say it is ironic that although she has little personality of her own, she takes the sexual initiative with John, something that many people think only a strong woman can do. Huxley implies that this is not uncommon in the brave new world, though it seldom happened in real life in his own day.

13. John is different in many ways, starting with his birth: he was born from a woman, not decanted from a bottle. He grew up an outsider among the Savages instead of a member of a defined group. He grew up without conditioning, but with a knowledge of Shakespeare and of the Savages' religion. He grew up loving and hating his mother. He knows the value of suffering and pain.

Many Utopias contrast civilized and "savage" behavior. John has the full range of emotions that citizens of the new world lack, and this enables him and you to see how hollow some of the virtues of the Utopia are. If you look at several feelings in particular, you will find that each one provides a new perspective on a different aspect of Utopia. John's feelings about his mother's death, for instance, give you a dramatic insight into the new world's conditioning about death.

14. Look up the dictionary definitions of "prophecy" and "prediction"; then look at what Huxley says in his Foreword. The novel is an inaccurate prediction of specific facts; it never mentions atomic energy, for instance. But 15 years after he wrote it, Huxley thought it was a good warning of the dangers of certain developments in biology and psychology, a good prophecy of changes in sexual morality.

15. They all offer escape from the routine of everyday life, and their use is encouraged by the state to keep citizens happy. Individuals play or watch sports more compulsively than we do because they've been conditioned to like them, but they don't get as much pleasure from sports as they do from sex, and not quite as complete an escape in sex as they do in *soma*. Sex still requires two people, while *soma* is a solitary experience in a world that offers few of these. The state seems to regard all three as necessary but to give *soma* the highest priority, with sex second and sports third. Look for quotations about each experience. At one point, Lenina sings, "Love's as good as *soma*." Do you think this is literally true from the worldlings' point of view?

Term Paper Ideas

Utopias

1. Compare *Brave New World*, Huxley's bad Utopia, with *Island*, his good one.

2. How does the society prophesied by *Brave New World* compare with today's reality?

3. Why do the creators of Utopias introduce savages into their new worlds? (Hint: looking at ideal states through the eyes of a primitive stranger provides deeper and more colorful visions.)

Community, Identity, Stability

1–3. How is each one achieved in the brave new world? (Hint: see the section of this guide on themes.)

Science

1. What scientific developments did *Brave New World* foresee? How much of its scientific prophecy has come true?

2. Why did Huxley emphasize chemical and psychological conditioning rather than make super weapons or nuclear energy elements of his new world? (Hint: he was interested in science that could affect man without killing him, and his Utopia took other advances for granted.)

3. How does the controlled breeding of *Brave New World* compare to the recent changes in genetic engineering in the real world?

Conditioning

1. Why does the Utopia use chemical and physical conditioning on embryos in bottles? (Look at the specific conditioning achieved.)

2.   Why does the Utopia use hypnopaedia to condition babies? (Distinguish between teaching facts and teaching moral attitudes while you sleep.)

3.   In what ways are we "conditioned" today? By what? Whom? From what motivations? For what purposes?

Sexual Pleasure

1.   Why does the Utopia encourage people to be promiscuous?

2.   Would I like to live in a world where everyone belongs to everyone else? (Analyze why and why not.)

3.   Would Malthusian drill be something we could borrow from *Brave New World* to deal with teenage pregnancy? (Again, why and why not?)

Soma

1.   Why is this drug a supreme necessity in the brave new world? (Hint: keep people happy by enabling them to escape.) Why is this a perversion of Huxley's hopes for a perfect drug? (Hint: it doesn't help you achieve knowledge of God; see section on Themes in this guide.)

2.   How does the Utopia's use of *soma* compare with real-world use of alcohol, tobacco, marijuana, and cocaine?

3.   In what ways can and are drugs used in a positive way today? In a negative way? What dangers does Huxley want us to avoid?

Other Pleasures

1.   How would I feel about the Feelies?

2.   How would I feel about *Brave New World* sports? (Include your thoughts about Huxley's failure to give details and on his using the names as a joke.)

Religion

1. In what way is "Ford" in *Brave New World* like "Christ" in our world? In what ways are the two different?

2. Why do you think Huxley chose to mythologize Ford (and briefly Freud) in *Brave New World?*

Family

1. Why does the Utopia make family an obscene joke or a crime? (Hint: Huxley says it's because families produce neuroses. Could it also be that the family is a focus of loyalty that might compete with the state?)

2. Compare the idea of family in *Brave New World* with a Utopia you create that redesigns a family to make people happy. (What changes would you make in your own family?)

Death

1. Death as a natural process—how the Utopia sees it, and how I see it.

2. Why the brave new world tries to eliminate the sense of loss and grief.

The Costs of Utopia

1. What are the costs of achieving the good aspects of the brave new world? (Describe the benefits of the world and their costs—including costs like the loss of family and the loss of art. Estimate whether the costs are high or low, and compare your estimate to Huxley's.)

Further Reading

AUTHOR'S OTHER WORKS

Many of Huxley's other books are worth reading. Listed here are those that provide particular additional insights into *Brave New World*.

Crome Yellow, 1921.

Point Counter-Point, 1928. Like *Crome Yellow*, this book gives you an earlier view of some of the ideas developed in *Brave New World* and provides characters to compare with those of the Utopian novel.

The Perennial Philosophy, 1945.

The Doors of Perception, 1954. In this book and in *The Perennial Philosophy*, Huxley explores the ideas of mystic communion and drugs.

Brave New World Revisited, 1958. Huxley treats in essay form many of the same topics he explored 25 years earlier in his novel: overpopulation, overorganization, propaganda, and chemical conditioning, among other subjects. "The nightmare of total organization . . . has emerged from the safe, remote future and is now awaiting us, just around the next corner." The book ends with two chapters on what people can do to prevent the nightmare from becoming reality. Huxley wanted to lower the world birth rate, increase food production, renew the environment, and decentralize political and economic power. He also wanted to create a system of education that would make propaganda and conditioning more difficult to abuse.

Island, 1962. This novel about a good Utopia shows that Huxley never gave up his belief in the benefits of science or of a drug that would enable man to transcend the limits of the self and know God, despite the warnings he gave against the misuse of science and drugs in *Brave New World*. The people of Pala, a fictional island in the Indian Ocean, enjoy a stable population, healthy agriculture, marvelous preventive medicine, no heavy industry, and an economy that is neither capitalist nor socialist. They also use *moksha*-medicine, a perfected version of LSD, to have religious visions that enable them to achieve a union with God. And, as in *Brave New World*, they use chemicals to condition babies—but with a major difference: on Pala such techniques are employed only to eliminate aggression or to raise the intelligence of retarded children to within normal range.

OTHER WORKS ABOUT UTOPIA

Three novels by other writers can be compared to *Brave New World*.

Orwell, George. *1984* (1948). A novel of an even grimmer future than that portrayed by Huxley.

Wells, H.G. *Men Like Gods* (1923). The novel Huxley intended to satirize in his own Utopia.

Zamyatin, Yevgeny. *We* (1959). A portrayal of the future inspired by the repression within the Soviet Union, the book bears some resemblances to *Brave New World* and influenced George Orwell.

CRITICAL WORKS

Bedford, Sybille. *Aldous Huxley: A Biography*. New York: Alfred A. Knopf, 1974. Essential to understand how Huxley's life related to his writings.

Bowering, Peter. *Aldous Huxley: A Study of the Major Novels*. New York: Oxford University Press, 1969. One of the more useful critical studies.

Brander, Laurence. *Aldous Huxley: A Critical Study*. Lewisburg, Pa.: Bucknell University Press, 1970. Another useful study.

Firchow, Peter. *Aldous Huxley: Satirist and Novelist*. Minneapolis, Mn.: University of Minnesota Press, 1972. One of the more useful critical studies.

Kuehn, Robert E., editor. *Aldous Huxley: A Collection of Critical Essays*. Englewood Cliffs, N.J.: Prentice-Hall, 1974.

Meckier, Jerome. *Aldous Huxley: Satire and Structure*. London: Chatto and Windus, 1969.

Watts, Harold H. *Aldous Huxley*. New York: Twayne, 1969.

Glossary

Anthrax An infectious, often fatal disease of sheep and cattle that can also kill humans. The Utopian state was established after a war in which anthrax bombs were used as a weapon of germ warfare.

Bokanovskify; Bokanovsky's Process Method to make a human egg bud by arresting its growth, producing up to 96 identical people.

Caste One of the five groups into which all citizens of the brave new world are divided by heredity and conditioning, each with its own rank and intelligence range. They are Alpha, Beta, Gamma, Delta, and Epsilon, from the Greek letters that English schools use as grades.

Community Sing An observance of the Fordian religion for the lower castes. The Arch Community Songster is the equivalent of an Archbishop.

Condition To put into a desired state by chemical, physical, or psychological action.

Decanting Process by which embryos are removed from the bottles in which they grow; equivalent of birth.

Ectogenesis Reproduction outside the human body, for example in bottles.

Emotional Engineering Designing propaganda for use on citizens. The Utopia's closest equivalent to writing poetry.

Fitchew A Shakespearean word that John uses to curse Lenina. Literally a polecat, but in Shakespeare's day it also meant a prostitute.

Flivver An old, small, or cheap automobile. Henry Ford's original Model T was often called a flivver, so the word takes on religious meaning in the Utopia.

Freemartin A sterile person; the Utopia makes 70 percent of its females freemartins by dosing the embryos with male sex hormones. They still have female sex organs, but they also have beards that need shaving.

Gametes General term for reproductive cells of either sex.

Hypnopaedia Teaching people while they sleep. In the book, suitable only for moral suggestion, not facts or analysis.

Ova Female reproductive cells.

Podsnap's technique Method to speed the ripening of human eggs, making it possible to multiply the number a single ovary can produce.

Predestination The process of determining which embryos will grow up to do particular jobs in particular places. The word has religious overtones; it once meant God's decision as to who would be saved and who would be damned.

Pregnancy Substitute A medical technique that floods a woman's body with all the hormonal and other physical changes it would undergo during pregnancy, which she will never experience.

Savage A person who is born and raised outside the Utopia and does not know how to behave according to its rules. Savages live on Reservations surrounded by electrified fences. The Savages who appear in the book resemble Indians of the Southwest United States.

Scent Organ An instrument that plays smells the way a piano or a pipe organ plays music.

Solidarity Service A Fordian religious observance for the upper castes, usually 12 people who eventually unite in a sexual orgy.

Soma A drug that both tranquilizes and intoxicates without hangovers or side effects. It provides citizens of the Utopia with escape from self and surroundings. The word comes from the Sanskrit language of ancient India. It means both an intoxicating drink used in the old Vedic religious rituals there and the plant from whose juice the drink was made—a plant whose true identity we don't know.

Spermatozoa   Male reproductive cells.

Surrogate   Something selected as a substitute. Embryos grow in blood surrogate instead of real blood because they grow outside a mother's body. Morocco-surrogate is imitation leather. Violent Passion Surrogate floods the body with the same hormones that fear and rage would.

Viviparous   Bearing live young rather than eggs, as mammals, including humans, do.

Zippicamiknicks   Women's underwear, one-piece but sexy.

The Critics

The Price of Utopia

A life-span without war, violence and the dread of cruel disease—is it not worth the silly slogans, the scent organ, the Feelies and the lack of an unknown freedom? But the price—in our terms—is also the freedom to reject servitude, the freedom to choose, to grow, to change. The price is deep and graduated human relationships, is virtue, is courage, endurance, faith exchanged for uniformity and spiritual squalor. There is no doubt on which side Aldous comes down.

—Sybille Bedford, *Aldous Huxley: A Biography*, 1974

The Worship and Enslavement of Science

In the World-State man has been enslaved by science, or as the hypnopaedic platitude puts it, "science is everything." But, while everything owes its origin to science, science itself has been paradoxically relegated to the limbo of the past along with culture, religion, and every other worthwhile object of human endeavor. It is ironic that science, which has given the stablest equilibrium in history, should itself be regarded as a potential menace, and that all scientific progress should have been frozen since the establishment of the World-State.

—Peter Bowering, *Aldous Huxley: A Study of The Major Novels*, 1969

A Choice Between Squalor and Spiritless Happiness

The core of the book is the argument on happiness between the Controller and the Savage. They argue like a couple of Oxford dons on the name and nature of happiness in society. The Savage reveals a power in dialectic for which his past life, one would have thought, had hardly prepared him. Huxley is right. It would have been better if the Savage had had another background, something worth preferring. As it is, he has to choose between the squalor of the Reservation and the spiritless shallow happiness of the world according to Ford.

—Laurence Brander, *Aldous Huxley: A Critical Study*, 1970

America—the Brave New World?

. . . For Huxley, it is plain, there is no need to travel into the future to find the brave new world; it already exists, only too palpably, in the American Joy City, where the declaration of dependence begins and ends with the single-minded pursuit of happiness.

—Peter Firchow, *Aldous Huxley: Satirist and Novelist*, 1972